RITUAL

RITUAL

Rivets & Runes

Book 1

F. Arburg

Published by ClickPrint, an imprint of DoxaNous Media, LLC
Marion, Indiana 46952
www.doxanousmedia.com

This book is a work of fiction. Names, characters, businesses, organizations, places, events, and incidents are either the product of the author's imagination or used fictitiously. Any resemblance to actual persons, living or dead, events, or locales is entirely coincidental.

Cover Design and Illustrations: Susan Spiegel
Interior Layout: Eric M. Bumpus
Editor: B.B. Lauriat

ISBN: 978-1-952375-03-3 (pbk)   ISBN: 978-1-952375-04-0 (ebk)

First Edition: August 2022
10 9 8 7 6 5 4 3 2 1

For the Blacksmith and Poet who helped me believe this
could be written and to the band of warehouse rats who
encouraged me along the way.

CHAPTER 1

THE CHAPEL BROTHERS SAY that the Holy, who spoke the world into being, has a Grand Epilogue in mind to cap off the story of history. The story is that somewhere along the way, Creation, drunk with free will and a little tipsy with temptation, took the plot on a few unnecessarily awful and dark derails. Undeterred, the Holy just watches, nods, and compassionately works with the new stories. Squint hard enough and you'll find the sparks of redemption that the Holy scatters, which will one day become blazing stars. That is the story that the Community of the Chapel has preached for as long as anyone can remember. Awful stories unfold, but they eventually transform into good ones.

This was a night that promised to be the start of one of those awful stories. When the gloam was devoured by the gloom of night, the seas turned to ink while darkness, black as charcoal, unfurled across the sky. The lighthouse pyre struggled against the murk; struggled to defeat the assailant's attempt to snuff out its light.

Ships out at sea weren't the only ones looking to the spire for guidance. Down in the markets, Sophie gazed up, using its light as an anchor to guide her tired trek towards home. Her feet felt grimy against the cobblestones.

She had never liked the feeling of the sand on the beach: much too coarse. Philip told her there were more excellent beaches beyond these shores with finer sand, but she had never seen them and probably never would. She wondered if there was better salvage on those more pleasant beaches. As it was, all she had to show for today's haul were a few gnarly yams, traded for with baubles and intact bottles on the beach, and a misshapen breadfruit that Mrs. Selma had given her out of pity.

Sophie didn't look any different from any other young girl entering adolescence. She was plain and tanned, with patches of skin peeling from sunburn. Her hair dropped just past her shoulders and was as well-kept as it could be for someone who didn't own a comb. Her limbs were long and lanky, bony even. Malnutrition had been a lifelong companion.

She walked past homes where lanterns dimmed in the face of the approaching night. She heard mothers and fathers coaxing their children to bed. Sophie did not smile. She had no memories of such things. It had been just her and Philip for as long as she could remember.

"Don't think like that," she grumbled to herself. Frowning, she went to brush something off her coal-black hair. She grimaced when she produced a length of seaweed. Had Selma seen that? Why didn't she say something? Ugh. She flicked it away and then trotted off as if it would try to nest in her hair again.

The harbor came into view. Most of the docks were empty, but a sullen, one-masted merchantman was on one of the piers. She'd find Philip there. Sophie heard him before she could see him, and it sounded like he was arguing.

Chapter One

"Don't get yourself fired, brother," she sighed to the uncaring, salty wind.

She found a crate to wait on. Philip would notice her sooner or later. He acted as if he noticed everything and it was infuriating at times.

Did he even notice she wasn't a child anymore or was he always seeing a child when he looked at her?

"I've been getting good enough to bring home yams," she griped to herself. "That's better than those awful potatoes we used to have to settle for."

A gangly palace official walked past her, pushing a cart loaded down with treasures meant for the Regent. Most of it was locked away in chests, but one item caught her eye as it unfolded while the cart bumped and jostled among the cobblestones. It was a book covered in writing she couldn't understand, but the pictures were quickly figured out. There, on the page, was the most beautiful blue butterfly she had ever seen even though she didn't know what it was.

"What are you gawking at, urchin?" the official cracked, noticing her gaze. "Don't you be getting any ideas. Stealing from the Regent will get you hanged faster than you can squeak."

Sophie pointed at the book. "It's pretty," she said.

"It's a book, girl. And you'll never be able to read it, so why are you even interested in it?" he sneered as he and the cart rolled away and off into the night.

Sophie sighed dejectedly, fidgeting with her frayed and much-patched dress. The man didn't have to say such awful things to her, even if she knew they were true.

***

A GROUP OF LONGSHOREMEN idled on the docks watching a small ship disappear into the darkness. Confident that neither the wind nor waves would carry their words to unwanted ears, they began to talk and grumble to each other. Doom and desolation were coming to their city. Reyais was on the brink of catastrophe. The laborers were sure of this. Idleness and years of cynicism have a way of turning workers into prophets, and prophets would be out of work without an impending disaster.

The trio here – Theo, Raymon, and Philip. The men were forgettable, cheap labor, dressed in functional, worn, and ragged clothes, as well as a healthy layer of grime. They were sunburned, grizzled as the clothes they wore. And rather untidy in appearance.

"There goes more of our hard-earned wealth," Theo, the foreman, lamented bitterly. The pipe in his mouth let out a momentary billow as he pointed it at the leaving ship. "Parasitic Arazumi, taking more and more from us. We were a great empire once, you know?"

"I thought Captain Gunderson was a Raermak," Philip, the youngest of the bunch, interjected.

"Raermak, Arazum, they're both allied, so they're all the same."

Chapter One

"But, Captain Gunderson complains about Arazum all the time and he says they're making his life harder, too. And, his first mate is Arazumi!"

"Quiet, Philip. You don't know what you're talking about," Raymon scolded. "You're still wet behind the ears and haven't worked around the docks as long as we have."

Philip opened his mouth to speak. He wanted to point out that ever since he had started working six months ago, he had done most of the heavy lifting, pulling the cargo from the holds to the docks, while Theo and Raymon were doing a lot of supervising. Self-preservation nagged at him, telling him this was not the appropriate time to speak up. Philip held his peace.

"And it's not just Arazumi. Danarians are coming in with their fat galleons and men o' war. They're always buying up rigging and lumber for repairs too," Theo complained.

"Can't outfit our ships with that going on," Raymon said, shaking his head and frowning with a protruding lip. "We'll never have an empire again if we keep doing that."

"But don't the Danarians pay our craftsmen for those repairs? Besides, our Regent seems more interested in handing out letters of mark to free captains rather than building his private fleet," Philip replied.

"Quit your foolish talk, boy," Raymon snapped.

"They're bleeding us all dry; they are. Taking our money and our people. Just the other day, I watched nearly twenty of our dockhands take passage on a Dhaliese ship. I doubt we'll ever see them again," Theo moaned.

"That's because it's easier to make higher wages in Dhalinur," Philip cried, growing more exasperated.

"Yes! Because they took our money!" Theo growled. "No one in the city sodding cares anymore. Our young ones don't take pride in our history. They just go off and leave, joining those other nations of parasites and thieves and stealing all the more from us."

Philip wanted to point out that many of his childhood friends had died in the plague that burned through Reyais two years ago, and it was doubtful that they were stockpiling money in their sea burials. However, indignation swallowed up any motivation to continue with this sullen company, so he upped and left. The grim prophets could prophesy to each other for all he cared.

"I think we're done here. I certainly don't need to listen to your foul mood. I bet my sister is waiting for me, anyway," Philip declared. He stamped down the planks and headed home.

"See what I mean? No respect, no common sense anymore," Theo grunted and emptied the cinders from his pipe.

"Right you are, boss."

Theo could remember when the harbor teemed with merchants, and stevedores like himself could take home a decent wage. He recalled

Chapter One

his elders having spacious and well-maintained homes with bustling families to fill them. Now, those houses had been subdivided and rented out to smaller, more desperate families; the buildings falling into disrepair even as every room was filled.

Stevedores broke their backs to unload the ships and struggled to bring home good pay. When the work was over, too many of them spent their evenings lost in a bottle of rum or opium pipe. Their livelihoods and city were slipping away, and that raised uncomfortable questions about their future.

The stones of the buildings and cobblestones seemed to grow darker and more filthy while their ships grew smaller and their sails more tattered. Even the sands on the beach seemed to be eroding into the sea.

What was happening here? Why was it all coming apart? How could this all be fixed?

Theo turned his head abruptly and stared sharply into the night. Still gazing into the night, he spoke out of the corner of his mouth to his comrade.

"Do you see that shape in the dark, Raymon? Is that a ship coming?"

Raymon squinted into the gloom. He could see movement, but it was hard to identify it.

"If it's a ship, its crew is taking quite a risk coming into harbor on a night like this," Raymon murmured. "Wait, I can see it now. The wood, sails, and rigging tell me it's Danarian."

"Typical Danarian arrogance," Theo spat. "They'll probably want us to start unloading immediately and have it done before sunrise."

"Boss, I don't think she's slowing down. Her sails are still full," Raymon said, alarm in his voice.

"Well, she better furl them and wait for a pilot to come to her. She'll run aground bad with the path she's taking."

It was a slow-moving disaster but an inevitable one. Theo and Raymon could scarcely believe what they were watching. No one manned the wheel of the wayward craft; not a soul was above deck either. The ship bore down on them. Frozen where they stood, the men stared as the vessel seemed to miraculously come in parallel to the pier and then, with a loud and ominous rumble, ran its keel deep into the mud.

"What the Abyss just happened?" Theo spat, still quaking in his boots.

A rope ladder rolled down from the side, and one by one, four people robed in white descended it. They stood on the dock motionless, silent as if waiting for yet another to join them. The stevedores were invisible, just another plank on the pier as far as these strangers were concerned.

Theo remembered to be angry, not just to stand there. Feet stomped on the boards as he stormed up to them. "Who's the captain of that ship? Huh? What lunacy drove him to do that? The docks could've been ruined! People could have been killed!" he bawled.

Chapter One

The small group remained silent and still. They didn't even acknowledge him. Their interest seemed fixed on the city and the distant mountain beyond. Theo felt his temper surge again.

"No one seems to have died. Not yet," a voice, flowing like silk, said in the night.

The laborers saw a woman so beautiful that they struggled to recall anyone who could compare to her in their memories. Her long black hair, adorned with many elaborate braids, shone in the light cast by the lighthouse. Eyes, large and dark, gazed at them as if reading their every thought. Her dress was well-made, decorated with jewels inlaid with gold. It clung to her body, highlighting it, and the men could not look away. To the dumbstruck longshoremen, she seemed to float gently down from the deck to the dock in one graceful movement. They failed to notice that was precisely what she did, the rope ladder neglected without a glance.

"L-lady! You—where is the captain? We're going to need to have words with him!" Theo protested.

"Shh, shh," she shushed them gently. Before either man could argue, she started to sing something softly under her breath, something just below what they could make out. At first, they were confused but were soon occupied with the coughs that came from their chests. It started gently but then grew more intense until their bodies convulsed violently. Both collapsed, their spasms growing weaker just as a thick, red mist began to escape their lungs.

The strange, beautiful woman finished her chant abruptly, the chilling silence of the night only interrupted by the last desperate gasps of

Theo and Raymon before they died. The crimson haze hovered lazily in the air until the woman beckoned to it with a single finger. She inhaled it through a broad, ivory smile.

"Such a pitiful, if amusing, welcome," she said as she turned away from the bodies.

"Would you have us bring more people out to you so that you may be properly welcomed, Lady Mara?" one of her white-clad attendants asked solemnly.

"That will not be necessary. No, the arrival could not be helped, but we can put this lack of attention to good use. This will suit my plan nicely," Mara said. The landing had been left to luck and luck had smiled on them. First Reyais and then, the rest of the island would easily fall into her grasp. Doom had come to the city.

***

CAPTAIN MIRABELLE VELLHUSE LOOKED every bit like a successful, enterprising captain of her own private ship. Her eyes were brilliant emerald green, and she kept her shiny hair cut short, though it found ways to keep itself perpetually ruffled. The coat she wore matched her eyes and did nothing to conceal the collection of wheellock pistols she kept on her person. A long, jaunty plume plucked from an exotic bird kept one side of her wide-brimmed hat pinned up. Corsairs or storms, she looked ready to handle whatever the sea could throw at her. Unfortunately, the same could not be said about her ship.

Chapter One

Under normal circumstances, the *Lauria* was a beautiful ship. A thirty-gun frigate made of bright timbers that practically glowed in the sun, she easily flew over the waves when at full sail. At the moment, she hobbled along over surly waves. Some of her sails were blackened with scorch marks, while a few of the yardarms lacked sails entirely. There was also the matter of her portside bow. A healthy, impressive section of it was missing.

"Burned clean off," she observed in disbelief.

"From witchcraft, no less," Gilroy, the pilot, commented as he swung the wheel to starboard. His hair was a rich blonde, but his dark eyes were becoming hooded, wrinkles crept into his face, and his beard was starting to lose its color. His hands were two large calluses from too many years fighting the helm through storms, waves, winds, and battles.

"I've seen more than my fair share of cannon fire, Lady Captain," Gilroy said with a mirthless chuckle. "But that was the first time I saw witch fire, let alone on the high seas."

"And I certainly hope, for all our sakes, that's the last time you and the rest of us see it," Mirabelle told him.

"I agree, captain, but if we're to take that sentiment seriously, we have to reconsider taking orders from that man," Gilroy murmured, pointing to someone with a flick of his chin. The figure in question stood at the furthest point on the bow staring calmly out into the horizon. He was clothed entirely in black.

"We have to follow his orders, Gilroy," Mirabelle chided the older man. "He's the Witch Hunter, and he's commandeered our ship. We are good and loyal subjects of our Empress Nathalie Caladhar, so we'll listen to what the good Witch Hunter tells us to do."

"We could toss him overboard, Lady Captain, say that he went over in a storm or in the fight. Unfortunate for the witch hunter, but that's what happens when inexperienced landlubbers come aboard ships. Not a soul aboard would tell a different tale, Lady Captain."

"No more of that talk, Gilroy. No more. I don't like the danger any more than you do, but we're being compensated for our troubles. Besides, we're loyal Danarians, and the Witch Hunter commands with the Empress's authority. Not another traitorous word or sentiment. Am I clear, Gilroy?"

"Yes, my lady."

"Good man, now work your own magic and get us to Reyais. Our Witch Hunter thinks his witch is headed there, and who are we to say otherwise?"

She had not been at sea as long as her pilot, but Mirabelle had led men long enough to read beneath Gilroy's words. The Witch Hunter was an unwelcome passenger on the *Lauria*. Crews have mutinied over lesser things. Mirabelle stalked towards the ebon-clad inquisitor. She made sure to encourage and praise the deckhands rushing to drain pails of seawater over the side as she passed. The *Lauria* never behaved well when she was wounded.

Chapter One

"Have you found your sea legs, sir Witch Hunter?" she asked with artificial cordiality.

"I'm quite well, Captain Vellhuse," the man replied calmly, eyes never leaving the horizon. "I will be even better when we capture our witch."

The Witch Hunter called himself Seth Glethrun of House Caladhar. He looked young, but there was a certain world-weariness in his posture and gaze. His eyes and hair were as dark as the clothes he wore. He was clean-shaven, and his skin was so pallid it seemed to glow despite the overcast skies. Mirabelle knew there were many who would have called him handsome. Personally, she found him unsettling and wanted him off her ship as soon as possible.

"What makes you so certain this witch is headed to Reyais? It seems like an odd place to flee to," Mirabelle said conversationally.

"I have my sources. I've been tracking her a lot longer than when I had to press you and your ship into my service."

"Can you even do your witch-hunting in Reyais? Wouldn't that cause some sort of diplomatic incident?" the captain asked quizzically.

"Are you questioning my competence?" Seth shot back.

"Not at all," Mirabelle answered quickly. "I'm just curious. It's not every day I have a Witch Hunter on my ship, let alone get to ask one about their trade."

"The less you know, the better. If it helps you sleep better, I know how to operate beyond the Empire's boundaries," Seth replied sternly. "Besides, Reyais is a lawless place."

"On that, we can both agree," Mirabelle said with a knowing nod.

"I'm led to believe that a private ship captain like you wouldn't mind going to Reyais. I hear an enterprising captain can spin quite a profit over there," Seth said, keenly observing Mirabelle's reaction.

"It's not my favorite port," the captain admitted. "But it's my favorite port to go to when the usual business is drying up."

"Ah. Pirating."

"No, it's privateering. There's a difference. They give you a letter of mark, so it's all very legal," Mirabelle explained stiffly.

"Wouldn't you rather limit your sailing for Danarian affairs only?"

"Not every merchant is looking to pay for an escort, and privateering is more profitable than navy work."

"I see…"

"Last question; are you going to ask that we wait in port while you go and burn your witch, or will we be free to go once we drop you off?"

"There will be compensation for bringing me here to Reyais. There will also be compensation for waiting and bringing me back to

Chapter One

Danaria," Seth offered, still gazing out into the horizon. "I understand that money is a concern of yours, Captain?"

"It is," Mirabelle nodded with a smile. "Most people don't realize it, but it takes a lot of coin to keep a ship like the *Lauria* running."

"Then the incentives lie in you waiting for me. I won't keep you on a tight leash, Captain Vellhuse. You can pursue your own affairs in port while I tend to our wayward witch."

Mirabelle began to turn on her heels, making her way back to the wheel. Seth didn't react. He kept still, staring out past the prow and into the horizon. Mirabelle wondered if all Witch Hunters were this unnerving.

"Did you have a good talk with him, Lady Captain?" Gilroy asked, hands moving confidently as if following an invisible turn in their plotted course.

"As well as any discussion with a witch hunter could go, I imagine," she admitted. She crossed her arms and sighed. The whole situation made her uncomfortable. Yes, she had an incentive to wait now, but she couldn't help but see it as a metaphorical anchor holding her to the city. The only anchors she liked worked with her schedule and didn't protest when tossed into the water.

"We may work on a longer leash than he's expecting," Mirabelle speculated. "But in the end, I suppose the only right thing to do is wait till he's done, or till he orders us to leave him behind."

"Your loyalty to the Crown's officials is commendable, Lady Captain," Gilroy grunted.

"Apparently, it's the only thing keeping this ship from going full corsair," she chided.

Early the next morning, the *Lauria* limped into Reyais' harbor. A small army of laborers, sailors, and port officials were still working on the derelict ship that had crashed into their docks the night before. Seth was probably the only soul there happy to see it.

CHAPTER 2

A STRANGE SIGHT ROLLED down the wooded mountain trails and towards the gates of Reyais. Noisy and moving without the aid of a horse, most onlookers thought they were the work of sorcery. The druids up on the mountain certainly found them diabolical. To their Arazumi operators, they were just another expensive tool to be maintained with care and then used to bombastic effect. They called them "armored auto-buggies."

The Arazumi had a small encampment up on the mountain to study it and run their esoteric experiments. The druids, who haunted the mountain and woods beyond the city, took offense to their incursion and laid siege to the camp. Since no one knew the language of the druids, the exchange was always going to end with thrown spears and, in the case of the Arazumi, rifle fire. The armored auto-buggies ensured their escape with the precious data. Blowing the encampment up with dynamite as they left was just protocol they had to follow; and out of spite.

One last obstacle awaited the convoy. As the machines lumbered into the city and through the narrow streets, locals began to stop and stare. And then they began to gather, eyes wide with boggled wonder. The war machines stopped, powerless in the face of crowded amazement and a lack of anything else better to do this early in the morning.

The door on the back of the rear car opened with a crash of metal on metal. A guard in a navy blue uniform stumbled out and trudged towards the front. The pith helmet he wore was, in fact, molded steel, and a cuirass of steel plates could be spied underneath his jacket. He leaned his rifle above his right shoulder while idly scratching his beard, analyzing the crowd that blocked their way. Gray was starting to creep into his trim facial hair, and his dark eyes seemed to rove around constantly. Two snapped arrow shafts jutted from his bloodied left sleeve.

"It would be helpful if you lot made way," he called. No one stirred.

"I'd rather not have to ask twice. You're free to admire the buggies as we pass along. Come on now; get! Make way!"

"Having trouble, little man?" a gruff voice barked from the rear buggy.

"No trouble, just a little too much native curiosity. Perhaps if you graced us with your presence, Jord, they'll make way."

A much taller, heavily built guard appeared. The blue tattoos on his face marked him as a Raermak. His voluminous beard only seemed to amplify his presence.

"Can do, Otto. Can do," he rumbled.

The locals recognized the uniforms, Arazum's Long Steel corporate guards. The Long Steel Company preferred to be known for their quality metallurgic products and the professional conduct of their guards. Most people throughout the Three Lands and Archipelago talked about their blunt and effective methods instead. The sound of

Chapter Two

trepidation swelling in the crowd could be heard over the sound of the idling engines.

"Move!" Jord roared. The crowd began to disperse.

"You're too polite, Otto," Jord told him.

"I'm better at more surgical predicaments," the shorter man groused.

The auto-buggies rumbled along behind the two guards leading them. Inquisitive, marveling eyes watched from windows, porches, and other hidey holes along the street. The guards kept their longarms shouldered, the occasional shout or scorching glare enough to wither any clot of gawkers. The turret hatch of the auto-buggy behind them opened up, revealing yet another Long Steel man, his face obscured behind a cold and ominous gas mask.

"I'm sure a few blasts of the rotary gun would've done the trick."

"Absolutely not, Derek," Otto snapped. "Do that, and then the company lawyers would have a field day censuring us. Then they'd hand us over to the judicial litigators. Do you want to be at the center of an international incident after Long Steel terminates your employment?"

"I meant over their heads, Mr. Gurman," Derek grumbled huffily. "Also, you got a few arrows sticking out of your arm. You better have that taken care of," and with that, he retreated back under the hatch.

"I'm going to find a way to have him sent back to HQ once things have calmed down," Otto muttered under his breath. "Bloody kid's a bloody liability."

"He was marked well in combat training," Jord said indifferently.

"Sure, because he's a psychopath."

"Agreed, but I doubt you'll find a time when things have 'calmed down.' I don't know which embassy you're stationed at, but things are heating up around here."

"I wonder when the company will contract me out to somewhere nice and quiet," Otto quibbled.

"The day after you retire."

Eventually, the convoy made it back to the walled embassy that served as Arazum's nexus of influence on Reyais. Thick concrete walls insulated it, and at night the locals could see the eerie glow of electric lamps shining within. Many said that the Arazumi were a nation of magicians, but the Arazumi denied this. "It's only science," was the over-worn refrain. Clearly, this science was a form of magic, and its users were in denial of it.

The guards called for help as soon as the heavy gates shut with the arrival of the auto-buggies. Injuries needed mending, and sensitive information had to be preserved and transmitted. A disheveled, breathless man stumbled out of one of the vehicles; a hefty briefcase clutched to his chest. Jord and Otto followed closely behind him.

Chapter Two

"All of this fuss to save you and your data, Mr. Feldsworth," Jord said, another briefcase in one hand and his blunderbuss in the other.

"No, more like all of this fuss because some primitives needed to act out their destructive impulses. We didn't even cast the first stone," Mr. Feldsworth grumbled, adjusting the glasses on his sweaty face.

"The mountain is probably sacred to them. We regard some groves as sacred in my homeland," Jord speculated.

"At least your people are civilized and recognize the benefits of becoming a commonwealth of Arazum."

"Perhaps you should hurry that data back to the research ship, yes, Mr. Feldsworth?" Otto butted in. He didn't like the look that emerged on Jord's face. The giant was scowling, and his movements were abruptly stiff.

"And you should have that arm looked at, Mr. Gurman," a woman said, stepping out from the vehicle. She was slender, round glasses framing a face of delicate features and a dusting of freckles. Her eyes were green, and she kept her braided hair tied up in a bun. She also carried a case, but the noise it made when it rattled suggested there was more than just papers within.

"A few minutes more won't hurt it, Miss Norwis," Otto reassured limply.

"Finish your work here and then head straight for the surgeon, Otto. You don't want an infection to set in."

"Yes, Kassia."

"Do that, little man, then hurry over to meet Axle. I'm sure he's going to want our report quickly," Jord instructed, tossing the last of the briefcases at Mr. Feldsworth. Some people didn't need one more second of help than was strictly necessary.

***

THE RESEARCH SHIP *PROJECT WONDER* was moored to a semi-temporary pier. Other important custom-built vessels were likewise docked to it, providing essential services to the embassy. It was a miniature reflection of the Arazum Republic on Reyais. A generator ship provided a limited pool of electricity, tankers kept the small flotilla of naval vessels fueled, and a communications ship hummed with countless telegrams invisibly buzzing to and from its many antennae. The research ship mirrored Arazum's compulsive endeavors to tinker, experimenting with curiosities often overlooked.

On foreign shores, the locals often paid no heed to the quaint, probing, clockwork instruments that spat esoteric figures. They cared even less for the odd detritus the Arazumi strangers would steal away back to their research ships. This was where people like Kassia came in. Some of the more astute locals accused her of being an alchemist. She preferred her actual title of "chemist."

Kassia told herself not to be too hopeful about these samples they gathered. Unique properties and their practical applications were not so easily teased out of elements and compounds. Sometimes, despite whatever imagined promises a glittering surface may have, a shiny rock was just a shiny rock.

Chapter Two

The military wing of the Bureaucracy kept commissioning more research for even more "efficient methods of neutralizing the Republic's threats," but statistically, the oldest method was still the most effective. Fastening a metal cone over a lump of combustible powder and then igniting the mix had yet to fall out of fashion. Maybe a new shiny rock would eventually prove to be a more effective way than the tried and true bullet, but that had yet to happen. The scientist within her speculated that attaining peace through inventing more toys of war was a flawed methodology. But, no one ever asked for her opinion on the matter. She doubted anyone would.

"Miss Norwis?" one of the scientists called. "Before you go, some company guards need a few items from the special armory. Could you accompany them?"

Kassia knew that ultimately it wasn't a request. And "company guards" in this context could only be one thing. Long Steel wasn't the only company with trained guns for hire. She recognized the four newcomers by their green uniforms, company repeaters, and cavalier manner: Comstock Company Night Riders.

"Please follow me," she told them and turned on her heels.

"I'm Garrett Blauestein," the oldest of the group said. His silver mustache sprawled across his immaculately groomed face. A plain but well-weathered dark hat sat on his head, and a half cape hung on his shoulders. Kassia recognized his name. It meant he was active enough to remain successful and hadn't gotten himself killed yet.

"What items will you need from the hold?" the chemist inquired, eyes never leaving the floor in front of her.

"Silver bullets," Garrett said.

"Ah. Of course."

"Some Long Steel men offered regular bullets from their armory," a young man at the back of the group chuckled derisively. "What good will those do against monsters?"

"Anomalous creatures, you mean," Kassia corrected. "Also, the bullets they're issued are sheathed in copper."

"So? All regular bullets are, but everyone knows you need silver bullets."

"Actually, copper sheathing only became standard three years ago. Also, copper is in the same family as silver, and it's deadly toxic to them." There was also yet another, less mentioned fact about copper: it was far cheaper than silver.

"The young miss is right," Garrett interjected. "I was hunting ghouls once west of Moraine. The ones that got hit with silver dropped and died in an instant, but someone on the team was careless with their revolver and hit one with a regular copper sheathed round. Worse, he didn't hit the bugger in the middle mass, just the meaty part of the thigh."

"What happened to the ghoul?" the young guard asked with morbid fascination.

"It was still alive when we got to it, so I was obligated to bring it in for study. Did you know those things will sometimes learn our

Chapter Two

language? It was too weak or in too much pain to resist us. It just lingered on for a couple hours before it finally died. I could hear it whispering about how it felt its blood burning."

"That was not a clean kill," another one of Garrett's team said sternly. She was a Raermak woman, tall with braided hair and intricate blue tattoos on her face. Kassia could not help but be impressed with the bow she carried.

"Correct, Siggy," Garrett agreed. "And that's why we only use silver on my team now."

The chemist nodded and then noticed they were about to pass a particular locker, its contents a relatively new addition to the Republic's arsenal.

"We have warding grenades," she suggested. "You're eligible for a small allotment of them."

"No, Miss," Garrett replied with a firm shake of his head. "In my experience, if you're using warding grenades, you're already in deep trouble."

"I understand. Now, I'll warn you all to mind your steps. There's not a lot of traffic down here, so they wired fewer lights. All for the better because some things they store down here can be photosensitive."

Kassia led them down into the deepest part of the hold. Shadows danced and leered as they walked. A thick, gloomy door made of layered metal blocked their path. The chemist pulled three different keys to unlock it. Each bolt slid back reluctantly. When she opened it, the door groaned, a casket for forbidden tools.

The lockers had labels chronicling the most sinister inventions of the Republic's imagination: Everfire rounds, for when standard explosives were too abrupt; canisters of Reaper Gas, which had brought the Black War to an end and convinced Danaria to give lenient terms for the cease-fire; or, the silver bullets, which were nestled in the back behind the Carnifex grenades. Kassia thought the bullets were probably the most merciful instruments inside this sorry compartment.

"How many will you need?"

"Four cases, miss. One for each of us. I'll make sure the proper paperwork is forwarded back to Comstock," Garrett said.

As the cases were handed out and the group hurried out of the vault, Kassia began to turn the locks that bolted the door shut. The riders were already leaving her behind.

"What will you be hunting?" she asked their retreating footsteps.

"Werewolf," Garret answered.

"Werewolf? Out here?"

"Allegedly. Villagers over at Klimmick's Hollow said they heard howling coming down from the mountain a couple nights before. Since there aren't any more wolves on the island, they figure that can only mean one thing."

Chapter Two

***

OTTO SAT PALE-FACED on a medical table. Two bloodied arrows lay in a pan nearby. Arrow wounds were becoming old news between the Black War three years ago and the countless contract assignments afterward. He also knew the worst was yet to come.

It surprised him to see Jord arrive before the surgeon. Jord also brought a familiar face: Axle Greerson, the head of the Long Steel guard assigned to the embassy.

"Axle wanted to have a meeting with you here and now," Jord announced, taking a seat across from Otto.

"This couldn't wait? I'm about to get the amber treatment," Otto replied in exasperation.

"It'll be short. It's regarding another assignment I must hand off to you as soon as the doctor gives his approval," Axle smoothed over. Otto was not impressed.

"If I didn't know you any better, Axle, I'd say you've been at your desk too long. It's been a while since you've been on a contract. We just got back from an awful fight up on the mountain, I have two holes in my arm, and you're putting me on another so soon?"

"This is one of those unexpected surprises, Otto," Axle admonished.

"Very well. I'll believe it's been just as turbulent here as it was on the mountain," the wounded guard muttered.

The surgeon interrupted their talk with his sudden arrival. A fist-size vial of yellow medicine gleamed in his hand. Otto's jaw tightened at the sight of it.

"Is this your first amber treatment?" the surgeon asked.

"No."

"Good, then you know what to expect. Would you like something to bite down on?"

"Yes," Otto sighed dejectedly. A thin strip of wood was given to him, which he promptly placed across his mouth. Jord nodded knowingly.

"Seen too many pups bite their tongues during this."

"Let's get this over with," the surgeon proclaimed. Holding the guard's arm still, he began to pour the fluid onto the open wound. Otto howled through the stick and impulsively tried to pull away. Miraculously, beneath the splashes of the liquid gold, muscles began to stitch together, and skin grew over. In moments, all that was left was a sad, purple scar and a winded, gasping guard.

The medicine colloquially called "Amber" made its debut three years ago during the Black War. The Republic's medical community preferred to call it by its patented name "Vurixide." During the war, Otto found it puzzling that their Danarian enemies called them "Clockwork soldiers" and initially thought it was because of how they marched into battle in disciplined formations. It wasn't until later, he found out it was because the Danarians couldn't understand how men that they had grievously wounded were able to come back battle after battle. Those "clockwork soldiers" and "machine men," instead of

Chapter Two

being fantastic automatons, were just regular men greased with Vurixide.

"It should be safe for you to return to your duties after an hour or so. Just take it easy in the meantime," the surgeon pronounced.

"Excellent," Axle said. "That'll give me plenty of time to explain what you'll be up to next: corpse transport!"

"Corpse transport?" Jord grunted with a raised brow.

"The poor sod cursed with the position of sheriff in this part of the city had two corpses dropped on him. All I know is that he's a little curious as to how they died, and he figures we have people who are the most qualified in the city to get him an answer. He's commissioning us to find out."

"We're not part of the city, and the embassy is technically a piece of Arazum, and in my opinion, we're better experts at making corpses. Why does he think we're qualified?" Jord asked.

"It won't be you two figuring it out; it'll be some scientists from the research ship," Axle explained. "Besides, there's no point wondering about it. The diplomats have already given their agreement since it'll give the locals more reasons to feel warm and fuzzy about us."

"The *city* locals, at least," Otto cut in as he fastened on his armor. "The druids up in the woods? I think we burned that bridge. Shame we're making enemies of them."

"That's something for the diplomats to worry about. In the meantime, be ready to go in an hour. I'll have the rest of your team prepared. You'll collect the bodies, bring them here for examination, and hopefully, it'll just be a matter of returning the stiffs to their owners," Axle ordered then, got up to leave. He gave Otto a friendly slap on the back on the way out.

"I've started to hate him ever since he got promoted to a desk job," Otto said.

"Little man, you've always hated him," Jord chuckled.

A little over an hour later, Otto and Jord trudged through the streets of Reyais, two junior guards following in their wake. The juniors were Derek and a guard who only introduced himself as "Michael: telegraph operator."

Otto almost felt sorry for the man; the mobile telegraph he dutifully lugged looked like an oversized backpack nearly identical to his torso. The antenna rose a meter into the sky and started to droop pathetically towards the end. A faint buzz could be heard coming from the pack.

"How's that supposed to help us?" Derek asked, motioning towards the clumsy device. "Are you going to drop it on anyone who attacks us?"

"Shut it, you misanthrope," Otto castigated.

"The embassy wants fast and constant communication with all outgoing teams now," Michael elaborated, adjusting the glasses on

Chapter Two

his nose. "It sounds like things are becoming a bit unstable here in the city."

"And why's that?" Derek inquired.

"I'm afraid that's above my pay grade," Michael confessed with a shrug.

"Focus, pups," Jord told them. "We have a mission to do. Conversing can wait till we get back."

Otto didn't like the street they were walking on. There was too much detritus on the ancient stones, and it was too empty for his tastes. Instead, he could feel eyes watching them from gloomy windows nearby. Some buildings were so dilapidated, they were more ruin than shelter and yet, many showed signs of being inhabited.

The stench of human excrement, molding scraps, and even death hung in the air. He had grown up in Arazum City. He was used to walking and occasionally sprinting through unhappy streets. Something told him this was the most unhealthy one he had ever trod on.

"Almost there," Jord said quietly.

The guardhouse seemed to appear out of nowhere. It didn't look much better than the other buildings around it and was all the more sullen for it. Otto was perplexed by the corroded cross spear sign that hung above the door and then remembered most people were not literate. Jord was positive he'd seen picket stations in the war that looked prouder than this establishment.

"Should we knock?" Michael asked.

"Knock, but never go inside unless you must," Otto whispered and promptly rapped on the door.

The stranger that emerged visibly jolted Michael. Derek gasped in shock and disgust. Jord and Otto seemed to regard the short, wry man warmly. Jagged scars crossed the man's face, each one screaming a muted story. His balding hair was cut short, not that there was much left for him to cut. His breastplate had grown dull; no amount of polish would ever bring a shine to it. Dents and gouges pockmarked it. There was a slight limp in his step.

"Arazumi. Good. My men are bringing the bodies. I've been doing this shite so long; I can't tell you how many corpses I've seen. Not even dreaming about them anymore. But these two? I don't like the look of them, so that should tell you something," he whinged.

"Your name, sir?" Otto asked.

"Sheriff Hector. It's really a curse, but someone's gotta' do the job. The ship vermin would've carved their own little kingdom here if not for me."

"What didn't you like about them, the corpses that is, sir?" Otto pressed.

"Two dockhands found side by side on the pier where that derelict ship crashed-"

"A ship crashed recently?" Jord interrupted.

Chapter Two

"You must be snug; real cozy behind those embassy walls. Yes, a blighting ship crashed into one of the piers last night, and those two were dead with their money still on them and no wounds to speak of."

"None? No wounds?" Derek asked incredulously. "Are you sure you checked?"

"I've been doing this shite longer than you've been shiteing. I'm fuggin' sure I checked," Hector growled. Otto made a noise somewhere between a snort and a cough. Their swear words were so quaint.

"Anything else unusual about them?" Otto added, a hand over his mouth to imitate thoughtfulness when he was trying to hide a smile.

"Yes. They were light."

"Unusually so?"

"Yep. Like I said, been doing this for years. Something's wrong with how light those bodies are. Like they're missing something," he grimaced at the cart two of his guards brought up. A bleached white sheet did its best to obscure two ominous forms underneath. Otto walked up and lifted the fabric so that only he could see. The inspection lasted for but a moment.

"It all looks in order. I don't know how long it'll take for our scientist to do an autopsy, but we'll get you the results as soon as we can. We'll also return the cart with the bodies so they can be reclaimed," Otto explained.

"Burn 'em when you're done," Hector stated.

"Wait, burn them? But what about their families?" Michael squawked.

"No one to claim them, and those bodies are going to smell once you're done. Besides, whatever happened to them can't be natural. I feel it in my bones. Burn 'em and the cart; just get your findings back to me."

"Are you certain? We can do it, but this is something you can't change your mind on," Jord cautioned.

"I'm certain. You boys just do your job, and I'll get to doing mine."

"Keep up the good work then, sheriff," Jord told the man, shaking his hand. "Are you a pipe smoker?"

"One of the few pleasures I have left in life."

"Ah, then have one of my bags. '*Plantation Island*' is my favorite, but it's too expensive to get all the time. What I gave you is '*Jeremias' Finest.*'"

Hector chuckled heartily as he studied the bag of tobacco. "You can never get any of the good stuff on this side of town. I usually just get what I can afford and hope for the best. Thank you, sir Raermak."

The guard station couldn't even afford a donkey to bear the cart. Otto volunteered to drag the contraption while the others formed a column

Chapter Two

in front and behind. It wasn't until they were further along the decrepit street that conversation began again.

"That arse looked like several kinds of ugly," Derek grumbled.

"The sheriff? Long years of guarding will do that to you, especially in a place like this," Otto replied sympathetically.

"Scars and wounds are the steep price that must be paid so that society can remain in order," Jord added.

"You two don't look too bad. Besides, didn't you both serve in the Black War? What about contract wars?" Michael asked.

"We've been lucky," Jord said darkly. "Or we've been marked by Archangel Vutan."

"You can't see the scars on me because of my uniform, and you don't know how much worse some of our friends have had it," Otto added.

"Viktor lost an arm, Joseph his leg and joy in life. Karl gave up some of his fingers to frostbite. Horace caught a glimpse of Brother Grinn, and his mind has not been the same since," Jord recited.

"And those are the ones that are still alive," Otto sighed.

"That all sounds...awful. I'm sorry," Michael said.

"They knew what they were signing up for," Derek muttered. Otto shook his head in disagreement.

"They thought they did. We all thought we did. We were foolish."

***

THE SCIENTISTS ABOARD *PROJECT WONDER* had all but concluded their examination of the bodies by the early morning hours. There was only so much they could do with the limited equipment on hand. Fortunately, at least for the scientists, there were several glaring problems. Both cadavers had been completely, unnaturally exsanguinated. After that discovery, it became a matter of trying to determine how that occurred. All signs pointed towards an uncomfortable conclusion. Kassia waited for the final tests to conclude.

"Miss Norwis, are you sure you're properly heating those samples? Giving them enough time to mature?"

"I'm positive, Dr. Linton," she replied quickly. Dr. Linton headed the biological team on the ship. Professionally, she respected his expertise in biology. She disliked his tendency of barging into other fields beyond that. While related to biology, chemistry was its own field, and more importantly, it was hers.

"Are you seeing anyone, Miss Norwis?"

Kassia made sure not to look away from the beaker she was carefully studying. "I don't see how that's important to the job."

"Just making conversation. Do you have a preference in jewelry?"

Chapter Two

"There are some metals I'm allergic to, and honestly, that's none of your concern. More importantly, I think we've reached the conclusion of this test," Kassia announced.

"And? Are you able to make anything of it?"

"None of the suspected poisons we tested for were present," she said.

"And none of our culture samples are showing any promise either," Dr. Linton sighed. "So what else would cause blood to pool and then rush out of the victims' lungs?"

"I hate to say it, but from the evidence we've been given, we have to consider anomalous activity," Kassia decided.

"Yes. Magic or the paranormal."

"It's called 'anomalous activity,' Doctor. You'd do well to remember that," Kassia criticized and then left the room. Some doctors weren't worth the credentials given to them.

CHAPTER 3

LAST NIGHT, PHILIP LISTENED to Theo and Raymon complain loudly about anything and everything. It's what they usually did, and he had other things to worry about. There was always something causing him anxiety. He didn't have the emotional bank to afford "other people's complaints." Then, to top everything off, someone murdered Theo and Raymon.

That's all it took, the straw that broke the longshoreman's back. Now, the anxiety was gone. It was odd without that old friend Worry hounding his mind day in and day out. Initially, he thought finding out about Raymon and Theo's deaths would've made it worse but only served to crystallize a plan he had long entertained. He and his sister were leaving.

There was always something to worry about. Was Sophie safe? Where will their next meal come from? Would either of them fall sick this month, and if so, would it be bad enough that they would need medicine? Would they have enough money to afford the medicine, food and then have enough left over to bribe off any thugs or officials? Were they finally going to catch their death of cold sleeping in this ramshackle excuse of a house? Would some big wig claim this abandoned hovel and drive them off? No one would ever take pity on them. Mewling babes at least had a chance of garnering sympathy. He and Sophie looked like grubby street urchins that needed to be kept at arm's length.

"We're leaving, Sophie," he told her as he picked a splinter from the heavily calloused sole of his foot. He worried that his feet would get infected one day, but shoes were a luxury they couldn't afford. Having three meals a day was another one. They could barely justify having two in a day, and sometimes they made do with only one.

"Do we have the money now?" Sophie whimpered uncomfortably. She was doggedly cleaning one of her spare dresses.

"Probably not, but maybe I'll be able to find a smuggler who'll take what we have. We can't stay anymore."

"That's dangerous, Philip! I heard there are bad smugglers who just take your money and sell you to the Tersians, or the Kholoti, or force you to work on a plantation until they're done with you."

"My boss died last night, Sophie," Philip protested. "Someone must've killed him right after I left! What if it had been me? If we stay any longer, something *will* happen to me. You'll be all alone."

Neither said anything for a moment. Danger and desperation had slowly but surely been tightening a noose around their necks all their lives. Sophie knew deep down that this day would come sooner or later. This was too soon, though.

"I'm not a child anymore, Philip. You don't need to talk down to me," Sophie grumbled before shaking her head and softening her tone. "Maybe you're right. I watched Arazumi soldiers taking bodies away in a cart today. Doras said they take people away, cut them open, and 'eksperiment them.' It's scary, Philip."

"I know, all the more reason we have to leave! I don't like the idea of trusting a smuggler either, but we don't have a choice. We can't stay any longer," Philip sighed.

Chapter Three

"Everything is scary. Every day that we both worry we won't make it home. We worry that there will be no food. We're scared we'll get the pox, or consumption or, or-"

"Sophie," Philip held her close and patted her head. "That's why we're leaving. We get out of here, and things can only get better."

"But this is our home!"

"We'll make another one. If we stay here, we'll be buried in it," Philip whispered. He gave her one last pat and then left. He'd do his job on the docks today and keep an ear open for smugglers. Even indentured servitude was starting to look acceptable. Death was coming to the city; he could feel it.

***

TWO YEARS AGO, MIRABELLE got tossed into the deep end of sailing. It was the best thing her late husband ever gifted her. When he joined the wrong side of a failed coup against the crown, she fled to the estate's frigate with her loyal servants.

The old seadogs under her employ had told her that she was a quick study at captaining a ship, but they neglected the financial aspect. Mirabelle quickly learned that running a vessel and crew takes money; a lot of money. Some days she felt more like a floating accountant than a frigate captain. Her men worried about rough waves, high winds, and battle damage. She had to worry about all of that, plus their cash flow and stock of supplies. A bottleneck in coin was just as fatal as those storms they called "ship breakers." This explained the fit that she was currently throwing at the dock official.

Ritual | F. Arburg

A letter of mark was a document handed out by the port officials to a captain legalizing the capture of any ships they took. The details would vary, especially from port to port, but it was the only thing that separated a legal privateer from an illegal corsair. Plunder and ships they took had to be brought back to the harbor and paid for at an agreed upon prize rate. Mirabelle was horrified at what she saw.

"The prize rate of most ships has dropped seventy-five percent! Foodstuff and commodities are down by twenty-five! Oh, I'm glad to see that *slaves* remain at their old rate," Mirabelle spat at the desk worker. "This is ludicrous! Just six months ago, the rates were better!"

"The Regent has seen fit to adjust the letters of mark. If you don't like the rates, don't take a letter," the port official sniffed. He was young, remarkably clean-shaven, considering his peers, and already so cynical.

"I just don't understand; I'm not seeing a flood of prize goods causing a glut in the market here," Mirabelle jabbed a finger in the direction of the docks.

"Regent's orders. If you don't like it, I'm sure a Danarian like yourself will have better luck with Arazum's Southern Traders' Company, or maybe even the Shah of Dhalinur might find a job for you!" the official chortled. "Maybe, if you're really lucky, the Iron Sultan of Tersia will sooner employ you in his penal fleet than outright hang you!"

Mirabelle glared at him coldly for a moment and then, an icy smile crept across her face.

"A letter of mark, please," she conceded with manufactured sweetness.

Chapter Three

"Pleasure doing business with you, Captain Vellhuse."

A man fell in place behind her as she stormed away. He wore a breastplate and plated gauntlets but otherwise, his clothes were bright and neat. A thick mop of curly brown hair erupted from his head, and his face would have been handsome if half of it wasn't marred by a wide, angry scar. He lazily balanced an intimidating two-handed sword on his shoulder. Jacques was her bodyguard from when she was a young maid. The only time he strayed far from her was when he was summoned to fight in the Black War.

"Bad news, I take it?" he asked.

"Prize rates are the lowest I've seen them. No specific targets are listed in the letters, so that's at least encouraging," Mirabelle moaned.

"There could be trouble trying to privateer the tribals in the Archipelago. None of the men will agree to attack the Kholoti because they sacrifice those they capture. Fellow Danarians, Dhaliese, and the Arazumi are out of the question," Jacques listed.

"That leaves rogue corsairs and the Tersians then. Still rather difficult targets."

"It's not easy being privateers with scruples," Jacques muttered.

"It's better this way," Mirabelle reasoned. "We'll wait for a target to get careless and isolated. Better to have a letter of mark and not need it than to want one and not have it."

"Are finances that bad, Lady Mira? Are the repairs that insurmountable?" Jacques inquired quietly. "I know you spend a lot of time tallying the money we make, and I always thought we were fine."

"We are fine, Jacques," Mirabelle answered with a diplomatic smile. "We're just going to have to be a little innovative. Also, Reyais doesn't seem as helpful as I remember it. I wonder what changed."

"People tend to be less helpful when they've fallen on hard times. Or when they're selfish," Jacques answered.

"I wonder if a society can be both," the captain murmured, her gaze going up the city until she spied the Regent's palace up on the hill.

"That sounds…rather deep coming from you, captain," Jacques said with a chuckle. "Since when have you been like that?"

"I'd say it started ever since we had to flee the estate in the name of loyalty to the Crown, Jacques."

"Does it still bother you?"

"Not at all."

Mirabelle's gaze darted around the rest of the harbor. The usual craftsman and yards hadn't given her an agreeable estimate on repairing her ship, and storm season was coming. Bringing the *Lauria* out into open water, especially in her current state, was out of the question. Despite her best efforts, it didn't look like there were any out-of-work carpenters loitering around either.

"Lumber ain't cheap, ma'am," they told her when she raised a fuss. "Not enough to go around, haven't had any good shipments recently either."

Chapter Three

They were in a tight spot. She could feel the metaphorical anchor weighing her down with a threat of permanence. Time spent in the harbor was time not making money, and free crews had a habit of simply leaving if payday kept getting pushed forward into the indefinite future.

"I need to take a walk, Jacques. You're dismissed," she announced.

"Are you sure, my lady?"

"I can take care of myself," she told him, patting the hilt of her sword.

"Very well, I'll head back then," he replied reluctantly.

Mirabelle strolled until she was away from the piers and out of sight. The city walls jutted straight up from the cliffs and made them look more imposing. The sandy beach was filthy and sullen. More importantly, it was deserted, and that was the way she needed it. She kept glancing over her shoulder just in case.

She reached into her coat pocket and produced a scrap piece of parchment and one of those fancy metallic fountain pens made in Arazum. Such a wondrous thing, a quill with a built-in inkwell that you could carry around with you. She was going to be sad when it ran out. Still, desperate times called for desperate measures.

"I'm here," she scribbled on the parchment and rolled it up. Scanning the rubbish all about her, she spotted a bottle that, judging by its smell, had once served as a receptacle for someone's homemade rotgut booze. The foul contents were dumped and replaced with her note. Mirabelle tossed it into the sea. The bottle splashed the surface, floated for a moment, and then unnaturally dropped into the depths.

She didn't have to wait long. Three dark, sleek shapes rose to the surface of the waters. Three pairs of glowing eyes gazed at her. One by one, the mermaids showed themselves.

Mirabelle knew from previous encounters that the mermaids could change their appearance into beautiful seductresses of the sea. Other times they revealed themselves to be brutish, ghastly carnivores with chilling razor-sharp teeth. It reminded her of the fish that lived in the dark tomb of the ocean's depths. For this meeting, they appeared to be something in between deep-sea monstrosities with webbed hands and ghastly voices but a hint of human familiarity. They never told her their names, "Your tongue could not speak it," they told her, so she silently named them by the fish their scales reminded her of.

"She calls again," Bluegill hissed.

"Another favor she needs? Another debt?" Salmon rasped.

"Another debt we will remember," Perch spat with an animalistic sneer.

"I already owe you a heavy pile in cash. This time, I just need a little information, just some foresight. I'm not looking to add another chest of gold to the debt," Mirabelle shot.

"Impertinence," Bluegill gasped.

"Such arrogance," Salmon growled.

"Your debt is tallied at 500 bars of gold because you would not give us the 500 souls of the galleon we asked. Should we take your ship and crew instead?" Perch shrieked, her voice piercing through the air like icy razors.

Chapter Three

"They were kidnapped; slaves bound for the sacrificial temples of the Kholoti!" Mirabelle objected.

"So, they were dead anyway," Salmon fired back, forcing the words through her fangs.

"I gave you the treasure that was already aboard. You didn't need their flesh."

"They were strange meat. New meat. Succulent meat," Perch salivated.

"Sailor flesh is old, salty; tastes of pitch and fire and disease," Bluegill said, flashing her teeth.

"You must pay your 500 bars of gold or 500 souls of those who never knew the sea or 1,000 of those who have," Perch demanded.

"Then, what information can this bag of coins get me?" Mirabelle demanded, revealing the bulging pouch and wagging it in front of them. She had been keeping it for a rainy day and a bottle or two of brandy. It pained her to part with it, but she didn't see a lot of choices anymore. The mermaids drew in close and sniffed it like feral cats before a juicy fish.

"This does not lighten your older debt," Perch hissed, snatching the bag from her.

"I didn't expect it to."

Bluegill grabbed the bag from Perch and tore it open with her razor-sharp claws. Salmon grabbed a handful of coins and swallowed them down in one gulp. Bluegill did the same and disappeared back under the waves. Perch took her share and ate each coin one by one, as if savoring them.

"Disaster is coming," Perch said between gulps. "Ships burning on the water; smoke and thunder on the waves. Stones and iron and fire will be thrown into the deep."

"Sounds like a battle," Mirabelle speculated. "I suppose I could take advantage of that."

"It comes soon," Perch repeated. "See that your ship doesn't sink before your debt is paid. We will feast on you and your crew if it does."

The mermaid's tail slapped the water as she left. Mirabelle was left soaked and stewing silently in her thoughts.

***

> *Spells are dangerous, and those who use them are*
> *too dangerous to be allowed to live.*

THIS WAS THE UNDERLYING PHILOSOPHY of the Danarian Witch Hunters. If you asked some random soul to describe a 'dangerous spell', however, most people would make up absurd scenarios, like summoning fireballs hot enough to reduce an armored knight to molten slag or perhaps, mind control to turn nobles or even the Empress into hapless puppets. These would be diabolical enough, in their own right, but the Witch Hunters knew they were mere toys. The arcane offered far more disastrous spells and rituals to the unscrupulous.

Chapter Three

Diggo's Hammer could flatten a whole city while *Walking Pestilence* once ravaged an entire province with an incurable, virulent plague. Other spells were technically still 'theoretical', but the Witch Hunters couldn't allow any witch to attempt them. With names like *Vutan's Engine*, *Mountain Breaker*, and *Army of the Damned*, Witch Hunters had nightmares of a rogue sorcerer slipping through the cracks and completing such a ritual.

There were many of these forbidden spells and rituals locked away in the Witch Hunter's archives. Someone had to read these diabolical instructions and memorize them. How else would they be able to recognize a sorcerer about to attempt one? And, if a witch hunter feared that a sorcerer was about to attempt such a disaster, they'd be willing to chase the miscreant to some backwater island in order to stop them. Far more was at stake than the Danarian Crown.

The tavern was musty, smelled of pitch, mildew, cheap alcohol, and body odor. Seth was the only sharp-dressed patron in the establishment and the only thing keeping the cutthroats at bay were his confident demeanor and nasty-looking sword. It also helped that his eyes kept darting about him.

Currently, they were scanning the body language of a guard he was interrogating. Fortunately, the guard, along with everyone else in the establishment, were oblivious to the interrogation. A menagerie of empty glasses sat in front of the guard, which had been full when Seth bought them moments before.

"And you say that two dock hands were dead the next morning?" Seth inquired.

"Quite so, quite so, yer lordship," the guard slurred. "Guard captain of the district even had their bodies sent…sent away to be exam…exam…looked at."

"And whom did he pay to examine the bodies, this nice guard captain?"

"The A-a–ara…the Zumi. The Ara-s-s-sumi."

"They're around, too? Interesting," Seth murmured to himself. Dark theories bubbled thickly in his mind; chilly terrors fermented there as well. He remembered that the island's geography resembled a rune, an unsettling shape that blasted a melody of panic inside his skull.

"There wouldn't be any sort of new gang or cult causing trouble lately, hmm?" Seth prodded.

"New cult? Trouble? Naw, the only new cult is the Prosperous Light. The priestess has been schmoozing the nobles who live up the hill," the guard wobbly gestured towards the general direction of the regent's palace. "My fellows are saying she'll conv…coniv…hmm, tell those rich arses to share some of their wealth with us. Might as well, don't know why they have to take all our wages."

"Yes, how hopeful for you," the Witch Hunter said.

So indeed, there was a new cult of trouble makers. They didn't have to declare outright, that trouble would be their intent; they all ended up as trouble makers, sooner or later. Apparently, Mara had evolved past her usual tricks and experiments. It would now seem that she had a frightening new goal in mind.

"'*Mara's Chalice,*'" he muttered to himself, his face growing dark.

Chapter Three

"Who, what? Can I have another drink, friend?"

"Of course," Seth agreed, sliding the guard a few coins. In time, there wouldn't be any more drinks for the guard to enjoy. The Witch Hunter left the tavern. He needed to think.

The island on which Reyais sits, is the rune; she'll simply have to empower the ley lines to activate it. How did she write it down in her notes, again? 'A sacrifice of the masses, a sacrifice of an immense ancient, and the sacrifice of a powerful young life.'

It occurred to him that all the pieces were here. He could guess at two of those sacrifices, but what exactly was the third one? How could he stop her?

***

SOPHIE LAY DOWN UPON her bed, staring at the crumbling ceiling. Philip said he found a smuggler that would get them off the island. She asked if he trusted the smuggler. He only said they didn't have a choice. She hated this.

All their lives, they had never had a choice. They had no choice when Mom and Dad died, no choice for Philip but to work as a dockhand, and no options for her but to scrounge around during the day for food or valuables. Philip was too afraid of something happening to leave her in the employ of a shop somewhere. "For now, at least," he'd always say.

How long could that last? Her stomach growled. She ignored it. She thought back on the water-logged page she had found today, while on the beach looking for crabs, dead fish, or a bauble that she could bring home for Philip to pawn off. Sophie couldn't read, but on the page was a painting of the most beautiful insect she had ever seen. It had two enormous, deep-blue wings with intricate, pretty patterns. She wondered where they lived. Maybe she could find them where the smuggler would take them. Sophie tried to fall asleep. Philip said they would meet the man early in the morning.

While she slept, she thought of the pretty insect. On the ceiling, right above her bed, a blue butterfly took form. It flapped its wings and tumbled out the window. The insect didn't make it far before it burst into incandescent azure dust and evaporated away.

Butterflies are not native to Reyais.

CHAPTER 4

GULLS CRIED TO EACH OTHER over the early morning surf. Sleepy fish glided placidly below the water's surface. They immediately scattered upon hearing human voices. Two dinghies drifted side by side, far from the docks on this otherwise calm morning. Two men were having a rather pointed discussion across from each other, bobbing about in their respective boats. The pungent smell of coffee hung in the air.

"Right, so that's that on Auntie Nyook. Are you almost done then?"

"Not by a long shot, Cousin. There's still Uncle Geos, Auntie Tia, Cousin Jif-Jif, Grandma-"

"By the Holy, get on with it then, Samir."

"Of course, Cousin Leon, though it'll go much faster if you stop interrupting."

Captains Leon Kasamir and Samir Temeng differed in their uniforms, the nations they served, and their mannerisms. The only thing that united them was that awkward shackle called "family" and a passion for coffee. Their mugs grew cold and salty as Samir caught Leon up on how the family in Dhalinur was doing. Leon was running out of parchment, as well as patience.

"Last of all, is little Nephew Al-Al. He took ill with a fever, but he's much better now. Little rascal loves his bananas, kip-kip," Samir reported with a smile.

"Wonderful," Leon mumbled as he put the last of his notes away in a water-tight container.

"All right, your turn then," Samir told him. "Tell me about Auntie Lina, Uncle Bernardo, and Cousin Ignacio."

"They're fine. Auntie Lina still works at the local granary and cafe at home. Uncle Bernardo still works for the post office. My brother Ignacio has also decided to join the Republic Navy and will begin training in a month or so. That's it."

"That's it? Cousin Leon, you're either a lousy storyteller or your family doesn't know how to have fun!"

"I would argue that it's more a matter of the other side of my family to not know how to stay out of trouble," Leon argued, folding his arms in front of his chest.

"Bah, Arazumi are just too serious for their own good. You get that from Uncle Bernardo. All right, you've seen my beloved Mouse-Deer. Did you notice the new cannons I put on her? All bronze! I worry less about a gun blowing up on me now," Samir boasted.

"Just make sure your gunners use good powder and don't overload them. When are you going to upgrade to something that isn't rowed? I'll worry less about you when you get a ship that can fit more guns on it," Leon said.

"Firepower isn't everything, Cousin, especially when you're hunting Archipelago corsairs and Kholoti. You should know that, kip-kip. Now, tell me about your ship!"

Chapter Four

"The *Defiance*? Well, what did you see of her?" Leon returned cryptically.

"I counted four cannons and many small rotary guns. I saw a rack of tubes on its center, I don't know what for, but it can't be good. I know nothing is ever what it looks like with Arazumi clockwork, so what else is that ship hiding?"

"I can't tell you anything else about it, Samir. Republic Navy policy, you see," Leon said.

"I see, I see. I suppose I understand," Samir replied, his enthusiasm only slightly dampened. "I do hope I get to see those cannons in action. They must be exciting to fire."

"Pray that you don't. I find them terrifying," Leon admitted, then eyed the burlap sack in his cousin's boat.

"So when are you going to hand over the good stuff? You know how hard it is to find properly roasted coffee beans outside of Dhalinur?"

"As soon as you hand over the coin, gingerbread, and clockwork knick-knacks for Auntie Tia's shop, Cousin," Samir chuckled. The two men gingerly wrestled over their respective goods. With the boats rocking in the waves, it wasn't an easy endeavor, but it was one done with the utmost care.

"Do you think you could get these purple yams to Auntie Lina before they go bad? I threw them in as well since I know how much you all like them," Samir offered.

"Probably not, but I'll eat them," Leon lied. The truth was they could quickly be brought back in time to Auntie Lina, but Leon saw no reason to share these goodies. "I also snuck a couple of cans of condensed milk for you all as well. Auntie Lina also gave me a bottle of Edalan Red."

"Also, don't forget the special green plumed pigeons," Samir said, pointing to a cage of the exotic birds. "You know, just in case you need to send a message directly to me while we're here. You remember how they work, right?"

"Of course."

"Excellent, excellent! You know, Uncle Baruum said you were foolish switching over to your Republic Navy rather than staying as a company privateer, but you're all right by me, Cousin."

"The Navy is offering favorable terms to captains who served well as Traders' privateers. Besides, at least you and I are still respectable."

"I agree, but Uncle Baruum only thinks on how a man can grow wealthy by capturing ships," Samir lamented.

"Sure, but as I said, we're still respectable," Leon said before lowering his voice. "Not like our cousin Davos who's gone full corsair."

"That's just a rumor, Cousin," Samir replied hesitantly. "He's still welcomed at Dhalinur harbor; it's never been proven he took a ship without a cause."

"That's because he auctions off the more embarrassing prize ships here in Reyais, where they'll give a sleazy letter of mark for it."

Chapter Four

"Enough, Cousin Leon, it's bad enough he's on our side of the—speak of the devil—I do believe those are his ships on the horizon," Samir cried, pulling out his spyglass to better study the sight he had been watching.

"What makes you say that?"

"Something about the formation. He likes sailing his squadron of five like that; then he trails whatever newly captured ships he takes behind them." Samir explained as Leon fished out a pair of binoculars. "And, if I'm reading those shapes on the horizon right, it seems like he took a massive new ship."

Leon's jaw set in a way that Samir didn't like as he studied the sight on the horizon. It was enough to make the Dhaliese captain nervous, and it resembled the expression corsairs wore on their faces plodding to the gallows.

"What's wrong, Cousin Leon?"

"That new ship he captured. The hull appears to be made of Tersian Ironwood. The sails and rigging look Tersian. Oh—and the rows of cannons and their bore size? Tersian."

"Tersian ships are popular targets for privateers and corsairs. They've made themselves so unpopular, even the Shah will tolerate a captured Tersian ship, if the captain says he took it with a justifiable cause."

"Samir, it looks like a Tersian fortress ship," Leon breathed sharply.

"A f-fortress ship? How did Cousin Davos take one of those? You must be mistaken, Cousin Leon."

Leon handed Samir the binoculars. Samir cursed in a Dhaliese dialect.

"We better head back to our ships, Samir. There's going to be trouble," Leon hissed, already reaching for the oars on his boat.

"Trouble? That's putting it very lightly, Cousin. Terribly sorry, but I must let the other sea-clanners in the harbor know. Cousin Davos could be bringing a squadron of Tersians right behind him, looking for retribution."

"Do you think they'd chase him this far with a squadron? I'm sure the Tersians have other troubles to deal with," Leon said uneasily.

"It's a fortress ship. They're going to want it back."

"Leave it to Davos to cause an international incident."

"What was that, Cousin Leon?"

"Nothing, now get out of here, Samir! Trouble is coming in on the waves."

The awkward shackle called "family" promptly jerked in an unexpected direction. The old chain tended to do that.

***

SOPHIE DIDN'T LIKE THIS. She didn't like where Philip was leading her. She didn't like how foreboding the streets were, even by Reyais's standards. And, she definitely didn't like how there seemed to be few people around. Sophie didn't like any of this.

Chapter Four

"Philip, lets…let's find someone else…or go back home. I have a bad feeling about this."

Philip stopped dead in his tracks. When he spoke, he didn't look at her. "Food shipments have been growing less frequent, Sophie. The ones that come in are almost completely designated for the Palace. You do know what this means, right?"

Sophie trembled. "Food is going to become more expensive, isn't it?"

"Remember that winter when food was scarce? Remember when we trembled all night, and we couldn't tell if it was because we were freezing or weak from starving? Remember when that man grabbed you and…and what if I wasn't there?"

"Okay, okay!" Sophie whimpered. "I'll be brave. You're right, we have to do this."

Her older brother walked with a marked deliberateness. He scrutinized the doorposts they passed. There must have been a secret sign or symbol for him to look for. All Sophie saw was one dilapidated building after another. He abruptly stopped.

"This one."

Philip knocked with a trembling hand. Paint cracked and crumbled off its beams. A moment of silence stretched an eternity of heartbeats too long. He was about to knock again when the door opened. The room beyond was dark as pitch.

"H-hello?" Philip called meekly.

"Get in," an icy voice hissed.

Philip tugged on Sophie's arm and they rushed in. The door closed with a slam. The world was dark until a dim lamp was coaxed to life. They saw eyes and faces in the gloom. Sophie's breath caught in her throat. They must have inadvertently stepped into the Abyss.

Blindfolds were roughly tied around their heads. Rough, leathery hands pushed them to the floor. It was gritty and smelled of mouse.

"I-I thought we were being smuggled out of Reyais! I paid you what I had!" Philip protested. "I was promised we'd work the rest of our debt off on a plantation for the Southern Traders Company!"

"That's mostly true," an unfeeling voice said cryptically. Sophie realized all this time there had been the faint hiss of a fire somewhere below them.

"You will work off your debt on a plantation, and you will be smuggled there as agreed. But first, you need to be marked."

"Marked?'

A burning hot brand slammed into the base of their necks.

***

THE EMBASSY WAS ABUZZ. It didn't take long for the news to get out that the two corpses in their custody were killed by anomalous activity. "Magic" was a dirty word in the Arazumi lexicon. It was too barbaric and backward. The wisdom of sages and then, early scientists said that magic was too chaotic, too specific to an individual to be meaningfully studied.

Chapter Four

Contemporary Arazumi researchers took to calling it "anomalous activity" instead and they insisted that the rest of the population follow. Give it a modern name and a modern approach and hopefully, enough data points would arise for a pattern to emerge. So far, the pattern said more data was needed.

It was one thing for Comstock Night Riders to be called in for a werewolf. They specialized in the anomalous, hunting those that dabbled with the arcane and unnatural creatures. Peasants in foreign nations could be a superstitious lot and it wasn't unheard-of for Night Riders to return with only the pelt of an oversized wolf to show for their troubles; giant wolves tearing through livestock and terrorizing peasants were a tragedy, but they weren't anomalous creatures. Two verified corpses with the evidence to back it up, and Guard Captain Axle Greerson upped the security protocols.

"Looks like another morning out there in Reyais if you ask me," Jord said, watching the streets below. The watchtower over the main gate allowed for a commanding view. Unfortunately, Reyais was overbuilt with buildings and small branching alleyways. Makeshift and alarmingly temporary stalls, lean-tos, and other urban detritus only added to the mess. A commanding view of urban chaos only allowed you to better appreciate just how much could be hidden in plain sight in front of you.

"Another day for Reyais, but I wonder if the Druids up on the mountain would feel the same. We left a proper mess up there with all that dynamite," Otto muttered.

"Hmm," Jord rumbled.

"Anyway, we now know there's an anomalous manipulator out there somewhere in the city. We always assume magic users are the aggressors, don't we?" Otto continued. "For all we know those two stiffs down there tried to attack said magician and were killed in self-defense."

"Magic is treated with respect in Raermak. In most places, they just burn a witch or wizard at the stake. Raermaks don't do that unless you give us a reason to do so. Their neighbors will be a little wary of them, though," Jord said.

"Similar in Arazum. Innocent until proven guilty."

"A sentiment I believe you all learned from us. If I remember correctly, there have been one or two witch hunts in Arazum," Jord replied with a cheeky smile.

"Yes, but then the rebellion happened, the monarch was deposed –"

"Beheaded."

"Yes, and then shortly after that came the First Great Plague, and when that was over, there were so few people left it didn't make much sense to burn anyone else. Everyone was needed, anomalous manipulator or otherwise. The Republic decided magic in itself wasn't a crime under those circumstances."

"But, it does look like a crime of some sort was committed outside these walls here," Jord said, pointing at the durable ramparts that protected the embassy. "So now we especially need to keep our eyes open. Tell me, little man, do you think some magician would want to magic his way into these walls?"

Chapter Four

"I doubt it. A lot of foreigners seem to be under some mad fantasy that we take such individuals away then cut them open and probe their insides," Otto chuckled nervously, taking another sip of coffee.

"Don't your scientists do that already with ghouls, werewolves, basilisks, and the like?"

"Well, yes, but those are different," Otto explained.

"Arazumi seem to be able to tell the difference between those two. Most other people don't."

A bell on a wooden panel next to them began to ring. Jord squinted.

"I do believe that's Derek's station."

"He may be a misanthrope, but it sometimes serves him well in sentry work," Otto conceded begrudgingly. "Sometimes."

The guard connected the line and then picked up a heavy receiver and mouthpiece.

"This is Cobalt Sentinel. Speak."

"I have a big procession of locals dressed in white. Looks like some sort of parade," Derek's voice flickered and sparked through the copper wire.

"Do you expect trouble?"

"Not yet, but they're getting closer. I'll report it at my discretion."

"Understood. I'll go over to investigate," Otto replied before hanging up the receiver.

"What was that about?" Jord inquired.

"Stay here; young Derek has spotted something interesting."

Otto moved at a hurried trot along the rampart. A strange parade with no immediate or apparent reason was worth an observation. Most of the guards stationed at the embassy, while well-trained, were still pups. Only Jord, Axle, and himself had seen combat. He finally stopped having night terrors about the Black War, and that had ended three years ago. These days they were just unpleasant dreams.

Derek watched the procession of white-clad people below the wall. There weren't many of them, but they walked with a self-assurance that Otto believed no one should have.

"Have they said anything?" Otto asked, beginning to study the parade with his binoculars.

"'Alms for the Prosperous Light. All will be welcomed in Reyais's Prosperous Light,'" Derek recited.

"How quaint. I wonder which arrogant charlatan decided more of these poor people need to be parted with what few coins they have left."

"Alms today to fund arms for when they get uppity," Derek said. "That's quite astute of you, Derek. Have you had any experience with cults?"

Chapter Four

"No, I just don't like groups of holier-than-thou types asking for my money to then tell me how to live. How about you?"

"Just one. It wasn't positive…well, looks like they're passing on now. I'll write up the report. Carry on, young guard."

***

LATER THAT MORNING, Jord, Otto, and Kassia were sent beyond the walls to carry out another chore assigned by the Republic. Flanked on both sides by armed and armored guards, Kassia felt overprotected. Personally, she would have preferred going alone and inconspicuously. She was perfectly capable of protecting herself. Regardless, protocols were protocols.

They made their way towards the dock avoiding the busier roads where they could. Abandoned alleyways were still out of the question. The embassy had no way to measure the amount of violent crime in Reyais, mainly because the city's decayed organ that passed for its judicial system had no interest in keeping track of it.

"All this trouble," Otto began before pointing to the satchel that clung to Kassia's shoulder. "For a bag of medicines."

"You served in the Black War, Otto, in addition to how many other contract wars. You should know how important a simple bag of medicines should be," Kassia replied with a smile.

"If we're going to be treating it that importantly, then we should be in an armored auto-buggy and there would be more than one bag."
"By the Holy, I'd hate to fight a war here," Jord grumbled. "All these streets and alleyways. It'd be worse than when we fought the Kholoti in the jungles."

"Bad memories, Jord," Otto reprimanded.

They arrived at the docks and made their way towards a quaint wooden shack. Around the building, the docks bustled with the usual day-to-day traffic. A lot of eyes stared out towards the horizon, where a group of ships fought the wind trying to pull into the harbor. The shack stood apart from all this, and yet the boards by the door were well-worn from a steady stream of traffic. With a rusted iron symbol, it advertised itself as a place to get medicines. Kassia rapped smartly on the door. An older woman with primitive, round spectacles opened it. She managed a smile upon seeing the three foreigners.

"Welcome, right on time! Are you here for samples, or did you bring more medicines?"

"Both, Mrs. Selma," Kassia replied, handing her counterpart the leather satchel. Selma took the package gingerly, almost reverently.

"It's the same as the last one," Kassia said. "Bandages, medicines for the 'Chills' -- we call it 'Malaria,' by the way -- tablets for scurvy and syringes for the Pox. You're not doubling up on those syringes, are you?"

"Of course not; you said a man or woman or child is good for one dosage, but my patients are a little skeptical of it. They don't really understand why they need one if they've never had the Pox before, but it's no good if they've already had it."

"That's just how it works, Mrs. Selma. Are your patients showing improvement with what we've given you?"

"It's hard to say. A lot of sailors come in, and I never see them again," Selma shrugged and then lowered her voice. "And most of them just come in for the mercury treatment. You sure you don't have a fancy Arazumi treatment for that?"

"None that would be more effective than wishful thinking. And, Arazum aren't in the business of putting that in a bottle and then deceptively selling it as a cure. Do you have a recent, uh, sample?"

"Just this," Selma replied, handing the chemist a dark bottle. "Someone was selling crates of them at the market; said the medicinal herbs in it made it a cure-all."

"I bet they did," Kassia spat, uncorking the bottle. "Jord, may I borrow a match? I'm quite certain I know what the main ingredient is."

"No bother, Ms.," Jord said, snatching it and taking a quick swig.

"Jord! There could be poisons in it! Toxic metals!" Kassia gasped.

The large man shook his head and wagged a gauntleted finger at her. The brew swished back and forth between his cheeks.

Otto made a noise somewhere between a chuckle and a snort.

"You shouldn't have done that," he told an exasperated Kassia.

The Raermak spat and wiped his lips with the back of his sleeves. "Ugh, it's something of a mix between poor vodka and even worse absinthe with some added fruit in there to sweeten it."

Kassia wrestled the bottle out of his grasp and threw it in her bag. "We'll be running a far more precise analysis of that back at the ship, though I suppose my friend's taste test will suffice for now," she scowled. "Thank you, Mrs. Selma. A good day to you."

"And to you as well!"

They noticed a man approaching them, a large sword resting on his shoulder as they left. The guards instinctively smiled. Otto subtly brought his hand close to the holster at his side. It didn't help that the stranger wore plate and clothes that looked remarkably Danarian and a ghastly scar that raged on half his face.

"Abyss take you, Arazumi!" the man threatened, spitting at their feet. "Abyss take you, just like you took so many of my countrymen!"

"Nothing personal, sir. I believe you forced us to sign the cease-fire anyway," Otto replied conversationally.

"You poisoned a whole army! The very air it breathed! It burned my face!"

"Three years ago. Gone along with the war. Time for you to walk along and have a good day, sir," Otto smiled. His posture growled.

"You as well! And choke in the Abyss!" the stranger cursed with a feral grin.

The rest of the walk back was uneventful. Kassia seemed the most shaken up by the event. She tried distracting herself by studying the bottle they had taken from Selma. Otto decided to break up the silence.

"Why are we taking those fake medicines and testing them? It seems unnecessary."

Chapter Four

"Who knows?" Kassia shrugged. "All I was told was that the Republic wants to keep tabs on how our neighbors are handling their medical affairs. Reyais is a mess, so this is the best we can do. And that man? Do you know him?"

"Not personally," Otto replied. "Maybe in the war, I shot at him. Maybe he knew someone I shot at in the war. Who knows?"

"The sooner you let go of resentment, the sooner the poison leaves your soul," Jord lectured.

"Easier said than done," Otto said.

"It always is."

***

WAS IT NECESSARY FOR YOU to do that?" Mirabelle asked, as her bodyguard came back on board the *Lauria*.

"What?"

"Antagonizing those Arazumi. Those were Long Steel guards, right? They could have shot you! What got into you, Jacques?"

"You didn't fight in the war, my lady, so you'll pardon me for letting my anger get the better of me."

"That was foolish, Jacques, and impolite."

The bodyguard didn't do well with his captain's displeasure. Instead, he gazed out towards the horizon. A formation of ships were pulling in. Mirabelle also saw them and pulled out her spyglass.

"By the Holy!"

"What is it? I don't like the look of those ships; whose are they?"

"That's Captain Davos' flag on their mainmasts; can't mistake that ugly collection of blades he calls a flag. He's captured a Tersian fortress ship!"

"C-captured? How?" Jacques sputtered. "Those things are, well, fortresses. If the cannons don't blow your ship apart, the men aboard will stop you from capturing it and then board yours! How did he do it?"

"I always knew he was a crazy man but...wow. He just became a rich one as well," Mirabelle said, eyes still as wide as saucers.

"But...but there's no way the Tersians would just allow that. They'll want their ship back!"

"Then let's hope they didn't follow him," Mirabelle murmured. She sounded more confident than she was.

CHAPTER 5

THE CITY OF REYAIS STARTED on the shoreline. In fact, that's where most of the population lived and where visiting sailors tended to lurk, never straying further into the city. From the harbor, it climbed up and followed the slope of Mount Letixis, the same mount the druids hold sacred. At the very top of the tired sprawl sat the Regent's Palace. Technically, the regent served as an official of the Kingdom of Ta'Geh across the sea to the north. Ta'Geh hadn't checked in on Reyais in decades.

The palace wasn't just built on the top because of its splendorous vista and the quip of looking down upon the poor. The stream Diphon ran down the mountain and made a convenient source of freshwater for the Palace. From there, having first served the regent and his house, it continued on to water the rest of Reyais. Admittedly, by the time the Diphon got to the shoreline, it could only be optimistically described as "water" and had long ceased to be potable.

Seth managed to get into the Palace and even landed an audience with the Regent. It turned out to be a lot easier than expected. For one, a polite Danarian Witch Hunter was considered an important official. Second, from what Seth observed, it didn't look like the Reyais nobility was very busy with matters of state. There was a lot of wine flowing, rich food being gobbled, and even a lot of rambunctious talking, but none of it concerned administration.

A chalice of wine sat in his hand. He brought it to his lips. Strong. He heard that the traditional method of serving wine in Reyais was to water it down, enough to take the edge off. This cup wasn't diluted in the slightest, and it came from a particularly strong vintage.

"You seem surprised, Witch Hunter," a cold voice said. Seth weighed his words carefully.

"This is a delicious wine, Regent."

Regent Mateo Iskander was of average height, barrel-chested, balding, and his skin was heavily wrinkled. Nevertheless, he held himself tall when he walked, and his voice still spoke with authority. Seth told himself to avoid irritating the man if at all possible. Considering the subject he was about to bring up, he didn't think it was possible.

"Thank you. It came from my own personal vineyard," the older man bragged, taking a seat next to the Witch Hunter. Seth noticed that the Regent wasn't drinking. He didn't like that. He took another sip to pretend he hadn't noticed.

"However, I assume you didn't request an audience with me just to sample my wine and give me a warm salutation. That's a diplomat's job. You're a Witch Hunter," Iskander said with a faint smile. It lacked warmth.

"There is, in fact, a witch that I've tracked all the way from Danaria to your city. Simply put, I request that you aid me in her capture and, if necessary, execution."

"Has she committed a crime here in Reyais?"

Chapter Five

"There are two dead longshoremen who I suspect are her victims. The evidence is circumstantial, but to assume it wasn't her doing would be the highest in folly."

"Longshoremen die every week, if not every day. Besides, you admit you don't have proof. Are there any crimes she may have committed, or are suspicions all you have?" Iskander demanded. He was calm, but Seth could tell his mind was already made up.

"I'm afraid I have nothing more concerning crimes she may have committed here. In Danaria, however–"

"This is not Danaria, Witch Hunter, so I don't care. If Reyais were to have scruples with every one of our visitors' pasts, we'd be a poorer city."

"Yes, I can see that," Seth nodded in agreement. The Palace certainly appeared to be doing well for itself. Was there anything in this room that didn't scream of expense and vanity? Seth didn't want to admit it, but it was all very gaudy to him, and he'd seen many, many palaces back in Danaria.

"Come to me when you have an actual crime to pin on her. Otherwise, do not waste my time. Now, if it's any consolation, I won't impede your pursuit of her so long as you don't give me a reason to do so. Now, are there any other complaints you'd like to fill my ear with, Witch Hunter?"

"No, I believe that is all, your Excellency," Seth relented with a smile and a bow. "I will be taking my leave of you."

"Formalities must be kept, Witch Hunter! The unspoken agreements must abide!" Iskander bellowed at him as he left. Seth forced himself to nod as he swallowed the bile rising in his mouth.

"Indeed, they must."

He knew that there would be no easy way out of this now. The hunt would continue. Mara, of course, would have been working on the ritual all this time. *A sacrifice of the masses, a sacrifice of an immense ancient, and one of a powerful young life.* The masses couldn't be helped. The immense ancient couldn't be controlled. He would have no choice then, but to move said young life off the board. But, where was it hiding?

***

EVERY EYE ON THE DOCKS WATCHED the fortress ship. Captain Davos captured other smaller vessels that needed to be audited, but they were ignored. The sailing behemoth that was the fortress ship was anchored away from the piers since none could accommodate her. Cargo was lowered from its top deck to waiting barges below. The laborers worked as fast as possible while the weather and pleasant waters allowed. So much loot had to be unloaded.

Winternalia had come early to the harbor town. Mirabelle, along with every soul around, took stock of the plundered cargo. Loud cheers rose when casks of coconut wine arrived on shore.

Among the usual exciting things already scattered along the docks, sat a few chests of coins intended for the payroll of Tersian sailors, but would now be the lucre of pirates; a few rolls of expensive and vibrant Tersian rugs; jugs of the exotic Lu'han purple dye; even quite

Chapter Five

a few shells of the Jeweled Sea Turtle that lives south of the Archipelago. Their shells were like giant pearls and were valued accordingly.

Less flashy, but still significant items included the small stock of spare lumber that arrived. Mirabelle watched it hungrily. Stores of gunpowder, shot, and extra guns were also delivered. Then, came the supplies of medicine and bandages. No one ever made sea shanties of them, but sailors and corsairs alike would hoard them as if they were gold and liquor. Next, came the rice. Bags upon bags of rice. It wasn't extravagant, but a full belly could be just as satisfying as treasure. This was followed by boxes of tea, burlap sacks of coffee beans, and jars of honey; things which enterprising local merchants could readily spin for a profit.

Then, there were the things that no one could be quite sure of; paraphernalia so niche to a Tersian war vessel that it was hard to put a price on them. Books and tomes covered in bizarre symbols came in, all written in the Tersian script, so that only a very few individuals would be able to read them. Fewer souls would dare try, for there was no telling what a magical tome could do to an unprepared reader. There were nautical maps showing the currents around the Lu'han Empire, but to get there, a ship first had to sail through Tersia, and not many of the captains here were interested in that. Then there were the manacles, clubs, and whips used in the business of keeping human chattel in order. No one liked to admit it, but some individuals would be interested in purchasing those items once the sun went down, and there would be fewer judging eyes to watch.

Mirabelle paced around the dock, trying to track the stock of lumber she saw. She watched it more intensely than any prize ship she spotted on the open sea. Relief flowed through her like a heady wine. She could get the lumber, strike some deals, maybe take on a little more debt, but she then could get the *Lauria* seaworthy again. That was all that mattered. Once the sails were full and her ship was roving, she could make all the money she needed.

She heard shouting. Bystanders were pushed aside. Sailors cursed hard enough to turn the air blue. Mirabelle was fluent in swearing, and this was the kind that raised alarm bells. She rushed towards the source of the commotion.

"Make way for the Palace Guards! Make way!' someone announced.

Most of the city's guards purchased their armor or made do with what they could; in the worst cases, a rusting helmet and a hefty wooden club that may have once been a table's leg were the only things signifying their occupation. The Palace Guards were a different species altogether. Their armor was uniform and well-maintained, made of steel plate with a bronze finish. Many carried broad shields as tall as a man and an equally robust pike to go with it. A sword at their waist served as a backup weapon. Those that didn't have the shield, pike, and sword carried a matchlock instead. Theoretically, the combination was deadly; the men with pikes acted as a barrier while those armed with matchlocks rained death from afar. The tactic had never been tested against invaders, but quite a few riots were swiftly snuffed out in the face of it.

The formation of guards descended on the assembled store of treasure piled on the docks. Words were exchanged with the harbor clerks. A courier was dispatched and scurried on a boat to Captain Davos' ship, paddles frantically spinning with haste. A while later, Davos Temeng was spied on the boat's return trip. Mirabelle met him once before and promised herself there and then never to cross him. Davos was a taciturn and ambitious Dhaliese man who fought like a demon. He always seemed to have a collection of knives and blades on him, a collection that only a man of his size could pull off. Davos arrived and was immediately led to a discussion with the clerks and the lieutenants of the Palace Guards. A hush descended on the docks.

The negotiations were quiet and quickly resolved. Chests laden with gold and a cart loaded down with grape wine were stowed onto boats destined for Davos' squadron. In turn, the Palace Guards began to take away the bulk of Davos' plunder.

"Wait, wait, are they going to leave any for us?" Mirabelle demanded. Other sailors began to voice her concerns but in a much louder tone. The guards ignored them. The clerks returned to their stations and started double-checking their figures, the bureaucrat's way of sticking his head in the sand. Piece by piece, the plunder was carted away to the Palace. Resentment threatened to ignite the air.

Privateers are an egalitarian bunch. Talent and the invisible claw of profit were their driving forces. Everyone understood there might be a small tax on what a privateer captured, but most of the booty was to be doled out and distributed among the crew and then unleashed into the community. That natural order was now stymied like a sinking ship. The ramifications began playing out all over the harbor like a virulent cough. Mirabelle could hear it.

"You, Captain Lizario, are you still going to pay me for those repairs?" a carpenter yowled peevishly. "You told me you were good for the money!"

"I'll get you your damn money once I damn well get paid! I can't be paid until someone purchases my cargo and no one is buying!"

"Well, me and my boys will be ignoring your ship until the payments come in again!"

"How about I send my boys to go and slap your boys in chains and hold them at blade point until you finish the damn job we agreed to!"

"You...you wouldn't!" the carpenter snarled, turning red in the sun.

"Oh, I would! You try me!"

Nearby, Mirabelle watched a tavern owner forlornly disappear inside his establishment before coming back with a "closed" sign and then barring the doors shut. Elsewhere, a surgeon returned his tools to their bag and then took a long swig from one of his cure-alls. Street vendors packed up their stalls or got into heated arguments with sailors who had outstanding debts with them. The saddest sight Mirabelle saw was an older matron standing in front of a building that advertised itself as "Dame Clara's Seamstresses." Dame Clara shook her head and hurried up the steps of her building.

"Sorry girls, it looks like they'll be no one who'll be paying to get their sails stitched. Just tell the others to expect some customers in our other line of work instead, and that's if we get lucky," Clara told the women waiting by the door. The girls began hanging red lanterns by the windows instead.

Mirabelle paced around dejectedly, helpless at what to do. It felt as though someone had jammed her rudder. Then, she remembered she was angry, a rage that ignited in her head. She needed that lumber, and now it was gone, all because of the Regent!

"What in the Abyss does the Regent need that lumber for!" she hissed furiously.

"That was good hardwood, milady," Jacques said. "Maybe he needs construction done at the Palace?"

Chapter Five

"We needed that lumber more than he did!"

"I agree, but it looks like the Regent had the money for it. Did we have the money for it?"

"Irrelevant!" Mirabelle belly-ached. She stomped off to her cabin, slamming the door loudly behind her. She needed to think, preferably with a bottle of brandy.

***

CAPTAIN LEON WAS SUFFERING his own paroxysm of agitation. The man marched aboard the communication vessel *Serene*, moored in the embassy harbor. Wireless telegraph communication was a very recent development and the Republic was practically tripping over itself trying to get the technology to run efficiently. The *Serene* carried all the messages from the embassy to the Republic and back. It also handled most of the messages bouncing around the region. If the *Serene* lost the antenna array that made it look like a multi-masted monstrosity, this whole map square would go mute. The Republic would go into a panic once it noticed that. Information was as precious as gold to the upstart nation.

Thanks to wayward cousin Davos, Captain Leon needed one antenna explicitly reserved for a particular gunboat in his flotilla. On his orders, carried out by a very confused crew, that gunboat had left its usual patrol to scout the waters to the southeast. He couldn't tolerate any messages it sent getting lost in a backlog.

"Operator, I need...why is a Long Steel man operating one of the telegraphs here?" Leon demanded. Most of the other men working the machines were clerks, the green in their ties or armbands marking them as employees of the Comstock Company. It made sense;

Comstock virtually owned the telegraph industry in Arazum. This operator wore Long Steel's blue uniform. Now that he was looking, he could see a few other Long Steel men in the room, scraps of blue within an assembly of green.

"Hi, sir! The name's Michael. Right now, they need as many operators as they can to transmit a report back to Arazum. It's a big one and we can't shorthand any words. It's the geological survey that we pulled off the mountain before the druids decided to go all hooligan on us. Apparently, it's our top priority," Michael elaborated helpfully.

"Do you know who I am, young guard?"

"One of the gunboat captains?"

"Captain Leon Kasamir of the gunboat destroyer *Defiance* and flotilla commander of the embassy squadron," Leon recited icily. The hapless guard smiled nervously.

"I take it this is a matter of embassy security?"

"Indeed, it is. You will listen for any messages from gunboat G-57. You will then immediately relay them to me until I relieve you of this duty. Am I clear?"

"Yes, Captain. Are we expecting trouble?"

"I am, and as far as you're concerned, that's all that matters."

***

Chapter Five

MIRABELLE AND JACQUES SAT on some forgotten cargo boxes on the docks, eyeing the pitiful scraps left behind by the Palace Guards. It was mostly rice, a few banged-up kitchen utensils, a funny-smelling bolt of cloth, and a water-stained box of salt. Mirabelle sulked. Jacques wasn't doing much better, but he felt the need to rein in his captain's more belligerent fantasies.

"I still say we have a chance at stealing the lumber back," Mirabelle huffed.

"That's the brandy talking. There's no way we could break into the palace, take the lumber, and then, get the ship patched up. It's just not realistic, Captain," Jacques scolded.

"We raided that warehouse in Sudev," Mirabelle pointed out.

"For bags of powder and shot that were, arguably, rightfully confiscated from us. The spices we found and stole were taken out of opportunity because it would've been a shame to leave them there all alone. Furthermore, and this is important, the warehouse was practically next to our ship. That's much different from the situation we're in now. Also, and I must point this out, we no longer return to Sudev!"

"Because it's too cold up there," Mirabelle prevaricated.

"Of course. I imagine the harbor authorities might still be a little unhappy with us as well!"

"What are we going to do, Jacques? What are we going to do?"

"We could wait."

"I hate waiting."

A chilly silence descended upon them. The smell of the sea beckoned to Mirabelle, singing of freedom. The stench of rotting, discarded refuse told her she was bound to a broken ship like an Arazumi bear trap gnashing at her ankle and that the insurmountable debt was strangling her like an iron pillory garroting her neck.

"If it's any consolation, I heard that Davos didn't feel he was adequately compensated for his plunder. The treasure he was allowed to keep was nice but didn't really cover the full monetary value of what he captured. He just took it because he knew that if he didn't, then there wouldn't be any pay at all," Jacques said.

"It's ridiculous," Mirabelle sniffed. "Corrupt officials can take what they want by slapping something they call a 'law' on it. Then suddenly, it's a 'tax'. But they dare look down on us and call us 'bloody pirates' and 'worthless thieves?'"

"Maybe we should pose as sea roving tax collectors then," Jacques quipped dryly. Mirabelle smiled, but said nothing. Another rough moment of silence passed.

"A lot of the captains look like they're preparing their ships for departure. The wind isn't in their favor, so they'll probably wait till tomorrow or later. Maybe with them gone, it'll be easier to spot an opportunity," Mirabelle sighed.

"It's our only choice."

"Maybe our Witch Hunter will leave a stipend which I can use as a bartering chip. Hopefully, the carpenters will listen. Even then, that

Chapter Five

doesn't solve our lumber problem. Perhaps the inquisitor can look into that."

"I doubt it, but if we're his ticket out of here, maybe he'll help. Or maybe he'll just commandeer a different ship back, leaving us stranded."

"Where is that spook, anyway?" Mirabelle wondered. She hadn't seen hide nor hair of him for a worrying amount of time.

Further out on the docks, Otto strolled up to one of the stalls. He heard there was some sort of excitement earlier in the day but didn't see what all the fuss was about. The vendor displayed a burlap sack of green beans. The script burned on to its side suggested that it was Tersian in origin. Otto's eyes went wide, especially when he saw the price the vendor was asking for it.

"I'll pay you half that amount," Otto declared, hoping the little experience with haggling he had at the markets of Dhalinur would pay off.

"The asking price or nothing else, foreigner scum," the vendor growled.

"That's a bag of tar tea. Who here is going to buy tar tea? I'm practically doing you a favor, even bothering to buy the whole bag off of you!"

"Asking price or nothing!"

"Fine, you'll regret it when the stuff rots on your stall and you get nothing for it," the guard prognosticated and began to trundle off.

"Wait!" the vendor called out after he had taken a few steps. Otto smiled darkly to himself. A few minutes later, his coin bag was a little lighter, but he had a whole burlap sack of tar tea.

It was grown down south, in Tersia and the Southern Archipelago. Those are also the places where it was popular. Most of the people of the northern countries: Danaria, Arazum, Gavendar, and Reyais had not warmed to its flavor. There were only a few niche northern individuals who enjoyed it. Otto developed a taste for it during the Black War; it gave a flavor of some sort to the water they boiled to keep warm during the winter when tea ran out.

Otto hated how everyone called it tar tea. Coffee was a much better name for it.

***

SOPHIE WAS TERRIFIED. Life was incredibly dark with a blindfold around her head and there was only so much her ears could paint for her. She could make out that there were others like her, people duped by the smugglers, and now they were being held in cages. Bland slop was parceled out to everyone twice a day, and you had to gulp it down from the wooden bowl they shoved into your hands. She was positive a splinter was behind one of her lips, but she didn't dare pick at it.

She couldn't know where exactly Philip was. It sounded like the smugglers separated the men from the women but didn't hold them too far away from the surrounding voices. Maybe they were all in one building with nothing but a good couple meters to separate the two groups. Who keeps people chained like commodities in a warehouse?

Chapter Five

They were told not to talk, and anyone who broke that order faced a brutal whipping. It didn't stop people from whispering, if only for brief moments at a time. Someone, a girl who sounded a little older than Sophie, whimpered with fright, saying the rune burned into their necks would be used to turn them into zombies. Sophie could still feel it painfully smoldering under her hair.

"Not zombies," an older-sounding woman croaked. "That's a different ritual. You need a potion for that. No, these runes are for tracking us if we ever escape."

"Quiet!" one of the smugglers shouted.

Her blood ran cold when she heard movement. It sounded like a work gang's worth of footsteps. A woman shrieked when she was roughly hauled away. A heavy blow quickly shut her up. Sophie didn't know whether to be terrified or relieved that she couldn't see anything. What was going on? She could hear the smugglers leading them away one at a time. Was she going to be separated further from Philip?

Then came her turn. She was tugged along across rough floorboards and then out into the open air. There was the smell of seawater, and the chill told her it was night. Gnarly gravel turned to rough wooden planks again. A prick erupted under her heel. Now there was another splinter to torment her, but she didn't dare complain. She didn't like being hit. Someone dragged her up a slanted plank; more wooden boards. *Was this a ship?*

Musty air, pitch, and body odor told her she was down in the hold of a vessel. What Sophie would have given for just a couple moments to make a break for it and swim to safety. She was forced to lie down and shoved into an enclosed space. One shoulder felt open air; it was the only thing that told her she wasn't in a casket. She strained her ears. Somewhere outside, she could hear the smugglers grumbling to each other. They were in a hurry.

They were leaving tomorrow.

***

LEON STOOD ON TOP of the *Defiance's* bridge. At a passing glance, it looked like he was staring out to sea towards the southeast. That wasn't the whole truth. He was waiting to hear back from the gunboat that he had sent out. So recent was telegraph technology that Leon was still making peace with the fact that a distant message could get to him regardless of whether he was looking out for it or not.

In the olden days, which really weren't all that long ago, you had to keep an eye out for a nearby ship and then check its halyards for whatever signal flags it flew. It was a system he worked with for years. Now, a message could come from a ship far beyond the horizon and arrive at its destination almost the instant it was sent. Leon couldn't blame foreigners who thought telegraphs were magic. It sounded like magic.

What was Davos thinking? It still made his blood boil. This was supposed to be a routine, easy assignment, but he could see the storm clouds that threatened to spin it all out of control. Leon kicked an imaginary rock that failed to vent his frustrations adequately.

Attacking a Tersian fortress ship? Plenty of corsairs fantasized about capturing such a vessel, but a little more thought would reveal the problems that would pile on afterward. Yes, you'd have a ridiculous amount of firepower at your hands, but they were massive ships hardly built for speed, and speed was a corsair's bread and butter.

86

Chapter Five

Without it, you couldn't chase down merchantmen weighed down with treasure and more importantly, you couldn't outrun the navy.

The navy always had more firepower than you did, but that made them slow and less maneuverable. Then, there was the matter of where would you moor your newly, foolishly captured fortress ship? How would you repair it or refit it? These vessels could only be berthed at certain Tersian harbors.

Finally, there would be the matter of the Tersians wanting it back. *How much were the Tersians willing to spend to get their fortress ship back?* This last detail weighed most heavily on Leon's mind.

"Captain!" one of his aides called, running up the stairs. "Telegraph received a message from *G-57.*"

"Right on time." The worried captain took the message and read it with anxious eyes.

```
HAVE PLOTTED A RETURN COURSE BACK TO REYAIS
STOP TERSIAN SHIPS SPOTTED STOP DESTINATION
REYAIS STOP COULD NOT COUNT ALL THE MASTS
STOP TOO MANY STOP
```

CHAPTER 6

CAPTAIN CYRIL GUNDERSON WATCHED the sea from where he stood on the rigging, clinging to the rope like a bird perched on a branch. He was bald, his skin was beginning to wrinkle, and his ivory white beard only seemed to be getting longer these days. His pale blue eyes were as cold as the winters of his Raermak home.

"I know we've discussed this before, Captain," Charles, his first mate, called from the deck. "But I don't think we have enough whale oil to justify the trip to Dhalinur. We'll be making this voyage at a loss."

"No one was buying it at Reyais," Gunderson carped. "At least some Dhaliese still buy whale oil because their old folks won't change their old lamps."

"Everyone is buying kerosene these days," Charles lamented. "It's killing us whalers. We can't fish kerosene."

"I believe it was you Arazumi who invented it. Besides, we do more than whaling these days. We don't have a choice anymore."

"I'm not responsible for my country's inventions. Bugger it; I'm the one facing a loss in pay too, sir!"

"I know. That was unfair of me," Gunderson admitted and began to make his way down from the rigging. "We'll go to Dhalinur. Maybe we'll get lucky and catch another whale or other large fish along the way. We'll be able to turn its bone into trinkets. They still love whalebone jewelry down there-"

"Sales for those are declining too, sir."

"Damn it, Charles, I'm getting too old for this. We'll get to Dhalinur, we'll sell what we can, and then while we're there, we'll be able to find some trouble in the jungles or take out a rogue corsair for a bounty," Gunderson explained.

"I don't understand why you don't retire, sir. You're always complaining you're too old for this."

"I can't go back to a life on the land. I can't die warm in a bed, Charles."

"Why not? What's wrong with that?"

"That's not the life I've led."

They heard the lookout shuffle on his post up in the crow's nest. A second later, they heard his call. "Ships, Captain! Lots of them!"

"How many and who?" Gunderson demanded.

"Tersians, sir! And there are more ships than I've ever seen!"

"By the Holy and Vutan's Anvil, how many times have I told you I'll have you tossed overboard for drinking at your post!" Gunderson yelled.

"I'm stone-cold sober, sir!"

Gunderson hurried up the rigging to have a look for himself. Age was taking many things from him, but it hadn't stolen his eyesight yet. He could also throw the man out of the crow's nest himself once he got up there.

"You better prepare yourself for a swim, pup!" Gunderson scowled.

"I'm serious, sir! Look for yourself!"

Gunderson opened his mouth for a retort, and then nothing came out. He stared transfixed at the horizon. Filling his field of vision and riding on every wave were masts, and each carried the Tersian flag. The old mariner's mind clicked and trembled, measuring and weighing each possibility he could think of. He very quickly arrived at one.

"Pilot, turn the *Osebirk* around! We're going back to Reyais!"

"Aye, sir!"

"We're doing what, sir?" Charles demanded.

"We're chasing an opportunity, Charles!"

***

THE MESS HALL IN THE EMBASSY was quiet this morning, though a few guards were already swapping rumors. An important-looking navy man passed by earlier along with Guard Captain Axle and many diplomats. Frowns and clenched jaws on their faces meant no one was going to enjoy that meeting. This was all it took to get the guards talking as soon as the delegation left. Speculation jumped like arcs of lightning from table to table. Guards had to make their entertainment, usually at the expense of others.

Off on his own, Jord quietly wrote a letter. For all their talk about "equality," "meritocracy," and the long history between their nations, there were still plenty of Arazumi who believed Raermaks to be simpleton brutes. The popular stereotype held that Raermaks were content languishing in the forest, hunting bears and swilling homemade ale with no interest in more sophisticated things like the Arazumi. Never mind that the bear hunts were a rite of passage and, in Jord's opinion, only his countrymen knew how to make a wholesome, proper ale. However, the notion of being a simpleton got him incensed the most. His writing was undoubtedly slow and at points agonizingly careful, but that didn't mean he was intellectually deficient. He had to be mindful of his penmanship. Ma and Da's eyesight wasn't as good as it used to be, and Da had recently broken the only pair of spectacles they had between them. Da may be a lumberman, but he was also too much of a penny pincher to get a new pair yet.

Nearby, Otto roasted his recently acquired beans on an iron skillet. He kept the pan in constant motion, the rattle of beans on iron making an oddly musical accompaniment to his conversation with Kassia. So far, no one else was showing interest in the beans, and he most certainly wasn't offering.

Jord folded up the letter and slipped it into an envelope. Breakfast didn't feel complete yet, and he knew what could fix that: a cup of tea. Off to the kitchen, he wandered. Judging from the smell and the sound of grinding, Otto was almost done with his brew. Jord passed the ship captain returning from the meeting. The captain noticed the aroma from the beans and sidled over until he found Otto in the middle of his project. He watched with critical interest and then spotted the Tersian letters on the nearby burlap sack.

Chapter Six

"Tersian? Do you even know which mountain those beans grew on?" Captain Leon asked.

"No, I just picked the bag up from the markets," Otto admitted.

"There's probably only one mountain in Tersia whose beans I would even bother with; Mount Ulru," the captain explained.

"Does it matter? Coffee is coffee," the guard shrugged. Leon stared at him for a moment. His jaw moved, his frown deepened, but no words came out. He turned and left.

"I wonder what his problem was," Otto grumbled, pouring the fresh coffee into a mug.

"Some people take their tar tea seriously," Kassia said with a shrug.

"You probably could have learned a thing or two from him, little man," Jord chuckled as he headed for the door.

"When you're stuck out on the march, or you have to stand guard outside of a building in the freezing cold, and there's only one place selling coffee nearby, you learn to make do with what you have," Otto vented. "Coffee is coffee."

Jord's mug shattered loudly just beyond the door. People turned to look only to see the towering Raermak standing stock still staring out into the horizon.

"You okay there, Jord?" Otto called.

He hurried over when the Raermak didn't reply. The air outside was cool, and the wind was picking up. Spilled tea turned to mud while the broken ceramic shards shone in the morning sun.

"Jord, what's going on?"

The giant's gaze was fixed on the sea line. On the horizon, bobbing with the ebb and fall of the waves, was a forest of masts. This was not a fleet approaching; it was an armada, and Jord recognized the flag those ships sailed under.

"Bloody Tersians."

***

CAPTAIN LEON WAS ALMOST THIRTY years old. Half of his life was spent working on ships. Ten years ago, the first coal-fired ones were made. Leon remembered there being many teething problems with them, exploding boilers included. The first blueprints for all metal ships were drafted down five years ago. Last year the Republic launched its first all-steel gunboats and the larger gunboat-destroyers. The technology involved was overwhelming, so much so that younger, more open-minded men were prioritized to command them over older sailors.

He could see it in the four subordinate captains before him. They were all younger than him, clean-shaven, and clearly from the Capital Province. Leon was used to seeing Edalan captains such as himself. He expected the men from the Capital region to send him paperwork, not work the decks, let alone command the ship.

Chapter Six

"Let's get to brass tacks," Leon started. "None of us were briefed on the possibility of the Tersians showing up, and yet here they are. Lots of them. Have any of you fought against Tersian corsairs?"

The other captains shook their heads except for Captain Sydney, who raised a hand.

"I thought the Tersians didn't use privateers, sir, let alone corsairs?"

"Sometimes, a Tersian captain or two will go corsair. The Iron Sultanate has its share of internal problems. Since none of you have fought a Tersian corsair, I expect you're all thinking it's no different from fighting a Danarian frigate or man o'war?"

This time they all nodded.

"And that's where you'd be wrong."

"Why's that, Captain? Their cannons look like they have a larger bore, but that just means they're slower to reload, and the cannon ranges can't be too different from a Danarian," Sydney interjected.

"Correct on both observations, Captain Sydney, but Tersians sail their ships differently. They use magic," Leon expounded darkly.

"Isn't 'magic' a bit of a bad word these days, Captain?" Sydney replied.

"Sure, but that doesn't stop them from using it. We may not understand how they do it, but they do, and we must be prepared."

Captain Milrose, a quieter, more contemplative man, raised his hand. "How exactly do they demonstrate this anomalous activity, sir?"

"Good question," Leon replied. "Not every Tersian ship has a sorcerer on board. There's just not enough to go around. Smaller ships, if they have any at all, tend to have one or two, and even then, no sorcerer is alike in power. Sometimes they'll cause a strong breeze to fill the sails giving the ship an edge in speed and maneuverability it otherwise wouldn't have. When it's time for boarding, sorcerers will probably use the standard fare of spells to help out: fireballs, shards of ice, blinding spells, use your imagination."

"You said 'smaller ships,' sir. That implies larger ships are different," Milrose inserted.

"Correct. It's the larger ships you have to worry about," Leon warned. "Sometimes, they'll gather a whole cabal of sorcerers who'll work together to cast ever more devastating spells. Few stories are confirmed, but I've heard privateers claim they've seen cabals remotely detonate a ship's powder stores or summon a massive wave to pull a vessel down into the deep. But remember, that's just hearsay and speculation."

"But, what's a spell that you can confirm, sir?" Sydney asked.

"The worst one. It's been called 'Jumping' or 'Blinking.' One second, the Tersian is too far away for either of you to fire. She's stalking you. You know it, they know it, but neither of you can shoot, and maybe you still have a chance to get away from her. Then all of a sudden, she disappears…"

Leon abruptly stepped into the assembled captains' faces, looming uncomfortably close to them. His voice became as cold as iron. "And then she reappears right off your side. She's too close for you to get away. Her sailors are already throwing cables to snare you, and worse, her big guns are ready to fire, and she's too close to miss."

Chapter Six

"Then, how come these bastards haven't taken over the seas yet?" Sydney said in shock. Leon looked at him.

"It's not always perfect. Sorcerers make mistakes. Also, magic, so I've heard, is hard to control. I've seen a Tersian frigate blink, but she only traveled a few meters from her starting point and didn't make any more attempts after that. The worst case I've seen was a sorcerer who blinked the top deck and sails of a man o'war. The bottom decks and keel stayed at their original point two kilometers behind. Very dramatic way for a crew to scuttle their own ship."

"Danarian and Tersian guns have to get below half a kilometer before they have a chance at hitting you," Milrose said to no one in particular, clearly thinking aloud. "Our guns have a maximum range of ten kilometers and can make short work of a target in half that."

"Bear in mind our ships' hulls were designed with fighting Danarian cannons or smaller in mind," Leon cautioned. "Tersians prefer their cannons to be twice the bore size of Danarians, and then they're going to try to fire at you from point-blank. Remember that when you're out on your patrols. We're not to leave the immediate waters around the embassy. We are not to provoke the Tersians unless otherwise directed. I want each of you counting as many Tersian flags as you can see, so we can get an accurate report back to command. Any further questions? No? Then you're dismissed."

With his subordinates gone, Leon made a heroic effort to ignore the Tersian armada off in the distance. He tried to enjoy the weather and identify the various sea-fowl overhead. There was also the schedule to think about; maybe some last-minute changes to the watch were in order. But those thoughts kept coming back, the ones that reminded him that a Tersian armada was right off his starboard. Leon heard the rumble of footsteps trotting up to him. He could already feel the bad news he was about to hear.

"Report, radioman," the captain ordered wearily without turning to face the man.

"Captain, an urgent telegraph just came in. The Tersians dropped off some declaration leaflets at the harbor. They're written in their language with their script. They didn't translate it into Northern, you know, the language everyone else can read. One of the embassy's agents got a copy and the diplomats are busy translating it. The important parts they've got so far states, as follows: 'Reyais and the surrounding towns will be under a blockade until further notice. There is to be no traffic going in or out. The Tersians will use deadly force if necessary and without warning.'"

Leon sighed and stared daggers out into the horizon. There would be a deluge of reports, orders, and meetings now. A major multinational migraine was about to flare up. And all because Cousin Davos had to steal a capital ship.

"And I suppose the Tersians consider it a courtesy that they even bothered to warn us," Leon muttered.

"In my opinion, it doesn't seem like they did an outstanding job at it, sir. At the very least, they could have translated it."

"They're Tersians, radioman," Leon said, turning to the man. "As far as they're concerned, we should either learn their language or just get out of the way. And then, they wonder why everyone resents them."

***

Chapter Six

"HAVE YOU EVER NOTICED there's a repeating pattern of events everywhere we go?" Otto asked out loud as they maintained their watch on the tower.

"Phase one: we're sent to a new place strictly to guard and impress the locals. Nothing bad will happen, the boss promises! Phase two: unfortunately, it's important that we blow up the locals' neighbor, the one they really hate. We hit that phase yesterday, by the way. Phase three: despite what we were promised, something rather bad happens anyway."

"That's where we are today," Jord growled, his gaze still fixed towards the sea.

"You know, Jord, we're supposed to watch the city, not the ocean. That's what the flotilla is for," Otto advised.

Jord said nothing. His posture didn't change. It was as if the Raermak intended to set fire to the whole Tersian fleet with his glare alone. Otto searched deep into his memory to remember the last time his friend was this agitated. Memory lane turned into a roundabout with no exits.

"You've always been pretty laid back and jovial, Jord," Otto said carefully. "You don't even seem to harbor any ill will towards the Danarians despite the Black War, so…did something happen between you and the Tersians?"

Jord relaxed his posture for a moment. He idly began to scratch at his beard as he brushed away the sands of time. He was quiet when he spoke.

"When I was young, younger than the pups we're ordering about, I helped my Da on a voyage to Tersia. He wanted to sell lumber to them because he heard they were building ships, lots of ships. This was during the reign of the late Sultan -- before your Republic began buying up all of Raermak's spare lumber. Da was having trouble finding a favorable deal, but it gave me enough time to fall under the spell of a Tersian maid. She'd come down by the docks to buy goods. By the end of the week when Da had given up and decided to go home, well, she and I decided to elope, so she snuck off with us."

Otto stared, his lower jaw hanging in the breeze. "You never told me you were married!"

"Yes, yes. We got married. I built us a house. We had a son. I was happy for a few years or so," Jord paused for a moment, a second of foreboding silence but just long enough for Otto to narrow his eyes and wonder if he heard a choked sob. His friend carried on with the story again.

"And then, the current Sultan took power and, as we all know, he and his policies are a real piece of work. See, my wife had worked in the Harem. She wasn't a proper Harem girl, but that was enough for the Sultan to want his lost property back. Tersian goons came to my house one day while I worked at the lumber yards..."

All Otto heard was the mournful cry of seagulls on the wind for a while. Jord still stared at the distant masts of his enemies. Otto jumped when Jord immediately slammed a fist down on the railing. He coughed and finally spoke again.

"They killed her. They killed my wife, Ela. They took my son, Harun. I lost my way for a few years. I drowned the pain in tankards ale and my work. I took too many risks on bear and elk hunts. It was scary for

Chapter Six

Ma, Da, and my siblings to watch. That's what they tell me, at least. In a way, it frightened me as well. That's probably why I eventually sobered up, but home didn't feel like home anymore. And then I heard that Arazum and her Long Steel Company were looking for recruits to fight in this little war they had with Danaria. You know the rest from there," Jord murmured.

Otto took a deep breath and a swig of coffee. It wasn't every day that he had to confront his ignorance.

"Damn. I knew the Tersians did things like that. I just thought they did it elsewhere, in other countries. Not-"

"Raermak? Moraine? Not them because they're right next door to nice, civilized, powerful Arazum? Tersians do their body-snatching everywhere, little man. I bet they've even snatched Arazumi but covered their tracks real good."

"Right, but remember, Jord, we're representing Long Steel and the Republic while we're here at the embassy. You can't pick a fight with them for no reason; you know that, right?"

"Yes, I know."

"And let's hope nothing terrible happens. The world doesn't need another Black War."

***

KASSIA LED DR. LINTON and his assistant, Mr. Walburg, away from the docks. Her two colleagues looked around nervously. Dr. Linton kept one hand in his coat pocket where Kassia knew he had stowed away a tiny, single-shot pistol. It drummed up her anxieties.

Otto had managed to defuse a potentially hostile situation the other day by talking the man away. If something similar happened today, it was clear that Dr. Linton would resort to the pistol first and miss, judging by his twitchy muscles. It would all go downhill from there.

"You got to keep an eye on these foreigners, Mr. Walburg," Dr. Linton murmured. "They're jealous of our prosperity, even if they don't realize it. It's their poor moral character that keeps them from attacking us. The very thing that makes them avaricious and stupid also causes them to be cowardly and lazy."

"Right you are, sir," Walburg agreed. Kassia furtively scoffed.

She had more important things on her mind. First, they dropped off the autopsy report to the district sheriff and then headed to the docks to visit Mrs. Selma. Kassia had to explain what they found in that latest bottle of "medicine" and then picked up Selma's report on the actual medications they were supplying her.

Kassia was pleased with the encouraging results Selma gathered. They showed Arazumi medicines were consistently working. On the other hand, what sort of desperation was driving people to cook up the "cure-all" that Selma had given them, the one Jord so carelessly took a swig of? A chemical analysis revealed that Jord's crude taste test was uncannily correct: mostly alcohol and aromatic herbs. However, Kassia felt vindicated to learn that trace amounts of lead were also in the mix, though she didn't bother telling Jord about it. The Raermak faced death in various ways and he probably only cared about lead when it was fired at him.

Someone bumped into her. Startled, Kassia turned to apologize, only to feel her bag ripped from her shoulder. Shock gave way to indignation. First, she shouted and then stormed after the thief without

Chapter Six

a thought. Dr. Linton's protests were ignored until they drowned away into the bustle of the crowd.

She knew she was breaking a few rules, namely, "Don't get separated from the group." Dr. Linton and his assistant didn't amount to much, but it was still a broken rule. Another significant rule was, "Don't chase after thieves who duck into hidden alleyways." That was a universal one, but she was giving it a thorough breaking. Each step she took smashed it into smaller pieces. Iconoclasm, in whatever form it took, had a thrill to it.

The alleyway ended. It was a dead-end, and three men were loitering in it. The one immediately in front of her was casually examining the contents of her bag while the other two were sidling further into her peripheral vision. All those broken rules had become chickens, and they were madly returning to roost.

"You a doctor, miss?" the bag inspector mumbled.

"I have medical knowledge, yes," Kassia replied coldly.

"Good thing my organization needs people with those skills; otherwise you'd have ended up as one of the cargo."

"Ah, so you're a smuggler then," Kassia deduced.

"Call it what you want," the thief grunted. "Starting today, you'll be working for a different organization."

"No, no, I won't," Kassia said and then held out her hand for the bag. "Instead, you'll give me back what's mine, and you'll let me go if you know what's good for you."

"Ain't no one going to rescue you, miss."

"I don't need to be rescued."

"Oh, hahaha! Well, that's where you're wrong, miss."

One hidden alleyway over, a passerby would have suddenly heard the sound of screaming abruptly end in muffled snaps. It was a small mercy that no one was around to listen to that.

***

"AND YOU JUST ABANDONED HER?" Otto hollered.

"We were just following protocol," Dr. Linton protested. "Something Miss Norwis so jauntily broke when she took off like that."

"Right, of course! And who allowed you, civilians, off on an errand without an armed escort?" the guard snapped venomously.

"It was well within protocol, considering the time of day and the nature of–"

"Forget him, Otto. We better start looking for our missing chemist," Jord interposed.

"I agree, but we can't forget him because he needs to lead us to where they got separated,"

"I'm sorry, gentlemen, but with all the people around and since I'm rather unfamiliar with these streets, I'm afraid I won't be able to recall–"

Chapter Six

"Oh, you better start recalling quick!" Otto snapped and began to lead Dr. Linton by his ear. "Or you'll be jaunting around a little funny by the time I'm done with you."

"Trouble, gentlemen?"

All eyes quickly turned to Kassia, who was as flabbergasted as her audience. The gentlemen slowly, awkwardly, settled into postures more befitting gentlemen under Kassia's stare. Jord slipped his pipe into his mouth out of habit.

"See!" Dr. Linton declared. "I knew she'd be alright. You trigger-happy guards are always underestimating the intrepid spirit of our people."

"You're free to go be useless elsewhere, doctor," Otto cut sharply, watching the man leave before turning back. His eyes fell upon a spot on the chemist's clothes. "Is that blood, Kassia?"

"This? No, it's not mine," Kassia said quickly, noticing the red stain on her jacket. "I grabbed my bag back and winged the thief in the face with it. You know how nosebleeds can be. Well, no harm done, I better get back to my duties!"

Jord narrowed his eyes as he lit his pipe. The Raermak was starting to suspect something was going on between those two. He saw it in the glances and how they somehow managed to find ways to gravitate towards each other throughout the day. It was all very romantic in its needlessly overcomplicated way; he was a guard for the Long Steel Company, she was a chemist for the Comstock Company. A very Arazumi love story. Or maybe he was becoming a romantic sod as he got older. However, Jord caught that look she gave Otto, which said this unexplained circumstance could easily be explained by some...secret. Jord wasn't one to pry, but his gut told him there was something sinister about this. Blood may have been on her jacket, but none was on her bag. How was that possible if she had bashed a man's nose in with it?

***

SOPHIE HELD HER BREATH in the dark, musty hold. It wasn't hard, considering the traffickers had gagged everyone. The timbers creaked and groaned in unison with the gurgling of the water outside. Just faintly, she could hear the occasional flap of the sails. They were, as Philip would say, underway.

She could tell there was something wrong. The smugglers were strangely quieter compared to the last couple of days, and Sophie wasn't convinced it was because they were leaving. Reyais didn't have a coast guard to police the waters around the city, and she knew well enough that smugglers made their living by not being seen. Their ships were supposed to look as inconspicuous as possible if they were spotted. Her ears were picking up less evidence of abuse vented towards her fellow prisoners as well. There was a time when this would have brought her relief. It only served to be unsettling now.

There were a number of reasons why the smugglers could be nervous. Taking a ship out in the dark without warning lamps was always a risk. Philip had told her some dreadful stories of when even small ships collided. She guessed that there would be no moon out either; the blindfold was playing with her sense of time, so the limited visibility would always fray a mariner's nerves. Maybe they were worried about rival corsairs and privateers? Everyone heard stories about them. Rivals looking to steal someone else's smuggled goods were unlikely to be this close to Reyais, but it wasn't unheard of and Sophie reminded herself that they could be further out than she

106

Chapter Six

realized. Could it be a storm? Hurricane season was just a few short weeks away. It was unlikely their kidnappers would deliberately face a hurricane, but even a small squall could be dangerous. Philip had told her so many scary stories. Why would anyone in their right mind go out into the open sea?

Thunder! She heard it! So it was a storm, something familiar. She relaxed, much to her surprise. There would be a lot of rocking and heaving and maybe some motion sickness, but she felt strangely confident in the traffickers' seafaring abilities. It would all be fine.

Thunder. Thunder again. Louder now. Sophie frowned. Thunder wouldn't erupt so quickly like that, practically overlapping. No, that wasn't thunder. That was the sound of cannon fire.

Something thumped the overhead deck so hard the whole ship shuddered. Through the boards, they could hear men screaming. The thump she heard was the sound of a cannonball skipping across the top deck.

A minute later, the world exploded around her. Sophie felt rather than heard the blast. Her whole body hurt; the concussion still echoed in her bones. Her shackles were knocked from their fastenings. For one brief moment, she was elated that she could see again. That only lasted for a second.

The entire hold was now a charnel house. Gaping, jagged holes riddled the walls. They showed her that Tersians were boarding the ship. Men were brandishing lamps and waving weapons. There was yelling, screaming, musket fire, and it filled her with terror. Sophie went to move, only for her hand to slip in something slick and sticky. Blood. She was surrounded by blood. As for everyone around her—

well, she wished they had all their parts together. Philip! She had to find Philip!

She knew about this, more of Philip's stories. It was why you saw sailors hobbling about on a peg leg or with a sad, empty sleeve. The cannonball smashing through the hull wasn't the only thing you had to worry about. The projectile crushed and fragmented wood as it ran its deadly course through the ship. That one cannonball immediately became hundreds of sharp missiles, and all of them were liable to do something catastrophic to the body. Where was Philip?

It didn't take long. It was the birthmark she found. She'd recognize that distinctive, stringy-looking birthmark on his right forearm anywhere. So, she had an arm but only an arm. You could live without an arm, right? She kept looking around despite the shouting and wailing around her and all the death and blood she was standing in. She had to find her brother. He wouldn't leave her, right?

The wind blowing through the battered hold was salty and cold. The tears flowing down her cheeks were burning hot. Another wail drifted across the waves.

Several things happened so quickly that they appeared to be a singular event. In a moment, one frightened girl's grief ignited as a lightning crack of hate. The very next heartbeat, all three ships were unnaturally torn apart, scattered across the deep until only flotsam remained.

It grew quiet. Scores of bodies were consigned to the depths that night, but a single soul still wept somewhere on the unforgiving waves.

CHAPTER 7

THE AIR OF THE YOUNG DAWN WAS CRISP as Mirabelle made her way to the alehouse. Hang out with enough free captains, "privateers" as they called themselves, and you'd learn they were a loose fraternity of sorts. There weren't many dogmatic rules: you helped each other where you could or at the very least stayed out of the way. If your letters of mark brought you into conflict with each other, well, that was just the nature of business. You didn't go corsair, raiding targets without a letter of mark. That made everyone appear bad. You also didn't become a navy regular; that was the opposite side of the corsair coin. Corsairs were the enemies of all nations, but the Navy was just another finger in the iron fist of governments that occasionally threatened, and always inconvenienced, honest free captains.

Flickering lamps burned pungent whale oil in the sullen air. Mirabelle immediately made her way to the counter and ordered a mug of tea. A few other captains were lurking here early in the morning. Only the ambitious, interested in organizing something important, came at this hour to meet. To do so, you either went to bed at a decent hour, or you ordered your aide to note the time and interrupt you from a night of vice. Either way, it was how the others would know you were serious about business.

She saw the usual faces. There was one-eyed Hernan Corba, an Arazumi who had little good to say of the Republic and had garnered a reputation for being a slippery, ornery bastard. She saw Ivan Vernovis of House D'sarin, a fellow Danarian who was sometimes known as the "Assassin." Samir Temeng, the cousin of the now-infamous Davos, sat quietly sipping a cup of tar tea. If Davos was the demon with a blade, then Samir was the lucky opportunist, but not one to be underestimated. Mirabelle had seen him end fights without ever drawing a sword, his fists a deadly flowing weapon in their own right. The mysterious Blind Captain was present as well. No one knew his real name, nor did anyone know where he was from, though it was rumored he came from Ta'Geh. And then there was the aging Captain Gunderson, the wry, crusty Raermak who somehow had all his eyes and limbs despite his many decades at sea. Some were starting to say Brother Grinn had forgotten about him.

Blind Captain had one of the many Tersian proclamation leaflets in front of him. Above the paper, he cupped an orb of magical energy while a quill slowly but surely wrote of its own accord on a nearby sheet of paper.

"How's the translation going?" Hernan asked while loudly popping open a bottle of rum.

"Slowly," Ivan grunted, eagerly watching the progress.

"Can't you translate faster, you blind magician?" Hernan complained. The quill flew over and rapidly wrote an elegant "no" on Hernan's napkin before hurrying back to its original work.

"They just dumped dinghies loaded with those scribblings onto the shore," Gunderson murmured while running a whetstone along the blade of his ax. "No helpful translation to go with them, no ceremony either. They're looking for a fight."

"Did anyone hear that explosion last night? It sounds like there may have been a fight already," Mirabelle said.

Chapter Seven

"It could have been a smuggler trying his luck and ending up the worse for it. It sounded like a big explosion, though. Maybe too much powder to be a smuggler then," Ivan speculated.

"The Tersians are here and we're here," Mirabelle said loud enough to get their attention. "Proclamation of theirs or no, they're legitimate targets according to our letters of mark. We're here to talk about taking their ships together, right?"

"Who said anything about fighting?" Gunderson replied, eyes open wide in mock surprise. "Perhaps we should wait for Blind Captain to translate these here writings first."

"They'll want their fortress ship back," Samir interjected moodily. "Come on, let's not pretend it's anything but that. I bet the moment Davos hands it back to them they'll all turn sails and leave, *kip-kip.* "

"Maybe you should talk your cousin into doing that then," Hernan suggested and then took a long, noisy swig of rum.

"I'm not fond of him, but if he does that, they'll take the ship and then hang him on one of the yards. I'll be less fond of that."

"Then all he needs to do is not get caught," Hernan shrugged. Samir cussed at him in Dhaliese.

The tavern door swung open, and a man strolled in purposefully, heading straight for them. Mirabelle thought the newcomer was a fisherman all wrapped up in oilskins and a broad, floppy hat. Instead, he slapped a large sheet of paper beside Blind Captain and tugged off his hat. It was Captain Leon Kasamir.

"There's your translation. Our diplomats have been working on it all night," he said. Immediately the others gathered around to read. Blind Captain simply stopped, the quill clattering onto the counter like a de-stringed puppet. He was motionless, but everyone could tell he was somehow reading the message despite his blindfold.

Mirabelle got to the end of the translation first. "'Total blockade of Reyais? Lethal force will be used without warning? All traffic will be treated as the work of corsairs or those who aid and abet them'? They're not even trying to be diplomatic," she groused.

"'And the blockade will remain until our ship is returned and the corsairs, who took it, have paid with their lives,'" Samir read. "Davos will just spit in their faces, *kip-kip*."

"Now, let's wait one second here, folks," Hernan growled. "I do believe it's only free captains who are welcomed to these meets. That means you ain't welcome, Leon," he spat.

"I have no reason to lie to any of you, Hernan," Leon snapped.

"You will call me 'Captain,' navy dog!" Hernan howled, drawing and cocking a percussion cap pistol.

"Hey! Put that away; no need for guns here!" Samir interjected, storming up from his seat.

"I am curious," Mirabelle said carefully. "Leon, why did you come here knowing you'd no longer be welcomed?"

"A Tersian blockade affects us all," Leon explained. "This has just been a courtesy for old time's sake. I'll also add that Arazum will remain strictly neutral in this matter."

Chapter Seven

"Of course it will," Henan said bitterly, pistol still pointed at Leon. "That's what the Republic does: nothing if it means the coin will keep flowing."

"I think it also means they won't be taking the Tersians' side. Therefore, they won't order Leon and his scary-looking flotilla to start firing on us in the harbor," Mirabelle pointed.

"Correct," Leon assented.

"You're still not welcomed, Mr. Kasamir," Captain Gunderson said. "But we thank you for your courtesy, don't we, Hernan? And thankful people stop acting like silly drunkards."

"You still need to turn around and get out," Hernan growled.

"I'll do that," Leon nodded. "As soon as you lower that gun."

"You'll forgive me for not lowering my guns at navy dogs."

Blind Captain raised his hand and made a swift gesture. A bottle of rum leaped from the table and made a satisfying *thonk* on Hernan's head. Leon bowed and made a quick exit as the hapless drunk massaged his aching skull.

"I have no love for the Tersians," Captain Gunderson sighed. "Neither do I fear death. However, I do not see a reason to die here. This is Davos' folly and, as long as we behave, it will remain solely Davos' folly."

"But, who's to say the Tersians won't overreact?" Mirabelle said with both hands raised in a desperate shrug. "They always overreact!"

"They would be risking a war with a kingdom and several nations," Blind Captain spoke. "Reyais may not seem like much, but there are Dhaliese sea-clanners here like Samir. Danaria may not look kindly if you or Captain Vernovis become casualties. And if the Tersians accidentally or intentionally harm the Arazumi? Imagine what the Republic will do."

"I'll fight you, you oversized bat, as soon as my head stops hurting!" Hernan threatened from the floor.

"Don't be a fool, Hernan," Ivan Vernovis guffawed. "And that goes for you too, young Mirabelle. Was it not your House Courmont that attempted a coup against our Empress? Impatience will be the death of you."

"My house was only a vassal to House Courmont," Mirabelle snarled. "And more importantly, I remained loyal to the crown. Don't forget that, Ivan!" She threw the rest of her mug at his face.

"Perhaps this is why young Leon became a navy regular. Look at us," Gunderson said gloomily, polishing a sword now. "We squabble and fight because the money is drying up. Fewer government men are paying out letters of mark, and fewer targets are showing themselves. When was the last time any of you 'mistook' a Southern Traders cargo ship for a corsair?"

"Our luck will turn around! It always does!" Hernan grumped.

"Will it?" Gunderson asked. "It's getting harder and harder for my men and me to make a living off of selling whale oil. Whalebone jewelry is losing its charm. More and more shipping is done by companies unwilling to contract out to free captains. I fear our days are almost gone."

Chapter Seven

Mirabelle sighed and shook her head. She didn't have time for them to turn into a self-pitying choir, as much as she loathed to agree with the old sea dog. If she didn't get the Lauria patched up soon, her days would be over before these idiots would. She could see there wouldn't be any chance organizing these buffoons into something she could spin into a profit, not just yet. Mirabelle needed to find a different lackey to drag into an alliance of convenience.

She slammed the door in a huff and was immediately glad she had. Mirabelle recognized that self-important swagger anywhere. All the young, free captains had it when they first started and racked up their first few prizes.

"Captain Novault! What a pleasure it is to see you!" she smiled. Here was her lackey.

***

SETH FELT LIKE HE WAS GOING IN CIRCLES; frustrating, futile circles. Mara's fingerprints were all over the new cult in town. Infiltrating the laity of the Prosperous Light was easy enough, but Seth couldn't find anything too out of the ordinary there. The same usual half-truths and comforting nothings that all cults offer to the desperate. Deciphering where the money flowed was harder.

It took a little more sneaking around and sleuth work, but he figured out most of the money wasn't migrating up the cult's ladder. Against all cynical expectations, a healthy portion of it was used to help the cult's general laity.

"I'm almost proud of her. She hasn't stooped to something so banal as a common scam," Seth said to himself as he used a stone to scribble on a forgotten piece of alley wall. "Unfortunately, that means she's

115

keeping people here for the ritual, but I can't find her in the city. Where has she gone?"

More furious scratches were made, the stone grumbling roughly as he drew out where he had been. He stared at the diagram he made of the city, foot tapping impatiently. If his brain were a muscle, he'd be trembling with strain right now. He couldn't waste time being stumped. What was her goal? The ritual, of course. He drew the rune and the mountain outside of Reyais.

"Context, context, context. I've snooped, investigated, and combed so much of the city with nothing to show for it. It's almost as if she isn't here anymore. If she's not in the city, then she's out on the island. Why would she be in the villages? There's nothing there but more ritual fodder. That's the cult's job. No, then she has to be with the druids. Why?"

Seth dropped the stone and began to walk away. He needed to follow the new mental thread with his feet. He found himself feeling nostalgic, a warm, sickly sweet emotion. This was Mara's end game, the goal that she had worked for all these years. Each time she got careless or perhaps created a fire too big to hide, he would come running to catch her. Oh, how many times did he get close. How many times did they duel face to face, only for her to fly away when no other choice was left for her? He'd put the fire out, clean up the mess, and she'd go into hiding and disappear only for it to start up again later.

And now it was all going to end. Relief. A weight lifted from his shoulders with that knowledge, but there was also sadness. How much of his life had he spent on this chase? How many forlorn roads had he ridden on, how many strange places had he seen all because he was obligated to catch this woman? And now, one way or another, it was all going to end. How long had they been doing this?

"Ages," he muttered to himself as he walked along, plotting his next move. "Too many ages."

He was running out of options, though. Mara did a good job shutting him out. He glanced around, making sure no one was watching. You didn't become a Witch Hunter without picking up a little magic. He drew a rough outline of Reyais and the island in the sand. Two interesting stones were procured from within reach and then tossed without apparent ritual. He watched where they landed.

One landed just outside the circle that stood for the city. Of course! That made sense. He shouldn't have used magic to figure that one out; he should have deduced it from last night's explosion. Seth decided he was more tired than he wanted to admit. Confirmation was good, though. He immediately hurried off. This was his last chance.

***

"THIS DAY JUST KEEPS GETTING INTERESTING," Leon grumbled. His mood wouldn't improve regardless of how much coffee he sipped. "Are we sure that banner they're flying is the one they use when they wish to parley?" he continued.

"It's a yellow field displaying a quiver of arrows. The book says it means they want to parley," one of his officers replied. Helpfully the official book was there in front of him.

About half a kilometer off his portside, a sizable squadron of Tersian rowboats moved directly towards them. Every binocular and spyglass on the *Defiance* was pointed at the Tersians, and yet even this didn't feel like enough scrutiny.

"Sound the men for general quarters," Leon murmured. "But I don't want a single gun to move. They are to man their stations, nothing more."

There wasn't much to do but watch, wait, and speculate. As the collection of boats was closer, another banner was raised. A brief consultation with the book showed that particular insignia was the Tersian way of asking permission to board. It was uniquely Tersian in that it wasn't so much of a request as it was a warning, a polite way of saying you will be boarded whether you like it or not, but you're not suspected of being a corsair. Yet.

The tension began when the first boat pulled alongside to be brought up, and it came from an unexpected source. There was a brief but vehement discussion among the Tersians in the vessel. The argument ended with a bark from the one in charge just as they were winched up .

"Do you speak Tersian, Captain?" the officer asked Leon.

"No."

"So we're hoping they'll be uncharacteristically polite today and speak our language instead, sir?"

"Correct. Besides, it's a little too late to call for a diplomat."

The boat came parallel to the deck. The leader—only the leader—stepped aboard. Leon noticed just how rigid the subordinate Tersians

Chapter Seven

were, hands tight around their weapons while eyes strained to catch the first sign of treachery.

"Welcome aboard the *RNV Defiance*," Leon said. "I am Captain Leon Kasamir. Whom do I have the honor of addressing?"

"I am Grand Admiral Oruz Bazeer. I am honored to be welcomed by you, Captain Kasamir. I request a meeting with you to discuss the matter of our respective fleets and where they stand. Is this acceptable?"

"Yes, yes, of course," Leon sputtered, still surprised at how fluent Admiral Oruz Bazeer was in Northern. He motioned towards one of the wings on the bridge where they could be watched but out of earshot. The Tersian sailors were glaring harshly at him. He knew why. Grand Admiral Bazeer was one of the most highly ranked and decorated men in the Sultan's navy. Sailors from all nations and professions talked about his escapades and tactics. Leon himself remembered training other men to emulate some admiral's tactics. He felt small enough to wash away in a drain.

Oruz Bazeer was a middle-aged man with a prominent forehead and nose and piercing brown eyes. A very practical turban wrapped around his head. Most of his beard had gone gray, and his swarthy face was wrinkled and leathered from years of harsh sea salt and the relentless sun. Like other sea dogs, he had a bandolier of many wheellock pistols across his coat. A heavy scimitar rested at his hip. Every tool the admiral needed in a fight was readily within reach. Muscle memory would do the rest.

"I do not mean to disrespect you, Captain Kasamir, but I am not altogether comfortable with your language," Oruz explained. "Would it be acceptable for me to summon a translator just to be safe?"

"By all means, Grand Admiral. If I may, you speak my language fluently, so I commend you for that. It's not what I've been led to believe is the norm among Tersians," Leon complimented.

"It isn't, but many of my countrymen mistake arrogance for strength. It is a sad state of affairs."

"Shall I call for your translator back at the boat then, Admiral?"

"No. My translator is here. Please do not be alarmed by what you are not accustomed to," Oruz warned. A green bottle was pulled from the sash around his waist. A handful of barnacles still clung to the dark, murky glass. Oruz gingerly pulled the cork stopper.

For a moment, Leon thought the sun had become painfully brighter and squinted. Shadows of heat thermals rippled wildly on the wall beside him. As soon as the burst of light died away, he saw a woman standing by them. She was dressed modestly in rich jade robes and a matching headscarf, but her skin was glimmering. She was a goddess of liquid gold mingled with sunlight. Leon tried to process what had just happened.

"This is Yera."

"A...jinn?" Leon asked hesitantly.

"Correct. Do be careful not to make wishes around her. Yera, would it be acceptable for you to translate our words so that we both understand?" Oruz inquired politely. Yera nodded and produced a ball of magic that hung in the air right above their heads. The jinn, her task completed, leaned on the railing and admired the seascape.

Chapter Seven

"You've had a jinn watching over your shoulder this whole time, A-admiral?" Leon stammered, mouth flapping.

Oruz chuckled. "Not my whole career, no. I take the warnings and legends seriously, Captain Kasamir, so I do not make wishes to Yera. All I do is make requests, and she is free to honor them or not. Jinn make a difference between the two."

"I see. I...I thought they were merely legends."

"We are not here to discuss jinn. We have corsairs to talk about," Oruz moaned. He really would have rather liked to talk about jinn instead. "Corsairs, pirates, they are the enemies of all nations. Will you not help us in this conflict against the pirates squatting in the harbor?"

"I understand it's a bit more complicated than that, Admiral," Leon answered firmly. "Reyais issues letters of mark, and the private captains take them and consider your ships legitimate targets. Arazumi ships are no exception, but we cannot make war on free captains with just suspicions. We cannot help you prosecute what is all being conducted within the bounds of understood law. Letters of mark, while infuriating to navy men, are still recognized as legal here in Reyais."

"I was afraid you'd say that. I remember a time when I benefited from those laws myself," Oruz said wistfully. "If you will not help us, then I can assume you will not actively hinder us either?"

"That is correct. My flotilla is here to protect the embassy and Arazum's interests. We're not here for war."

"Then that concludes our business here. The decrees of the Sultan say there is nothing left for us to discuss. An unnecessary restraint and a pity if you ask me. Now, would it be acceptable for me to speak as one former privateer to another former privateer?"

"I suppose. I will admit that you've caught me unsure of what else you may want to talk about, so all I can say is that I'm listening, Admiral."

"It is in my experience that privateers and free captains band together, especially in the face of a common enemy. I do not delude myself: I am that common enemy, but my fleet is capable. Do you fear for your cousin, Davos?"

"I must honor my family but also my country. Davos chose his path, stealing your nation's fortress ship."

"And yet you say nothing that might betray a weakness Davos may have," Oruz chuckled. "As I said, some habits don't change and worry not; I respect you all the more for that. May I offer you some friendly advice, Leon?"

"I'm listening, Oruz."

"The Sultanate of Tersia is a tired, rabid dog," the old sailor said regretfully. "Our leaders only worry about their personal enrichment and pleasures; our people are divided between being apathetic or fanatical. Our wars with Lu'han and the nomads bleed us dry, but the Sultan can only imagine peace by waging more war. When I was your age, I chose the path you have chosen. Sometimes I regret it."

"Are you telling me I should give up my naval commission and become a privateer again?" Leon scoffed.

Chapter Seven

"I suppose I wasn't clear. Let me repeat; Tersia is a rabid dog. A desperate, rabid dog that snarls over the smallest of slights. I was sent here with this fleet. So were Sorcerer Doruk and Erdem the Whaler and many other reprobates in military clothes. You commended me for my politeness, Leon, and I have always tried to be a virtuous man, even to my enemies as the Proverbs command."

Oruz then pointed towards the forest of masts and sails waiting on the horizon. "I cannot say the same about them. And what will happen when the privateers in the harbor start attacking my ships? It's not a question of 'if,' young captain, it's a question of 'when.' You and your Republic may not want conflict, but I'm sorry to say it is here, and it will drag you in. Do not be in denial of it."

There was a flash of light, and Yera was gone. Oruz was already walking back towards the boat of fidgeting sailors. "That is all I wish to discuss, young Captain Kasamir. The prophets watch over you."

Admiral Oruz and his boat descended back into the sea. Before long, the small flotilla was rowing back to the fleet. Their shapes grew smaller and then disappeared altogether. Leon watched his crew sigh in relief with the Tersians gone. He shook his head, knowing they were far from being safe.

***

MARA SAT ON A DEER HIDE RUG with bone-carved runes scattered in the dust before her. A small fire cast a rich orange glow on the tent flaps. Her circle of attendants waited quietly for her instruction while the druids respectfully stood guard outside. It wasn't a castle, but it was a keep in its own right. Mara smirked to herself. Her attendants were loyal and, for the most part, competent, but they lacked imagination. They doubted her ability to win over the druids, but Mara knew she wouldn't need magic to do it. All the druids wanted was her assurances that she'd help restore their old lands back to them. That's what these quaint forest folk requested, but it wasn't what they wanted. No, what they really wanted was for her to hurt as many of the Others as possible. Mara hadn't lied when she said her ritual would do exactly what they wished. The Druids didn't seem to think they might be caught in the blast when that happened, but Mara saw no reason to dispel them of that illusion. That would require her to tell them an uncomfortable truth.

One of the druids stooped into the tent and whispered something to one of Mara's underlings before quickly leaving. The lieutenant was quick to report.

"The druids say they are close to connecting the ley lines as instructed, Lady Mara."

"Good. Until they are connected into the shape of the rune, then whatever deaths occur will be meaningless. "

Mara tossed the bone runes and watched where they landed. Some of her aides sat nearby, motionless in a telepathic trance. One finally stirred.

"Our agents in the cult report that all is proceeding as planned," she announced, voice still groggy from coming out of the trance. "They also report that they suspect the Witch Hunter has attempted to infiltrate their ranks."

"Ignore him," Mara replied gently. "I trust everyone is doing their jobs properly, and I see no reason to take a more direct approach. Let him think he's being obnoxious."

Chapter Seven

"My lady, may I ask why you're not using more magic to ensure as many people as possible are brought into the ritual? I say this because I am worried for your safety and only want you to be successful."

"I appreciate your concern, Dimia, but you should not fret. I will need all of my magic for the final part of the ritual. Besides, I am using more basic, but no less effective magics. Appeal to peoples' need for belonging and hope, and you'll get them to stay where they are. Pique their fears and the worst of their nature, and they'll do the blood-letting for you," Mara explained. She scattered the runes again.

"Is everything still in place?" another aide asked expectantly.

"Sacrifice of the masses," Mara said, pointing towards where the majority of the bone runes fell. "The sacrifice of an immense ancient is also in its proper place. And there is the powerful young life," the sorceress showed them. "All are where they should be."

The rune that stood in for the powerful young life suddenly, violently rolled a couple of centimeters until it touched a black rune. Even the fire quieted down as if it too felt embarrassed. Mara steepled her fingers and gazed thoughtfully at what they had just witnessed.

"My lady, should we direct some of the cultists to handle that?" another aide offered.

"No, no, that will not be necessary," Mara shushed with a wave of her hand. "Human nature will always find a way. I trust it more than I trust my magic."

***

SETH WAS A FIRM BELIEVER in human nature. It had its bad parts and worse parts and, worst still, its disappointing parts. Seth did not believe in expecting the worst in people; that just led to self-fulfilling skeptical cynicism. No, he learned to expect the usual in people. There were the bad parts, the worst parts, the disappointing parts, and the good. People could behave well if you put the proper sticks and carrots in the way: social pressure, religious systems, even institutional charity. Sometimes you even found someone who was genuinely compassionate, someone who genuinely cared even without those carrots and sticks. You had to watch out for those folk. They could do enough good to ruin the plans of the cynics trying to game the system for themselves.

Tonight, he was hoping that the best in people would win out. It hurt to admit, but it was all he had left. The night was cold, dark, and a storm brewed overhead. *Stick.* He produced a frantically scribbled message; one that he knew would act as yet another stick. The person he'd send along to deliver that message? *Stick.* The bag of gold, stolen off the cult, included with the messenger? *Carrot.*

"Hurry along to that gate, child. You're not well, and they'll know what to do. Give them the note and package I gave you," Seth breathed above a whisper. Here in the shadows, he was practically invisible. It helped soothe the knowledge that he was also completely helpless as he sent the courier stumbling away.

The messenger tottered and limped towards the heavy gate. It was the only brightly lit place on the street. Seth held his breath and continued to expect the usual in people. He listened to the blue-dressed guards.

"Hey, who goes there? What are you doing, miss? You need to run along home! You'll catch your death of cold in this rain!"

Chapter Seven

"Fletcher, she's not supposed to be this close. Hey, look at her; she doesn't look well at all."

"Clemson, bloody Abyss man, what are you doing? Put your gun down; she's just a sick girl. Look, it can't hurt if we help her, right? We won't even leave our post. Young miss, get over here. What's this you're carrying?"

"I don't think this is protocol, Fletcher. Also, she's– catch her! She's freezing, Fletcher! What do we do?"

"We protect her, Clemson."

"But she's a local! We can't just take her! That's definitely-"

"No, we protect her because that's what the message she was carrying says. I think this is what Mr. Gurman said is an 'ad hoc contract.' Someone just paid us—um—an awful lot, to keep her in Long Steel's protection."

"Oh, well, then it's settled. Jolly good! It would be a shame to send this poor thing off alone and shivering like she is. Fletcher, I think she's delirious. She's definitely not well."

"Get her through the gate and call for help, Clemson. I'll stand guard here. Damn the consequences and the yelling; we can't turn her away. It wouldn't be right."

"Right you are, Fletch!"

Seth watched and smiled.

The gate closed and the young guard called Fletcher waited until Clemson returned a few minutes later. Seth turned and left. He wasn't so helpless anymore.

CHAPTER 8

THE WORLD LOOKED STARTLINGLY SMALL from here. There it was, the whole of it, so serene and far away. It didn't quite resemble the maps he studied. It was the clouds; you didn't draw clouds on a map, and the human eye caught the world's features far better than any hand could.

There was also white, but not the clouds; this white was more than that. There was so much of it, like a flood and a blanket. It collected and condensed more heavily in some places but never too far away from anywhere. It was like an overwhelming cosmic cloud. It moved, made shapes, and then folded away again warm and luminescent. A swarm of buzzing insects materialized and then faded away. A robust creature, one he didn't recognize, with a long nose and broad ears, emerged and then dissipated like mist. Below him, a translucent whale flew through the void and sang its forlorn tune.

And there was nothing but void below, dark, cold, and foreboding. It was a sea of darkness so thick that pitch would disappear right into it. He saw people dimly in the gloom reaching up to him, but they were weighed down by chains fastened to great anchors. Above him was...peace. It was bright and warm, and a marvelous celestial light shone from it. He saw people rise to it or gently come down to watch the globe. From the gloom below, one chained figure ascended, each link of the chain shattering as if it were ice, and the once captive soul was free to walk above the abyss.

The Abyss. So, below was the Abyss...

"And above is Paradise," a voice told him.

He turned and saw a mariner with ancient clothes, darkened and tattered with age, looking down at him. The mariner wore a floppy, wide brim hat, his face was bleached white, and his eyes were empty sockets. His grin was eternal.

"You're...you must be the Ferryman. And I...must be dead."

"Your culture calls me the Ferryman. Others call me Brother Grinn, Messenger Last, Reaper Grim, Angel of Death, and many, many other names. Death is not my deed; it is only an action the living can do. Your name is Philip, and you've arrived into my care."

"What do I do now?" Philip asked breathlessly.

"Anything you like," the Ferryman said calmly.

"Anything? What, no chaining to the Abyss to choke out my sins? No bliss in Paradise?"

"Our heavens and our hells tend to be of our own making. No chain weighs you down to the Abyss for transgressions most grievous; Paradise is not a prison that its inhabitants may not leave. You are free to do what you will."

"The bright cloud, mist, thing? I saw animals in it. Is it some sort of spirit?" Philip blurted. Cognitively, something told him he should be beside himself with sadness or fear. Instead, the siren call of curiosity was too strong.

Chapter Eight

"The Holy is the giver of life and creation yearns to live. Not all souls are the same of course, but nonetheless, life remains holy," the Ferryman explained patiently.

"I don't understand."

"Neither do I; not fully, at least. You may spend as long as you wish contemplating it."

"Does this mean the Holy is in, well, everything?"

"I am the Ferryman; theology was not the path allotted to me. However, I have observed that it is very tragic when unholy things are done to what the Holy has given life to."

"This isn't what I imagined the afterlife to be," Philip said. "Abyss or Paradise, you go there, and that's just it. That's how it was always explained to me."

"Of the people who told this to you, how many of them went here and returned to confirm their statements?"

"That is a good point. I suppose it's a little unfair to be angry then. Once you're dead, you're dead. Still, why would anyone wish to leave Paradise freely? What's stopping some of those in the Abyss from just ignoring their punishment?"

"Eternal peace becomes less peaceful once you realize that others are suffering on the former side," the Ferryman said. "And while many will suffer in the Abyss until their appointed time, it is foolishness to think that the ocean of eternal darkness is the be-all and end-all of torments."

"I don't think I quite understand."

"You believed in spirits and ghosts on the former side, correct?" the Ferryman quizzed patiently.

"Well, yes. Sort of, I think."

"There's a surprising number of souls who take a startling interest in the former plane despite Paradise being available to them. So their spirit wanders the earth. Just as you felt like you could only cast mere echoes into eternity while you were on the former side, so do spirits feel just as subtle when trying to interact with the former plane. And yet you can feel them if you pay attention," the Ferryman said. He made a sound that would have imitated a chuckle, but it hit like the weight of a judge's gavel.

"I have watched warlords spend more time being disparaged by the souls they slaughtered, only to watch their successors waste away the petty kingdoms they worked so hard to build. Their sons who are still alive feel the weight of their fathers' sins and achievements but cannot grasp the regret of their souls. So, they continue to do more acts of madness. Only once they've whispered enough of their guilt into the ears of the living do the history books change, and the healing begins.

"Those who were angry and abusive in life still shout their venom at the living long after they're gone, not having learned the error of their ways as they continue to wander the earth. They become more demonic than some of the demons of the Abyss. Until, finally, something causes them to regret. Then, love awakens within them, and they can begin the journey back to the Holy. A few of the wretched in the Abyss aren't chained down by anchors but by all the accumulated, shiny matter they piled on in life. They are denied Paradise until their grip releases the weight that torments them."

Chapter Eight

"Wait, they're the ones holding to the wealth they refuse to let go?" Philip inquired incredulously.

"Yes. Love in shiny matter somehow causes it, in turn, to begin holding on to you. Love gives life. Love the right things, and they will hold you up. Love shiny matter, and it will come to life and latch onto you. Consider also regretful liars who spend their eternities dredging up the truth to undo the harm they are now all too acutely aware of while the unrepentant scream out their falsities to whichever sensitive ears will listen. The hating, fearful and bigoted refuse Paradise because the ones they deemed unworthy somehow got there before them, so they wander the earth pretending it's the best they'll ever have. As I said, we tend to create our own heavens and our own hells."

Philip stared at the Ferryman, aghast at what he had learned. "Is everyone's afterlife so...dramatic?"

"Not quite. Many linger watching their loved ones for a time. Some try to mend small mistakes they made while they breathed. Babes will follow parents and peers they never got to know while those who were crippled in the former side go to experience what they never could. All those stories you heard about ghosts lurking in houses? Sometimes they stay because that's where they feel most at home and aren't quite ready to ascend to the Holy yet."

Philip thought for a moment. "Well, Reyais wasn't what I would call home. If I'm going to linger, it isn't going to be there. Ascending to the Holy sounds nice."

"That too is a journey of its own right," the Ferryman nodded.

"I see. Well, I haven't quite made up my mind yet, and you make it sound like there isn't any rush."

"There isn't. The living have a quaint saying: 'You have all the time in the world.' Now, you do have all the time, indeed. "

"I wonder what I should do," Philip murmured, rubbing an incorporeal chin.

"Are there, perhaps, any loved ones you'd like to check on before you go?" Ferryman suggested slyly.

"Sophie! That's right, is she still alive? But we were on the schooner, and then all of a sudden, I was here!" Philip cried.

"She is not here."

"Well…well, then I must do something!"

"Then, do as you wish," the Ferryman said with a respectful bow.

The form that was Philip turned and hurried towards Reyais, incorporeal feet echoing silence as he ran. Eternity was before him, and yet he could only think about one thing. The Ferryman's words still echoed in his head.

"If this is what I want to do, is it my punishment or my paradise?" Philip asked as he ran. The skeletal mariner kept pace with him while somehow standing completely still.

"The depraved and the saint suffer differently though they undergo the same trial. Deeds, intentions, and attitude all hold their own weight. Ultimately, whether it is punishment or paradise is up to you," the Ferryman said.

"I have to fix what I left behind!"

Chapter Eight

"Infamous words spoken here on this side."

This side. Philip never really had time for spirituality on the former side. Staying alive took up most of his time and effort, and now here he was: dead but still speaking. The Chapel brothers had a phrase they often repeated: "Till all is made new." He always thought that was the Holy's job, cleaning up the mess people made until everything got a bright new shine. Now it looked like the Holy invited you to help out, and if you didn't have time on the former side, you had all eternity in the hereafter.

CHAPTER 9

MANY ARAZUMI HOLD THE BELIEF that their society alone holds the rule of law sacred, obsessively so. Worse still, they were quite proud of this. The Reckoning brought that ideal to a head, an event that had happened not even a decade ago, where the Republic ruthlessly crushed the organized crime families that plagued it. Like so many other events in Arazum's history, it was a bloody time. In the end, the corrupt politicians and lawyers associated with the mobsters were given their own metaphorical chopping. On some of those occasions, the chopping was literal.

The Republic's neighbors would argue that Arazum was not uniquely blessed with an interest in following the letter and spirit of their laws; it was only Arazumi arrogance that led them to believe in their superiority. It wasn't the law they were sticklers for: it was contracts. Otto was giving a stellar and noisy demonstration of this in the early hours of the morning. It had interrupted his morning coffee, so he had plenty of frustration to vent.

"Let me get this straight," Otto said wearily, grumpily massaging his temples. In front of him dejectedly sat the guards Clemson and Fletcher. Behind Otto was guard captain Axle, who had the look of a man who knew he should be concerned, but his ignorance limited his capacity to do so. Otto was the most versed in the company's bibliography of contract regulations. Axle's job was to consult with him, not study the esoteric knowledge.

"You brought in a foreign girl—unauthorized to do so by the way—into the embassy without consulting a diplomat or a bookman. You did so because you decided that this slip of paper the girl had constituted a contract and that the gold in her possession was a down payment. And, this was good enough for you to break—only the Holy knows—how many various regulations and protocols?" Otto demanded and then took a desperately needed gulp of coffee.

"She was cold and sick, sir!" Clemson protested.

"She practically passed out as well, Mr. Gurman. It wouldn't make the Republic look good if we just let a young girl pass out in front of our doorstep," Fletcher added pointedly.

"No, it wouldn't look good, but you also put the company and the Republic in an uncomfortable situation. Protocols exist for a reason, gentlemen!"

"She was dying, sir," Clemson replied firmly.

Otto sighed heavily and scanned the girl's note. The whole situation was a nightmare and the letter, written like a contract, only threw more petrol on the fire. Whoever wrote it knew just enough legalese to hold Long Steel responsible for the girl's safety, and by taking her into their care and accepting the money, Fletcher and Clemson had unwittingly sealed the contract. Otto's mind screamed words like 'subterfuge,' 'sabotage,' and 'liability.' He took another sip of coffee.

Admittedly, and no one would outright state it, Clemson and Fletcher made the right decision. When so many lawyers were hanged, burned, creatively lacerated, and generally abused during the Reckoning, they were done so on the grounds of abusing the spirit of the law while barely upholding the letter of it. "Laws are meant to protect life, not to be some silly game," an old saint taught. The common masses appropriated this ideal by declaring the corruption they witnessed

Chapter Nine

violated "bloody common sense" and proceeded accordingly and excessively.

"This is just my reminder to you two to follow protocol. Are we clear? You have a wire there to quickly contact someone who would know. Use it. That's all I have to say," Otto grumped, lightening his tone. Axle nodded.

"You two are dismissed. Get some rest, gentlemen," Axle said. Clemson and Fletcher shuffled out like the exhausted who got saddled with unwanted overtime but wore the smiles of those who knew they won anyway.

"How bad is it going to be, Otto?" Axle asked once the door closed.

"The diplomats will make a fuss, but due to the language in this note, that girl is now technically in Long Steel's custody, not necessarily the Republic's," he said. "What's her name? Sophie?"

"Correct. So she's in our protection then? And you said the note is pretty locked tight in its wording?" Axle pressed. Otto was still busy digesting the rest of the paperwork.

"Just Sophie? No last name? My question is, what legal mind with this much money to spend decided to use their resources to protect a street urchin?"

"Very perplexing but again, the wording, Otto."

"Yes, Axle, it's very binding in every sense. However, I don't think we should be so eager to turn this Sophie loose back onto the streets. It will not be the easiest thing, but I think the company prides itself in doing right, not easy."

"Ahh, so Mr. Gurman's idealism shows itself. Apparently, you do have a heart hiding somewhere under that breastplate. Well, I'll prepare myself for the inevitable complaining and hand wringing from the diplomats. They have to pretend they're somehow in charge. But I need you to write up a report explaining why we're bound to this decision," Axle ordered, a finger tapping on his desk. "I'm going to get an earful about 'liabilities' and 'possible international incident,' and 'public relations' and Holy knows what else."

"I'll get right to that," Otto said tiredly before glancing into his mug with a suspicious eye. "After I get another cup of coffee."

"Out of curiosity, under what circumstances would this current situation become more difficult?"

"Realistically, it'll only be if the rulers of Reyais demand their misplaced citizen back," Otto replied after a moment of consideration.

"Well, I doubt we'll have to worry about that then. She is, as you observed, a street rat with a mysterious benefactor. What's their name?"

"One 'Seth G.O.H.C.' Whatever that means," Otto murmured. "Legally, we're on pretty defensible ground. However, the whole thing still feels wrong, like there's a trap somewhere."

"Well, Mr. Gurman, you better start puzzling that out. I'll expect several reports from you later."

"I will get several cups of coffee."

***

Chapter Nine

CULTURE SHOCK HIT SOPHIE like a jet of steaming hot water. Literally. She feared they intended to drown her creatively. Germ theory was a recent development in Arazumi society and while they didn't see witches and demons everywhere like their neighbors, they instead saw bacteria. It didn't help that all their instruments confirmed their worst fears; like witches on occasions, microbes were indeed everywhere. Sophie was tossed into a small enclosed space with a strange pipe sticking out of the wall. Two scientists with rubber coverings accompanied her and subjected her to "the shower."

The strange Arazumi women pulled her out, strapped her down, and gave her "the inoculation." Sophie was sure she was going to die. She gasped in horror as they jammed several needles into her arm and watched the strange fluid disappear inside her. How long would it take for the poison to kill her?

They waited for her to recover her strength. Sophie wasn't sure what to expect. Her arm still hurt, but she wasn't convinced death felt like this. One of the women took her by the hand and walked her outside and across the compound.

"Are you hungry?" she asked cheerfully.

"Yes," Sophie mumbled numbly.

"What's your name?"

"Sophie."

"My name is Kassia. Let's get you some food. You'll feel much better after you've had breakfast."

"Thanks for the new clothes, but they look so expensive, and I don't have money to pay for them," Sophie admitted shyly. "Can I please have my old ones back?"

Kassia suddenly had the expression of a person caught with their hand in the cookie jar. "Oh, the clothes are for you, no charge. You won't need your old ones back." Unbeknownst to Sophie, the staff had taken one glance at her clothes, tossed them into the furnace, and began sewing together new ones.

"Oh. Well, thank you, Miss Kassia."

"Just Kassia will do. Let's find you a seat, and I'll go get you some food from the kitchens."

Sophie meekly followed Kassia into the spacious mess hall. Her knees went weak, overpowered by the smells of so many kinds of food. Her stomach didn't growl; it shrieked. Fear told her to keep quiet and follow Kassia. It also did an excellent job of drying up her mouth. Kassia motioned for her to sit across from two men already at one of the long tables. Sophie recognized them as soldiers.

"Keep an eye on her, you two; I'll get her something decent."

Sophie instinctively tried to make herself shrink. Life was scary without an anchor to hold her in place, and she still felt like she was bobbing in a stormy sea. The memory of last night felt like a jigsaw puzzled strewn about the room of her mind. First, she found...well, then there must have been an explosion because the ship was gone, and she was frantically paddling to a floating piece of wood. She could thank Philip for teaching her how to swim; that was far more useful than all the nautical horror stories he filled her head with. Then what happened? She woke up on the beach, slipping in and out of consciousness. She remembered vomiting water. There had been a scary man dressed in black. He gave her...something? She remembered walking up to the embassy. Now here she was, and she didn't know whether to panic, run off with a stolen plate of food, or both.

"Here, have a biscuit," the giant in front of her offered, scattering her internal monologue. Sophie reached for it. "Don't forget the butter," he added.

Butter! Only the aristocrats up in the palace could afford butter! She had never tasted butter before. It nearly knocked her out of her seat.

She studied her table mates a little more closely. The man next to the giant had finished his food but was busily writing on a sheet of paper. Occasionally he would stop to sip from a mug of coffee. Another cup of tea sat by him, neglected and forgotten. Across from her, the giant was finishing off what remained on his plate: sausages, fried potatoes, and hard-boiled eggs. Sophie felt her mouth-watering around the half-chewed biscuit in her mouth.

"Here, kid, I don't know why the cook keeps giving me a mug when he knows I won't get to it," the writing man said, pushing the tea towards her. He never once looked up from his work.

"Don't forget the sugar if you want it, pup," the giant added, motioning towards a small porcelain cup of it nearby.

"Jord, Kassia will get grumpy if she finds out you offered her that."

"One spoonful never hurt, Otto," the giant said, rolling his eyes.

Sophie stared at the sugar. There was a long story behind the simple sweet that she couldn't have known, but it affected her nonetheless.

In Arazum, whole industries sprung up overnight with the creation of sugar. It was grown in the Southern Archipelago. Land was leased from the Shah, and the local Dhaliese were hired to work the fields. Sugarcane was processed into powdered sugar and molasses, and from there, the possibilities were endless. Rum, new kinds of sweetened baked goods, and a plethora of candies burst into the world.

The field of dentistry found itself becoming more sophisticated and flooded with sugar money from the spike in tooth decay. Toothbrushes, mouthwashes, and all kinds of surgery had to be developed, spilling yet more money everywhere. Arazumi and Dhaliese bakers led the way in dreaming up new kinds of sweets while Arazum's Southern Traders Company brought the white gold to the tables of those who could afford it in every known port. Prices rose with the distance it traveled.

Sophie had heard of sugar, but she never had it. It was inconceivable. Many wealthier neighbors would save and penny-pinch for months just to purchase a small bag of the stuff to show off during the Winternalia parties. You didn't dare bake with it; oh no, far too much money had been spent just to waste it by putting it into your mouth. Sugar was a showpiece on the table unless you lived in the Palace, not something you dared to eat.

She turned away from the sugar. It was too much, too overwhelming. What was Otto doing? She watched as more and more strange lines were marked into the page and stared bug-eyed at the text. Quietly, she leaned in closer towards Jord.

"Is...is he a warlock? Are those spells he's making?"

One of Otto's eyebrows jumped like a kicked dog. "It's just a report, girl. There's no magic here."

Jord shook with contained laughter. "Ahh, but there is a magic of a sort here, young miss."

"Jord!"

"Calm down, Otto. You forget most people don't know how to read, let alone write, and when they see someone writing, it can be intimidating. No, young lady, he's writing a different sort of spell. No fireballs, no summoned demons, but he is making instructions to people who will never see him and it will stay around longer than words simply spoken. That's a magic all its own."

"Oh. Well, I guess that isn't so dangerous then," Sophie said hesitantly.

"Ah, but it can be very dangerous when used by the wrong men and read by those who don't fully understand. But that is no different from the magic you're thinking of, young miss."

"Is he one of the good ones then?" Sophie whispered again.

"Well, he can be an arse at times, but he's one of the good ones."

"I can file a complaint about you in this report, you know," Otto said.

Kassia showed up at that moment, and the plate she brought made a hearty bump on the table. There was buttered toast, a hard-boiled egg, a bowl of warm porridge, and a whole orange! It was enough to make Sophie weep, but that could wait till after she ate.

"Help yourself," Kassia told her. It was all she needed to say.

"So what's the verdict? Is she staying with us?" the chemist asked as Sophie began the project of clearing her plate.

"All circumstances considered, she has to. Long Steel Company is responsible for her now. Axle wants me to lay it all out in writing just in case the diplomats get fussy. They'll probably draft up a waiver and have Axle sign it," Otto explained.

Kassia looked over at the street urchin. "All right, I understand you're hungry, but if you keep eating like that, you'll choke. Slow down and chew. There's no need to rush; you'll be fed again at lunch."

Sophie looked up with her bug-eyed stare. "You mean I can have breakfast and lunch?"

"And dinner, too. But, you won't get any if you eat too fast and choke."

"I think she's more confused about getting three meals a day, Kassia," Otto said. "I mean, you remember what it was like."

"No, no, I don't," Kassia replied quickly. "And before you say anything, neither do you. How could you remember those days? We were too young."

Jord's eyes rolled back and forth between Otto and Kassia. Just how far back did their history go? Otto caught his gaze.

Chapter Nine

"We were both in an orphanage in Arazum City. You've heard of the term 'Children of the Fire?' We're both survivors of that disaster."

It wasn't a happy term. A surprising number of young adults from Arazum City were Children of the Fire, orphaned during the inferno two decades ago that reduced whole districts of the city to ash. Most of the victims were workers trapped in the factories and sweatshops that dominated the burned sections of the city. The poor suffered the most in the aftermath because it was their homes and jobs that went up in smoke. Then the crime syndicates swooped in to establish their own fronts and projects while politicians found excuses not to put the city's resources into helping the afflicted. The seeds for the Reckoning were sown there in the broken lives and scorched rubble.

"You can't say that for sure, Otto. There was also a pox epidemic going around at the time. We don't know how we ended up in the orphanage because we were too young to understand," Kassia cautioned.

"I stopped having nightmares about the Black War. I still have nightmares about fire."

"Well, I still don't remember going too hungry at the orphanage," Kassia retorted.

"It got better as time went on, but I remember the first couple years being bad," Otto said.

"I don't have a lot of memories of that time. I remember you. I remember Sister Therese, and I remember you getting in trouble a lot. Most of my memories begin after I was adopted," Kassia admitted. She then furtively motioned for Otto to lend her a spare sheet of paper and his pen. She began to scribble something on it.

"Otto, a trouble maker? Now, this is a story I got to hear," Jord announced.

"There were a lot of street gangs during that time in Arazum City, and it wasn't just Children of the Fire. The orphanage kids couldn't be cooped up all the time either. The Sisters were very adamant about children learning practical skills to help them get adopted. Otto took it upon himself to get into scrapes with any of the street gangs that got too threatening," Kassia snickered.

"I never understood why the Sisters were so set on swatting my knuckles for getting into fights when they could've been using those very same rulers on the gang kids," Otto griped.

"If I remember correctly, Otto, your attitude towards them probably contributed to your punishment," Kassia tutted.

"Of course, I had an attitude about it! I'd have fewer black eyes if the Sisters helped me out instead of trying to hold me back!"

"So you've been in touch with each other all this time?" Jord asked. "I didn't realize you both went that far back."

"It wasn't easy, but yes, we sent letters back and forth to each other. I also recall Otto being a little lax with his replies," Kassia said with a wry smile.

"Stamps and stationery weren't cheap, especially when the Sisters had me on a strict allowance!"

Sophie put down her silverware with a clatter and hiccupped. She used a napkin to wipe her mouth, but quickly picked up another one

Chapter Nine

to dab at her eyes. "I'm sleepy," she moaned. "And...and I miss my brother."

"Here, let me show you to your bed," Kassia soothed, leading the girl up from her seat. She stopped when Otto furtively grabbed her free hand.

"Find out what you can about her brother," he whispered. Kassia nodded and then pushed a note towards him. Jord and Otto waited until things were quiet again. Otto tried to make sense of what he saw on the paper.

"Poor pup," Jord murmured, shaking his head.

"Look at this note," Otto said furtively, showing it to Jord. "Sophie has some sort of brand burned into her neck. It looks like a smuggler's brand."

"It's also a rune," Jord said.

"A rune? We're dealing with magic now? Do you know what it does?"

"If memory serves correct, it combines a shape that signifies 'eye' and another that means 'rope.'"

"Should we be worried?" Otto asked quickly.

"It's a sodding rune, little man. Of course, we should be worried."

***

HECTOR LIT HIS PIPE. Decades of doing this shite and suddenly, the bizarre was brazenly showing itself all in one week. It wasn't that he didn't believe in coincidences; they sometimes happened. The problem was that they didn't come in like a parade. Bodies shouldn't keep showing up with unusual causes of death.

"They're smugglers, sir," one of his guards announced.

"What makes you so certain?"

"The tattoos. We've had to deal with this group before. Body snatching, contraband running, murder even. Someone did us a big favor by killing these three."

"Hmm, yes, but murder is still murder. Especially if it's done in such an unusual fashion," Hector grunted, his pipe billowing thickly. "Did your examination reveal anything else? I'll be disappointed if all you tell me is the obvious."

"I'm glad you asked," the subordinate guard grinned. "Something was surprising. All the bodies have a strange series of gashes on their jaw and cheek. Can't really tell what might have caused that."

"I'd say that's where something grabbed them. Grabbed with such force, it punctured their skin. Like a hook, maybe."

"That makes sense but then what sort of thing was it? I've never seen a weapon that does something like this."

"Shite. Just a couple days ago, we found those longshoremen dead by magic. Now we got three dead bodies because of strange arse reasons," Hector said and took a long drag from his pipe. Smoke flowed from his nostrils.

Chapter Nine

"Start warning the people," Hector commanded. "They need to know that some sort of devilry is about, and if they know to look for something, maybe they'll start giving us tips."

"As you command, sir. I'll let the others know."

"And have someone come and dispose of these bodies. Get them covered before they're removed. We want people to know, not get hysterical."

"Good idea, sir."

Hector gave the bodies one last glance. There were too many uncertainties, too many unanswered questions this week. However, there would be no need to consult the Arazumi on the cause of death for these stiffs. The living cannot lie on their stomachs and face skyward at the same time.

***

LEON PULLED OUT HIS POCKET WATCH and counted the seconds ticking by. The manufacture of clocks was not a uniquely Arazumi enterprise, but their clocks were considered the most accurate, dependable, and affordable. Pocket watches found their way into the possession of all kinds of folks, even Danarian peasants. Sea captains of all nations paid heavily to purchase an Arazumi nautical clock out of their savings. Without one, it was impossible to determine longitude accurately. With the transcontinental railway and telegraph network across Arazum running without rest, the Republic had no choice but to create standardized time zones. The phenomenon of scheduling was born. All this naturally caused headaches, grief, and confusion, especially among the elderly, but the Arazumi cog of progress ground on.

The passage of time is an unrelenting phenomenon that laughs at all things, but scheduling is a human attempt to capitalize on it. It is a usual tool but an artificial one with its strange drawbacks. Consider the number of herculean efforts people will go through to make a meeting, a task that is universally hated but engaged in nevertheless.

Leon closed the lid on his watch and returned it to its place. The water having boiled long enough, he began to pour it over his coffee grounds meticulously. Human construct or not, scheduling had its uses.

The *Defiance* never fully slept, but it was waking up from the sleepy stupor of the evening. The small night shift began to trade places with the much larger day shift. Men were roused from their sleep, given a quick breakfast, and then sent to their duties. Leon, long used to seeing ships manned almost entirely by fellow Edalans, realized that the *Defiance* had a shadow resemblance to the Republic.

Most of the sailors handling the day-to-day duties were Edalans, the province steeped in maritime shipping and agriculture. Down in the engine room, most of the men came from the northernmost province called Tenethar. Scions of miners and blacksmiths, they felt right at home in the cramped, sweltering quarters shared with noisy machinery. Then, there were the cerebral men from the Capital province in charge of his gun turrets, communication system, and ordnance lockers. He trusted them the least, the gunnery men especially. They spent so much time consulting charts and crunching the numbers on hitting hypothetical targets, Leon wondered if they would be able to do it on actual ones.

The coffee was made. A pinch of cinnamon, brown sugar, and milk was added. Scheduling was a flawed miracle but a wondrous, flawed miracle nonetheless. Outside he could hear the turrets hum as they rotated, right on time. It had to be done to prevent rust buildup. The whistle screamed to ensure it was working correctly. Topside work crews brushed the deck while rotary guns were oiled, just as they were done every morning. He could hear the shanties sung so the men would keep in pace. The ship was waking up.

"Captain, we got a situation," a sailor from the bridge announced. "Unidentified brig just beyond the embassy's waters but close enough to be a concern. It's not Tersian, though. Orders, sir?"

"Let me have a look," Leon said, taking his coffee with him.

The scene from the bridge would have been pretty enough for a painting. On one side was the city of Reyais, old to the point of venerable and made of impressive stonework. On the other side were a gorgeous seascape with rich sapphire waters, ivory clouds, and the call of seagulls. It would have been perfect if that ugly Tersian armada wasn't on the horizon. Leon spotted the brig rolling along the waves, trying to keep a safe distance from the trigger-happy Tersians. Leon squinted; he recognized that ship.

"Helmsman, bring us to quarter speed and set a course to bring us alongside that brig. I'd like to hail that ship."

"Aye, sir!"

It took some time, but the warships were eventually sailing in parallel, undoubtedly watched by Tersian spyglasses in the distance. The sailors on the brig were tense, but no one appeared to be running for the guns yet. Leon decided not to keep them waiting.

"Blind Captain! I know you man that tub! Where are you heading off to?"

Ritual | F. Arburg

Leon raised an eyebrow when he was first met with silence. It raised further when he saw a bottle erratically floating through the air towards him. You never knew how Blind Captain was going to flex his magical talents. There was a rolled-up note. Leon carefully grabbed it and peered inside.

> *Greetings to you, young Captain Kasamir.*
>
> *I intend to run the Tersian blockade. We will wait for the currents and wind to favor us. No need to wish me luck. I can't approve of your decision to become a navy regular, but I know you're one of the good ones. Fair winds and seas to you, and may we next meet under better circumstances.*
>
> *– B.C.*

CHAPTER 10

THE CORSAIR'S CREED WAS TO NEVER get into a fair fight. Instead, you ran down helpless, under-gunned merchantmen weighed down with cargo. If those merchantmen happened to have no guns, all the better. When the navy showed up, you raised all the sails, put your back to the wind, and outran them. If you absolutely had to fight, then you didn't fight fair.

Mirabelle was doing everything to ensure this wouldn't be a fair fight. Captain Novault was one of those young captains willing to try any dirty trick to give him an edge. Mirabelle heard he stalked in the waters of the Southern Archipelago where a free captain could cheat and cut a living by raiding hapless indigenous tribes.

Along the way, he scavenged from the jungle's natural bounty to sell to the highest bidder and lay in wait for any opportunity that blundered his way. He had even modified his ship to suit his favorite hunting grounds. Additional davits were built along the hull, and even more boats were stowed on the top deck. The overall appearance made the aesthetically minded cringe, but the results couldn't be opposed. Anyone who tried to attack Captain Novault found themselves quickly surrounded by large custom-made attack boats ready to board from an unexpected angle and often sporting an uncomfortably robust cannon. Precisely what Mirabelle needed.

"I still can't believe you agreed to this. What's the catch? You get the captured ship, and I get ninety percent of the profits from the plunder?" Novault exclaimed, grinning like an idiot. Mirabelle smiled at him.

"It's very simple. I need a ship, and you want gold. I need your boats to help me catch a target, and you need my experienced crew to take a ship."

"My men and I have taken ships before."

"How many of them were Tersian?"

"...None," Novault admitted sheepishly, grin wilting.

"That's where my crew and I come in."

"How many have you taken then?"

"Five," Mirabelle lied confidently. It was closer to two, and the Tersian crew of the first one were so sick they barely put up a fight.

"I'm impressed! Then I'm pleased you'll be helping."

"Of course," Mirabelle smirked. She would have felt sorry for him, but she had little sympathy for captains that preyed on tribals. Besides, it was Novault's fault for being so easily impressionable.

"Last question," Novault announced. "Why are we waiting in this cove when we could be tracking down our target?"

"Because of the currents," Mirabelle explained and brought a map up. Gilroy had helpfully scribbled in his own notes and markings. This particular map showed the currents around the island. Gilroy's commentary showed that the map wasn't quite accurate, knowledge he had gleaned the hard way. She learned a long time ago always to trust Gilroy over the map, no matter how up-to-date it claimed to be.

Chapter Ten

"We're expecting the Tersians not to be very well versed with the local currents. My pilot tells me a ship can find itself getting pulled close to the island if they don't know what they're doing, a blunder those Tersians are bound to commit," Mirabelle said.

"An omnibus of blunders, if you will," Novault chuckled. Mirabelle desperately held on to her wooden smile.

"We'll wait for one of the Tersians to fall into this particular current and get separated from its allies. From there, we'll use your boats to descend on them in the darkness, when they may not even realize the danger they're in, and then get the ship back to Reyais."

"So...we could be here a while?" Novault asked nervously.

"You're no stranger to waiting. It'll all be worth it, I'm sure. Now, if you'll excuse me, I need to go check on my men," She wasn't going to wait for him to figure out that they wouldn't know what their target was until it fell into the trap. That meant it could be anything from an attractive frigate, a disappointing sloop, or an imposing man o'war.

The sand felt soft under her boots, and the water looked inviting enough to swim in. Most of the sailors lounged around along the shore, relaxing with the lack of any duties to occupy them. Mirabelle didn't like the idleness, but they could do little until a target showed itself. She made her way back towards her men and sat by one of the boats. There was a bottle of brandy stowed away somewhere in here.

"Just how big of a fool have you played Captain Novault?" Jacques inquired quietly.

"As big of one as he deserves. If he seriously thought he was going to be making easy money without a hook attached, then he only has himself to blame," Mirabelle huffed.

"We also don't know what kind of ship will fall into that trap."

"Yes, but we fully expect the risks and accept them. Novault just saw his share of the take and stopped listening. Now he's along for the voyage whether he likes it or not."

"You can be quite cruel, my lady."

"I think I'm being more than generous if you ask me. He gets an opportunity to work with some of the best boarding and capturing sailors I've ever seen, and then he gets to have ninety percent of the plunder. I'm practically giving him money!"

"And we get an easily manipulated patsy who is giving us ships we otherwise wouldn't have had."

"And he's being more than adequately compensated for it, especially if a great big man o'war or transport galleon falls into the currents."

"You think he'll back out if that happens?" Jacques asked quietly.

"After telling his men how much they'll be getting paid? He'll be a coward if he backs out, and respect is a currency he can ill afford to squander," Mirabelle said.

"You are quite scary, my lady."

"I'll take that as a compliment."

Chapter Ten

***

GUNDERSON BALANCED HIMSELF on the rigging, scanning the Tersian ships he could see. During the meeting he had publicly said it was best not to interfere with the Tersians. He didn't expect the other captains to listen. Young Mirabelle was most certainly looking to pounce, but the old man knew that with freelance privateers and rogue captains, you sometimes had to tell them to do the exact opposite of what you wanted them to do. Besides, the Tersian sailors and captains were a savage lot. Spend enough time being a free captain on the open seas and, if you were lucky, you'd hear a plethora of horror stories about the Tersians. If you were unlucky, you got a starring role in one of those horror stories.

"Are the Tersians as bad as everyone says they are?" one of the young deckhands asked. Gunderson looked at him quizzically and then decided this must be the pup's first voyage.

"You know how most navy men will fire a shot across your bow as a warning? It'll be a near thing, but you know they intentionally missed, and more importantly, the navy man knows he intentionally missed, right?" Gunderson explained patiently.

"Yes."

"With the Tersians, your warning shot is when they've intentionally fired a few whirling bolas of chain shot at your sails to slow you down. They don't ask permission to come aboard. They just do. If they suspect you're a corsair, they hang you on the spars of your mast. And that's if you're lucky," Gunderson said darkly. Old memories bubbled up from the dark tar of history. It made his ax hand itch.

Ritual | F. Arburg

"And if you're unlucky, Captain?" the deckhand asked timidly.

"Pup, is this your very first voyage?"

"Yes, sir."

"By the Holy, you have the worst luck. Well, if you're unlucky, you run into Erdem the Whaler."

"Who's he?"

"A twisted ghoul walking in human skin," Gunderson spat. "He likes to play with his victims, cuts up and mutilates them. They say–"

"H-how does he cut them up, sir? Are they still alive when he does it?"

"Don't ask questions whose answers you're not prepared to hear. No, Erdem the Whaler is a demon, and not many people survive fighting him."

Gunderson's fists clenched and trembled. He had fought Erdem once, about ten years ago. The Tersians had come upon Gunderson's convoy of whalers, honest men making an honest living. Erdem, commanding the squadron, must've decided they were carrying contraband instead. Or maybe the Tersians just wanted a fight and steal away some of their cargo. Either way, Gunderson remembered being shocked by the sadist. Shaking with rage in his waterlogged boots, he saw how Erdem eviscerated and flayed the men before him, and before he knew it, he was fighting for his life against this demonic Tersian. It had been a long time since someone put terror into him.

Chapter Ten

The only reason Gunderson was one of the few men to cross blades with Erdem and live was due to the ship heaving violently in a sudden swell, and Gunderson being too close to the edge.

First, he tumbled overboard; then he spent a week drifting on flotsam. The sun baked him alive, the salt scraped his flesh raw, and his brain teetered on the brink of dehydration. Eventually, he got picked up by a passing Arazumi merchantman and was nursed back to health. That was more than could be said of the corpses they found later in the voyage, corpses Gunderson recognized as old crewmates whom Erdem had gotten to first. His knuckles went white with rage.

"You...You don't think Erdem is in that fleet out there, do you?" the deckhand quavered.

"Oh, I hope not," Gunderson lied. Let the pup have hope, and Gunderson could continue to count the many ways he'd kill Erdem when he crossed paths with him again.

***

HECTOR STARED AT THE STACKS OF PAPER before him. This was the last chance to have second thoughts, so naturally, he started to have them. The years of being a lawman and town guard had not been kind to him. The lawbreakers hated you, the sailors on the dock made your life hell and the people you were supposed to be protecting treated you with indifference or distrust. The Palace barely paid their wages anymore, let alone equipped them. He once put in a request for armor from the Palace. The letter sat on a desk for nine months before being promptly rejected. Then, they deducted a fee from his pay for some asinine reason.

Sometimes, he wondered why he kept doing it. He didn't have to; he could simply drop his badge, what little good it was worth anymore, and walk away. The door, slightly ajar, looked so alluring. He sighed and lit his pipe again. Maybe he'd find an answer in all this smoke.

What was he going to do? That was five deaths this past week or so under unnatural circumstances. He had no choice; they had to warn the people that there was some dangerous boogeyman about, and if they spotted anything suspicious, they were to let the city guards know. Simple, right? An educated populace would act sensibly, be vigilant and cooperate with the authorities, right? Ah, but even he knew therein lay the problem.

Individuals, rare ones at that, may act sensibly, but mobs do not, and Reyais looked more and more like a mob each day. Hector couldn't blame them. The Palace didn't care for them; the ever-changing sailors had no allegiance to them, and a very alien nation with ideas they didn't understand had built a veritable fortress in their city and called it an embassy. When people figure they have no allies left, they either turn to each other or turn on each other, and that new cult out there was telling them to band together. That was a good thing, right?

Hector couldn't help but feel that he was about to throw pitch and gunpowder onto a roaring fire despite his best intentions. But he couldn't ignore it either. He couldn't leave the population in the dark about this in good conscience. Could he trust people to act sensibly? Absolutely not, but conscience left him no other path. It wasn't the easy thing to do, but it was the right thing to do, and he was going to do it. It was why he kept taking up that badge every day. While there was still something to salvage in this city, there was still a reason to do the right thing.

Chapter Ten

"Are we ready, sir? It cost a lot to get these posters painted," A guard said.

"Do it, son. Make sure the others also announce what's on the posters so those who can't read can at least hear about it."

"Of course, sir. Do you think this'll help us catch the monster?"

"We can only hope," Hector sighed.

"Uh, what happens if they find the monster? Are we going to have to take care of it? I've never fought a monster before, and well, I saw what it did to those three smugglers and the two longshoremen."

"Son, we'll cross that bridge when we get there. Right now, the step we need to take is getting these posters up. No more lollygagging! Get to it, all of you!"

***

THEY WATCHED A TERSIAN SHIP fall out of formation and drift close to their cove, just as the sun was descending on the horizon. The ocean currents, just as Gilroy predicted, presented their victim. Countless eyes watched the wayward vessel with ravenous eyes. For some, it was payday. For others, it was their ticket out of here.

The boats came out the instant the waters' hue matched the midnight sky. Oars were muffled with soft cloth around the oarlocks to dampen unnecessary noise. The predators glided over the sea like sharks after a crippled whale. One by one, they fell into position circling the hapless ship. Hearts caught in throats.

The silence and absence of gunfire suggested they weren't spotted, but it could have also meant their prey was setting up a trap for them instead. Grappling hooks launched onto the top deck. Still, no alarm. One by one, they began to climb the ropes.

Mirabelle waited on the cable beside Jacques. She and her crew had this sort of operation practiced until it was a macabre ballet. Silently climbing over both sides of the ship were the throat cutters led by a man named Bartrand. He wasn't the most sociable individual and Mirabelle always felt uneasy around him, but he knew how to train the throat cutters into silent assassins. If all went according to plan, they could slowly but surely decimate the crew of a small ship. Mirabelle, Jacques, and the other heavy hitters would never be needed.

No one said anything. No unnecessary movements. The most effective, and at this point only, way they could help the assassins now was to be silent and not interfere. Besides, the throat cutters were skilled enough to hold their own until reinforcements arrived if the situation unexpectedly went out of control.

Mirabelle's hands quickly tightened around the rope when there was a shout, a scuffle, and then the blast of a pistol. Jacques cursed under his breath. They heard a loud, chirruping whistle: Bartrand's signal that they needed help. Mirabelle and her team started climbing as fast as they could.

"That noise came from the second deck. Do you think one of the throat cutters botched it?" Jacques hissed.

"Personally, I think one of Novault's men got a little over-eager," Mirabelle said in exasperation.

Chapter Ten

"Damn them; that does sound likely."

Mirabelle rolled over the side and into a scene of blood and despair. Bartrand and his team were finishing the rest of the Tersian crew on the top deck. She could tell from the noise below, that is where the real trouble was. Sword at the ready, she headed down the stairs, the rest of her crew right behind her. Her fears were verified; Novault's men couldn't sit tight and tried to "help" the throat cutters. Now the Tersians were on the verge of pushing them out of the gunports and regaining control of the floor. Mirabelle charged into the melee, sword searching for a target. Her other hand kept a pistol at the ready and if she fired it, there were many more to take its place.

Never get into a fair fight. The Tersians were fighting back, but they were disorganized and had only moments to discern friend from foe. It became even more chaotic when someone lit a lamp, and everyone's night vision evaporated with the flash. Mirabelle and her men moved methodically together, controlling what they could. Blood splashed on the walls while swords clanged and wheellock pistols whirred then boomed. The sounds of battle roared within the rapidly foul-smelling hull. Then, with a final gurgle, silence drowned the ship.

"Help the wounded," Mirabelle bellowed, stiffly wiping blood off her sword. "Toss the dead overboard. Men of the Lauria, help me get this ship underway!"

"What about our plunder?" someone demanded. It had to be one of Novault's men. No one on her crew had a habit of talking back to her at a time like this.

"We can worry about that when we get back to port. There'll be no plunder if a Tersian catches us. Jacques, make sure the men follow Gilroy's instructions on how to get out of this current."

"Aye, my lady! You heard her, get to it, men! Get the sails up to catch the wind and get this tub headed due south!" Jacques snapped.

Mirabelle scribbled a quick note in the darkness and scrounged for an empty bottle. There was a footlocker, now without an owner, and within was a bottle. Someone had been building a model ship inside it. Mirabelle sighed and stuffed her note with the incomplete ship, splintering it. She tossed the bottle out of a nearby gunport. The mermaids were invited to dine well tonight.

***

BLIND CAPTAIN GRITTED HIS TEETH. The wind howled hard on the sails, and the rigging groaned under the strain. His hands shook, using as much magic as he dared to push the ship as fast as he could muster. It wasn't enough. Two Tersian warships were gaining on them.

Then it all went wrong. Both ships blinked and were suddenly next to him. The Tersian guns roared, vomiting noxious black smoke. Beneath him, the ship shuddered and buckled. Gunsmoke surrounded them. Then the enemy ships emerged through the wall of oily smoke. He heard the Tersians boarding them. Blind Captain lowered his hands, gave them a shake, and then began hurling fireballs at his assailants.

He sensed that his enemies were no strangers to boarding actions. For a moment, he used magic to give him true sight, painting an image around him sharper than any eye could see. Men armed with cutlasses rushed to board the stricken vessel while musketeers remained at the

Chapter Ten

gunwales of their own ships, firing in volleys at his men. He could do little to directly intervene in the melee just meters from him, so he focused on the enemy musketeers. The true sight went away; he needed his magic for something else. Concentrating, he twirled a finger around and around in a slow, deliberate movement. Gunpowder smoke, so abundant despite the few shots taken, began to gather around the gunmen. It would be a while before they could see out of that haze.

The fighting turned desperate, a frantic flurry of activity where a man could forget his training because he was fighting for his life. Blind Captain could tell that something awful was happening up front on the bow from the chilling clashing of weapons and screaming. He heard his men shrieking that Erdem the Whaler was aboard. He couldn't help because he recognized the footsteps of multiple Tersians who knew that the best way to stop a sorcerer was to overwhelm him with numbers.

Blind Captain bellowed, straining his limits. Those who wielded magic knew about control, how to will magic into being. Those who wanted to be magicians for long learned not to lose control. If you were lucky, a minor slip-up would only turn half your arm into a charred stump. As for a bad mistake, Blind Captain had heard of sorcerers spontaneously immolating themselves, transmuting their bodies into water or turning half a village, and everyone in it, inside out.

Blind Captain screamed and released the magic he had been building, praying it wouldn't take him in the process. Every Tersian in front of him fell away as cinders, their weapons dropping as slag. He wobbled and leaned on his knees, gasping for breath. He heard clapping.

Clap. Clap. Clap.

"Well done, well done! Blind Captain, I assume? We've all heard of you."

He perceived a man staring down at him, a ball of magic suspended in the air above his head doing all the translating. Blind Captain straightened up and raised both hands to incinerate him. The cheeky Tersian was probably grinning.

"No, you will not do that," the stranger declared, a hand pointing at him. Suddenly, Blind Captain was paralyzed, his body refusing to obey him.

"Perhaps you've heard of me? I'm Doruk the Sorcerer. I've wanted to see your work, Blind Captain, and such an impressive display it was! You must forgive me for having ordered my men to exhaust your powers, but you must understand, the Sultanate demands your execution. It's the only thing corsairs deserve."

Blind Captain could only let out a gurgle of rage. He heard his men screaming. It wasn't the sound of dying men. No, that sounded like torture. He struggled against the force holding him captive. Small, harmless bursts of fire erupted from his hands.

Doruk snapped his fingers. Blind Captain was violently thrown onto the floor, his face roughly pressed into the wood. He felt Doruk weaving something in his other hand, moving it through the air as if knitting something. A rope began to twist around Blind Captain's neck. He heard the other end anchor itself to one of the mast yards.

"Rejoice, Blind Captain. You and your crew will be the first warning for your friends. It is more than they deserve," Doruk proclaimed. Blind Captain's body moved in sync with the warlock's hand when he flicked it. The rope whipped violently and then, fell taut.

Chapter Ten

***

MIRABELLE THOUGHT SHE WAS STRAINING her face muscles, trying to keep the smile up. Experience taught her to wear it both during and after the haggling. If you didn't get the best deal now, it might help if you had to negotiate with the same person later. It was also why you didn't intentionally try to burn anyone too badly during a deal, either. Sure, you might have the upper hand today, but what if tomorrow you were shipwrecked, fighting the endless ocean to keep from drowning, and the other party happens to have the upper hand then?

She and Jacques waited on the pier while one of the port officials consulted with a team of carpenters inspecting the Tersian ship she brought in. Further away, they could hear the merriment of Novault's crew celebrating their easily liquidated plunder. It wasn't a bad haul. Mirabelle got her ten percent, all of which went towards her crew's payment. The rest of the cash, a rather sizable amount, went to Novault's. Reyais's ravenous port quickly bought up the other valuables; medical supplies, stores of powder, shot, and rations were always in demand.

Mirabelle smiled sadly to herself when she watched some of Novault's crew. Some were in the depths of bliss and debauchery, but she could see the emptiness in some of their eyes. She also saw it in Captain Novault. It was that nagging old hag in your head that asked why weren't you happy despite the wealth in front of you?

Funny how "just a little more" was never enough no matter how much more you acquired. This was a harsh lesson some people never learned. Mirabelle learned it long ago among the ranks of the nobility. It was why so many wealthy nobles she knew felt so empty inside.

They hoarded and cherished treasure, but treasure would never cherish them back.

"I hope this'll pay off. If you break parts off a ship for repairs, it always hurts the sales price. But with the lack of lumber supplies around here, we'll have no choice but to cannibalize some of the wood off our prize to repair the *Lauria,*" Jacques sighed.

"Don't worry too much about it. I have ideas," Mirabelle replied softly.

"Now, don't get me wrong, my lady, I know the crew is loyal to you, and they know you always deliver in the end. Morale is strong enough that they'll weather a little delay in a decent payout."

"Don't fret, Jacques."

"I can pass out a few hard knocks and stern words if anyone talks about mutiny, my lady. You won't have to worry; I'll make sure the crew doesn't do anything discourteous such as walking off–"

"Jacques!"

"Right, right. Sorry, lady captain. I just hate being stuck here on land so close to the Arazumi," Jacques said dejectedly.

"I hate wallowing here too, Jacques, but even if the Lauria was in sea-worthy shape, we'd still have to wait for our Witch Hunter. Besides, what do the Arazumi have to do with it?" Mirabelle asked curiously.

"You've never had to fight them, and I don't wish to go through that again. Yes, everyone in the Empire sings General-Patriarch Calistus's praises, how he defeated the Arazumi and forced them to terms by

Chapter Ten

besieging Arazum City. No one talks about how the Arazumi put two out of every three men in our army into the ground, how every battle was us getting mowed down. We only took ground from them once they stopped firing. Do you know what we found out? They only retreated because they were running out of ammunition! You've never heard a rotary-gun fire and pray to the Holy you never do!"

Mirabelle bit her lip, searching for the right words to say. It was a relief when Jacques began talking again.

"We're lucky they're not interested in war. They only want to tinker with their clocks, their alchemy, and make money off the trinkets they sell us."

"So, you feel safer on the *Lauria* because, at least, that way we can steer clear of the Republic?"

"Correct, my lady."

"Well, I spy the carpenters coming our way. Perhaps we can grant your wish soon enough," Mirabelle said.

The lead carpenter had an intimidating grin of brown, gnarly teeth, but he was excited. He couldn't even help himself from laughing as he got close to Mirabelle.

"So, we gave the ship a look and you're in luck! We can raze off the top deck, use that lumber to patch up your ship, and convert this captured Tersian into a faster, but heavily armed warship. Several buyers are already waiting to bid, so for you, captain, we can do it free of charge. You even stand to gain a little in prize money on top of it all," the craftsman chuckled before scratching at an interesting scab on his neck. "Unless, that is, you got any objections."

"No, no objections at all," Mirabelle beamed. "How soon can you get started?"

"The boys have been itching for work and pay, so I'm sure we can get her patched up before the week is out!"

Mirabelle's tired smile became genuine for a minute or two. She dismissed Jacques to go back to the *Lauria* and spread the good news. She was going to need some privacy to deal with the mermaids.

***

FAR FROM THE HARBOR, the Tersian armada was busy with the constant duty of communication. A series of signal flags began snaking their way towards the fleet's center one by one. An important message had to be passed to the flagship.

Humming a shanty under his breath—a reminder of simpler, happier days—Grand Admiral Oruz watched the signal get ever closer to him. Before long, he spied the designated pennant raised on the ship and by then, it was so close he didn't need a spyglass to read it.

"One of our ships has gone missing," he murmured to himself, thoughtfully stroking his beard. He shook his head sadly.

"I'm pretty sure there's our first victim," his first officer said. "Abyss-cursed corsairs couldn't help themselves."

"Of course they couldn't," Oruz agreed. "One was bound to be in a desperate situation, and our fleet isn't familiar with these waters. A privateer was going to pounce as soon as possible."

Chapter Ten

"I believe you mean 'corsair,' sir. What are your orders, Grand Admiral?"

"Raise the crimson stallion ensign. Let the fleet know they're to be aggressive in their search for targets of opportunity. Have a few scouting parties come ashore and probe for weaknesses," the weary admiral said in resignation.

"Why not raise three and signal them to attack, sir?"

"Because this isn't an all-out war yet, officer. We're just tightening the noose. The Sultan's decrees dictate that we must equal the scales of justice."

Thousands of Tersian cannons gleamed in the morning light. Before long, they would grow dull under a layer of soot.

Chapter Ten

CHAPTER 11

THE TENT WAS QUIET. Smoke from the fire lingered in the air, reluctant to drift out into the sky. Gouged into the dirt floor was a diagram of Reyais and the island. It needed to be regularly re-drawn due to the repeated consultations. More rune-carved bone pieces became necessary as well. Despite all this, Mara remained the picture of quiet confidence. There always seemed to be a smile on her lips.

"Scrying tells us that the Tersians are beginning to make their move on Reyais. There's been bloodshed already," one of her servants announced gloomily.

"A pity," Mara nodded sympathetically. "Ideally, we would have had the ley lines completed before this, but I am not worried. The lives lost are a mote compared to the number still alive on the island. Are the druids almost done with this task?"

"They assure us it will be done today, my lady."

"Excellent. Once that is done, you may inform our leaders in the city to proceed as planned."

"What about the powerful young life, my lady?" another servant asked. "Isn't she out of your reach, now?"

"Do not fear; we still have time," Mara said soothingly. "Though, I suppose it couldn't hurt to let the Regent know that one of his citizens is held unlawfully at the embassy. He must be notified of this breach of his sovereignty. We should hurry a concerned citizen to him."

"As you wish, Lady Mara."

***

KASSIA STUDIED THE VIAL in her hand as she walked down the street. This particular one was an inoculation against the Pox. She remembered growing up in fear of the disease. You'd hear stories of the dreaded blood-red blisters tearing through neighborhoods and villages. By the time it was done, somewhere between a third to half of the infected were dead, and the survivors were left dazed, struggling to clean up the nightmare. Now, a whole generation of young Arazumi were growing up without ever seeing someone infected by it; the Pox, a bogeyman told only in stories by their elders.

She recalled the Raermak myth of a monstrous, world-destroying wolf restrained in the Abyss by a chain of links constructed of impossible things. The roots of a mountain, the spit of a bird, and sunlight cold as ice, to name a few. She wasn't in the business of chaining apocalyptic wolves, but, in a way, she was in the business of impossible things. Strange potions to ward against disease, black blood of the earth to power fantastic engines, threads of metal to carry messages faster than any bird could fly. Sympathy washed over her. No wonder foreigners thought they were a nation of magic. It wasn't magic, not in the typical sense, but it was still the work of stealing fire from the gods. They were turning myth into reality, making their impossible things. And what they stole from the gods, the Holy now made them responsible for with their new knowledge of good and evil. She wondered what they could make if they ever found a handful of selfless politicians.

There was tension in the air as they neared the docks. A procession of those strange, white-clad cultists calling themselves the Prosperous Light marched past them. "Charity for Reyais! Scorn for the Greedy!'

176

Chapter Eleven

they chanted while marching. Kassia couldn't help but feel the cult was singling out the embassy, but why? Selma was doing so much good work with the medicine they supplied her.

The docks were unusually quiet when they got there. Despite all the ships tied to the moorings, few sailors were found and even fewer dockhands. They still felt eyes watching them.

"Hurry this along, will you, miss?" Jord urged, looking down at Kassia.

"I'm not looking to make this a social call, either," she replied. The embassy staff had similar feelings. They sent her escorted by Jord, Otto, Derek, and Michael. They were fully armed.

Kassia helped herself inside once Selma opened the door. Selma, for her part, glanced out the door just as the chemist closed it. Selma looked up at her with a face full of worry.

"I'm glad you have four guards with you, Miss Norwis. I don't know how safe it'll be for all of you to keep coming back here."

"What's wrong, Selma?"

"The Tersians, for one."

"We're aware of them, but they're keeping to their ships," Kassia chided.

"There's also the cult. I'm sure you've heard of them. The Prosperous Light hooligans? They're singling out the Arazumi; I just know it," Selma said while stabbing her finger to emphasize her point.

"That's quite an accusation. What led you to that conclusion?"

"You heard the chanting! 'Scorn for the greedy?' Young miss, I may not be clever like you, Arazumi, but I ain't stupid either. Everyone has been describing you all as greedy, tucked away in your walls with your food and magical science lights. I try to tell my patients about your miracle cures, ones that actually work, unlike the snake oil the charlatans sell, but you know how people are. Unless they're the ones sick as a dog they assume good health is just something you're always supposed to have."

"All right, so there's a well-organized group of box-top preachers looking for a scapegoat, the Republic has dealt with worse–"

"It's not the Republic that has to deal with them, Miss Kassia. It's you that has to deal with them," Selma chastised. "And if that wasn't enough, the local watchmen are warning people that there's a nasty monstrosity about!"

"What sort of 'monstrosity,' Ms. Selma? Did they give any specifics, or is this just more fear-mongering?" Kassia asked, eyebrows narrowing.

"Only that it was strong enough to wring the necks of three men."

"Ah."

"So, please, Miss Kassia, I'm one of the few people here in this city that actually likes you, strange foreigners. You must be careful when you go strolling out here. Do you think four men armed with guns will be enough to protect you if that monstrosity shows up or if the Prosperous Light tries to stir up trouble?"

Chapter Eleven

"Yes, you're right," Kassia relented. "Very well, I'll show you the medicines I brought, and then you can show me whatever hilariously optimistic snake oils you found on the markets."

Outside, the four guards stood in a half-circle by the door, looking out towards the docks. Guns were held loosely but ready to be shouldered at a moment's notice. Michael kept a finger conspicuously close to the tapping mechanism at his waist, ready to clack a message to the embassy at a moment's notice. Eyes searched for trouble.

"We need to stop bothering with these people," Derek grumbled. "It's becoming obvious they don't care for our help."

Otto gave him a sideways glance. He felt unusually thoughtful at this moment. "Where are you from, Derek? Any family back at home?"

"No, no family. I grew up at St. Rowena's Chapel. Couldn't wait to leave the place. The only good thing the brothers and sisters did for me was to vouch for me at Long Steel."

"...Is Sister Claire still there?" Otto asked curiously.

"You know her? She wasn't so bad, but she could be stern in her own way. I don't think she's really the big sister, motherly type she plays. She would tell me I was lucky they don't swat knuckles with rulers anymore," Derek complained.

"Yes, because when you do that, you're just toughening a young man's knuckles, all the better to punch street gangers with. Use the rod often enough, and you'll end up doing a young street fighter a favor."

"Wait, you're the reason they have that rule now?"

"The very one."

"So all this time you were also a—what did you call me—a misanthrope?"

"It pays to grow out of it, Derek."

"Yeah, bugger that. Life has been too much of a disappointment to give it a chance anymore."

"Some disappointments in life go away as soon as you stop seeing them as disappointments," Otto said quietly.

The door opened, and Kassia marched out, bag clinking with a new handful of snake oil bottles. The guards instinctively fell into formation around her.

"I'll have to write up a report for the embassy," Kassia announced. "The locals seem to think there's an anomalous beast about."

"Here? In the city?" Jord asked incredulously. "I wonder what set off that rumor."

"Selma said the guards of the district made up some flyers and posters warning about it."

"So maybe Sheriff Hector has a better idea of who or what killed those longshoremen," Otto said.

"I doubt it," said Kassia. "Apparently, they think whatever killed the longshoremen has learned a new trick: wringing necks."

"Or, Holy forbid, there are two awful beasts about," Jord suggested.

Chapter Eleven

"I think that's something the watchmen will have to figure out," Kassia said. "We should still report it to the embassy, though."

The walk back was silent but tense. Catching sight of the closed embassy doors didn't bring any relief. A familiar group of individuals loitered by the gate.

"Isn't that the hard-arse sheriff? Hector, was it?" Derek asked. The old watchman wasn't alone; he had a handful of his men and a scruffy horse-drawn cart beside him.

"We were just talking about him, too," Jord said tiredly.

"I do believe we're waiting for you, louts," Hector boomed as they approached. He was met with quizzical looks.

"Why exactly are you waiting for us?" Otto asked, befuddled.

"I'm sure your boss man on the inside will let you know," Hector grunted. "Your monster hunter came back all in a Blighting tizzy, and from what he tells me, I don't like what he found any more than he does. We'll need every cutthroat we can hire."

The doors rumbled open, and the sentry shouted for them to come in and for the locals to stay away from the gate. Jord, Otto, and the rest had no choice but to do as they were told. Once inside the courtyard, the answers came.

There were four horses in the courtyard. Kassia furrowed her brows upon seeing the animals. Two of them each had a large rolled sack stowed behind their saddles, the shape of their contents eerily familiar.

"I recognize those horses," Kassia said.

"Oh?" Otto asked.

"They're the Night Riders. I wonder if this means they bagged that werewolf they were hunting," Kassia speculated.

"You mean two werewolves?" Jord injected. "Why else would they have those two bodies on the horses?"

Garrett Blauestein emerged from one of the buildings. He looked worse for wear, his half cape tattered, and his once green clothes now speckled with mud. Stubble carpeted his face. His eyes flashed with menace, looking for a fight. He spotted Otto and Jord and began marching towards them, reloading his repeater the whole time. The bullets weren't silver-tipped.

"You must be the men the guard captain said we're waiting for," Garrett said, his voice hollow.

"We're not trained to hunt monsters," Otto replied quickly.

"We're hunting something worse than monsters; we're hunting men," the Night Rider said grimly.

"Hold up now; I'm confused. Why are we hunting people?" Otto shot.

"Because the nice Night Rider is in a bit of trouble," Axle's voice boomed, appearing in the courtyard. The faces of the other Long Steel men fell. Otto clenched his eyes shut in exasperation, looking as though he was trying to summon a mug of coffee into existence.

Chapter Eleven

"He's found an awful threat to the island, or so he claims," Axle continued. "And he's enlisted the help of the earnest Guard Captain Hector waiting outside, and both tell me they want whatever hired guns we can spare. I'm choosing you four."

"Is anyone going to explain what exactly we're being sent off to do?" Otto asked testily.

"I've only had light combat training," Michael butted in.

"Understood, but you're also the only one with combat training that can also operate a mobile telegraph pack at the moment," Axle explained. Then he looked at Jord.

"You're in charge. Keep the pups in line and assist the city guard the best you can. The Night Rider will explain the situation along the way. Off you go to the cart now. Move, move!"

The Long Steel men piled into the cart provided by Hector and shared it with his local guardsmen. The ride through the streets, normally a tedious affair, was greatly shortened by Hector yelling to make way, followed by whatever creative verbal abuse he could come up with. The Night Riders, Siggy, and Garrett rode silent and grimly by the cart. Jord waited until they were beyond the city gates before he said anything.

"I think you owe us an explanation now, Comstock man. I remember there were four of you when you started. Something tells me those bodies I saw earlier are your two comrades, not two bagged monsters," Jord grumbled. Garrett drew in a deep breath and let out a sigh.

"You're very astute."

"Thank you. That's still not an explanation."

"Right, so a few days ago, we began our search at Klimmick's Hollow. There wasn't a lot to go on, but the locals were insistent that they heard the howl of wolves, so we persisted. We didn't find any signs of werewolves, no matter how much further we trekked into the forest. Instead, we began finding signs of the druids who live there."

"Blighting forest bandits and murderers," Hector spat.

"We knew well enough that they weren't friendly, so we couldn't keep going further into the forest, but we didn't want to give up the hunt either," Garrett said. "So we started off in a different direction, away from the druids' mountain. We still couldn't find any signs of werewolves, but oddly enough, we kept finding signs of druids."

"Going away from the mountain?" Hector asked skeptically.

"Yes, and that didn't sit well with us. Everyone knows the Druids don't stray too far from there. So we kept following the clues until we left the forest and came to one of the roads. They were doing some sort of...ritual. We had to intervene," Garrett growled.

"You had to?" Otto inquired, an eyebrow raised. "You could have left them alone to do their little worship service."

"You don't know what you're talking about," Garrett snapped, turning on him. "This wasn't a bunch of island tribals rattling clamshells and chicken bones! We're talking about a sacrifice, blood-painted ritual circle, glowing balls of magic, real dark magic! I've been doing this long enough to know that if you see stuff like that, you shoot first and ask questions later."

Chapter Eleven

"Is that how your team members died? Overwhelmed when you kicked a hornet's nest?' Jord asked stoically.

"Yes," Garrett admitted. "We rode in thinking we could easily disperse the ritual performers, but there were other druids in the woods nearby. I should have realized from the tracks they left that there were far more of them than we initially set upon. That's how Ambrose and Nicholas died; we kicked a hornet's nest."

"Arrows? Clubs? What got them? I need details, man," Jord prodded.

"Arrows and slings, but they also had stone spears and axes as well."

"All right," Jord said thoughtfully. "I think we need to set up our own ambush. Stop us when we're about two hundred meters from the ritual site. I will look around and find a suitable place."

"We may not have that sort of time left!" Garrett protested.

"You already tried charging in," Jord said as neutrally as he could. "We don't need to make that same mistake twice. You may be hunters paid to move in for the kill, but the rest of us here are just guards. We're paid to do a job, and we prefer to stay alive."

Garrett led them along the road until they got close to a bend that ran beside a shallow slope. He signaled for them to stop and looked at them.

"We can charge in now and stop them all before they complete the ritual. We have the numbers now," Garrett said.

"Your suggestion is noted, and I'm rejecting it," Jord replied. He didn't even look at the Night Rider. Instead, his eyes were taking in the broader scene beyond the ritual sight.

"You fool! Don't you understand the situation you're in? Siggy and I are Night Riders! We're trained to track and kill anomalous creatures and those who practice anomalous rituals! When we say this is dangerous, and we need to attack now, we need to bloody well attack—"

"Mr. Blauestein, I'm not questioning your competence as a Night Rider; I'm just rejecting your ability as a tactician. No, I have a different plan. Now, you shut up and everyone here, listen to me."

The group waited in silence as Jord explained the situation and began to hand out instructions to the Riders, the Long Steel men, and the city guards in separate groups. There was no more room for further comments. The groups began to carry out Jord's orders, which required them all to go in different ways.

Jord led the men of his company quietly up the slope and then along the trees. The city watchmen followed at a distance and took care to keep low. The Night Riders stayed where they were but remained on their horses, Garrett looking as grumpy and anxious as ever. Siggy, to her credit, was calm and collected as she readied her bow.

Jord brought them to the edge of the trees and motioned for Otto to go ahead. "Attract their attention and make them bleed as much as you can."

Otto gave a quick salute and stalked forward; rifle leveled at the scene before them. Off in the distance were the druids still engrossed by the ritual. It was a macabre sight. A circle of eight druids chanted in blood chilling tones while remaining motionless. A bulky rock was in their midst upon which a brutally carved corpse rested. Lines of glistening blood were painted in bizarre patterns around it on the grass. Otto found it hard to still his breathing as he concentrated on his aim.

The rifle barked, and the stillness cracked. Metal rattled on metal as another round chambered, and then the gun fired again. The first round struck the rock, producing a small geyser of fragments. The second round struck a druid who wobbled but remained in place. It wasn't until the fourth shot that the druid fell over. The fifth round screamed downrange, and Otto was forced to reload.

"What are we waiting for?" Derek asked.

"The inevitable counterattack. Don't watch the ritual; watch for the other druids," Jord hissed, his blunderbuss pointed towards the darkness in the forest by them.

"Is that movement?' Michael suggested, pointing towards another part of the trees. Jord's gaze snapped in that direction. "Good job, pup, but pointing a finger won't stop them. Use your rifle."

Otto rushed back to join them once he heard the shots behind him. Thunder echoed through the trees as ears began to ring. Gunshots produced flashes of light on the ground. There was no time to fully comprehend what was before them because the forest was suddenly swarming with druids, and flint-tipped arrows rained around them. Their enemies were close enough to read the rage on their faces. Jord's blunderbuss punctured a red crater into the druid leading the charge, and he let out a bellow that echoed into the trees. Hector and the city guardsmen emerged from cover with a voracious war cry of their own and rushed into the fray.

The fighting became instinctive, visceral, and blunt. The flint axes, clubs, and spears of the druids were frightening things and used with deliberate prejudice. Those with slings swung their loaded weapons like whirling clubs. Unfortunately for them, the city guardsmen, armed with a motley collection of weapons and shields, had frustrations of their own to vent. Years of knocking sense into belligerent pirates and street gangs made them well versed in the school of dirty fighting, and a lot of it was on display in the melee.

Otto and Derek made use of their bayonets, surgically thrusting whenever there was an opening. It was often fatal to whoever was on the other end. Jord merely held the barrel of his blunderbuss and dropped the butt of it down like a club producing gory results. One of these cranial explosions finally caused the druids to route and disappear back into the trees. Their enemies' sudden withdrawal left the guards bewildered as they took the unexpected opportunity to catch their breaths.

"Who's wounded, and who's dead?" Hector popped. His subordinates began sounding off. Jord looked to his own men. Derek was in a giddy daze, shaking hands struggling to reload his firearm while bullets dropped to the ground. Otto squatted beside a prone Michael, lying up uncomfortably from the telegraph pack still on his back.

"Talk to me, pup, what happened? I don't see any blood on you," Otto asked calmly.
"I heard a big 'thunk'. I landed on my back and a rock bounced off my chest," Michael recited from his memories. Otto rapped his knuckles on Michael's jacket. The breastplate underneath sounded with each knock.

"Are you flabbergasted, or are you in actual pain?"

Chapter Eleven

"I guess...I'm...fine. By the Holy! I got hit by a sling!" Michael blurted.

"A rock more accurately," Otto suggested.

"Someone tried to kill me!"

"That's just a job hazard."

"Bu...bug…I mean, pardon my- oh f-, er, I mean, da-"

"Listen, Michael," Otto interrupted, waving his hand as if to stop the younger guard. "I've been pin-cushioned by Danarian arrows, taken a couple blows to the helmet, even had a Danarian mace land me flat on my back. I know pain, and listening to you try to cuss has definitely been one of the most painful experiences I've ever had."

"Oh. Sorry, sir."

"Don't think any more of it, rookie. Just let us know if you start feeling sick or something," Otto said, helping the man up.

"And what about those creepy chanting druids?" Hector said, marching up to them.

"I told our Rider friends to handle that," Jord replied, looking towards the ritual site. "Let's head over there. It looks like they've done their job."

The guards found the makeshift altar in an even more distressing state than when they first spotted it. The eight druids had died where they stood, some riddled with bullet holes while others had Siggy's long arrows sticking out of them. The Night Riders ignored the bodies, their attention transfixed on something else.

"Well, did you get them in time?" Jord demanded, marching up to them.

"Can't say. I'm not well versed in rituals," Garrett admitted. "But I do not like how that altar is glowing."

The stone on which the sacrifice rested was indeed glowing, shining like a block of condensed light. The surrounding blood began to congeal, being drawn with the red ritual circle slowly receding towards the stone.

"We were not successful. That stone looks like it is a focal point for two ley lines that have been activated," Siggy said.

"What does a ley line do?" Otto asked curiously.

"Many things," said Siggy. "In this case, it seems like it is meant to capture and hold magical energy. I cannot tell you anything beyond that."

"Well, the Blighting forest hooligans are dead. That's a win in my book," said Hector. "Can't tell you how many times I've had to pick up the corpse of a poor villager who got ambushed by this lot."

Derek, who had been quiet, shockingly doubled over and vomited up his lunch. The city guards were already headed back towards the cart, their interest in the scene long gone. Michael seemed to be in a world of his own. Derek, no longer retching, took a few steadying breaths.

Chapter Eleven

"Combat wasn't like what you were expecting, pup?" Otto asked.

"No...no, it wasn't."

"It never is."

"Come on, let's get out of here," Jord ordered. "Regardless of whether we stopped them in time or not, I know well enough not to linger. They might come back looking to finish what we started."

***

After multiple interviews, the subject's account remains unchanged and consistent with each telling. We conclude that there is only one extraordinary aspect of the report; that the subject, a prepubescent child, survived what seems to be an explosion of the ship she was on.

The subject displays no injuries that we can detect and, until physical evidence suggests otherwise, we must assume that the vessel suffered an explosion.

The possibility of anomalous activity vulgarly called "magic" must be considered for these reasons. We will be keeping the subject under observation.

We do not recommend any further tests, and unless otherwise directed, we will refrain from provoking the subject from demonstrating anomalous talents.

Due to the diplomatic complexities surrounding the subject, her safety outweighs any scientific curiosities we may have at this time.

Report conclusion submitted by:
Dr. Kassia Norwis

CHAPTER 12

MIRABELLE SAT ON A ROCK in the quiet morning. The sun hadn't risen yet, but she dared not go back to her ship. Earlier, a sharp had noise rudely scattered her sleep, and she had wakened with a start. Peering over the corner of her bed, she saw a bottle rolling on the floor, one she did not recognize. Within was a note with a scrawled diagram showing her this rock. The message underneath, written in ghastly letters, told her to go there soon. The mermaids wanted to meet.

On a sandy beach like this, she had first met them and made the pact. They were in the Southern Archipelago, and she knew they were pressing their luck with how close they were to the Shifting Sea. The *Lauria* caught on a hidden sandbar and refused to budge no matter what they did. Then they waited. The Shifting Sea, living up to its name, shifted. Perpetually. Whole tribes of indigenous folk lived their entire lives wading and fording the ever-changing expanse of salt water, sand, and foliage. They learned to live with a landscape that had a life of its own. But the *Lauria* remained stuck where it was, and her crew couldn't live there. Weeks became a month, and the fear of scurvy rose as rations became smaller.

Late that night, the mermaids had found her. Mirabelle had decided to take a stroll to clear her mind and plan. Truth be told, dehydration, starvation and despair were the real demons slithering through her brain. The men were becoming too weak to forage for food, let alone try to cut through the jungle back to civilization. Then in the darkness she found the mermaids staring at her, rising from the water to surround her. Mirabelle remembered laughing. Death would've been a relief at that point.

"Desperate, are we?" one asked gently. She couldn't tell which one was which in the gloom.

"Do you need help?" another inquired. Their voices were like honey.

"My...my ship is stuck, and we can't get off," Mirabelle replied quietly.

"We could help you," the third offered kindly.

"But...but you're mermaids, and you eat sailors, and I'm probably just dreaming this."

"Shh, shhh," one of them shushed soothingly, a soft pink finger on her lips.

"Tomorrow morning, your ship will be free. There will be some fish and turtles washed ashore for you all to eat," a mermaid said. "And then, after that, we'll talk about how you can repay us."

"Thank you, thank you," Mirabelle chanted, confused tears falling down her face. She remembered kissing, slobbering over the hand of one of them. She cringed at that memory now. It wasn't long after that the ghastly voices and blood chilling notes began to appear in their meetings.

Perch, Bluegill, and Salmon slinked up the shore later. The mermaids decided to wear more alluring forms this time. Mirabelle's eyebrows narrowed, and she fought the urge to reach for her sword. They wore the erotic shapes mermaids were infamous for, a sight that would

Chapter Twelve

cause most men and women to forget themselves and lean too far over the side of a boat. Mirabelle knew that under those delicate lips were fangs that could rip through flesh and bone. They were tempting now. What were they planning?

"She came; the prey did as instructed. Can she keep doing it?" Bluegill rasped. They may have looked beautiful, but the voices were as soothing as an ear canal full of broken glass.

"Tell me, do you prefer that voice? It's been a while since I've heard any of you sound melodious, and I'm starting to think I only dreamed it," Mirabelle asked.

"Like this, you poor, lost thing?" Perch cooed, staring dreamily at her. This time Mirabelle didn't try to hide the hand that came to rest on her sword hilt.

"You brought us a hundred and two sailors two nights prior. We watched you. There were others with you, others' flesh you could have given us," Salmon stated, hauling herself up the sands until she was uncomfortably close to Mirabelle's boot. The captain raised an eyebrow at her.

"Stabbing my fellow captains in the back at every given opportunity would not be good for my career. In fact, it may just cut it short."

"You fear your fellow humans, but you don't fear us?" Salmon asked sweetly and began to massage Mirabelle's foot.

There was the ominous whir and grind of a wheellock being cocked. Mirabelle's glare was as cold as the pistol pointed at Salmon's skull. The mariner's eyes were orbs of hatred in the sunlight.

"Don't underestimate the fear I have for you. Let go of my foot."

"Such foolishness," Bluegill hissed. "You claim fear, but you draw your weapon on us."

"A wise woman once said, '*If you're going to be afraid, get angry as well.*' I'm putting that in action. Let go of my foot! Now, I doubt this is a social call. Why did you summon me here this morning?" Mirabelle snapped.

"You sent a hundred and two pieces of flesh to us, but your crew had help. Our pact was made with you safeguarding your ship and crew, no one else. Since another ship, captain, and crew helped you, your payment must be re-balanced. It will only be counted as fifty-one souls instead of a hundred and two," Perch said.

"Excuse me?" Mirabelle fired back. "What difference does it make whether I had help or not? The payment doesn't need to be 're-balanced' or whatever you want to call it."

"Your complaints matter not!" Bluegill howled.

"There will be no negotiations, little lost thing," Perch said with a shrug. She turned and began to slink towards the water. Bluegill followed her sister. Mirabelle's jaw clenched until her teeth hurt. She knew it would be pointless to argue. She looked down at Salmon.

"Aren't you going to join them?"

Salmon grinned at Mirabelle, exposing her fangs. Then, she sank her teeth into the meaty part of Mirabelle's calf and slithered off like a slippery Abyss-spawn towards the ocean. The hapless captain was left clutching her wound and growling through clenched teeth, waiting for

Chapter Twelve

the bleeding to stop as she thought about what had just happened. Mermaids weren't like vampires, right? You didn't turn into one if they bit you, right? Her teeth ground further against each other as she began to bandage the hole in her leg.

Payments be damned, these leeches were as bad as money-lenders and only half as evil. Their arrangement could not go on much longer like this. She was going to have to find a way to end it. With her wound bandaged, she limped back towards the docks. Perhaps it was time to do a lot of thinking.

***

ARAZUMI WARSHIPS, WITH THEIR ESOTERIC internal engines, made a mockery of the winds and currents. It wasn't uncommon for the crews of sailing vessels, struggling against the wind, to pout and shake their heads at passing Arazumi merchant ships steadily chugging along as if the laws of nature didn't apply to them. That was why this morning had an odd sight for all to see: two Arazumi warships cautiously, painfully shadowing a listless brig driven only by the currents. Two picket boats, one from each warship, closed in on the stricken derelict.

"With all due respect, captain, don't you think it's safer for you to be back on the ship? Leave this work for us marines?"

"Maybe, sergeant, but I think I should come with you on this one. I know this ship," Leon admitted. Besides, he admired the efficiency-minded marine sergeant, but he doubted any of them had boarded a stricken vessel before. They'd need an experienced eye.

"Is the captain of this ship a friend of yours, sir?"

"'Friend' is a little too strong of a word; more like, 'Respected fellow professional.'"

"I hope you'll forgive me for saying this, captain, but I'd start worrying about your fellow professional. A ship shouldn't have that many gaping holes in her side. Also, we saw...things... hanging from the yards, sir."

"Thank you for stating the obvious, sergeant."

The boats lined up along the hull, and once again, they hailed the ship for a response. The silence forced the men to board. Heavy climbing ropes were thrown, and the marines began their ascent up the hull.

"See any survivors, any signs of life, sergeant?" Leon asked as he began his climb. The sergeant was further up the line, and he lingered a little too long near one of the jagged blast holes on the side.

"None whatsoever, captain. It looks exactly like what you'd expect to see from multiple cannonball hits."

Leon heard the sergeant yell for his men to make sure their blunderbusses were loaded and to search the ship as the marines got on the top deck. The lack of footsteps told him that the marines were hesitating for some reason. Not a good sign. Leon redoubled his efforts to make it to the top. He found out why once he joined them.

Someone had turned the mast yards into a gallows. Bodies hung by the neglected sails, necks at odd angles while the ropes creaked in the wind. A few marines walked around gingerly as they tried to navigate the floorboards; the late crew didn't have enough time to dump sand on the deck before the killing began. One soldier hollered, saying he'd found more bodies near the bow. His comrade behind him rushed for

Chapter Twelve

the railing and became sick. Morbid curiosity forced Leon to walk closer.

"Why...why are their bodies like that?" someone asked.

"Because Erdem the Whaler got them," Leon said, a disgusted frown on his face.

"I don't know who that is, Captain," a marine said.

"Erdem is a sadist masquerading as a loyal Tersian soldier. Not many people survive a fight with him. Have you ever watched a whale get processed for its meat and blubber? The whaler cuts a deep line along the body and then removes the blubber all at once or in strips. That's why these corpses look the way they do," Leon explained. The marines gaped in horror; one or two began to unconsciously back away.

"Those sailors were lucky," Leon continued. "They were dead when Erdem started doing his playing."

"Enough standing around and gawking, men!" the sergeant bellowed, remembering why they were there. "Search the ship! Make sure it's secured before we scuttle it!"

Leon turned back towards the bodies hanging from the yards. He recognized the lone one far in the back behind all the others. He shook his head.

"I had hoped you'd get away, Blind Captain. It's a shame we can't give you all a proper send-off. Fair winds and seas wherever you are," Leon said.

"The men reported no survivors, sir. Here's the ship's log. There's nothing valuable to salvage, either," the sergeant said hurriedly.

"Have the men ballast the bodies as best they can, then we'll plant some dynamite down by the keel. We can't leave this ship floating without a course."

"Aye, sir!"

Leon didn't stay around to watch the ship's last voyage into the deep. There were reports to write. Not all of them would go back to the Republic.

***

SAMIR TEMENG BELIEVED THAT YOU COULD tell a lot about captains by the way they kept their personal quarters. Cousin Leon kept his mostly neat if a little lived in; maps, logs, papers, and books in their proper piles. He even kept his old tricorn hat from his days as a Southern Traders privateer. It mostly hung on its hook and gathered dust. Samir would admit his own cabin wasn't the neatest, but the work areas, the desk for maps and charts, were always immaculate. He would also admit to having a few vanity things on display; a gold leaf scimitar he won off a Tersian corsair and the very first gold coin he ever plundered.

But, here he sat in Cousin Davos' cabin and he could tell that he was in a different world. Various blades of all shapes and sizes were racked and secured on the walls. Pouches bulging with coins sat on his desk while expensive Tersian rugs hung on display. *Was that a bloodstain on one of them?* Various necklaces of gold, silver, and precious stones sat on hooks evenly spaced around the room. There were a few nautical maps to be seen, but they paled in comparison to

Chapter Twelve

all the weapons and booty about. *Why in the Abyss did Davos have a human skull on his desk?*

Samir looked up from the skull to his cousin. Davos was imposing, heavily muscled, and covered in scars. A robust machete hung on one side of his waist. Opposite to it was the wavy blade known as a keris. Several large knives, in all kinds of exotic shapes, kept them company along his belt. Samir decided to get straight to the point, if only so that the skull on the desk would have less time to leer and grin at him.

"Cousin, what were you thinking!? A fortress ship? What madness drove you to take this prize?"

"It was there," Davos grunted.

"That's hardly an explanation!" Samir protested hotly.

"They were there and we watched them get isolated and pummeled in a storm. It was an easy fight and too good of an opportunity, *kip-kip.*"

"Well, I sure hope it was all worth it, cousin!" Samir said quickly, rising from his seat. "Now, the Tersians are here and they're bottling us in! There are twenty ships of us Dhaliese here! Eight families of sea-clanners are on those ships, and we can't leave. Captain Binidi missed his great uncle's burial because we're stuck here!"

"The Tersians will leave. And if they don't, I will lead the charge against them, *kip-kip,*" Davos rumbled.

"They'll kill you dead, then hang your body from the yards! *Kip-kip.* Can this fortress ship make it through an armada, you stupid cousin of mine?"

"They didn't expect to lose it to me. Besides, the captains here are no strangers to hardships. You are foolish, Cousin, for being bothered by such trifles," Davos scolded.

"Trifles? Trifles?" Samir hissed. "Cousin Leon sent me a message this morning by pigeon. The Tersians got Blind Captain and his crew."

"They killed Blind Captain?"

"Yes! I've already told the other captains. That's why I'm here telling you. Blind Captain was hanged from his mast yard, and Erdem had his way with the bodies of his crew. This isn't 'trifles' anymore, cousin."

Blind Captain was a pillar among the free captains, and awful things are unleashed when a pillar topples. Davos gripped the hilts on either side of him. A terrible expression settled on his face; an expression Samir had seen all morning on the other corsairs.

"I will make them suffer," Davos said. "And, if I finally find that son of the Abyss Erdem, I will hang him, still alive, from my bowsprit with butcher's hooks. I will watch the birds peck at his flesh and make him bleed. I will watch the sharks jump from the water to gnaw his bones. I will watch him die slowly. *Kip-kip.*"

"You'll have to get in line behind Captain Gunderson. In the meantime, come with me, later today, to the docks. The other captains would like to hear your opinions, *kip-kip.*"

***

YOU COULD FEEL THE RAGE in the air and see it in the sharp, quick movements on the docks. It radiated in the cleaning of cannons,

Chapter Twelve

the whetting of weapons, and the urgent tugs on the rigging. Common sailors from different ship crews were getting together to exchange ideas and make last-minute barters. A singular idea was burning above the harbor: how to bloody the nose of the Tersians.

"They'll be coming, you know," Captain Gunderson grunted, leaning on a pole. "The Tersians have already figured out you took one of their ships."

"How do you know that?' Mirabelle asked incredulously.

"I saw their signal flags change overnight," Gunderson said coldly.

"That could mean anything," Captain Vernovis said. "Do you even know what their signals mean?"

"I do not, but I doubt it's a coincidence," Gunderson replied.

"Either way, it doesn't matter," Mirabelle interjected. "What matters is that we find a way to drive the Tersians off and bloody them in the process. They need to pay for Blind Captain."

"And make a profit off it," Corba added. Mirabelle didn't know if she liked him any better sober than when he was sloshed. It didn't seem like he liked himself sober either.

"Any wrecked Tersian ship is worth gold to Reyais. It's in their letters of mark. Additional plunder helps as well. We should have no problems making a profit, but if we're going to do that, we need to be smart about it," Mirabelle said. "If we don't organize, we'll die."

The thunder crack of gunfire echoed through the harbor. The captains ducked and ran for cover. A thick cloud of spent gunpowder rose from one side of the docks. It was as if someone dropped a basilisk into the middle of the square. The crowds ran and screamed in chaotic directions. Gunderson kept a watchful eye, finally deciphering what was going on.

"A lot of musket fire is coming from the far end of those buildings there," he pointed with his ax.

"Any idea who's doing the shooting?" Mirabelle demanded.

"Open your eyes! It has to be the Tersians!" Gunderson hollered.

"How in the Abyss are there Tersians in Reyais?" Corba snapped.

"I don't know, but who else could it be?" Gunderson bellowed.

"Focus!" Mirabelle shrieked.

"They're firing in volleys, captain!" Jacques cried, quickly shambling up to them as best as he could while staying low to the ground. "Whoever they are, they need time to reload between shots. We can take advantage of that."

"They're coming," Corba said, just loud enough for them to hear.

The silhouettes emerged from the thick clouds of spent gunpowder. There were a good number of them, each in dark lamellar armor and a sturdy musket already primed to fire. All doubts were dispelled; the Tersians had made landfall and were already in the city.

"Those are skirmishers, captain," Jacques said. "You can tell by their equipment. They're just probing us for now, but they've gotten overconfident, showing themselves like that."

Chapter Twelve

"You know an awful lot about Tersian tactics, young man," Gunderson said.

"I'm still technically part of the Danarian army. We keep our eyes and ears open on whom we may have to fight."

"How likely do you think there'll be further reinforcements behind them?" Mirabelle demanded.

"The possibility exists, but that wouldn't fit their standard practices," Jacques explained. "They're just probing for weaknesses. I don't think they've spotted us, so if we hit them quickly, we may be able to overwhelm them."

The harbor was in chaos. You could hear the townsfolk screaming for the local watchmen who wouldn't come. A handful of bodies littered the streets. Cautiously, like a pack of wolves, the Tersians moved forward. A handful of civilians who lingered too long were shot down, and the skirmishers mechanically reloaded and resumed moving forward. Their eyes roved around, ignoring their bloody work and taking in their surroundings.

"They've reloaded; we can't just rush them now," Corba whispered.

"We need to do something," Mirabelle added. The other captains looked at her skeptically. "Come on; we can't just let them take in their fill and leave. They're scouting out where our ships are and our relative strength! Besides, they completely outmatch the local street guards. We're the only ones who can help these people."

"You can't put a price on local goodwill," Vernovis agreed.

"We still can't charge them yet, Mirabelle," Jacques advised.

A rolling thunderclap roared through the square. Several Tersians fell, and not all of them in one piece. The survivors desperately looked around, eyes falling on a Dhaliese sailor who saw an opportunity and fired a swivel gun from his ships' deck.

"That's our chance," Mirabelle declared.

"Wait, what?"

"Charge!"

Mirabelle didn't wait for their agreement. Sometimes, in order for action to be done, you need to do the acting first. Sword raised and bellowing loud enough to wake the dead, she rushed towards the closest Tersian she could see, praying she was moving faster than they could draw a bead on her. Behind her, she first heard the sound of confusion and then running footsteps. Her war shriek turned into a feral grin. She saw shock and then fear on her enemies' faces. A charge of corsairs is not a sight any soldier wants to see. They shouldn't have pressed so far into the harbor without backup. There was the explosion of muskets, the flashing of blades, and the screams of those in peril.

After some time, the red rage began to dissipate. Mirabelle began to piece together the jumbled smorgasbord of her memories, all of them soaked with adrenaline and instinct. The other corsairs were also pulling themselves together, staggering from wounds or exhaustion. Jacques wiped the blood off his two-hander in jerky movements, more concerned with cleaning his blade than his face. Vernovis had calmed down and helped himself to a wineskin he found. Corba waited nearby, hoping to have some as well. Gunderson squatted over a prone Tersian soldier. They appeared to be having a peaceful conversation. Suddenly, Gunderson drove his ax into the man's head.

Chapter Twelve

"He refused to cooperate," Gunderson muttered.

"Did anyone get away?" Mirabelle asked, stopping to catch her breath.

"Nope," Jacques replied. "Samir and Davos stepped in at the last minute and made sure of that. At least the Tersians won't get any intelligence from this squad."

"How did these mongrels get into the city? Did they just waltz right in?" Vernovis demanded.

"Is that so hard to believe?" Gunderson snapped. "The citizens here aren't going to go fight them. The watchmen aren't equipped for soldiers. The Palace Guards only concern themselves with the palace. Of course, the Tersians just walked right in."

Davos, Samir, and their crewmen began to return. The Dhaliese were eerily calm despite some of them carrying bloodied weapons. A good many of them had crossbows and matchlocks of their own. Those with the firearms had distinctive stains of spent gunpowder on their clothes.

"Everyone still all right, *kip-kip?*" Samir asked. "We need to do what Captain Mirabelle said and start planning attacks on the Tersians."

"Will you finally be joining us, Davos? Tired of sulking in your brand-new toy?" Gunderson demanded.

"I plan to use that 'new toy' to send many of them to the bottom. If we don't unify now, then the Tersians will kill us off one by one," Davos said.

"Kip-kip to that, you ugly sea dog," Corba grunted. He got a withering glare from Davos and Samir.

Someone clothed in a full robe of white approached them. Mirabelle turned to get a better look. It had to be one of the cultists she heard about, from the Prosperous Light. They seemed to be everywhere these days. In fact, they were all over the docks tending to wounded civilians and respectfully covering the dead.

"Excuse me," the cultist greeted them softly. "Thank you for your bravery and for driving these invaders from Reyais. All are welcomed who help the Prosperous Light. Your generosity will be remembered, unlike some who hide away and ignore the city."

"You mean the Arazumi?" Mirabelle asked after a moment's reflection.

"They and whichever witches and monsters are plaguing the city. Some of the watchmen have warned the people that there's a monster about, one that's already killed a few longshoremen and citizens. You must remain safe out there and continue to help us here in the city," the cultist said.

"That's enough sweet talk, lass," Gunderson grunted. "Off with you now."

"Very well. Thank you again, captains and sailors!" the cultist smiled, beginning to turn away. "Remember to continue giving so that all will be blessed with prosperity! Shun the ungenerous, burn the witches and beasts!"

"Burn the witches?" Mirabelle asked quietly. "Is that our Witch Hunter's work? I haven't seen him in a while, come to think of it."

Chapter Twelve

"Captain," Samir called to Mirabelle. "Perhaps you'd like to lead us in the planning? You've been leading so far."

"Yes," Mirabelle breathed, a smile coming to her. "Yes, I do think I have a couple of ideas."

CHAPTER **13**

SOPHIE DECIDED THAT THE GUARD, JORD, was the only sensible person in the embassy. He alone recognized that books held magic within them. Kassia had been teaching her how to read. She had even told Sophie she was a quick study! But Kassia couldn't be with her all the time, and Sophie was left in the library to practice her reading.

There were worlds out there, more than she imagined, ones that she wasn't equipped to imagine until now. The world grew wider because there were so many more places beyond Reyais, more than she knew before she could read.

The world became vibrant, more complex, and full of wonder because there was so much in it. Animals, different peoples, languages, plants, and *things*. So many things! She would have to read more, so she could understand it better! And the more she read, the richer everything grew because there was always more to learn.

The world grew deeper because she found a couple of books on history which showed why the world was the way she knew it today. It turns out that a lot of what she had heard before was wrong: people saying inaccuracies and then, others repeating those same inaccuracies. Sophie pitied them: they didn't know how to read.

And then, surprisingly, the world grew taller and branched out like a tree because there were books speculating, warning, and hoping of what the future could bring.

Books were magic. Anyone who said otherwise was either obtuse or had never quite seen beyond the pages. Sophie looked up from her book when she heard the door open behind her.

"Kassia! I'm glad to see you; can you tell me if I'm saying this word right?" She pointed to a rather daunting word on the cover.

"That's 'Entomology,' the study of insects. Whatever made you pick up that book?" Kassia asked with a chuckle.

"I saw a bug on the cover. It made me wonder if there were any I'd recognize."

"Any in particular you're looking for?"

"There was a sketch of a beautiful blue bug, I think it's a kind of 'butter-fly?' It had wings of the deepest blue I've ever seen and these soft, long white brushy things coming out of its head. I saw it a couple of days ago," Sophie explained, still reading through the book rather than leafing through it. "I've never seen it before, but I thought it was pretty."

Kassia could picture what kind of butterfly Sophie was talking about, an insect of such vibrant blue it was practically a jewel. It was a specimen you couldn't forget once you saw it.

"I think that's the Lapis Butterfly, famous for coming out in swarms when the moon is fullest, which is their breeding season. They live in the jungles of the Southern Archipelago, so they're a little hard to come by, here."

"You don't have one in a jar somewhere?"

Chapter Thirteen

"Nope. Sorry, little entomologist, you'll have to wait for your own grant to find one. Now, I just came in to check on you and make sure you had snacks to hold you over until lunch. I hope you like apples,"

"It's been a while since I've had one. I'm sure this one will taste much better. Thanks, Kassia!"

Kassia smiled at her and then shut the door. Sophie was a delight, she thought to herself. And to show such initiative by picking up a book on entomology just because she saw a sketch of a pretty butterfly.

She could still picture the Lapis Butterfly. It was practically right there above her head, flying ahead of her. *When did her imagination get so detailed?* She almost wanted to pluck it right out of her mind's eye. The butterfly burst, a cloud of blue that drifted away in wisps and then, it was gone.

She stared at the now empty space in the air. Beakers and tubes of thought bubbled and gurgled in her head. The epiphany struck her like a ball-peen hammer. That was no hallucination. She knew because of that one mild accident she had in the lab last year. Magic! No, 'anomalous activity'! Sophie could manipulate anomalous activity! She took a few unsure steps; the beakers in her head now began bubbling with anxiety.

"I already wrote that report. I suggested we leave her alone, but now...now we know she can manipulate anomalies. But, she's in Long Steel's care," Kassia argued with herself before breathing a sigh of relief.

"I didn't see this. I won't tell anyone and, until we have reason to believe she's doing more than just *'poofing'* butterflies in and out of existence, no harm done. I'll have to brush up on magic, though."

She'd get the books from the library after lunch. Fortunately, or not, there weren't any experts in this field attached to the embassy.

Unseen by Kassia, a ball of magical energy rose above Sophie's head as she came across a word she didn't recognize. The young orphan concentrated on the word. Her mouth moved as she tried to pronounce it. The ball of magic above her glowed brighter.

"My...mer...Myrmecology. Oh! The study of ants!" Sophie declared, proud of herself.

The ball of magic flickered and disappeared. It wouldn't show itself again until Sophie came across the next word she didn't recognize.

***

JORD AND OTTO SAT TIREDLY in Axle's office. Questions rolled through their minds. Why were they meeting so early? They had barely had time to eat, and they were still exhausted from the fight yesterday. Michael turned out to be all right, barely even a bruise on his chest. The Night Riders were camping in the embassy with little else to do other than tend to the bodies of their late comrades. They could comfort themselves with the thought of it being better to have a few survivors than none.

"Axle, it's nice sitting here with you pretending there's nothing to do, but I'm sure there's an actual reason you've called us here for?" Otto asked before obnoxiously slurping his coffee.

"We have a different problem," Axle said quietly as he chose his next words carefully. His eyes kept glancing at the door behind them. "Normally, it's a problem that only Otto would be trained to deal with, but I need you, Jord, here because the problem is more complicated than just book stuff."

"You should probably tell us what the problem is, sir," Jord murmured tiredly.

"I suspect there's a mole here in the embassy, one reporting to the Regent."

"Why's that?" Jord asked incredulously, arms up in a dramatic shrug. "Who here would want to report to him?"

Axle procured a letter from his desk and pushed it towards the guard. The parchment was written in crude ink scratched from a quill. The Regent's seal was stamped in wax at the bottom.

"A diplomat brought that in yesterday. The Regent is formally requesting our guest back."

"Sophie?" Otto asked.

"Indeed. So, how did the Regent find out? I don't think anyone here was eager to advertise that we had a guest in our custody because of bizarre events. Otto, didn't you say this was one of the few circumstances where we'd be forced to comply?"

"It is, it is," Otto said, scanning the paper in front of him. "Do you think one of the diplomats let it slip out? Maybe hoping for a favor or something?"

"It's possible, but I don't reckon our diplomats as the type to admit to something embarrassing on our part," Axle explained.

"I went over the history records of every person here in the embassy with you before we were stationed here," Jord told Axle. "I can't think of anyone who would let that out, especially to the Regent."

"Agreed. Something fishy is about and I don't like it. I also don't understand why the Regent would want the girl returned directly to him at the Palace. She was just a street urchin; what interest would he have in her?"

"Nothing benevolent or humanitarian, in my opinion," Otto interjected, putting the letter down. "We'll have to comply, but we don't need to be cooperative about it."

"Care to elaborate?" Axle asked curiously.

The door flew open, straining its hinges. The veterans stared wide-eyed at the newcomer, one of their junior guards. He was in a panic and spoke accordingly.

"Pardon me, sirs. Terribly sorry, sirs, but you're needed at the south gate! The sentries there are calling for backup!"

Chairs clattered to the floor as the guards took off and ran. Even Axle kept on their heels, seeing no reason to sit this one out. Out into the courtyard, they ran and then up the stairs to get to the top of the gate. Outside on the streets in a sandbag watch-post were two guards, Ausburne and Black, watching a lone figure clothed all in white across the street. The stranger looked agitated and was pacing back and forth. Occasionally, he would stop to bellow loudly at the embassy gates.

"Purveyors of greed and self-absorption! If you will not open and give to the Prosperous Light, then I will shake your very gates!"

Chapter Thirteen

Otto pulled on a nearby phone and buzzed the guards at their station. Black picked it up, although he and Ausburne kept their eyes transfixed madly on the cultist.

"How long has this been going on?" Otto asked calmly.

"About an hour or so, he's been watching us longer than that, maybe all morning. But then, he just started preaching and acting funny," Black said through the wire.

Eyes turned to the cultist again when they heard the sound of heavy wood hitting the cobblestones. The cultist was dragging a portly, full barrel from the alleyways. Ausburne raised his rifle.

"Guards, lower your guns! Do not fire!" Otto shouted and then turned to the man controlling the gate mechanisms. "Open the doors slightly; we need to let those two in."

"You're ordering them to abandon their post, Mr. Gurman?" Axle asked pointedly.

"Notice how the streets are empty? That doesn't mean there aren't eyes watching. Even if that's a cask of gunpowder, the gates can handle something like that. What we don't want are stories about Arazumi guards gunning down a harmless man in the streets."

"He's right, Axle. We still don't know what this madman is planning, but shooting him first will just make this worse," Jord agreed.

"Very well, not that anyone was waiting for my approval," Axle said, rolling his eyes.

"Guards! Get back behind the gate! That's an order, move!" Otto shouted. He didn't need to do it twice and the gates shut with a heavy bang.

The cultist stared flabbergasted at the empty guard post, somehow oblivious to the guards watching him high above on the ramparts. Disbelief gave way to frantic passion.

"Craven! Craven and tight-fisted! Destroyers through negligence! I will shake your foundations!"

The fanatic popped open the barrel and a pungent smell filled the streets. He began liberally pouring the goo on himself with abandon as the guards stared at him aghast. There was a desperation in those movements, a singular, idealistic goal that struggled with the man's own instincts.

"What is that fluid he's dumping on himself?" Otto asked. Axle and Jord glanced at him for a moment and then stared grim-faced at the cultist.

"It's whale oil, little man."

"Oh, sod me, is he going to…?"

They saw rather than heard the strike of a match. Then, they wished they couldn't hear anything at all. The shrieking pyre ran towards the gates then crashed into the heavy beams with a gut-wrenching smack. They heard a body fall onto the pavement, the crackle, and the susurration of hungry flames. The screams didn't stop. The victim was still alive, but too weak to do anything about it.

Chapter Thirteen

"Hey, bosses? Uh, what are we supposed to do about this?" a junior guard called to them, visibly trembling under his uniform.

"We could bring him in, get him medical attention!" Black offered.

"Keep those gates sealed. No one is going out," Axle yelled for all to hear. The guard working the gate controls pulled his hands away from the levers and dramatically showed them for all to see. They could still hear the cultist wailing as the fire continued to burn.

"Do you gents see an alternative? I'm open to ideas," Axle murmured just loud enough for Otto and Jord to hear.

"I don't like this whole situation. Someone is putting us into a trap," Jord hissed.

"We can't risk the whole embassy for that madman," Otto added.

"Make sure the men keep to their stations. Everyone is to be on high alert. Am I clear?" Axle demanded.

"Aye, sir!"

"Sir," Ausburne interjected, trying to swallow with a dry mouth. "Shouldn't we do something about that man screaming out there?"

"No one is permitted to shoot him and, until we deem it safe, no one is to open the gate under any circumstances," Axle said firmly.

The guards were left to man their stations, the gates locked, and their weapons gripped tight. Axle ordered more men on the ramparts and to remain on high alert. The streets around the walls remained empty, which distressed the guards all the more. Where were that cultist's friends to come and take him away? All the heightened senses of the guards were spent listening to a dying man's cries, and few of them knew just how long it could take for someone to die.

***

PHILIP'S SPIRIT SAT NEAR THE WEATHER VANE atop one of the embassy buildings. A memory from his mortal life told him the winds were bad for ships trying to pull into the harbor. Maybe that's why the Tersians were keeping their distance. All this would have been exciting, anxiety-inducing if he were still alive. Instead, he was left getting used to the afterlife. Most of the worries that previously hounded him were now laughably irrelevant. Hunger, fatigue, and even the desire for entertainment were gone. Time started to lose meaning; the ups and downs of the sun had as much weight as passing clouds. There were different things to occupy him.

For one, people looked different. He saw their spirits more clearly than he did their mortal appearances, and that took a lot of getting used to. It didn't help that their spirits didn't always bear an identical resemblance to their corporeal forms. What was that fancy word he heard someone say before? Caricature, yes, a lot of times a person was just a caricature of their spirit. Or was it the other way around?

He had found Sophie a while ago but then, he was at a loss. What could he do? Incorporeal forms washed like mist over and, sometimes, through corporeal entities. The worries of the former side suddenly seemed small and petty, and besides, Sophie was doing well enough for herself. There were many walls around her, keeping her safe. There were enough trained men with ridiculous firepower to back up those walls. His sister even had free reign of their food, more than he could have ever provided her while still alive. It made him smile, surprisingly, since he believed he would've been jealous if he

Chapter Thirteen

still had flesh on him. Sophie was more healthy now than ever before, and it reflected in her spirit as he watched it glow brighter with each passing sunrise and set. Maybe it was time to ascend to the Holy after all.

The weather vane groaned as the arrow shifted. The winds were still bad for ships, but storm clouds were gathering on the horizon. Not all of it was physical. You rarely saw a truly ugly spirit in a person, but it wasn't just people who had souls. Gatherings of people, gangs, organizations, and even a kingdom can take on a proto-soul of its own and those you had to watch out for because they swept people up in their influence like a rushing flood tide. A storm was rolling down from the mountain and then from the Palace. Philip saw it flow like a channel towards the embassy walls. What could he do about that?

He looked around and saw one spirit that...stood out in the city. It wasn't quite human, or it had been human once. Philip could tell that this particular soul had a memory of Sophie; he had saved her once. Philip knew there was little he could do about the coming storm, but maybe this specific soul could do something at least tangible for Sophie once more.

It looked like he was about to leave the city. Philip pulled up above the man's shoulder and tried to whisper into his ear. He kept insisting. What was this soul's name? Seth? Philip couldn't let Seth leave so soon. Sophie would need all the help she could get.

It took a while, but eventually, this particular soul hesitated and then looked back at the embassy. He turned around and headed back. Philip felt ecstatic. Maybe he had made a difference or perhaps, it had all been a coincidence, but that was fine. Every little good in the world mattered, regardless of which side of eternity you peered from.

***

THE STREET FILLED UP the next morning in front of the embassy. A formation of heavily armed and armored men waited there in the streets. It was the Palace Guards, their armor and spears gleaming in the morning sun. This didn't bring relief to the Long Steel men guarding the ramparts. It only compounded the headaches they had from the day before. Axle was summoned from his office to negotiate with the interlopers.

"What can I do for you fine gents this morning?" Axle called disarmingly.

"We're here for the girl! You must return our citizen to us! She is not yours!"

"All you Palace Guards for one girl? Were we unwittingly entertaining nobility this whole time?"

"That is none of your concern! Hand over the girl now!" the Palace captain roared.

"And after we transfer her into your custody, what will you do?" Axle pressed.

"Again, that is none of your concern! We–"

"On the contrary, it is, in fact, our concern!" Axle corrected. "That girl was handed to us to be protected under contract and the Long Steel Company must always safeguard its contracts! Now, we'll be more than happy to comply with you: once we know where you'll be taking her."

Chapter Thirteen

The Palace captain rolled his eyes and sighed heavily. "I don't answer to you, foreigner!"

"No, you don't. But, you and I both know we're just pawns to powers much larger than us. Now, I don't know about you, but I have a nice warm office I'd like to go back to, and you probably just want to get this assignment over so you can go back home. So, the sooner you cooperate with us and get the paperwork filed, so to speak, the sooner I can get to making sure you go back home with the girl."

The Palace captain paused for a moment before grumbling noises rumbled up his throat. "Fine, you win, foreigner! We'll be transferring her back to the Palace. From there, I don't know what will become of her. Now, hand her over!"

"With pleasure, sir!" Axle replied theatrically. "But, in order for me to do so, and this is something I've consulted with my company bookman, I must hand her over to you with a compliment of Long Steel's finest guards to make sure the transfer is done so safely."

"That. Is. Not. Necessary!"

"Sorry, my hands are tied! I'm merely following orders and protocol just like you are, guard captain!" Axle said without a hint of contrition. "It's not like this would interfere with any of your orders, would it?"

The Palace guard ground his teeth, and his eyes bulged in his sockets, but otherwise, he made no noise. Axle watched this and did his best to ensure his next reply wasn't too cheeky.

"There, you see! What harm could it do? More guards to make sure everyone is safe! My guards are gathering the girl and will travel with you shortly. Oh! One last thing; one of your citizens went a little barmy yesterday and immolated himself in front of our gates. Would you please make sure his body is properly, ah, cared for? He's on your side of the embassy after all."

"That is none of our concern!"

"You have a very limited reservoir of concern, fellow guard!"

"Shut up and hurry up!"

CHAPTER **14**

ADMIRAL ORUZ WATCHED as the captured smugglers were lifted off the deck by their necks and hanged until dead. A few words from the Prophets were read over them and their bodies were then consigned to the deep. It wasn't a pleasant deed, but it had to be done, especially since it was Sorcerer Doruk who had captured them in the first place. Doruk intended for the corsairs to be keelhauled until dead, but Oruz was not going to tolerate that.

"We're not savages; you will hang those smugglers, Captain, or I will!" Oruz thundered.

"We may not be savages, but these smugglers are, and they must be treated as such, Admiral!" Doruk contended.

"All the more reason for us, the civilized and enlightened, to punish them civilly! No, I will oversee their execution myself. I'm ordering you to transfer them to my ship!"

And that was how Oruz gave five smugglers a slightly less violent death. Landlubbers mistakenly believe the victim of a keelhauling just needs to hold their breath really long and deal with being buffeted against the ship's keel. They forget barnacles are often along the keel and hull, and those things are little more than jagged razors. Oruz knew Doruk took a peculiar glee in keelhauling the victim until they were ripped down to the bone or an extremity was lost. Oruz was not going to listen to another gruesome retelling about how a smuggler's head was ground down to a stump.

It irked him to remember that he had to host Doruk and a few more of that murderous bunch on his flagship in a few minutes. It couldn't be helped; guidelines demanded that the head captains meet with the Admiral to communicate better and give their reports.

"This assignment—just this last one—and then, I'll petition the Sultan for my retirement," Oruz muttered to himself, nursing a cup of tea as he did. He made sure the samovar was sufficiently warmed. Personally, he wouldn't have offered any tea to those mongrels masquerading as captains, but niceties had to be observed nonetheless. It's what separated those who heeded the words of the Prophets and those who were little more than animals.

And those disgraceful men came aboard, bowing to him and giving their empty words of respect. Oruz forced himself not to shake his head in disgust. Calling them mongrels was an insult to dogs. The admiral couldn't remember the last dog he met who was as depraved and murderous as this lot.

"Give me your reports, captains," Oruz said as he began to pour them each a cup of tea. He only listened for keywords or changes from their usual declarations. Blockade work was long hours of boredom punctuated by brief hours of drama, which inevitably drifted back to boredom.

He sighed when it was Doruk's turn. The admiral silently prayed that Doruk wouldn't have anything new to report.

"I was able to extract crucial information from the smugglers that will interest you, Admiral," Doruk said. Oruz silently prayed to the Prophets, begging that they would petition the Utmost Sovereign to have mercy on him and give him patience.

Chapter Fourteen

"Do continue, Captain," Oruz said quietly.

"I learned that the smugglers found out too late that there was a powerful sorceress in their clutches. They intend to take her back today."

"How could they not know they had a sorceress? And taking her back today? They are very confident to assume that," Oruz said thoughtfully, handing out the last of the tea.

"The girl didn't show any signs of magical talent until one of the smugglers' own wizards felt a strong resonance feedback on their branding runes, something that would only happen if the girl exercised her powers. It's possible she's not aware of her own talents. As for taking her back, the smugglers have their sources. They intend to intercept her as she is being transported through the city today," Doruk explained patiently.

Oruz sipped his tea and pursed his lips. "You intend to request that I sanction a recovery mission. You want this sorceress plucked from Reyais and brought into the Sultan's Corp of Magicians."

"It is our duty, Admiral, to obtain whoever has magical talent and bring them into the service of the Sultan. If this sorceress is as valuable as the smugglers believe her to be, then she will be an asset beyond measure."

"Do we have the resources for this, Doruk?" Oruz demanded, the disapproval heavy in his voice. "Does this not distract us from our mission?"

"Each magician is a precious resource, Admiral. You should know that. I've already assigned a few of our sorcerers to join the infiltrators we have in the city. They will know what to do," Doruk said calmly. "Worry not, sir; the sorcerers I've ordered to go ashore won't compromise the magical abilities of our fleet for long."

"Then it appears I have no choice but to give my approval," Oruz said bitterly. "Please, send your reports on this action to me as soon as you know the results. Are there any other captains here who have a request for me? No? Then that is all," Oruz commanded. "Off of my ship, all of you. Back to your duties."

***

SOPHIE WAITED SULLENLY IN THE COURTYARD while Kassia loitered by to keep her company. Kassia kept offering apple slices. Sophie ate them numbly, unable to taste them. She was going to miss Kassia, Jord, and the other guards and staff. She was going to miss the books and the food. She'd even allow herself to be subjected to another inoculation if it would mean she could stay, but Kassia repeatedly assured her it didn't work that way. It made her sad.

Jord and the other guards were dressed differently now, and it was frightening. In addition to what they usually wore, they all had leather pads on their elbows and knees. Belts of things called "bullets" were worn across their bodies. They never seemed to let go of their guns anymore either. It wasn't enough that they were expecting a fight; they seemed intent on stopping one with enough firepower to obliterate a whole building and everyone in it.

There were six guards standing by her and Kassia. She recognized only Jord and Otto. Jord, stoic as always, finished his smoke and emptied the ashes from his pipe. He gave her a reassuring smile as he did so. Sophie didn't smile. Axle strolled up to them, his face wearing an expression of disappointment. Otto was the first to speak as soon as Axle arrived.

"Are they still insisting on her return?" he asked.

"They still are. There's nothing we can do," Axle said regretfully. "It's all horse manure, of course, even though they won't admit it. The problem with that is that it smells. No matter what you try to call it, or how you try to hide it, or how much you try to re-package it, it still has an unmistakable stench to it. We just can't call them out on it, and they don't have the pride to be embarrassed by the smell of it."

"I'll be honest," Jord chimed in. "I think there should be more than just six of us. The city seems to be going through some sort of fey mood. You saw what happened yesterday with that cultist who went mad, and we know there's a strong presence of smugglers about."

Jord didn't say it out loud, but there was also the matter of experience. Other than himself and Otto, Michael, Derek, Fletcher, and Clemson were the only ones there. The last two hadn't seen combat at all, and as far as the veterans were concerned, Michael and Derek were still green.

"You'll be surrounded by a formation of the Palace Guards," Axle said bluntly. "Michael will be able to telegraph us the moment there's trouble, and the unfortunate truth is that I need every guard I have available on the walls here."

"Understood, sir. I take it we'll have to figure our own way back?" Jord asked.

"Probably. The Palace Guard said they'd escort you back, but I don't know if you can trust them," Axle said.

"We've made it through worse," Otto said numbly.

"All right, but I don't think we have," Fletcher interjected, motioning towards himself and the junior guards.

"Then follow Mr. Gurman and Mr. Krarkson. They dragged other sorry boys alive through the Black War; they'll do the same for you."

"Are we ready?" Otto asked and without saying a word, all eyes fell to Sophie. She wore Arazumi clothes and had grown healthier with their food and medicines, but now she looked even more lost than ever before.

"I'm ready," she said softly. There wasn't a sign of protest, not even a whimper. Acceptance came naturally to her; an old habit practiced so long it was a reflex. "Goodbye, Kassia," she said to the chemist. Kassia bent down and hugged her.

"Goodbye, Sophie."

No one was in a hurry, and the motions came to everyone like a machine grumbling reluctantly on low gear. Limbs moved forward, numbly running on torpid minds. The whole embassy watched but not a word was said. The gate opened wide enough for everyone to pass through in double file and then closed shut with a jarring bang. The Palace Guards, relieved, formed around them, and the march began.

"Why are we so worried, sir?" Michael asked Otto quietly. "We're carrying an awful lot of equipment to guard one girl. Is there something Axle knows that we don't?"

"Long Steel takes its contracts seriously, and we took a contract to protect her."

Chapter Fourteen

"That can't be all, sir, if you'll excuse me saying."

"You're right," Otto relented. "In case you hadn't noticed, the city is a little tense right now. A man just immolated himself in front of our gates yesterday. Only the Holy knows how many security risks are out there, and there are only six of us available to make sure we honor our contract. That's why we're armed for bears."

"Keep your eyes peeled, pups," Jord muttered as they moved along. The clatter of footsteps and metal armor was deafening. The junior guards swiveled their heads like startled cats.

"Don't just keep them at ground level either," Otto warned. "There are rooftops to worry about."

"And the windows?" Clemson sputtered.

"Those too."

" I suddenly hate the city," Fletcher grumbled, color draining from his face.

"Keep your heads," Jord said sternly. "We didn't ask for this, but if we're going to stay alive, we need to focus."

"I keep thinking some other locals will go mad and try to burn themselves up while rushing towards us," Michael admitted.

"Worry about it if you see it. In the meantime, only worry about what's in front of you," Otto said.

Progress was slow but steady and without interruptions. The locals knew to clear the way from the unmistakable tramp of the Palace

Guards. Alleyways and side streets passed by without number. Jord felt a small hand hold tight to his free gauntlet somewhere along the way. He didn't dare look down at her, it was too important to watch the streets, but he let out a shaky sigh of grief. None of it made sense. Why was a street urchin suddenly so important to a mysterious benefactor, one even Sophie didn't know, and the Regent? There was a whole armada of Tersians beyond the harbor and so-called privateers living within, and yet, the Prosperous Light seemed to have an ax to grind with the embassy. Why?

Why had Sophie gone limp?

Jord looked down, the girl's arm hanging in his grasp while she lay face down on the street. The only movement she made was from short, desperate breaths that wracked her body. Squinting, Jord saw a shape burning with an angry glow beneath her hair at the base of her neck.

"Get your heads down."

"What was that, boss?" Clemson asked.

"Everyone get your heads down now!" Jord roared.

The thunder of musket fire echoed across the streets. Civilians panicked and ran in every direction, confusing the eyes. Several of the Palace Guards dropped to the cobblestones in no discernable pattern. Thick in the air was the smell of spent gunpowder and blood.

Shields and pikes went up as the Palace Guards at the boundary of the formation reacted to the sudden chaos. Eyes searched for the plume of gunpowder. The Long Steel men closed around the prone body of Sophie and readied their weapons. Derek was the first to fire.

Chapter Fourteen

"Rooftop to the left!" he shouted.

"And the right!" Otto hollered as he saw a group of men emerge above them. There was barely any time to react before another volley of muskets vomited smoke in their direction. More of the Palace Guards fell dead or screaming.

"Who's doing this?" Fletcher demanded.

"Smugglers," Jord growled, pointing towards the glowing rune on Sophie's neck. "They want their misplaced commodity back."

"We can't stay out here in the open; they had this ambush planned out," Otto snapped.

"I'll telegraph the embassy for help!" Michael cried and furiously began tapping on the device by his waist.

Jord looked around furiously for an escape route. The Palace Guards didn't move, too intent to make a stand and fight. It was foolishness. The smugglers were using muskets, sophisticated weapons that meant business, and were waiting for them to arrive at this exact spot before attacking. Staying here under the rooftops was asking to get massacred.

"Any word back, Michael?" Jord demanded. The technician listened breathlessly to his headset, a finger stabbing one earpiece further into his ear.

"They say return to the embassy!"

"Agreed! Squad, attention!" Jord barked and then made a series of curt arm and hand motions. The Long Steel guards watched and nodded. Jord pointed at Otto.

"Now, little man!"

Otto pulled a metal canister from his bandolier and tossed it over the heads of the Palace Guards towards the street. It clattered on the cobblestones and immediately began erupting a thick cloud of smoke. Jord hefted Sophie over his shoulder and began to move. The Long Steel men bullied their way through the Palace Guards in the opposite direction back towards the embassy. Another smoke canister was rolled and deployed as they made their escape. The Palace Guards weren't happy about it, but they were also unhappy with the salvos of musket balls raining down on them, and that was a far more pressing concern.

"Why does he call you 'little man?'" Michael muttered to Otto as they bounded along. "You're not that short." Otto glanced at him incredulously but then relented.

"Old war joke. Now, focus!"

"This street, this street!" Jord hissed, motioning towards a quiet avenue. The men piled in, running as if the demons of the Abyss were hot on their heels. Derek and Fletcher yelled at the locals to clear the way up front while the rest of the squad ran behind them. It boggled the mind; minutes ago, there was an eruption of gunfire and men screaming in mortal agony, but that was several streets down and not a problem for the people here enjoying their time spent on their rickety back doorsteps.

Chapter Fourteen

"Do you think we've lost them?" Clemson gasped. Their lungs were on fire, but no one dared to slow down. Just how far had they gotten from the embassy?

"Worry about it when we get back to safety. Michael, update the base on our status," Jord commanded.

"Aye, si–"

There was the crack of musket thunder followed by an ominous thump that sent a shiver down their spines. Michael brought his hand up to his face and began to scream. A gaping hole marked where a musket ball had hit his hand. Blood spilled onto the leather and metal of his gauntlet, the armor hiding his mangled fingers underneath. Behind them, they saw smugglers rushing up the alleyway.

"Fletcher, Otto, cover our retreat! Clemson, get Michael some amber! Keep moving!"

There was more screaming along with the sloshing of yellow medicine on the cobblestones. Jord followed closely behind Derek, who led the way. Behind them, Otto and Fletcher systematically pumped a hail of fire into the smugglers who were desperate to catch up with them. Jord chanced a glance back and was satisfied with what he saw.

"We'll protect you, pup," he whispered to the helpless Sophie, who was still gasping for breath. "You keep fighting your fight; grab the strength inside you."

"We need to hurry," Otto barked behind them, smoke trailing from the barrel of his rifle. "Hostiles cleared. For now."

"We got a problem, sirs!" Derek announced. "Up front! And they don't look like smugglers."

It was a fact as plain as day. The smugglers had been a ragtag bunch with no uniformity other than the fact they were pointing their firearms at the guards. This new group wore uniform dark lamellar armor, and the subordinate men each had a musket in hand and a curved sword at their waist. Ominously, their leader was armed with only a simple rod.

"Tersians!" Jord snarled.

"Get out of the way and lower your weapons!" Derek shouted at them. The Tersians didn't comply; they stalked closer. The Tersian lieutenant raised his hand and pointed the rod towards them.

"Wand!" Jord warned.

"Those work?" Clemson asked incredulously.

Derek reacted and shouldered his blunderbuss. The Tersians were quicker. A gunshot echoed through the alleyway, and Derek fell flat on his back. The remaining Long Steel men raised their firearms at once, but their guns remained silent. The Tersian sorcerer kept his wand pointed steadily at them. The triggers of their weapons refused to budge as if the mechanisms were fused in place.

"There doesn't need to be any more bloodshed, mercenaries," the wizard told them, speaking their language. "Just hand us the girl, and you may continue on your way."

Jord gingerly handed Sophie to Clemson. "Keep her safe. If it all goes arse up, run and get to the embassy," he said quietly.

Chapter Fourteen

The Tersian sorcerer watched with wary eyes. "Do you defy us?" he demanded. Jord glared daggers at him and drew his bayonet. He brought the blade up to the shoulder of his right sleeve and began to saw at the fabric.

"Dammit, Jord, no, that's not necessary," Otto groaned.

There was the protest of ripping fabric, and the sleeve fell away. Jord's whole upper arm was a mosaic of blue tattoos around a single black one. It was common for Raermak men and women to have important personal achievements inked onto their dominant arm. In the olden days, Arazumi villagers and militias quaked at the sight of a Raermak reaver party displaying the blue on their arms before charging with a blood-curdling war cry. In baring his sword arm, a Raermak wasn't just showing you his personal saga; he was declaring you were going to be his next tattoo. There were already five broken lance and arrows on his arm, the traditional symbol of the Tersian Sultanate.

Jord unleashed a venomous bellow of war that reverberated down the street. Grabbing a nearby discarded plank, he threw it at the Tersians before charging towards them. It was all Otto could do to keep up. The other guards were frozen in place, the Tersians not much better. There was a murderous glee in Jord's eyes, and he was not going to stop.

There was a crash of steel and muscle. The Tersians stood their ground but weren't expecting this much fury as Jord plowed into them, Otto right behind him with bayonet fastened. The fighting was desperate, and the sorcerer could do little to help, focused on making sure the firearms were useless. He swished his wand, strain visibly weighing on his limbs. It was the junior guards who noticed the change first.

"Our bullets are crumbling," Michael groaned, still nursing his ruined hand.

"What?" Clemson blurted.

"Look at your bandolier," Michael said. The bullet tips crumbled away like brittle powder, followed by a rain of inert gunpowder. Fletcher frantically tried to heft up Derek from the ground.

"He's still breathing and bleeding. Bugger this; we got to help those two, then get out of here."

The sorcerer flicked the wand up and all of the guards began to levitate half a meter off the ground, impotent as hanging string puppets. The Tersian soldiers, the three still alive, pulled away and caught their breath. Jord, bloodied and still raging, continued to swing the butt of his blunderbuss in wild arcs.

"Put them down," a new voice ordered. Everyone turned and looked at a black-clad figure casually approaching them from further up the alleyway. He wasn't Tersian, but he didn't look like a local either. Otto squinted at him.

"A Witch Hunter?"

"Last warning, body snatchers. Let them go, and I won't become unpleasant," Seth said with a stormy glare.

The sorcerer pointed a finger at the Witch Hunter and looked like he was about to cast a spell. Seth raised an open palm and hissed something in an alien tongue. The Long Steel guards crashed to the ground in a heap but were immediately pinned down again by an invisible force. The Tersian soldiers charged the interloper. There was

Chapter Fourteen

a morbid surprise when Seth began carving carmine tapestries out of them. The sorcerer was forced to intervene, and both of them began dueling with blade and spell.

Sophie watched with wild eyes where she lay, paralyzed like the guards around her. She was aware of everything from the beginning, from the Palace Guards falling from gaping musket wounds to Jord going berserk and being stopped dead with magic. Fear transmuted into anger. She wanted the rune on her neck gone, and she wanted these animals who saw her as nothing more than a commodity to be passed around gone too. How do you rip a magical device off your flesh? Sophie didn't know, but she felt compelled to try.

Seth and the sorcerer swung and jabbed at each other while grasping at every spell they could think of, only for the magic to fizzle out in the face of the mental duress of sword fighting. There was a clatter of steel and then a muffled burst signaling a blast of misfired magic. The two stared at each other, the Tersian magically stitching his flesh together where Seth's blade had found its mark. Seth looked down at his left hand, only to see a fountain of blood where it should have been.

"You're not normal. I've seen magics, many kinds, and you, you're different," the Tersian hissed desperately.

"Maybe I'm just strange. Still, I'm not a blighting body snatcher abducting children to be twisted into sorcerers like you are," Seth spat.

His vision swam for a second. Then he felt his legs give out under him, and he was pinned to the ground just like the Arazumi. He didn't realize he had lost that much blood, and he could feel a pressure building up at the stump of his wrist. The sorcerer was using magic to drain his blood faster.

"We shall see how different you are," the Tersian said, wand pointed directly at him.

"Go away!" Sophie shrieked. She was limping up towards the Tersian, her posture tortured as if weighed down with cannonballs but angry enough to continue plodding along.

"How did she get up?" Clemson demanded, still face down in the cobblestones.

"Have you tried pushing yourselves up harder, pups?" Jord said desperately.

"Have you, sir? Because if you can't, then we don't have a chance," Fletcher cut in.

"Hey, I'm still alive," Derek breathed. "Wait, can the surgeon do anything about gut wounds?"

"You're lucky, rookie," Otto said calmly. "A lot of men died in the war in order for the corpsmen to learn what to do for those. You'll be fine once we get you back."

"Thanks, that's a relief," Derek sighed.

"Could we focus on how Sophie is able to stand, and we can't?" Jord growled.

"That's a question I can't puzzle out, so it helps to focus on the ones I can," Otto groused.

Chapter Fourteen

The sorcerer turned to Sophie, bewilderment written all over his face. He raised his wand at her and began to chant in a language that the others didn't understand. Sophie stood fast and glared at him defiantly.

"I said, go away!"

Later on, the guards would debate on whether or not there was a sound. Some said they heard nothing, while the others insisted there was a terrifying popping noise. The aftermath was less ambiguous. The spot where the sorcerer once stood was now a grotesque red smear with a few piles of offal and, if any of them had been curious enough to investigate, utterly devoid of bones. The whole skeleton had been spirited away.

Sophie was on all fours and losing most of her lunch by the time the guards were up on their feet to collect her. Seth met them just as Jord hefted the hapless girl onto his shoulder.

"Why did you help us?" Otto demanded. "Don't Danarian Witch Hunters burn magicians and witches?"

"Uh, who said anything about Sophie being a witch?" Clemson asked. "I thought that sorcerer blew himself up."

"Yes, that's exactly what he did," Seth laughed mockingly, staring at the bleeding stump of his wrist.

"I don't believe so. I'm also starting to suspect you're the one who put us under the contract. What's your name? Someone with ridiculous initials?" Otto pressed.

"You want answers?" Seth said coldly, looking up at him. "You keep that girl safe, up in your embassy, and you get as far away from this island as possible."

"There's a Tersian blockade in the way," Jord said bluntly.

"Doesn't matter. Use that fancy Arazumi clockwork you have. Someone wants that girl and everyone on this island dead. You'll do everyone a lot of favors if you just leave and take her with you," Seth explained and began to walk past them.

"How do you know all this? That doesn't answer anything!" Otto pointed out.

"I'm a Witch Hunter. That's all you need to know. Now, get back to your embassy. I'll make sure no one else follows you."

"You're...missing a hand," Fletcher pointed out.

Seth didn't answer and hurried down the alleyway. He could hear the guards retreating towards the embassy. He listened hard but couldn't hear anything that would suggest more smugglers were on their way. The Witch Hunter chuckled hoarsely. He didn't know what tickled his intuition to come back one last time to check in on the girl, but he was glad he listened to it.

There was an unconscious smuggler at his feet, laid low from one of those Arazumi rifles. Seth could smell the copper in the wound, a little benefit from being "not normal," as the Tersian had put it. Ugly stuff, copper was. It was slightly uglier than what he would have to do next.

Chapter Fourteen

Seth fetched a simple goblet awkwardly from his satchel. He propped the smuggler up by the wall and made sure there was no one around to watch. Witnesses would've made this more awkward. Assured he was alone, he plunged a dagger into the dying man's throat and collected the flowing blood into his chalice. The cup was important. He had standards. Seth drank hungrily until the vessel was drained and then returned to the red fountain for seconds. His left arm jolted as a new hand emerged from the ruined stump. Seth ignored this little miracle as he drained the goblet a second time.

"You're right, Regent," Seth said to himself. "Formalities must be kept, and the unspoken agreements must abide. I wonder when you'll be forced to cast off the mask you wear."

CHAPTER **15**

MAGIC AND MONSTERS: HOLDOVERS FROM the olden days when man's collective memory faded and wobbled and was anchored by legends rather than evidence. Were the legends simply tall tales that grew over small fires when the nights were darker and the world more foreboding? Was there a small seed of truth hidden beneath all the exaggeration? Or was old magic real and simply gone into retirement as each new generation of man stayed forever young?

Seth would have told you the truth was somewhere between all of them and none of them. In the olden days there were more vampires, dragons, werewolves and all kinds of monsters haunting the lands. Magic was more prevalent and no one could say that the future belonged to man. It was a precarious time to be alive for everyone, not just for the mere human. No one remembers the tales of dragons obliterating packs of werewolves or the infamous Fey-Unicorn Incident. Seth still cringed at the memories of whole vampire clans learning their particular bloodline was susceptible to sunlight when no one was left the morning after someone threw strange herbs on the fire.

Then man learned to cast bronze. These days, man only remembers that he mastered bronze because it was easier to mold than iron. He never fully realized that copper, an essential ingredient in bronze, is silver's cruder, sadistic cousin. Silver will kill a monster before their body has a chance to hit the ground. Copper, on the other hand, won't kill as quickly, but you'd feel your unnatural blood boiling, your organs rapidly going necrotic, and a broiling fever in your head that no human could ever imagine. Then, finally but never soon enough, you'd die. It was a relief when humans discovered how much more effective silver was, but then the bronze age had turned to iron, and the damage was already done. Dragons no longer terrorized the skies, the fey retreated into the deepest woods, and the monsters learned to cloak themselves in night, as terrified of man as man was of them. Werewolves and vampires still stalked among men, but they were as much the hunted as they were the hunters. Even the demons had to grow up and start acting their age.

This was a time so long ago that Seth's memories of it were as fuzzy as the legends told of them. He knew Mara was around back then as well, though he could no longer remember which of them had first shed their humanity. They had been colleagues, rivals, family, lovers, and enemies again and again throughout the long years. Eventually, he and the other vampires of Danaria formed the Agreement, a similar pact that all the other monstrous creatures effectively abided by; you didn't stir the pot, you helped each other or stayed out of each other's way, and you never gave the humans a reason to suspect a vampire was about. The Danarian Witch Hunters were formed under the influence of several vampires, incognito, of course. Sometimes you had to clean up after an old colleague who got careless or put down a young, newly awoken vampire who couldn't control their hunger. And when an old friend decided he was done, that he tired of the long and lonely years, Seth was there to make sure the passing was as clean, merciful, and dignified as possible.

Seth wore many faces throughout the ages and just as many names. He knew one day Brother Grinn would come to visit him because while vampires persisted century after century, they were not immortal. Eventually, even a vampire's life will end, no matter how much blood they took. That was the natural order of things, at least on this side of eternity. But that wasn't enough for Mara; no, she wanted to steal immortality from the Holy. That was where the trouble

Chapter Fifteen

began, and as the Agreement demanded, Seth gave chase. He liked to think it's what proved he still had at least a single bit of his humanity left. Humans, bless and curse them, didn't need an immortal vampire in their midst.

***

MIRABELLE WATCHED AS CAPTAIN GUNDERSON furiously scaled up a grappling line and onto the deck of a Tersian mortar ship. Behind him were the Dhaliese sea-clanners he and his crew had joined up with, the sea-clanners' rowed galleys perfect for this mission. Mirabelle sighed with relief as Gunderson, and the Dhaliese began to make short work of their hapless enemies. The wind remained contrary to their assailants but a few of their vessels managed to beat their way close enough to be a danger to the harbor, and more importantly, the corsairs' vessels moored within. At least Gunderson and the Dhaliese were doing their part in keeping with the plan.

Mirabelle trained her spyglass away from the mortar ship and to another point on the horizon. She groaned at what she saw. Captain Corba and Novault were attacking a Tersian frigate. There was little doubt they would take it, but the frigate would take a toll on Novault's small attack craft. Novault probably thought of them as easily replaceable, but Mirabelle did not. The harbor was already pressed hard enough for resources, and captured Tersian vessels were practically cannibalized for repairs. It also didn't help that deep down, Mirabelle knew that Corba and Novault were thinking about profit while she and a few other captains were planning how to escape the blockade.

"It's not good out there in the city, Lady Mirabelle," Jacques said, sitting down next to her. She glanced at him with a wary eye and sighed heavily. Graphic blood splatters mottled Jacques' armor, and he was dragging a rag over the length of his two-hander.

"You say it's 'not good,' but all the red on you tells me you're underselling it," Mirabelle chastised.

"You always tell me to try to look for the positive side of things. I couldn't think of a positive, so I decided to go with softening the blow instead."

"Tell me what you've found out then," Mirabelle said tiredly, taking a seat across from him.

"The city has gone into a sort of revolt."

"Revolt?"

"Well, it's breaking down," Jacques clarified, fidgeting with his hands as he tried to explain it. "A lot of the carpenters that manned the docks are leaving now that they've gathered enough pay and don't see a point in staying anymore. It's not safe here, and a lot of them were threatened and brow-beaten by a few of the sailors here. Then, there's the auditors and quartermasters. With them gone from the harbor, everyone isn't sure how long the coin will keep flowing, and most aren't interested in bartering. The locals beyond the docks are outright hostile. You'll recall how everyone lost their tempers when the Palace Guard took Davos' plunder."

"We're mistaken as corsairs or worse all the time, Jacques. A little hostility shouldn't be anything new."

"This is more than just resentment, Mirabelle. A few sailors complained about bricks, stones, and bottles thrown at them when

Chapter Fifteen

they tried to go further into the city. One man was shot and killed by a crossbow. A few captains have their men maintaining a barricade around the harbor and shooting at anyone who tries to get close," Jacques admitted.

"By the Holy, has everyone gone mad? We're not the enemy; the Tersians are!"

"The locals seem to think we're part of the problem. They're not wrong on that part. The Tersians wouldn't be here if we weren't."

"And the sailors blocking up the harbor and shooting at people aren't making that better. We can't afford to waste ammo and bodies on Reyais."

"We don't have a choice. We can't have an angry mob pushing us out of the harbor yet. It doesn't help that some people think a monster of some sort was brought into the city by one of our ships," Jacques added.

"A monster?" Mirabelle sneered.

"Yes. We found some information posters hung up by the watchmen. They believe a monster or some other dangerous creature killed a bunch of their people in the last couple of days."

"That is such nonsense," Mirabelle complained. "Why would any sane ship and crew do such a thing? And how?"

"I don't think people are interested in reason now, Captain. They're more interested in simple answers with blunt solutions," Jacques sighed.

"This is madness," Mirabelle said, massaging her temples. "If we're going to get out of here, we'll need all the help we can get. We shouldn't be wasting our efforts on pillaging the locals for trinkets. There's got to be a way to placate them."

"Do we even have the time and resources to do that? I thought we were trying to get out of here as soon as possible and barring that, hunker down and hold out against a siege."

"Look at us! Gunderson had a point," Mirabelle said bitterly. "We can't organize. A few captains think they can have freedom and plunder, and others don't care; they just want that next payout, that next bottle of rum, that next fight and damn the consequences. We cannot withstand a siege!"

"So how do we leave? We need to decide how to do this now!" Jacques replied, thumping his blade to emphasize his point.

There was scattered musket fire and yelling from the barricades on the far side of the harbor. Mirabelle rushed over to investigate, if only to make sure the sailors manning it didn't overextend or, Holy forbid, use it as an excuse to go looting again. By the time she and Jacques made it, the fracas was over, just a couple of pirates rummaging through the bodies of dead Tersians.

"Lucky break this one. If Eagle-Eyed Jerry hadn't spotted these guys trying to sneak by, we'd never have bagged them," one of the sailors said gleefully. The one Mirabelle assumed was Eagle-Eyed Jerry was busy reloading his musket. Mirabelle narrowed her eyes.

"You can keep the coins you find, boys, but could you hand me any papers they might have?"

Chapter Fifteen

"Sure, not like they're worth anything."

Moments later, Mirabelle studied the grubby papers given to her by even grubbier hands. The captain examined each sheet with a critical eye. Jacques curiously watched over her shoulder.

"I didn't know you could read Tersian," Jacques said.

"I can't."

"Well, you keep staring at them, and they're all in Tersian script, so...why do you keep staring at them?"

"I'm trying to spot a pattern."

"Found one yet?"

"No, Jacques!"

They both held their breath when Mirabelle moved to the next sheet. Heads tilted at different angles as they each tried to make sense of what they were looking at. Jacques spoke first.

"That's an interesting doodle."

"It's a battle plan," Mirabelle breathed.

"Okay, but what are they attacking? That doesn't look like the harbor," Jacques shrugged.

"It can't be the Palace either. The shape is all wrong," Mirabelle murmured.

"Wait, can we be sure it's not the harbor? This bit looks like water and piers," Jacques said, pointing at the sketch.

"The harbor isn't curved like that, and the piers don't match, not by any stretch of the imagination. And if I understand this correctly, it's not an all-out assault. Why would they be attacking the harbor with so few numbers?"

"Are we sure it's not a doodle? I hear the Tersians really love their opium pipes," Jacques offered limply.

"Jacques," Mirabelle's eyes widened as an epiphany flowed through her. "It's the embassy."

"The Arazumi embassy?"

"Do you know of another one here?"

"Okay, so they're going to attack the Arazumi. Good for them; they can both choke on each other's blood for all I care."

"We can use this, Jacques," Mirabelle chided.

"How?"

"We won't know until we try to get this to them," Mirabelle told him. Jacques stared at her aghast.

"You are beside yourself, my lady. You're not seriously considering helping those butchers!"

"They could help us, Jacques. I'm not saying we just hand this to them. They'll have to help us in some way."

Chapter Fifteen

"They won't," Jacques snapped. "They're heartless butchers, clockwork demons who the Holy forgot to give souls. They won't help us, so why bother?"

"Even if they don't help, I can still learn something. Come on, Jacques, we're going on an adventure!" Mirabelle declared, already vaulting over the barricade. Jacques growled, stamped his feet, and scowled. Then he used his sword to help himself over the barrier. He'd been her bodyguard for years and dealt with enough of her fey-touched schemes. He was going to see this one through, too.

It took a while for Mirabelle to realize she'd been holding her breath. Could you take the pulse of a whole city from traveling on just one street? This one declared that Reyais was going mad. Houses were vacant, and the detritus of civilization were piled on the sidewalks as thieves took the opportunity to loot what they could. Even the district Watch station was empty.

"I wonder where they went," Mirabelle murmured. Jacques pointed further up the city.

"You can make out some barricades up on the streets. They coincide where the richer districts are. They've already lost control of this part of the city, so I imagine the nobles are trying to shore up what they can. The watchmen here probably got called up to protect the Palace and more affluent parts of the city."

"All the more reason we need to appeal to the Arazumi. They're trapped in the storm with us."

"Let's hope it's not a ship breaker, Mira," Jacques said grimly.

"You always have a chance to survive a ship breaker storm, but you'll never make it if you try to run from it. If you can't avoid it, you have to sail in and survive as long as it takes for the storm to pass."

They heard the embassy long before they got close to it. The pair instinctively stopped at the sound of gunfire, both crouching below an abandoned wagon while trying to analyze the situation they were walking themselves into. They decided on a roundabout route, and the two stalked accordingly. Mirabelle, ignoring Jacques' disapproval, was the first to glance around an alley corner towards the embassy.

"Devil in the Abyss," she hissed. "What's going on here?"

The street and houses around the embassy were a war zone. Oily plumes of gunpowder smoke erupted like geysers from the dilapidated hovels as citizens took potshots at the Arazumi. A mob of the Prosperous Light cultists stood out on the streets, the white robes eerie in the writhing torchlight. You could hear the vitriol in their protests despite the musket fire.

"Arazumi parasites! Arazumi parasites! Thieves and invaders! Prosperity for Reyais!"

"I have a question," Mirabelle whispered to Jacques. "Why aren't the Arazumi shooting back?"

"There's probably some rule of theirs that's keeping them," Jacques shrugged. "Let's just not be anywhere near when they decide to change their minds."

"We give our all for Reyais!" a cultist screamed from the streets. Jacques and Mirabelle watched in captivated horror as four cult members stepped out of the mob towards the embassy gates. Their

Chapter Fifteen

robes glistened with the sickly amber of whale oil. The torches they held painted shadows around them and on their faces.

"Get away from the gates!" a guard bellowed from the ramparts. The cultists ignored him and raised their torches.

"Prosperity for Reyais!" the cultists proclaimed and pressed the torches to themselves. Four people became standing, moving pyres.

"Bloody Abyss, bugger off! Keep away from the damn gates!"

Four burning cultists sprinted towards the sturdy, heavy gates, crashed into them, fell screaming, and began to die. More cultists began to step forward; more burning pillars started to light up the streets. More rushed the gate.

The embassy ramparts lit up with muzzle flashes. Fusillade after fusillade dropped the cultists on the cobblestones and then began to rain on the houses, furiously hunting for the musketeers. Mirabelle yelped and looked at Jacques. Her bodyguard turned away from the scene, visibly trembling behind the wall he huddled behind.

"Arazumi rifles," he mumbled. "They sound different from a musket. You can't mistake one for the other."

"When will they stop to reload?" Mirabelle demanded.

"They're always reloading; it's much different and faster than a musket. Just be glad you're not watching one of their rotary guns in action," Jacques said, a hoarse, mad chuckle on his lips.

"Okay, we can't do this," Mirabelle declared, stepping away from the alley and pacing. "There's another way, and better yet, since they're paying attention to this mob, they won't be focusing on where we'll be coming from. Come along, we can't waste time!"

Jacques fumbled after his captain, who made her way around the walls toward the shoreline. Staggering down to the beach, Mirabelle began swiveling her head every which way, looking for something that only she could see.

"The Arazumi have floated a chain around the shallow waters of their embassy," Jacques said, pointing to the buoys and the offending metal links peeking over the waves. "Even trying to row a boat through the shallows is a fool's errand, and besides, a guard may spot us."

"Listen, they're expecting someone to invade the harbor intelligently," Mirabelle explained, trotting towards some debris on the sand.

"So you're saying we need to invade it foolishly?"

"I'm saying we break in creatively!"

Mirabelle pulled out a broad sheet of wood, more than enough for the both of them. She even let out a small laugh of triumph when the makeshift raft floated beautifully. Mirabelle looked back at Jacques, face full of joy and excitement.

"You've gone mad, Captain."

How they made it into the embassy waters without getting shot at, Jacques would never know. They latched his sword to the raft to act as a balance and then carefully positioned themselves to stabilize the craft. It was an odd dance they did, maneuvering and staying afloat, but they did it. Jacques was even more surprised when they made it

Chapter Fifteen

through the chain with just a few coordinated footsteps and maneuvering. The embassy grew larger as they fumbled their way closer. Jacques refused to believe what he saw.

"This shouldn't be happening."

"You're right, and that's why it's happening. They didn't plan for someone to get into the harbor in the most unexpected way," Mirabelle giggled.

"You mean lunatic way."

"It's working! That's all that matters."

"Stop right there! Hands up!" someone shouted from the ramparts. Guards began to move down from the wall towards the beach. The chilling shape of rifles winked in the electric lights. Jacques and Mirabelle raised their hands and stood awkwardly on their raft.

"I believe it's stopped working, Captain," Jacques mumbled.

"We got in," Mirabelle growled dejectedly.

The next couple of minutes were full of shouting, pushing, and all in all, a jumbled, messy affair. A ring of guards stood and monitored them in the bright glare of the embassy lights. From the beach, a picket boat from the flotilla stood watch, the marines inside also clearly armed. As instructed, Mirabelle and Jacques waited in the sand on their hands and knees. Minutes passed. Mirabelle started to wonder if they were to become permanent beach ornaments.

Two guards came from the embassy, followed by a woman who Mirabelle decided wasn't a guard but couldn't figure out her occupation. The new guards radiated with annoyance. Most of the guards were irritable enough considering the circumstances, but these two looked sour enough to shrivel lemons. The taller one, a Raermak, wore a frown that extended to the tip of his beard. The shorter one drank a rather strong-smelling dark brew from a mug. It was angrily oscillating in his hand.

"Start talking," the Raermak said with a voice of stone.

There was a lot of back and forth over the next couple of minutes. Fortunately, Jacques let Mirabelle do the explaining, and there was a lot of it because the guards often repeated their questions, especially the one drinking from the mug. The Arazumi woman watched in interest the whole time and, much to Mirabelle's puzzlement, seemed to sniff the air periodically. It felt like an eternity before they allowed Mirabelle to produce the sheet of paper that had brought them here. The Arazumi woman took the note, lingered a moment longer than necessary, and then hurried it to one of the buildings.

"We expect to be compensated for that information!" Mirabelle called after her.

"Shut up," the Raermak said.

"And while you're doing that, let me explain to you what's going to happen in the next few minutes," the other guard announced, squatting down next to them to get closer. Mirabelle noticed his mug was empty. "We're going to take you away on that boat over there. They're going to take you somewhere far away, back into the city. Then you're going to leave, and you're not going to come back. By all accounts, we should have shot you both on sight since, in case you haven't noticed, the citizens aren't on their best behavior around here

Chapter Fifteen

right now. You two are alive, and you have a chance to stay that way as long as you don't come back. Am I clear?"

"Certainly, but we still did you a favor. We deserve compensation," Mirabelle replied calmly.

"That's not up to me to decide, plus we can't verify that your information is even genuine."

"This is a rather lunatic way to ask for coin, all for a fake note, don't you think?"

"The world outside is going mad, lady," the guard growled. "I don't know what to think anymore."

That strange Arazumi woman returned and, much to Mirabelle's delight was carrying a sizable purse bulging with coins. She, too knelt, by Mirabelle and handed her the hefty sack. The captain was surprised when the aide began to speak quietly to her.

"I've placed three white gold coins inside that bag. They're very valuable, extracted from Arazum's famous Stirling Coast Mines. You may find them useful for paying any debt holders you may have."

Mirabelle squinted hard at her. Questions raced through her mind as the Arazumi woman made sure she held onto the coin bag and patted her hand.

"Seems like the bosses were feeling generous today," the Raermak said in observation. "This transaction is complete, and it's more than I would have given you. Get up on your feet and get on the boat."

The better part of an hour later, Mirabelle and Jacques were unceremoniously dumped on a beach by the harbor and, more importantly, away from the embassy. The picket boat motored away, and the two were left waiting for their minds to catch up with what had just transpired.

"All those risks for a little payday," Jacques sighed, looking at the purse Mirabelle was numbly holding. "I suppose it's easier for me to do it when I'm not facing Arazumi guns."

"We got more than just coin, Jacques," Mirabelle scolded, looking at him.

"We did?" the bodyguard asked incredulously. "Pray, tell me, what else did we get?"

"Didn't you notice the way the Arazumi warships were moored at their embassy? They're all tied to their piers with their engines running. That can only mean the Arazumi are getting ready to evacuate at a moment's notice."

"So…?"

"So we'll try to run the blockade with them."

"My lady, you have gone mad, but now I'm starting to like it."

CHAPTER 16

THEIR UNIFORMS STANK OF SWEAT and spent gunpowder. Jord could smell it in his beard as well. Ears continued to ring even though the gunfire from last night was now only a memory. Feet hurt despite the well-made and equally well-traveled boots they sat in. The interior of their gauntlets felt moist and grimy. The guards looked awful, felt just as bad, and smelled even worse. It was an improvement when Jord lit his pipe and let the tobacco smoke billow into the air.

"What phase are we on now, Otto?" Jord asked wearily.

"We're on phase 'everything's buggered, stay alive, and pass the ammunition.'"

"You think anything will come of that note those sailors, ragamuffins, whatever they were, turned in last night? I can't quite decide whether to believe it or not."

"Not for us to say, at least not for now. Axle will have to decide what to do. Besides, it's not like we can be on any higher alert than we are now. I heard a rumor that the navy men are flooding the lines back to Arazum requesting we be allowed to evacuate."

"Really?" Jord asked, an eyebrow raising high enough to lift the dark circles under his eyes.

"Yes, but that's just a rumor. Now, we better go check on the wounded. Axle said anyone who can stand and operate a gun needs to be back on duty," Otto said.

"Awful business this is. I doubt any of the pups knew they were signing up for this."

"No one ever does. All they wanted to do was to look tough, maybe scare away a few hooligans, but otherwise just warm their spot on the wall and get a few marvelous stories to impress the folk back home. Then we told them they had to open fire on some maniacs in the street and stand in the line of musket fire. They didn't sign up for that; they couldn't have even imagined it because they're just children."

"You're waxing a touch eloquent there, little man."

"Sorry," Otto said quietly. "I was back in the Black War there for a moment."

"It happens to me too."

It was a small mercy that the embassy hospital wasn't a scene from the old war, but it was still a sad affair. The smell of disinfectant hung heavily in the air, almost strong enough to hide the stench of blood and gore. Surgeons and anyone who knew a thing about medicine from the ships worked like frantic bees on the wounded. Some young men confined to the beds tried to wave at Otto and Jord, and while their efforts were valiant, their wounds got the better of them.

One man sat at a nearby table and stared into the void, a space that started somewhere past his nose and ended beyond the horizon and where the universe just became endless night. If "dejection" were

Chapter Sixteen

ripped out of a dictionary and painted on a canvas, this man would have served as the model.

"Michael?" Otto inquired. The telegraph man swiveled his head haltingly, as if every muscle in his neck was brittle, and then stared right past his two superiors.

"Derek is dead."

Otto and Jord didn't reply; they just gave the sad frowns of men who had hoped for better, but were too acquainted with grief to have more optimistic convictions. The dead Otto and Jord were strong enough to mourn, but it was Michael's expression that was unnerving them. The living shouldn't look like the Abyss was poured into their head.

"They said he'd be fine and get better. So he went to sleep. He never woke up. 'Complications' they said," Michael stammered out. "You know what wasn't complicated?"

Michael raised his hands as if trying to shrug at the madness of it all. Only one hand went up; his left arm ended in a bandaged stump. The table began to clatter as Michael's limbs began to tremble violently.

"You know why I was asked to be a field telegraph man? My left hand was my dominant one. I could send a message faster and clearer than anyone else and with no errors. I wasn't even a half bad shot with my weak right hand. And now...and now..."

"You're alive, Michael," Otto said.

"Am I? Am I, though? I don't know if I can tap out a message with my right hand as well as I could with my left. This feels like a nightmare, and no matter how much I hold my eyes open, I can't wake up from it! This wasn't supposed to happen!"

"I know it wasn't," Otto said regretfully. "None of it was."

Jord and Otto left a little while later. None of the wounded would be pressed into service.

***

SETH HURRIED UP THE MOUNTAIN, hidden and out of sight, weaving between the trees. At first, it was an easy task, even without the help of his vampiric senses. Then the presence of the druids became too thick to ignore, much less avoid. Seth grumbled in frustration and then began to climb up a tree, awkwardly at first and then more smoothly, as old memories started to awaken. Soon he was bounding from tree to tree, always keeping concealed. He fought the urge to hang upside down. Again, he had standards. He wasn't a bat, dammit, and a thousand silver blades on the vampires that made that particular stereotype famous.

Up and up the slope he went, keeping in the tree branches and stopping when there were too many druids. He chewed his lips nervously as he waited for a roving band of the forest folk to move along below him. He could feel the magic in the air, and that meant Mara was in the process of initiating the final steps of her ritual. Did these poor druids know what she had in mind? Probably not. It was hard to believe they would willingly wait about on the mountain if they knew what Mara intended.

Finally, he was at the foot of the summit. Mount Letixis was hard enough to climb on foot, but it was an awful ordeal scaling it from tree to tree. The Witch Hunter took a few moments to catch his breath

264

Chapter Sixteen

and survey the scene before him. From his vantage point, he could see what remained of the Arazumi encampment, a blackened carcass that still smelled of harsh chemicals and smoke. There was also the path that led to the crater on top of the mountain. Seth grumbled when he noticed a few druids were guarding the trail. Bad luck for them, but he told himself not to feel too bad. He'd be joining them in the afterlife before too long anyway.

Within the cone of the mount, the walls were smooth, quiet, and cold. The sky above was clear and darkening. Mara stood silently while her companions drew the instructed ritual circle on the stone floor. There were a couple of things she wanted to make sure of. All the necessary ritual ingredients were more or less in place, but she needed to remove any uncertainties. Twisting her hands, she began to speak telepathically to the immense ancient. She knew what sort of creature he was, and they, for all their arrogance, could be easily manipulated.

***

SOPHIE SULKED IN HER CHAIR. The room was decent enough, but it was small, and the men arguing about her outside didn't have the decency to keep their voices down. She could catch most of what they were saying. One of the diplomats sat beside her, keeping her company. She missed Kassia. At least she was kind and didn't talk down to her. It was the ones who knew so little that assumed they were the smartest ones in the room. If someone doesn't recognize their own ignorance, they cannot truly begin the journey of learning.

"We'll keep you safe, young lady," the diplomat said, giving her a confident smile.

"Safe or imprisoned?"

"You've done nothing wrong. Why would you even suggest that we'd imprison you?" the diplomat scoffed.

"Because I can do magic and the men outside keep saying 'Miskgate Asylum.' That's where people are kept because that's what 'asylum' means," Sophie explained numbly.

"Young lady, 'magic' is a barbaric word and is beneath your station of a young woman. You will say 'anomalous activity' or nothing at all."

"But, there's magic everywhere, sir. I didn't know about my abilities until now. But, while I was on the streets, I did know that there's a much simpler, but more important magic everywhere."

"What did I just say, young–"

Sophie pouted and watched him marvel at himself while his tongue and mouth flapped, but no words came out at all. She wasn't quite sure how she did that either. She wanted him to be quiet, so now here he was: mute and bewildered.

"Real magic that everyone can do is when people take those big abstractions like Truth, Justice, Compassion, Bravery, Wisdom, Beauty—those sort of things—and make them real. You know what an abstraction is, right? When people do good things, bring beauty to life, and encourage others to do the same, it makes the world better. It brings magic into the world. That's the important magic. Do you understand?"

The diplomat stared at her aghast. Silent and jittery, he desperately began jerking his head in a nod, frantic to convey that he wanted his voice back.

Chapter Sixteen

"I'll let you speak again, but I don't want to talk anymore if that's acceptable to you?"

More frantic nodding.

Sophie let something go, and the diplomat let out a frightened squeak. Relieved to hear his voice again, he blathered something about needing water and quickly left the room. Sophie sighed. She was glad that she was friends with Kassia, Jord, and Otto. She worried about what she would have done to the building if she didn't like them.

***

OTTO STOOD WEARILY ON THE RAMPARTS, watching the battered street in front of the embassy. Periodically the cult would show up and begin chanting again but, thank the Holy, the shooting and self-immolations had stopped. By the looks of it, the Prosperous Light had more important things to worry about. Reyais was burning. Rumors ran like wildfire through the ranks, and the awful stories they told weren't far from the truth. Tersians scouts and skirmishers lurked in the city fighting with the militia, the city guard, and the sailors who had seized the harbor. Small isolated fires in the city streets and squares were beacons of tragedy as the terrified citizens turned on their neighbors. There was a monster loose in the city after all, and a fiery end awaited anyone on whom too much suspicion fell.

Otto shook his head. This had to be how the demons of old operated now. Push the right dominoes in the worst of human nature, and a whole society will happily destroy itself, all the while masquerading in the robes of righteousness and necessity.

He heard footfalls coming up the steps, too light to be one of the guards. Kassia rushed up to him and Jord, breathless and eyes flashing in the firelight.

"We have a problem," she hissed.

"What sort of problem?" Jord asked.

"I- I don't know, but there's something wrong, I can feel it. Could you get the men on higher alert?"

"Kassia, we're already frantic with paranoia," Otto said softly.

"I know, I know, but– oh no!"

Kassia immediately bolted back down the stairs and was gone before the guards could say another word. Jord and Otto glanced around, helpless with what to do with Kassia's warning. Jord frowned as he chose his next words carefully.

"She can be a little quaint at times."

"Jord, look," Otto whispered and pointed towards the courtyard. Sand was spread on the cobblestones, a habit copied from the sailors who did the same to their decks when they anticipated a battle coming. Something was disturbing the grains.

"Are those...footsteps?" Jord asked quizzically.

"They really want our miniature witch," Otto said darkly and shouldered his rifle. Thunder roared from the barrel, and they saw the sand mysteriously crater out in the shape of a man, blood spilling out of thin air.

Chapter Sixteen

The embassy exploded in violence. Guards fell screaming as plumes of spent gunpowder erupted from every direction. They couldn't see the invaders, but they were everywhere.

"Shoot at the gun smoke!" Jord roared. A bizarre firefight unfolded as guards shot at ghosts. Most of the time, a cloud of gunpowder would materialize, and another guard would fall. Sometimes blood would fountain and spill on the walls.

There was a yelp and a blood-chilling snap. Tersians materialized, ghosts becoming flesh in the blink of an eye. The Long Steel guards no longer hesitated. A more traditional and rapidly one-sided gunfight commenced as the guards hammered out their vengeance.

"Otto, go check on Sophie," Jord commanded. "There's something else I need to check on before I join you."

"Understood."

Jord stomped down the steps after Otto left. It was all going too fast. The Tersians were ruthless, but they weren't stupid. For a group of scouts to skillfully infiltrate the embassy while remaining invisible meant they needed a sorcerer to cloak them. And now their cloak was gone. Who got their sorcerer? Someone here knew something was up before everyone else did. Jord followed his memory of where that sound, the one that reminded him of the crunching of bone, came from.

His feet moved towards a dark corner of the embassy. To his surprise and horror, he could hear muffled screaming, savage growls, and a wooden crunch. Jord brought his blunderbuss up and steadied himself. Fear told him he didn't want to see whatever was around the corner. It couldn't be human. The thing in the shadows saved him the trouble. First, two halves of a staff flew from the dark and clattered onto the ground. Then came the sorcerer, landing in a heap by his staff, both wrists turned at odd angles.

"Help!" the Tersian cried. That wasn't the reaction Jord expected.

"You must help! Beast! Save me!"

"Shut up, hands in the air, and surrender!"

"Yes, yes, don't let it eat me!" the wizard blathered, raising two sad broken arms.

"I need a guard over here!" Jord said. " Watch this man and take caution. He can use magic!"

Jord saw a shadow move preternaturally fast from the dark and head into one of the buildings. His mouth dried as he waited for a subordinate to come and apprehend the Tersian. It was just a moment, but he recognized the clothes that made up the apparition's garb. Something was wearing a familiar chemist's clothes, but that's where the similarities ended.

Jord left the wizard under the angry supervision of two guards and hurried to the door where he saw that thing vanish. He found himself wondering why he had carefully pushed the door aside with the barrel of his gun. The guard didn't know what he expected to see, but somehow he knew to assume the worst.

The room was lit, but empty. There was no sign of struggle, no signs of distress; nothing looked out of place. This was one of the office buildings used by the administrative staff. A monolith of glacial ice formed in his stomach. Sophie was also in this building. He heard a

Chapter Sixteen

noise. Someone was approaching. Jord raised his blunderbuss just in time to catch Otto rounding the corner.

"All clear, Jord. Why do you have your gun pointed at me?"

"Is it, Otto? Is it all clear?" the Raermak growled.

"I just checked. What's gotten into you?"

"Better question: what's gotten into your Kassia?"

"My–? Jord, what are you talking about? We're just–"

"Shut up and stop lying to me."

"It's all right, Otto; he needs to know," Kassia said, emerging from the shadows. Jord immediately swung the gun towards her, and Otto hurriedly stumbled to block the line of fire.

"Get out of the way, little man. How long have you knowingly sheltered a monster here?" Jord snarled.

"First of all, Jord, that's unfair!" Otto protested. "Second of all–"

"What. Is. She?"

"I'm a person, Jord," Kassia scowled. "I just happen to have a fascinating case of lycanthropy."

"Werewolf?"

"Considering the different strains the virus can take, I'm blessed to have a mild version of it. Over the years, I've learned to keep it under control, and during a full moon, I keep in my room with relaxing music and a good book, so I'm not tempted to transform and rip a person's rib cage out," Kassia said and brought one of her hands into the light.

The arm and hand bulged with newfound cords of muscle but were quickly relaxing, melting away into their usual shape. The five wicked talons that jutted out from her fingertips fell out and before a minute had gone by, new ordinary fingernails grew in their place. Her hand back to normal, she brought it up and caught the two bloody fangs she spat out.

"I've committed no crimes, Jord," Kassia explained. "Yes, there were three smugglers whose necks I had to wring, but that was self-defense. When we were up on the mountain, I tore up a few druids in the shadows, but if I hadn't, the encampment would have fallen sooner. If I hadn't sniffed out that sorcerer just now, a lot more of our men would have died. I may be a werewolf, but I keep my worst impulses in check. That makes me a lot less monstrous than some normal people."

"Why did you break their limbs?" Jord asked coldly. "The druids in battle I can understand, but wringing necks and breaking arms is a curious calculation."

"If you disembowel someone with claws or rip out their throats, of course, everyone will start looking for a werewolf. But broken limbs with little if any blood? No one expects a feral werewolf to do that, much less a docile lady chemist," Kassia replied smugly.

A rumble rattled around in Jord's throat and came out as a sigh. The gun lowered, and he turned on his heels, heading back out the door.

Chapter Sixteen

"You can keep a secret, right, Jord?" Otto called behind him.

"I can keep what's going on between you two a secret; what's another one?"

"That's still just an allegation!"

"Don't push your luck, little man."

***

THE BEACH BY THE EMBASSY was stony silent or would have been if not for the lap of the waves and the tortured shrieks of the guards undergoing the amber treatment. Their unscathed comrades grimly wished that there were more wounded and fewer dead. Those who could still stand were staring daggers at a sorry dingy and its sorrier occupants. The wounded Tersians and those who surrendered were rounded up and curtly deposited within. It was flanked on either side by picket boats from the flotilla, the Arazumi marines brazenly displaying their guns while glaring at the defeated interlopers. The Tersian wizard was the last one to be dropped into the boat, both broken arms in hastily made splints. He kept yelling about a werewolf in the embassy, but no one listened to him. Guard Captain Axle spoke to the sorcerer directly.

"Good evening, you lot. Let's keep this short; it looks to me that you have just enough men who aren't bleeding, so they can row the little boat we're donating to you. This is after you've trespassed and discharged firearms in our embassy. That's an international incident, by the way. We'll also be having these strong and helpful marines tow you halfway to your armada, so you don't unduly tire yourselves before you get there. Isn't that nice of them?" Axle said, not even hiding the overchilled cheeky tone in his words. "Long Steel would also like to remind the Sultan's fleet, on behalf of Arazum, that so much peace and prosperity could be lost between our two nations over petty miscalculated ambitions, yes?"

"You don't know what you harbor, head guard," the wizard coughed hoarsely.

"I'm sorry?"

"The child you shelter. You think her just a lost girl. She is a powerful witch. More powerful than many of the sultan's long-time warlocks. Magic is chaotic fire, even when guided by strong minds. Who will guide her? You are sheltering dangerous fire, Arazumi."

"Well then, I suppose we must do our best to train her to be a good person, my good wizard."

"What? Explain!" the Tersian demanded, eyes wide with befuddlement.

"Weapons must be, as you say, kept safely harbored and inert, and the Republic does that every day. People, though, they're different. You train them and encourage them to be decent folk, and that's all you need to do with them. I'm sure that's what you meant to say, good Tersian. Well, that's enough talk and games tonight. Push off!" Axle ordered and gave the marines a wave. The men in the picket boats leaned hard on their oars and began to drag the Tersians away. Axle grinned at the wizard as his flabbergasted eyes eventually drowned in the gloom of night.

Captain Leon watched the three boats wallow through the harbor. He cared more about the marines than the Tersian captives. Yes, yes, rules of war had to be observed. It's what kept us all from becoming

Chapter Sixteen

savages. It just seemed short-sighted to prepare and be eager for war but then also expect your enemy to treat you courteously after the shooting stops.

There was also the matter of waiting to hear back from the Department of Armaments. Too much was going on, and he had requested multiple times for permission to evacuate. He even sent out another request updating the Department on the Tersian incident. That would be the straw that would break the camel's back, right?

"What else is it going to take?" Leon vented to the uncaring wind. "We can't hold the embassy any longer! We'll have to run the blockade, but we have a better chance of surviving that than holding out here losing a battle of attrition."

What would it take to run the blockade? On one hand, not every ship here was dependent on the wind and currents. Send an order out to put on full steam, and they'd outpace any ship the Tersians had. The range and firepower of his ships' cannons? They outperformed the Tersians' in every category. But he wasn't sure what would happen if a Tersian cannonball connected with the armor of his ships. Steel plating didn't mean they had immunity. Leon was convinced that even if the plates weren't punctured, they could still fracture and shower fragments into the interior. That would be bad news for sailors and sensitive equipment once that happened. The Tersians also had magic. And numbers. Numbers had a way of adding up.

"Captain, urgent telegram from the Department!" the telegraph man announced.

"Thank the Holy," Leon sighed in relief. "I bet the attack made them see the light."

"You should read it first, sir."

Leon rapidly scanned the paper. His face twisted into one of confusion. He looked back up at the radio technician.

"We're still ordered to evacuate, sir, there's that," the operator shrugged.

"Yes, and that's all well and good, but they want us to leave because of the findings from the geological survey," Leon explained.

"I just work the telegraph, sir. I don't understand rocks."

"It means they think the mountain is going to explode."

"Oh. We should probably leave, then."

"We will evacuate two days from now. We'll need to spend tomorrow processing the embassy before we leave. Let the Bureau know we've received the orders and will comply."

"Aye, sir!"

Leon hurried over to his cabin and pulled the green plumed pigeon from its cage. It was his last and emergency pigeon. A hasty note was scribbled and tied to the bird's leg before he tossed the messenger into the air and watched it fly across the harbor. Cousin Samir had to be kept up to date as well.

CHAPTER 17

THE THREE BRILLIANT COINS SHONE in Mirabelle's hand like drops from the full white moon. She had never heard of white gold before, but the Arazumi woman who gave it seemed sincere enough. And she said they would be useful for paying debts. How did she know? Was it all one strange coincidence? She kept staring at the coins. What did it all mean?

"Are those silver or white gold?" Gilroy asked, noticing his captain's intense stare.

"White gold, I'm told. How did you know?"

"I've seen it once before. A merchantman from Arazum was showing it off at a tavern one time while I was in Dhalinur. It's actually an alloy of gold and silver."

"It is?"

"Indeed. In Arazum, gold is less valuable than silver, and the Stirling Order of Knights controls most of the mining, so they have to get creative with their stocks. There's a story that a scientist from Moraine came across a vampire while doing their research deep in the heart of Gavendar. The vampire noticed the scientist's necklace and thought it was silver at first but wondered why he didn't feel any danger he normally associated with silver. The scientist told the vampire he could have her necklace, made of white gold, so long as he spared her life. The vampire took it from her and then declared he could do whatever he wished, and so he would take her gold and her life."

"What happened to the scientist?" Mirabelle asked. "She must've survived; otherwise, we wouldn't have this story."

"You're correct," Gilroy replied. "She pleaded and argued and negotiated with the vampire for about a quarter of an hour or so when the vampire noticed his hand was starting to burn. He promptly threw the necklace away, but the damage was already done. He burned to ash right before her eyes."

"Huh," Mirabelle murmured. "Interesting story." She stared at the coins again, this time in a completely different light.

***

SETH LEFT A TRAIL OF DEAD DRUIDS on his way towards the crater's rim. It bothered him, he was able to toss them aside without pause, without thought, but now that he was about to confront Mara, he found himself unsure and hesitating. He even had an impulsive thought about turning around and walking away. After all these countless years, why did she still have all this power over him? Like the undead, feelings could hobble along relentlessly long after they should have died.

The witch hunter strode down roughly chiseled stairs that hugged the interior wall of the crater. Below him were Mara and her aides. They all stood around an intricately-drawn ritual circle on the rugged stone floor. Mara's aides did not react even though he made no effort to conceal himself. Mara knew he was there even though she kept her back to him. Here he was strolling up to his fate, yet it only felt like he was walking up to greet an old friend.

Chapter Seventeen

"Greetings, Seth," Mara said.

"Greetings, Mara."

"Shall we have another dance, old friend?"

"Very well. One last dance before we step into eternity."

"Aha, I'm sorry, dear, but I fear I'll not be joining you for that," Mara chuckled.

"It's time to wake up, Mara. All things must come to an end, and for you and I, that should have been a long, long time ago. How many ages have we seen? How many lives have we stolen?"

"The difference between us, Seth, is that power seems to bother you. Very odd, especially for someone that's worn countless different masques all while holding to the role of Danaria's Chief Witch Hunter."

"The difference, Mara, is that I made my peace with death and lived accordingly."

Mara chuckled to herself, shaking her head. She turned to face him. "Foolish, sentimental man. All these years and that's never changed."

"Shall we have that last dance, Mara?"

"Let's!"

The aides did not interfere and did not dare to move as the two vampires dueled with magic as only two ancients can. Seth didn't bother reaching for his blade as he frantically raised his hands to focus the magic. Mara was matching his movements. Both dug their heels into the rock floor, anchoring themselves from the forces that were unleashed. The cascade of hostile magic erupted faster and faster. Seth howled. Flashes of light and heat cracked through the air. Eldritch noises howled within the crater. A pillar of lightning raced into the sky, and abruptly all was silent. When the dust settled and pupils adjusted to the dim light, only Mara remained standing on the crater floor.

"Such a shame, Seth. Such a shame. And now you've been rewarded for your conscience."

Suspended in the air at the very mouth of the crater was Seth, immobile and unable to protest. Mara held him trapped in an invisible cage. Wearily, he looked down at his counterpart and wondered if somehow he misremembered everything. How could they have ever been friends in those long eons past?

"That's a poor gloat, Mara," he sighed.

"And that sounds like the feeble protest of someone who knows they've lost, love."

"I still have my peace, Mara. All these centuries, and you still haven't found it."

***

DIFFERENT KINDS OF SMOKE HUNG HEAVILY in the air, and the corsairs could tell the difference between all of them. Fires from the city brought the harsh fumes of burning timber, detritus, and flesh. From the harbor and the battered waters came the smell of spent gunpowder. The aroma of pipe smoke was on the pier where the captains chose to meet. No one spoke, still processing the note that Samir Temeng provided. Behind him was Davos, who stared out at the horizon, glaring at the Tersian sails in the burning sunrise.

"I have an important question," Hernan snapped for all to hear. "Why are we to believe the information given by a navy dog? What's next? Are we all going to sign up to be Republic peons?"

"Why would he lie?" Samir asked bluntly.

"Maybe he was ordered to."

"Maybe you're stupid, *kip-kip*."

"He is stupid," Davos said bluntly. "Even if Cousin Leon is lying, and we nonetheless band together to run the blockade, we'll still stand a better chance of escaping the city than surviving a stand here."

"That's why we're proposing we all run the gauntlet behind the Arazumi," Mirabelle announced. The other corsairs quickly forgot she was the one who called this meeting. "I've seen their ships ready to leave. My men are already preparing my ship to follow in their wake."

"We have no other choice," Samir said. "Running individually means certain death. Together we have a chance of escaping with our lives."

"I'll only agree to go if we let the navy men go in first. Let them take the brunt of the Tersian fire," Hernan pouted.

"How strategically pragmatic of you, Captain Corba," Gunderson said. "Comforting to know you will happily allow your countrymen to put themselves in danger so you don't have to."

"Arazum is no longer my country, old man."

"How sad for you. Davos, I know the look of a man who is planning something. What is going on in that head of yours?" Gunderson asked.

"I have a plan, *kip-kip,* but I'll need volunteers. It's also one that the volunteers won't likely survive, but it'll help the rest of us escape. I know I want my fellow sea-clanners here to return home to Dhalinur."

"What is the nature of this plan, then?" Gunderson inquired, eyes narrowing.

"Well, the Tersians want their fortress ship back. I say we give it to them, guns blazing and all."

"But then they'll have all that blazing firepower back!" Captain Ivan protested.

"Will they? I have a plan for that. Besides, even if my plot fails, it'll take time for their sailors to get the fortress ship underway again, let alone maneuver to use their guns. Our fleet of blockade runners will hopefully be long gone by then," Davos explained.

"I volunteer," Gunderson said.

"You don't know the plan," Davos retorted.

"I volunteer nonetheless. I am getting old, and there's no bed on land that I can die sick and weak in. I will go in battle so that Archangel Vutan may find me worthy. Do not make me pull rank on you, Davos."

Chapter Seventeen

Gunderson's willingness seemed to shift the wind. First, a couple of the other captains nodded, and then others still voiced their desire to plan. Then came the captains and men who said they'd volunteer for Davos' plan so long as Gunderson would lead. It almost brought a tear to Mirabelle's eye.

"Are we really doing this? Is everyone going to cooperate on this? We'll need as many hands on deck as possible if this is going to work," Mirabelle said frantically, a smile coming to her face.

"We can't stay here. We'll lose to them on land, but we still have a chance on the sea. Also, I think we all want to bloody the Tersians for what they did to Blind Captain," Ivan said.

"Now, this hopeless plan of yours, Davos. Tell us more," Gunderson ordered.

Plans were coordinated and refined. Details were agreed upon and sorted out. Mirabelle made sure to steer them back towards the all-important goal when tempers or petty squabbles arose. None of the captains and their crews wanted to die in this place that the Holy had forgotten about. It took the better part of an hour, but the captains left for their respective ships when that was done, Gunderson joining Davos and a few others on their special mission. Mirabelle was curious, but she had more important things to worry about.

She sneaked off towards a secluded part of the beach. This sort of tryst was one she preferred to arrange during the evening or early morning, but she wasn't going to have the time, and the mermaids needed their due. She scribbled a note, jammed it into an abandoned bottle, and tossed it. She didn't have to wait long.

The mermaids came up from the water, surrounding the rock at the end of a small spit Mirabelle decided to wait on. They grinned at her like feral cats. The captain shuddered. How could these things choose to look so alluring and yet keep those vicious fangs in their mouths? Of course, it was an intimidation tactic.

"She calls again," Bluegill announced.

"What does she ask for?" Salmon sneered.

"She had better offer payment; otherwise, we may have to eat her debt," Perch said.

"I do have payment," Mirabelle declared. She reached into her pocket and pulled out a bundled-up piece of cloth. It was carefully unwrapped, and then the sun shone brightly off the metal in her hand as she held it out for the mermaids to see.

"I have a coin for each of you," she said. The mermaids jerked, shying away from it.

"Silver!" Bluegill screeched.

"No, it's white gold from Arazum," Mirabelle explained patiently.

"White gold? We've never heard of such a thing," Perch said, cautiously approaching the coin to give it a sniff. "It smells like gold."

"How much will these coins be worth then? Surely they must be valuable because they are different," Mirabelle argued. One of her hands wrapped around the hilt of her sword.

Chapter Seventeen

"They shall count for two bars each then. Your debt will be lowered by six," Perch decided, taking the coins and distributing them among her and her sisters. Mirabelle watched intently as each of the mermaids swallowed the precious metal and then turned to leave. She jumped when one of them suddenly wailed.

"Cheat! You cheat!" Salmon screamed.

The mermaids turned towards her, fangs and talons flashing. Mirabelle drew her sword and pistol but didn't move. It was one of the most upsetting things she had ever witnessed. The mermaids lost control and began to writhe and jerk violently, never getting close to her. She wished she had closed her eyes sooner.

In the end, all that was left was a growing cloud of ash floating on the water's surface and three sad skeletons laying derelict in the sand. Mirabelle sighed as she returned her weapons to their place and waited for her body to stop trembling. The waves beat on, and the surf called to the gulls overhead. Steady once more, she got up and waded in the shallows until she plucked each coin from the muck. There was nothing more to be done here. She made her way back to the ship.

"You should never have tried to take more," she said to the cold bones.

She found the ship buzzing with activity when she returned. The men were working in tandem to get the sails ready and the lines in place. It was all one big ballet of industry. Jacques supervised her orders to prepare for departure. She wasn't disappointed with what she saw.

"Report, Jacques."

"Everything is going splendidly, Captain. Are you all right? You look a little pale; you're not falling ill, are you?" Jacques asked curiously.

"I'm fine, Jacques. No, of course I'm fine! I have a good feeling about this. We'll get through this blockade and I think we can see it as a fresh start," Mirabelle said, a cheeky grin starting to roll out on her face.

"If you say so. The rigging and sails have been seen to, we have fresh sand for the decks, and the cannons and powder are prepared for a moment's notice. Morale is high, Captain. You can even tell Gilroy is feeling confident because he's doing his silly little jig," Jacques said.

"Yes, I can tell," Mirabelle said, watching her pilot do his personal odd quickstep. Gilroy swore it's what kept his limbs and body limber all these years.

"You know, Captain, I don't know how this is going to work, but I'm feeling good about this," Jacques said quietly.

"That's good. Now let's just hope the winds remain in our favor tomorrow morning."

***

Regent Iskander sat on his throne, his face stony and immobile. The nobles in the Palace were useless with fear and pettiness. The only thing they worried about more than their personal hoards were their own individual lives. He could hear them, whispering about which of their counterparts they'd gladly throw to the angry mobs if it increased their own chance of surviving. Never mind the fact that the populace of the city seemed more concerned with escaping or turning

Chapter Seventeen

on each other rather than making a dedicated effort to storm the Palace. Accusations began to fly in venomous whispers. The pure white marble of his Palace seemed to darken in the hostile air. Slowly at first, but growing in speed, he could hear the nobles turning against him. Fools.

There was another voice in his head. Old magic, telepathy. The witch who had fled to the city talked to him, daring to negotiate with him. He didn't care for her designs, her plots, but she did promise that if he traded her that one life, that one small girl she created so much trouble over, he could keep his hoard. And oh, how many years he had spent cultivating this pile of treasure.

He could do it all over again, if he needed to. He could begin somewhere else with a different persona. However, the defiance in the room, the insolence in the witch's tone, it was all too much for him. He deserved respect. He was more significant than these worms. Perhaps the world needed a reminder of the olden days. These young insects needed to be made an example of. Iskander stepped up from his throne. The nobles abruptly became quiet and looked at him.

Iskander's body began to twitch violently, unnaturally, impossibly as he stepped confidently down the dais. Quiet gave way to gasps and gasps turned into screams as his form changed and then finally, his skin ripped and was discarded like an old rag.

He was surprised no one had accused him of it earlier, but people these days thought legends were mere stories, myths to amuse children that couldn't possibly serve as a warning. An old creature, he was compulsively amassing riches to the detriment of a whole society, yet no one in all these years had likened him to a dragon. No dragon slayer came forward to stop him and now, it was too late.

Iskander torched the Palace with a mighty breath of flame and then crashed through the ceiling to take to the skies. Those petty baubles could be replaced; terror was the new currency he desired now. The new age would learn to fear dragons again.

***

IT WAS THE EARLY HOURS of the morning; the skies were dark as night, but the embassy swarmed with activity. Streams of personnel emptied the ramparts and offices of their contents and fed the ships moored at the piers. The Republic was obsessive about its equipment and documents. Drawers were pulled out of cabinets and tables left upturned on the floor to ensure they were empty lest a single secret be left behind.

One of the secrets to be evacuated also necessitated a heavy escort. Jord and Otto led a squad of eight men, two lines of four standing parallel to each other. Sophie stood in the center, a bit bewildered that it required so many Arazumi to walk her to the ships. She sighed and wished she was back in her bed.

"Squad, move with the objective," Jord said for all to hear and leaned down to Sophie. "Keep close, pup."

"Mhm."

It was going to be a short walk. Merely a stroll across the courtyard, down to the beach, along a pier and up to the research vessel. It would certainly be much shorter than that disastrous march through the city. Sophie wished they'd let her amble along on her own; she'd get there much quicker without a herd of guards crowding around her.

"Off we go then," Otto said.

Chapter Seventeen

They had made it across the courtyard when they heard a noise in the wind. A shout from the ramparts made the men jump and look around. Jord and Otto, hearing the noise, looked overhead. Eclipsing the stars in the sky, a massive, chilling shadow hurdled towards them.

"It can't be," Jord said, eyes wide in the moonlight.

"Well, here's something we don't have a protocol for," Otto groaned.

A nightmare made flesh and scale crashed into the courtyard, knocking the junior guards aside like scattered toys. Jord moved on instinct and shot at the saurian face he had only heard about in stories. A draconic arm made of scales like shields swatted him aside.

"Sophie, run," Otto hissed and began to empty his magazine at the dragon. The behemoth ignored him. Muscles thick as industrial cables moved the dragon's thundering weight at surprising speed and snatched up the fleeing child.

"Fire! Everyone, open fire!" Jord shouted, struggling to get back onto his feet. Guns lashed out like spears, bullets blossoming in clouds of sparks when they struck the ancient plates. The dragon turned and stood on its hind legs. It was now the tallest thing in the embassy, and it let out a roar that deafened the night. Smoke sprouted from its nostrils like twin geysers. The fusillade quickly wavered.

"By the Holy, he's going to flame," Jord exhaled.

A rolling boom erupted from the shore. Fire and smoke exploded off the dragon's back and the creature flinched, doubling over from the sudden violence. Back in the harbor, one of the guns of the *Defiance* vented smoke from the barrel. The embassy unexpectedly became quiet. For a moment even the dragon seemed unsure of what to do next.

The monster whipped its mighty wings like echoing thunder and the creature was gone. After a moment, it was abruptly still, and with only bruises and empty shell casings to show for their troubles, the guards began to gather themselves.

"Bloody Abyss, what was that?" one of the junior guards cussed.

"We all saw that, right? That actually happened, right?"

"Help me out, Otto," Jord rumbled, painfully nursing an arm that had become one singular bruise. "What does the book say about this?"

"It says," Otto paused and looked out into the unforgiving night. How could something so monstrous just disappear? "It says 'mission failed and contract breached due to anomalous events.'"

"Bugger that," Jord retorted, stomping towards the gates. "I'm getting Sophie back." Otto stared at him aghast as the giant stormed towards the gates. Thoughts began to jumble together in Otto's head, and he rushed after him.

"Jord, I care about her too but the ships are leaving. Our primary objective is with the embassy personnel, and how do you propose to track a dragon down on your own?"

"What do you know about losing a kid, Otto? You've never lost one and I'm not losing another," Jord shot.

"Jord, she's an anomalous individual. She's a witch. A potent one," Otto said, trying to catch up with the giant.

Chapter Seventeen

"I'm going to sodding kill that dragon!"

"Jord, by the Holy, listen to me! The Defiance hit that dragon with one of its main guns, and it barely flinched. What's your blunderbuss going to do? Now, think about Sophie. You saw what she did to those Tersians. If there's anyone here who has a chance against the dragon, it's her. Besides, you'll be killed out there by yourself!"

Jord stopped and became quiet. He trembled with rage, knuckles white around his gun while his internal debate threatened to rattle his head apart. Finally, he turned around.

"You're lucky I trust your judgment, little man," he said, voice shaking with rage while he jabbed Otto in the breastplate with his finger. "But you're right. The little pup is going to have to hunt on her own."

"She can do it, Jord. Now, we better get back to the ships because the last train is leaving the station."

In the shadows, teams of marines and navy technicians began unspooling long cables from one of the gunboats. They led the wires back to the abandoned buildings. More men followed behind them, and they carried heavy packs and were eerily very careful with them.

"It still doesn't feel right leaving her," Jord said.

"She'll find a way back. At least this way the diplomats won't be tempted to toss her into Miskgate Asylum."

"Hmm," Jord sighed. Whether deliberately or by reflex, he rested his gun on his shoulder as if he were on dress parade. He began to whistle.

It was one of the old war songs they played before the men marched off to fight in the Black War.

"Steel in name, steel in soul," Otto said. "Until Vutan calls us or we go home."

***

THE DRAGON SOARED THROUGH THE COLD AIR, wind roaring over his now tattered wings and roughened scales. Fury coursed through his veins. He could smell the toxic copper on his plates, and the surprise explosion the humans unleashed on his back still seemed to rumble in his bones. Where did they learn to do that? How did they release that kind of power? Something told him it was something utterly apart from magic, which made the hatred in him burn all the hotter still. Humans should've forgotten the power of copper. They shouldn't be allowed to have that kind of power. How did they do it? Why did they have to take it back?

Iskander tightened the grip on the human worm still in his grasp and brought her up to one of his massive, glaring eyes. How dare that witch. How dare those upstart humans. How dare everyone! His whole kingdom, his whole hoard, all for this tiny speck?

"You," Iskander boomed through vocal cords used to giving commands. "You are the cause of all this trouble. If not for you, the witch would not have come here."

Sophie's eyes, wide with shock from first being captured by a dragon and then being hauled high into the air, suddenly lit up with anger at her captor.

Chapter Seventeen

"I was just living my life! A normal life! It– it was you monsters who decided I was trouble! I had nothing, and now you've all shoved this on me!"

"I should kill you," Iskander said. "Kill you first and then, burn the witch for daring to threaten me."

Sophie's anger hit a snapping point. These creatures that meddled with her life had had years to learn their powers; she was still fumbling about trying to control hers. If harnessing magic was like playing with fire, Sophie did the equivalent of rolling a dry, petrol-soaked hay bale onto a pyre.

There was an explosion. A sonic blast ripped the branches off the nearby treetops on the mountain. A dragon's head, arm, and body landed in three very different locations, each slamming into the ground with the sound of thunder. Still clutched in the arm, Sophie struggled, pushed, and finally wrestled herself free. Dazed but in one piece, the girl found the lights of Reyais in the distance and staggered towards it.

"I don't know how I did that, and I'm not even sure I should have survived," she muttered to herself, her steps steadying and becoming more sure. "I think my guardian angel may have been looking over me."

Somewhere on the after side, Philip's ghost let out a celebratory whoop.

***

A sacrifice of the masses. A sacrifice of an immense ancient. A sacrifice of a powerful young life. That's what her ritual called for.

293

It's what was going to bring her immortality. All her plotting was to ensure the ingredients would be there to complete the ritual. So she cast the runes and watched.

Mara stared at the bone runes she threw to the floor. The dragon, the immense ancient, was carrying the powerful young life in his talons. They were headed towards her, right here at the mouth of the crater, and then the dragon inexplicably stopped. She watched his life fade. That wasn't a problem, she was probably going to have to kill him anyway, and regardless, his life was sacrificed according to the ritual. But now that child was free once again.

Mara scowled. She wanted to be sure. But she was standing on a lot of destructive power, enough power that would assuredly sacrifice the masses. It was a risk she was going to have to take and really, how much of a risk was it? Undoubtedly, the young life would die with the masses.

The witch stepped into the middle of the ritual circle she drew and then clenched a fist. She began to chant. The ground started to fracture around her; cracks glowing orange and red crept in every direction around her. Only the ritual circle remained untouched. Up above her, still suspended in his invisible prison, Seth looked down and smiled.

"Are we parting ways now, Mara? Is this goodbye?"

"It is, Seth. Take comfort in the fact that I'll do my best to remember that you amused me, at least."

"So you say, Mara. So you say. I still think we'll be greeting each other again soon enough."

Mara stared at him, her face hardening by degrees. The glow all around her reached a crescendo. A roar started to rise up the crater. Liquid fire began to climb up the walls.

"Goodbye, Seth."

The mountain became a volcano.

CHAPTER 18

THE EMBASSY WAITED WITH A SILENCE that practically loomed within its tiny enclave of Reyais. Frantic with their personal errands, the marine teams began to rush back towards the pier and board the gunboat. A naval petty officer and marine sergeant kept track of the squads reporting back. The navy man shook his head.

"We need to hurry or we'll fall behind schedule."

"It would probably go a lot faster if they didn't cut the power. Doing their jobs in the dark with only electric torches isn't easy. Or safe," the sergeant said irritably.

"Protocol is protocol."

The men grew quiet at the sound of footsteps pounding up the planks. One of the radiomen hurried to deliver a message. Even in the dim light, the two officers could see that the serviceman was pale.

"The captain says you need to get the teams back on the ship within ten minutes. We'll be taking in the lines, and the captain is not keen on leaving anyone behind."

"That's a pretty tall order. Several teams still need to complete their tasks," the sergeant replied.

"The timetable just moved up on account of what the lookout spotted a moment ago."

"And what was that, radioman?" the petty officer asked. The messenger said nothing but pointed at a spot in the distance behind them. The marine sergeant blanched and then frantically leaped into action.

"Finish up your objectives, men! We are leaving! Rig the last of it and get back to the ship! Now!"

"We haven't secured all the wires, sir!" someone cried from the direction of the office building.

"Throw the last of the packages and hope for the best! We need to get out of here now! Double time, men!"

The officers counted the men sprinting aboard the ship and, when the last man was accounted for, hurried aboard as well. Mooring lines slipped off the bollards, and the gunboat rumbled with newfound power. The vessel pulled deeper into the harbor and behind it trailed the long cable that snaked and branched into the embassy buildings. Finally, the line became taut and promptly snapped, a sharp crack echoing through the air. Across the waters, the embassy began to explode, the individual structures within blossoming like fiery clouds before withering away, leaving only sad ruins in their wake. Soon all that was left were the heavy walls, and those were going to be Reyais' problem.

Jord and Otto watched the demolition display with passing interest back on the Defiance. Otto slurped a mug of coffee with a jittery hand. Jord flipped open a pocket watch and squinted hard at the dials, trying to understand what he saw in the starlight.

"Do we always blow up our buildings when we leave?" he asked.

Chapter Eighteen

"Only when the locals evict us without advance notice," Otto said.

"Also, I might be reading the time wrong, but I think that happened a little ahead of schedule."

"Look above the city."

"Above? Ain't nothing there but the mountain and...oh."

Mount Letixis was burning.

***

SOPHIE HURRIED ALONG AT A LIGHT TROT. She didn't dare go any faster in the poor light. The lights of Reyais still seemed days away, but she didn't like the noise she heard from the mountain.

The air was getting warmer. Sophie saw smoke in the air but wasn't sure where it was coming from. Heat suddenly broiled her back, and an unnerving glow lit the ground. Breathless, Sophie turned around. A river of fire rushed towards her.

She began to sprint, frantically running where she could see, and tried to make it to a side where she would no longer be in the lava's path. The molten stream never seemed to let it happen, either getting wider or moving too fast. Sophie realized she couldn't keep this up for much longer.

She came upon a large boulder, one that would allow her to stand above the lava flow, and she fled to its farthest end. Just in time, too, because the lava almost had her. She watched the molten stream tumble pass and felt the intense heat on her skin. Now she had a different problem. She wasn't going to incinerate in an instant anymore, but now she faced the reality of slowly being baked to death.

"Think, think, think," she repeated under her breath. It looked like magic was her only option left. She only exploded things before this, and exploding lava would just fill the air with fragments of white-hot rock flying in unpredictable directions. No, she needed to do something else.

Teleportation? She never tried that before and something, a grim intuition cold in the pit of her stomach, told her she had to get it right on her first try. She couldn't afford to lose her nerve now. She could feel the blisters gnawing and multiplying on her legs, which meant her time was running out.

Sophie took a series of deep breaths and concentrated. There was a pop, like the world's largest cork pulled from a house-sized bottle. The boulder was empty.

***

HECTOR SIGHED. He was exhausted, the night kept dragging on, and there didn't seem to be an end in sight. Whole streets were barricaded, and their occupants shot arrows, musket balls and threw rocks at whoever got close. Not even the badge of a city guard provided safety, and Hector suspected it sometimes made it worse. Then the cult members declared that the parasites, the Arazumi, and the corsairs, had left. The embassy and harbor were abandoned, and now prosperity could finally come to Reyais. Prosperity could wait, Hector thought. He wanted order restored to the city he had spent his whole life in.

Chapter Eighteen

"Sir, you should see this," one of his men said, leading him towards the channel that shepherded the Diphon through the city.

"Have you ever seen the stream go dry, sir?" the man asked.

"Can't say that I have. Why?" Hector grunted.

"Because look, it is."

Hector's mouth became parched. The Diphon, always bloated with water, or mud if you lived further down the city, was bare. All that remained was the sad streambed and the forgotten refuse of the years that had been dropped in. Hector began to tremble.

"What's wrong, sir?"

"What's wrong? Screw me, did none of your grannies tell you the stories?"

"I hated my granny and didn't listen to a word she said. I was relieved when she finally dropped dead, sir," one guard admitted.

"Never had one," another said.

"I might have one, but–"

"Shut up, shut up, I get it; you lot didn't hear the stories. Listen, the last time the Diphon dried up, Mount Letixis erupted," Hector explained and then looked back at the mountain. His men did the same, and their faces fell at once.

"By the Holy, it's leaking burning rivers!"

"All that smoke coming from its top, that can't be good! What do we do, sir?"

The mountain unexpectedly bellowed. A head-splitting roar stormed down the slopes, and the cobblestones quaked under them. The guards struggled to keep their footing, staggered, and then steadied themselves when the tremors subsided.

"We have no choice, men; we must evacuate the city," Hector said.

The men protested. They made noises of disbelief and voiced their confusion. Hector stood quiet for a moment but began to march off, realizing what lay ahead of them. His dumbfounded men followed, and Hector waited until they were silent again.

"Not everyone remembers the stories, but they all warn that most of the fire from the mountain will fall down on the city. That's what happened last time there was an eruption and the time before that. It's the mountain's shape. We need to get as many people as we can far away from here. Come along now! There's got to be some ships left in the harbor we can commandeer."

The guards led a forlorn exodus of sorts. Folk of all kinds began to gather around them. Some had to be persuaded, and others simply sought shelter in numbers. In the end, Hector soon had a swollen posse that needed organizing.

Small dirty comets began to rain down around them. The volcanic rock made terrifying pops when they crashed into the ground or buildings. The refugees began to gather shields, boards, and any sort of cover they could carry. One of the guards looked down into the empty streambed of the Diphon again.

Chapter Eighteen

"Oh."

"Oh, what?" Hector grumbled.

"The Diphon is glowing, sir. I think it's on fire."

Hector poked his head out to see. The Diphon was now a stream of molten rock, a canal of broiling heat, and it glowed more angrily than a blacksmith's forge. The old man felt fear in his heart and found himself fighting back tears. What was happening to his home? Reyais wasn't merely slipping from his grasp; it was deconstructing itself in ways he never imagined. All he ever wanted was some peace and quiet in his small part of the city, and now he couldn't even have that. Memories boiled away with the lava flowing past him.

"We need to hurry," Hector said and picked up the pace. The people hustled to keep up with him.

The harbor was a picture of abandonment. Small sea craft rocked at their moorings while pumice continued to clatter around them. The corsairs and their ships were gone, but a few stragglers could be spotted in the distance, their sails catching the wind on a departure route.

"Orderly fashion, everyone," Hector hollered. "Keep together so you can keep your heads covered. We'll go boat by boat and make sure as many people can get safely aboard. Do as you're told, and we can all leave safely."

The old sheriff made good on his word. Vessels with adequate coverings were prioritized and then boarded by just enough people to remain sea-worthy. Hector was impressed. He expected it to be a lot more difficult, like everything else in this city. Instead, people did as they were told without question or complaint. Where was this sort of cooperation during the rest of his very long career?

"That's all of us, sir," his lieutenant said as they prepared the last boat. "Let me help you aboard, sir."

Hector pulled out his pipe, filled it with his best tobacco, which admittedly wasn't all that good, and lit it. He let out a smoky, satisfied sigh.

"You all go on. This is my home. I'll try to get others to safety."

"You're alone, sir, and you don't have anything to protect your head!" his lieutenant protested.

"I still have my helmet," he retorted. "Now, off with you. Keep the people safe!" Hector said, kicking the boat off with his foot before settling to watch them drift away. Tobacco smoke trailed into the night sky as lava boiled the Diphon and rocks rained from the sky. Hector turned and left. He didn't know where he was going; all he knew was that he was a free man. Tomorrow was unlikely, and all he cared for was drifting away with the smoke. He was a dying man, and there was nothing left for him to pine for.

A smile spread across his face as he returned to the old watch station. Yes, the world was burning, but he had nothing more to live for, so it all felt like a fitting, poetic end. He was a cat finding a comfortable place to curl up for the last time.

A boulder, wreathed in flames, crashed through the watch house and set the building alight. Hector felt the heat on his face, and in a moment, his courage, that unyielding pillar all these long years, finally failed him.

Chapter Eighteen

He had to leave. He had to get as far away as possible. Ass, the team's donkey, brayed in panic at her post. He couldn't leave her there; she worked too hard for the team just to be left to burn. Hector rushed over, unhitched her from the post, and mounted up, driving the pack animal through the dying streets.

Hector never thought of himself as a man who would whimper or get teary-eyed at the sight of so many houses burning, but the sky was raining stones, the stream was on fire, and everything he knew was turning to ash. The world was ending, his world was ending, and there wasn't a single place to rest his head anymore. The east gate, long neglected, was abandoned and unblocked. The old sheriff fled the city, the past painfully wrenched from his grasp to a future he could not know.

And so it was that doom came to Reyais, just not in the way so many claimed it would.

***

MARA'S WORLD FILLED WITH HEAT and the colors of red, orange, and yellow. Magma flowed around her protective cocoon. Her body was a ball of magic and light, changing and on the verge of fully transforming. Just one last thing, and then she could have immortality. The protective circle she drew was holding, and yet doubt began to chew at her mind. Everything had gone according to plan up till now, what else was there to wait for? How long was the young life going to hold out? It wasn't as if that little mouse of a girl could have escaped. Yes, she was a powerful young life, but she was untrained, unsupervised, and most of all, unsupported.

The minutes dragged on, the magma glowed all around her, and she wondered how long it would take. She wished she could cast the runes again, but those had burned away along with her selfless aides, the druids, and Seth. Only she remained. She told herself to wait.

Her finely tuned sense perceived the thump of a distant magical discharge. Powerful magic. Mara ground her teeth. While she didn't know the details, she knew enough to realize that was the powerful young life doing...something. Something happened, and yet Mara remained unchanged. Her mind screamed. The child had escaped.

Bright, translucent cracks began to form in her protective barrier. Caught in a limbo state, Mara shrieked as she expended magic to hold up the barrier, magic she needed to transition to immortality, magic she couldn't afford to spend. Several meters of molten magma surrounded her, and now it was threatening to entomb her. The doubt chewed and gnawed and swallowed her. It didn't matter if the magma hardened or not. She was already buried but not quite dead.

CHAPTER 19

A SHOAL OF STEEL BEHEMOTHS lumbered through the waves, dark plumes of smoke rising from their funnels. The cloud of volcanic ash snaked through the winds above like the finger of Brother Grinn. The Arazumi squadron had no choice but to follow its gesture.

Captain Leon stood at the bridge, surveying the sea before him, and was surprised at himself. In a few minutes, there was going to be smoke and fire and death, and all he could think about was his old tricorn sitting in his cabin. It was a relic of his days as a privateer, and his head itched to replace the regulation cap on his head for that beloved hat. Alas, formalities had to be observed. He was a collared navy dog now. He allowed himself one privilege: he had his old sea blade at his hip.

"Do you think that will be of any use in the coming battle?" someone asked him. Leon looked over to see Mr. Cooper pointing at his cutlass. Leon fought the urge to scowl at the man. He had been fighting the reaction ever since the cretin stepped on his ship.

"You never know; we could be boarded."

"Do you suspect that to be a likely possibility?" Mr. Cooper asked, genuinely curious.

"Mr. Cooper, there's a maxim that a lot of Arazum's fighting men have been repeating ever since the Black War: 'Never underestimate the locals,'" Leon sighed.

"We have many technical advantages over the Tersians," Cooper replied.

"Do you have an answer for magic?"

"It's called 'anomalous activity,' Captain."

"I'll take that as a 'no.'"

"I have a further inquiry if you're done, captain? I've heard that there's a rather large squadron of, let's not be delicate, corsairs from Reyais following us, and yet you've only placed our gunboats between the Tersians and us. Shouldn't the corsairs also be a security concern?"

"Mr. Cooper, I thought you were confident in our technical advantages?"

***

ADMIRAL ORUZ WATCHED ALL OF THE SIGNAL FLAGS rising and falling among his ships. The sailors could scarcely keep up with all the information. Oruz wasn't surprised. They saw the fire and smoke coming from the mountain earlier in the night. Of course, the prudent were going to flee to their ships and try to run the blockade. Several of his sailors stood interpreting the signals and, in turn, clacked overworked abacuses firmly in their grasps. The signals brought in sighting reports and numbers. Oruz didn't need to see the final sum.

"They're all fleeing together. Very well coordinated of them."

Chapter Nineteen

"Do you think so, Admiral?" one of the sailors asked. "We never did get a good verification on the number of corsairs in the harbor. For all of them to band together like that-"

"It's what the corsairs would have done, the ones that matter, anyway. And they're following the Arazumi, letting them take the brunt of our fire. Very clever of them."

"The Arazumi aren't our primary objective, sir. We could order the fleet to ignore them."

"Alas, the Sultan was very clear in his orders, and we do not have permission to modify them. No one is to leave Reyais until we get our fortress ship back. And look at the wind. It's a southeast wind that favors them, and they know we'll be at a disadvantage because we need to sail into it to intercept them," Oruz observed, unable to keep himself from smiling.

"Admiral, a lookout has spotted a ship separate from the others. You may want to see for yourself, several degrees east of the corsairs," a soldier perched on the rigging announced. Oruz promptly produced his spyglass and scanned the sea. He stopped and stared.

"That's...that's the fortress ship! That's our stolen ship!"

"Aye, admiral! Do you think they're hoping to offer it to us and be let off without punishment?"

"I think it's a trap. Order the nearby ships to approach it carefully and not to board it until I've personally observed it myself," Oruz commanded. He noticed one of his signalmen grimace uncomfortably.

"Is something wrong, sailor?" Oruz demanded.

"This report just came in, sir; Sorcerer Doruk has ordered his ship to intercept it. Captain Erdem and several others have joined him as well."

Oruz knew Doruk. He knew that the ambitious wizard would have long ago summoned a wind to drive his ship towards the enemy and only then run up the signals to announce his intentions. By now, it would be too late to reach the sorcerers. Veins popped out on his fist, and the admiral slammed his spyglass into the railing.

"Damn them," he shouted. "Damn them all to the Abyss!"

***

CAPTAIN GUNDERSON MADE SURE the many, many blades on him were properly secured but easily within reach. His shield was strapped to his arm, and his ax was comfortably in his grasp. The familiar weight of the sword at his waist made him smile. Below him was the fortress ship. Davos had put him in command of this mad mission. Overhead only half the sails were in use, forcing the Tersians to come to them. With him was a ship full of what he could only comfortably describe as the callous and insane. Peg-legged Mad Marcus was at the helm, Sangil and his gang called the Iron Butchers manned the guns, while eagle-eyed Jan the Spider cleaned his musket up in the rigging. The rest of the volunteer crew knew they were headed for a suicide mission and didn't care. They all had a reason for their death wish.

Gunderson saw the Tersian sails in the distance, and a grim rictus came to his face. He raised his arms to the heavens and banged his shield and ax together three times. It was a traditional Raermak

Chapter Nineteen

invocation of Archangel Vutan. In the olden days, Vutan was the chief of the Raermak pantheon, and then missionaries from Arazum came bearing the word of the Holy. The Raermaks converted but insisted that their old gods bore an uncanny resemblance to the angels of the Holy. Vutan had to be the Archangel of Justice who ensured righteous judgment was met. The Arazumi missionaries enthusiastically agreed, surrounded by so many swords, spears, and axes. And now, to this day, many Raermaks and quite a few Arazumi called to Vutan on the eve of battle to watch them.

"Ready the cannon and powder, lads!" Gunderson called gleefully and beat his shield three times more. "Not long before those self-righteous hypocrites are in cannon distance."

The men on the top deck checked their weapons one final time and readied their boarding pikes. Gunderson heard the door behind him being nailed shut. It led to the lower decks. This didn't bother him. It was part of the plan, after all.

***

THE *DEFIANCE* AND HER SQUADRON of gunboats formed the vanguard of the Arazumi flotilla. Suddenly, the warships turned hard on their rudders and fanned out to meet the approaching Tersians off their port side, the flank bearing down hardest on their flotilla. The gunboat on the extreme end of the line began spewing thicker, oily smoke from her funnels. One by one the other gunboats started to do the same until a sable smog lingered on the restless waves. The civilian ships slipped into the oily curtain and were lost from sight. The warships turned again to keep up with their charges. Their guns remained fixed on the Tersians.

Eventually, the positions shifted, and the Tersian fleet was no longer fighting the wind. The behemoths of wood and sail gathered in speed, rigging creaking with newfound power. At five kilometers, each Arazumi warship fired off a single ranging shot. It was the only warning the Tersians were going to get. The Tersians, in turn, opened their gun ports, and cannons slid out with the rumble of heavy wheels on planks.

At three kilometers, strange racks mounted at the center of each Arazumi warship swung to face the sea, and mysterious canisters dropped into the waves. Lines of bubbles began to form ominous wakes on the surface, hurrying towards the Tersians. Soon vessels were exploding when the white path met them, great geysers of water, wood, and cloth erupting towards the sky before the stricken ships wobbled in mortal distress. Unmoved, the Tersian armada continued to close in, ignoring the dramatic fate of its sinking comrades.

Leon and Cooper watched the torpedoes launched by the *Defiance* race towards their Tersian targets. Cooper was just as interested in the lecture he was giving the veteran captain.

"The gunboats are equipped with the old version IV torpedoes. We've just launched the newer prototype version V. They're faster, have a larger fuel tank, carry a more explosive payload, and—"

"Are they by any chance heavier than the reliable version IVs?" Leon inquired.

"Hm? Well, yes, they are. Why do you ask?"

"Because I just watched all four of those torpedoes swim right under the targets we sent them towards," Leon glowered, turning to glare at Cooper. "And, this is the reason why creating overly imaginative

Chapter Nineteen

weapons and then, testing them on the battlefield gets us in trouble each and every–"

Leon's rant was interrupted when a giant Tersian man o'war, one that was behind the Defiance's target, encountered the new torpedo. A watery explosion ripped through the warship, and it began to list dangerously to one side. Cooper looked ecstatic. Leon was less than pleased. Ignoring the egg on his face, he pushed the mouthpiece of the new wired headset closer to his lips and gave the only command he had left.

"All ships: fire!"

He watched his warships bellow fire and metal at the Tersians. When the shells struck, gaping wounds opened on the wooden hulls. Still, more ships came to intercept them, more sailors ready to catch a shell for their Sultan. Leon tried to imagine the confusion gripping the poor men at this moment. They were being devastated at ranges they never imagined possible. Over his headset, despite the heavy static, Leon could hear the brazen confidence in his fire directors' voices.

"They haven't seen Tersian magic yet," Leon said forlornly.

Right on time, the first Tersian ship, a swift-moving frigate with a generous arsenal of guns, blinked out of formation. A second later, right between the battle lines, a chaotic tangle of wooden planks, rope and twisted metal materialized and began its journey to the bottom of the sea.

"Is that the Tersian anomalous activity you were so worried about, Captain?" Cooper cackled.

"Quiet, you fool!" Leon hissed. "There's plenty more of them!"

Suddenly, a handful of Tersians was all around them. The floor beneath Leon shifted fast, the helmsmen quickly turning to avoid a massive man o'war dead ahead of them. Cooper abruptly blanched, backing away from the railing.

"Captain, what's the effective range of Tersian cannon?"

"Less than half a kilometer."

"And how close would you say they are now?"

"Close enough to be worried."

***

GUARDS FLETCHER AND CLEMSON MANNED their posts on the deck of *Serene*. High above them, the forest of antennae hummed, a dense web of invisible messages running to and fro along their lengths. Fletcher and Clemson couldn't help themselves from watching the naval battle in the distance.

"I'm glad those naval boys know how to aim," Clemson remarked, licking his lips with a dry tongue. "The Tersians just keep coming."

"They've been firing for quite a while now, right?" Fletcher said numbly.

"What are you getting at, Fletch?"

"Well, when you listen to the Black War vets, they said the battles would always go our way up until the ammunition ran out. How much ammo can a ship hold, anyway?"

Chapter Nineteen

The two guards fell silent before Clemson decided to break it. "Naval shells are a lot larger than bullets, aren't they?"

They heard a sound, like the ripping of air under the edge of a lightning strike. Suddenly, right beside the Serene was a Tersian frigate. The guards saw the cannons bristle in their gunports. Clemson had just enough time to scream before the breeze was drowned out by suffocating cannon smoke and the roar of guns.

Fletcher opened his eyes, the haze of smoke still heavy around them. A quick mental checklist reported that all his body bits still seemed attached and in working order. He shakily got to his feet.

"Fletch, am I dead?" Clemson cried from the floor.

"You're still talking, you idiot."

"I'm not bleeding or missing anything, am I?"

"Not from what I can see."

"Is it safe to get up?"

There was a shriek of tortured metal above them. The communication lines began to fall and collapse into each other, forming a tangle of arcing rods and wires. They held their breaths until the cacophony died down. The humming stopped, and with it the lifeline transmissions they had back to the Republic.

"Oh, for the love of the Holy, Clemson, get up now!" Fletcher shouted.

"I don't think it'll ever be safe to get up!" Clemson wailed.

"You need to get up; the Tersians are getting ready to board us!"

The claws of grappling hooks were visible on the wooden deck. Tersians on the frigate were fighting to haul their ship closer. Swivel guns continued to pour fire into the Serene, causing deadly ricochets when they struck the metal plating and shattering glass windows. Long Steel guards emerged onto the deck. Rifles barked and began pelting the Tersians in turn. Yet, they kept coming, determined to cross the ropes. Tersian swivel guns and muskets answered the Arazumi rifles. The Long Steel men knew to keep their heads down. A musket ball was far more primitive than their copper sheathed bullets but just as deadly all the same.

The Tersians on the rope were about to make it aboard when an arrow impaled each, dropped from the sky like the wrath of Vutan. The guards looked up towards the crow's nest and saw the distant figure of Siggy, the Comstock Night Rider, who had decided that would be the best place for her. Her aim was deadly and never wavered.

"We need to cut those hooks, or we'll to have to murder a boatload of Tersians," Fletcher yelled. "And we don't have the ammo for that."

Several guards rushed forward, more confident now with Siggy helping them. One by one, the ropes tore off, Long Steel men paying in blood to cut them. The last one bogged down into a standstill, both sides unable to gain ground.

"Stop hesitating, you idiots," someone shouted. Fletcher turned to see Garret Blauestein, his fluttering half cap cutting a dashing scene but contributing nothing up until he shouldered his repeater. The gun began to pour bullets at the Tersians. Fletcher found it to be a waste of ammunition, all noise but no hits, but it kept the Tersians' heads down, and that was enough to allow them to rip off the last hook. The

Chapter Nineteen

frigate started to fall behind, unable to keep up with the industrial boilers of the Serene. The vessel was savaged; windows were broken, the wounded and dying scattered on the deck, and massive dents were in the hull where cannonballs struck.

"Keep your heads down," Fletcher bellowed. "We're not quite out of range of their guns yet!"

There was a gaggle of voices behind him. Curious, he turned around only to see the many reporters and journalists on the ship talking with Blauestein. Many excitedly took notes. The Night Rider looked more than happy to answer their questions.

"How come he's getting all the attention, Fletcher?" Clemson grumbled. "We did all the work."

"Because some reporters are a strange and occasionally brainless lot. Also, he's the one that's going to look best in the pictures, Clemson."

***

OTTO GRITTED HIS TEETH while securing the goggles over his eyes. He and Jord were sent to man one of the rotary guns on the *Defiance's* quarter deck. The whole affair had been a miserable experience.

"I'm grateful that those big guns are keeping the Tersians away," Jord grumbled. "But by the Holy do they rattle your bones when they fire."

"I don't think my ears will ever stop ringing," Otto said, eyes still wide from the skull-jarring gun concert.

"Look alive, men and guards," a marine sergeant hollered. "A Tersian magicked itself right by one of our ships. One could do the same to us."

"Over there, little man," Jord warned, pointing to a man o'war heaving about a kilometer off and so far untouched by the main guns. Otto swung the multi-barreled weapon towards it.

"What did you see, Jord?"

"Flashes of light coming off it. That tells me they're preparing some sort of magic."

There was a peal of luminance. It could only be described as a corona of purple lightning that rippled off the man o'war's hull. The Arazumi held their breath. And then the ship did as well. Everything fell silent. Even the hum below their feet cut off and died. Smoke ceased to pour from the funnels. Otto fought with the motorized controls of the rotary gun. The whole assembly refused to obey him.

"That's not good," Jord said. "Any idea what's wrong, little man?"

"The engines are dead, and that's what drives the main generator. There's no electricity to run any of our equipment," Otto explained, staring grimly at the inert gun.

"They're going to turn the electricity back on soon, right?"

"They'd better."

There was a blast of rapidly displaced air. The Tersian man o'war was suddenly right there off their port side, and they could see the cannons

Chapter Nineteen

shifting their aim. Jord dove, flattening himself on the deck. Otto had not, and his brain still had enough sense to tell him it was too late.

"Oh bugger," Otto cursed.

The Tersians replied with a full broadside.

CHAPTER 20

MIRABELLE STOOD BY GILROY at the wheel. Both of them focused on what lay ahead on the horizon. The *Lauria* glided over the waves at a brisk pace, her sails clutching the wind at their back for all their worth. Behind her were most of the corsairs, a gnarly-looking flotilla ready for a fight. The ships of the Dhaliese sea-clanners were in front of her, preferring speed above all else. And ahead of them, out of sight but undeniably heard, was the Arazumi vanguard.

Hearts pounded with anxiety, and people held their breaths. The Arazumi formation had fallen out of sight a while ago, their strange engines driving them faster than the wind, and then their ships hid themselves in a black smog. Only Jacques up in the crow's nest grasped the situation, and from what Mirabelle could tell, not by much.

"Jacques, you've been quiet up there. What's going on now?" Mirabelle yelled.

"Hard to say. There's fighting going on, and there's no mistaking an Arazumi cannon, but there's too much of that awful smoke to see clearly," Jacques complained.

"It sounds like the Arazumi are giving them what for, though," Mirabelle said. The grim echoes of the guns never stopped. Mirabelle was starting to understand Jacques more and more. You thanked the Holy that it wasn't you under the gaze of those guns.

"We got a ship coming out of the gloom dead ahead, captain!" one of the other lookouts warned. Dozens of eyes strained until finally, they saw it: a battered frigate displaying large holes in her hull and a broken forward mast. Mirabelle gulped at the sight of it in her spyglass.

"It's Tersian, captain!" the lookout called.

"And, they don't look happy. Or healthy," Mirabelle said, studying them still. She almost felt sorry for her enemies as they eventually passed by. The Dhaliese ignored them when the Tersians made no effort to attack, and the Lauria held her fire as well. It wasn't every day you saw a Tersian warship with the will to fight shot out of it.

"We got more Tersians, ma'am! It looks like the Arazumi gave them quite a beating, but we should remain cautious!" Jacques warned. Mirabelle nodded.

"Gilroy, keep us as far away from the Tersians as you can. We don't want to get bogged down in a fight. Load the cannons with double shot! We'll bite the first Tersian who gets too close!"

The order was dutifully carried out, but no further instructions came. The squadron of rebels and roughnecks plowed on, broken Tersian ships bobbing in their midst with their crews too battered to mount an attack.

"This is so...surreal," Mirabelle said, watching the floating casualties. Her men remained huddled around their cannons, waiting for an order to fire that would never come.

"Captain!" Jacques shouted. "There's a man o'war approaching from the north, our ten o'clock position! It looks like she's about to use some sort of magic!"

Chapter Twenty

"What's she doing that appears like magic?"

"There's an ugly purple glow all over her."

"Gilroy, turn us hard to starboard, do it now! Portside cannons, ready to fire on my command!" Mirabelle barked.

"What are you thinking, Captain?" Gilroy asked as he wrestled the helm as far as it would go.

"If I were a Tersian captain with all those guns to use and I saw a bunch of dirty corsairs trying to escape, I'd tell my sorcerer to blink the ship right in our path. However, I've never heard of a ship rotating while it blinked, so what's going to happen?"

"The Tersians are going to magic right into our midst and blast us with their guns, and since it's larger and slower, our more nimble line is going to go right past it, getting hit the whole time," Gilroy said fearfully.

"Yes, but they forgot one thing: their position."

The man o'war materialized amid the Dhaliese line, cannons sliding out of their gun ports. The Dhaliese sea-clanners scrambled on their ships, bracing for the worst and hoping they'd survive the inevitable volley. Having turned her side to the Dhaliese, the Lauria had all her port side cannons facing the exposed Tersian stern.

"Fire!"

Gleaming brass cannons roared fire, metal, and smoke. Hot cannonballs and smaller grape shot slammed through the rudder assembly, ripped through the wood, and then traveled the length of the ship. The Tersian cannon decks were suddenly unrecognizable and grimly covered in red.

"Swivel guns, aim for the pilot house! Keep them off their helm! Cannons, load chain shot and shred their sails! Gilroy, keep us on our course until we're out of effective range of their cannons. I don't think they enjoyed that, but let's not find out if any of their gun crews survived and want retribution," Mirabelle breathed, still processing the destruction she just watched.

"Nicely done, captain," Gilroy said, heaving the wheel yet again. "I don't think I've ever seen a warship that large knocked out as quickly as that."

"Let's just stay as far away from the navy, any navy, from now on."

***

UP THE LINE OF THE FLOTILLA, Samir stood at the prow of his *Mouse-Deer,* the long oars hauling the ship forward through the waves. His crew found themselves unconsciously clenching their teeth and feeling their hearts racing despite no enemies to be worried about just yet. It was the noise they could hear around them and the knowledge of where they stood in the flotilla that made them anxious. Up ahead in the vanguard were the Arazumi, taking the brunt of the Tersian fist. Behind the Arazumi were Davos and his squadron of five frigates, able warships in their own right. Samir was with the other Dhaliese captains who had ships built for combat, and they were all behind Davos' squadron. Immediately behind them were the ships of the sea-clanners, which weren't meant for fighting. These vessels were loaded with cargo, livestock, and families, including the children and the elderly. And Samir heard a broadside erupt from that

324

Chapter Twenty

direction. He could only hope Captain Mirabelle was watching them well.

The *Mouse-Deer* pushed through a curtain of gunpowder and mist. Samir gasped at what he saw ahead of him. Davos' frigates were viciously fighting two Tersian men o'war. Two of the frigates were sinking, and the other two worked on finishing off one of the Tersians. The last one, Davos' ship, was latched to her enemy, each vessel desperately struggling to gain control of the other.

"Row harder and aim us for the boarded Tersian!" Samir hollered for his men to hear. "Time to bail out Cousin Davos again, *kip-kip*."

They swooped into the fray. If the renegade convoy was to keep moving away from the Tersians, they had to regain control. No holdups could be tolerated at any point in the chain, and they could hear the Arazumi guns loudly holding up their end of the bargain. None of the Dhaliese fighting men wanted their family ships to fall under the glare of a Tersian vessel. The *Mouse-Deer,* smaller than the man o'war, fired a few rounds of grapeshot at the Tersian gun decks and then rolled alongside her. Samir led his boarding party onto her deck. To his relief, they were able to catch their enemies off guard, attacking from an unexpected angle. The fighting was fierce, visceral, and desperate.

Davos and his men carved a bloody red corridor across the deck, but they were outnumbered, and it was slowing them down. Davos could easily overpower any Tersian that crossed his path, but he was only one man and it would take only one mistake to stop him.

A Tersian sailor charged at Samir, noticing that he had not yet drawn his blade. Samir took a breath to steady his mind and raised both of his hands, still unable to draw his weapon. He didn't need to. The

Tersian swung his blade, and Samir struck, stopping the man's forearm mid-swing with his own and then landed a blow on the man's throat with his other fist. His enemy laid out on the deck, Samir finally drew his sword. He had a man o'war to take.

The fighting was intense but quickly broken, and then it was over. Davos, covered in blood and steadying his breath, looked over at Samir. He seemed unbothered by the whole ordeal.

"Cousin Samir, I must thank you for your help. How are my other frigates?"

"Well, the good news is you now have this ship, Cousin," Samir replied with a sheepish smile.

"Argh, what am I going to do with a man o'war? They're too slow to do the hunting I prefer. I've learned my lesson with that fortress ship," Davos said apologetically.

"Maybe sell it to the Shah and use the money to buy a brand-new frigate?"

"Good idea, but we're wasting time. Men! Get this ship back underway! We can't afford to drift here! If you're not part of my crew, get back to your own ships before more Tersians come!" Davos bellowed. Samir gave him a jaunty bow, and he and his men made their way back to the *Mouse-Deer*.

***

CLARENCE GILDERSCHMIDT WAS THE CHIEF engineer of the *Defiance* and was going through his mental checklist, trying to troubleshoot what was professionally understood to be a "major

Chapter Twenty

problem." The engines, for no discernable reason, weren't working. The entire ship, engine room included, was entirely in the dark save for the emergency lights that flicked on under their own battery power.

"All right, gents, we have a right, big kertuffle here, and all the usual solutions aren't working. Anyone have any bright ideas?" he demanded.

"Don't you mean 'kerfuffle,' sir?"

"No, I meant kertuffle because it's worse than a kerfuffle. My grandfather explained the many gradients of fufflery to me. It's right above 'kerfuffle,' but just below a, well; some of you are too young for the word. Now, hurry up and get me solutions, men!"

"My father up in Tenethar taught me a little blacksmith charm he'd do when making important bits of equipment," young Harold said. "He said it's supposed to keep the kobolds and other bad luck away."

"Well, seeing how none of you are offering any other suggestions and black magic is probably the only explanation we have left, young Harold is now in charge. Everyone, listen to him!"

***

OTTO BLINKED, his brain processing that, despite the sensory and literal bombardment he had experienced, he was shockingly still alive. There was a thick layer of soot covering him, but all his bits were still attached to him, just the way he liked it. That was more than could be said about many of the marines scattered all over the deck.

"You got lucky, Otto," Jord scolded, getting back on his feet.

"I'll face down a Danarian cavalry charge, but I never want to see a battery of naval cannon firing at me ever again," Otto admitted, still trembling on his feet. Jord tossed him his rifle.

"Time to do this the old-fashioned way until your electric comes back on."

The *Defiance* was dead in the water, and every gun on deck was frozen in place. The men could see the man o'war hauling ever closer, and grappling hooks were brought up to ensnare the ship.

"Clear their main deck!" the marine sergeant shouted, rallying the men who were still alive. "Aim for their helmsman when possible! We have to throw them off!"

The firefight became intense. Marines and guards dove for cover whenever a dreaded Tersian cannon swiveled towards them. Heavy iron balls would slam into the *Defiance's* hull whenever the main Tersians cannons fired, crumpling the armor plates and sending a deadly spray of steel fragments at anyone unlucky enough to be in the vicinity. The Tersians, in turn learned that Arazumi long arms could be just as devastating as their primary battery. Sailors fell from the rigging and dropped where they stood at ranges they didn't think possible. Not even the men manning the guns on the cannon deck were safe, and sailors were now hesitating to take hold of the helm, a grim pile of their fallen comrades accumulating around it.

"They keep getting closer!" a marine hollered.

"Then don't stop shooting!" the sergeant snarled. "If we force them to keep their heads down, they won't think to grapple us!"

Two grappling hooks and ropes eerily rose of their own accord from

Chapter Twenty

the Tersian vessel and shot forward like hydras. The snares caught fast on the *Defiance's* deck, and the ropes grew taut. The Arazumi stared in horror as they felt their ship drawn in.

"They're using magic!" Jord warned.

"Keep shooting, damn it!" the sergeant howled.

A deep, leviathan rumble jolted the *Defiance*. The funnels choked and coughed before a steady stream of smoke began to rise from them. No one on the deck heard it, but far below them, the engineering team and boiler men cheered with victory as the lights flickered on. Instead, the marines whooped and hollered when they heard the familiar hum of the main turrets moving. The Tersian man o'war quickly fell under the impassive glare of the two stern guns.

The man o'war began to break apart under the repeated high-velocity shelling. Even after the grappling hooks were released and the Tersian tried to escape, the main guns continued to fire. Soon there was only broken timber for the sea to reclaim.

"You know, I'm a little disappointed," Jord said as soon as the cacophony died away. "I was looking forward to operating the rotary gun."

"It's a bit hard to hear you, Jord," Otto said a little too loudly. "My ears are still ringing."

"That's just the rattling of the shell casings on the deck."

"I think it's both."

Jord didn't reply; his gaze turned back to Reyais as he thoughtfully prepared his pipe. His brow furrowed as tobacco smoke began to join the smell of sea salt and spent powder. The worst was over, but his anxieties wouldn't go away.

Up on the bridge, Captain Leon stared haggardly at the sinking derelict that had once been a proud Tersian warship. The whole battle had played out before his eyes, and there was little he could do other than wait for the power to come back on. Cooper had, thankfully, lost his nerve and gone off to hide.

"Our weapons are getting too industrial," Leon said quietly to himself. "People will forget what they're actually doing when killing a man becomes as simple as flipping a switch."

"Preliminary reports coming in, sir," his first officer announced, arriving on the bridge. "The hull took a beating but nothing that threatens our ability to stay afloat. We have casualties, though."

"Any word on the other ships?"

"*G-18* reports they expect to limp out of the blockade but will have to scuttle the ship once in safer waters. The other gunboats report casualties and light damage but nothing as major as *18*. As for the civilian ships, only the *Serene* took damage, but she's still afloat. Finally, we're just a few more kilometers away from evacuating the blockade."

"Thank you for your report, officer. Was there anything else?" Leon asked.

"Nothing else. I think we can call this one a victory, sir."

Chapter Twenty

"Agreed, but let's bring everyone home first."

***

ADMIRAL ORUZ GLOWERED at the helm, compiling every law and excuse in the Tersian law books he could use to have Doruk hanged. Charging after the fortress ship, solitary and on its own despite the rest of the corsairs escaping from a different direction? Why couldn't Doruk see that it was a trap?

Oruz turned to the sorcerer cabal behind him, the group of magicians hard in concentration. "Raise more speed, you dogs! We need to catch up with them!"

"We're putting as much wind on the sails as we can, Admiral," one of them groaned, veins standing out on his skin.

"Try harder!"

One of the sorcerers let out a gasp, paled, and then suddenly turned into air with a violent burst, his robes fluttering away into the breeze. His surviving comrades tried to ignore what they just saw and hoped none of them would likewise lose control.

***

GUNDERSON GRINNED AT THE TERSIAN WARSHIPS closing in on them. There was going to be a vicious fight ahead, because these ships were sailing steadily along despite the direction of the wind: sorcerers were coming. He beat his ax and shield together a final three times.

The sharks circled in closer. He marveled at their discipline; not a single cannon fired on the fortress ship. They wanted their treasure back unspoiled and in one piece. Gunderson didn't have any such compunctions for them. He stamped his foot hard on the deck three times. All the gun decks below him roared in response.

The Tersian warships around them shuddered, sloughing off timbers under the punishment of the fortress ship's heavy batteries. It was enough to make Gunderson cackle, the old man sniggering into his beard as the destruction played out before him.

The air seemed to ripple around them. Gunderson looked around and raised his shield and ax. You could feel magic in the air, but you never knew what it was going to do until it was too late. Shapes began to form around him and his crew of suicidal volunteers. Human shapes.

"Hold your fire!" the old captain roared.

There was a popping sound in the air, and suddenly they were surrounded by Tersian boarding crews. Heavy cutlasses flashed under the overcast skies, the hammers of flintlocks were fully drawn back, and boarding spears were raised. Standing at the head of the Tersians was the most cocksure sorcerer Gunderson had ever seen. The magician began clapping.

"Well done, well done, criminals and parasites of all nations," Doruk declared with a smile and raised his staff. "You'll now have the privilege of being executed by the very best of Tersia." The corsairs' response caught Doruk off guard.

"Now!" Gunderson shouted.

Chapter Twenty

The sailors armed with muskets rose from their positions on the quarterdeck, hidden by makeshift barriers for just this purpose. Musket balls pelted the Tersians. They weathered the fire, ignored the screams of the fallen, and charged in return. The deck became a writhing, desperate melee.

Gunderson made sure to hurl himself wherever he was most needed. Despite the chaos, he saw they still had the upper hand. Despite the eldritch fireballs tossed around and the momentary impossible physics imposed upon them by Doruk, the corsairs serendipitously fought with cohesion, a symphony of butchery.

Someone was sneaking behind him. Gunderson turned on his heels and raised his shield just in time to deflect a Tersian blade. He locked eyes with his attacker.

"Vutan's Anvil, but you are still one ugly whore's son. In fact, you've gotten uglier!"

His enemy's skin was a patchwork of scars, some of them self-inflicted with a ritualistic deliberateness. The overall picture made Gunderson think he was fighting a cobbled-together homunculus. Here was Erdem the Whaler.

Gunderson was taken aback by his opponent's attacks, relentless blows lashing out at him. It had been a while since someone made his shield arm tire, but now he would not be afraid. Gunderson waited for an opening and then struck out. Erdem pulled back and was lost in the melee. The old captain was thoughtful as he dispatched another Tersian that strayed too close to his ax. Now he understood. He had seen men like Erdem before, opportunists who only attacked men who were outnumbered or outmatched. Tersia's most infamous whaler wasn't just a sadist: he was a coward.

It wasn't a game he liked to play, looking like he was off guard, because it didn't come easy to Gunderson. He tried to keep his stance sloppy, his ax out of position, but he knew any soldier worth his salt would know it was all a pantomime, as if anyone would mistake a bear standing on its hind legs as a creature looking for a warm hug.

Perhaps Erdem didn't read all the signs. Perhaps he became overconfident. It didn't matter. Gunderson saw the whaler of men coming back, so he threw his ax. The heavy blade tumbled through the air and caught Erdem in the rib cage. Gunderson reached for his waist and produced another ax.

It occurred to him that the corsairs were rushing for the stern, where they threw themselves into the sea. The musketeers held on, pelting the Tersians where they could, but they too were slowly leaving.

"Why are we retreating?" Gunderson snarled. One of his escaping comrades was considerate enough to give him an answer.

"The men below deck slammed the gun port hatches shut!"

"Ah," Gunderson said. It was a critical agreed-upon signal. "All of you run then; old man Gunderson will buy you time."

"No, you won't," a voice declared. Gunderson turned and found himself staring at Doruk. "Your men are retreating, their discipline has wavered, and now you will die in the same manner that you've killed so many others."

"You can go to the Abyss, witch!"

"I'll send you there first, corsair."

Chapter Twenty

Gunderson scrambled across the planks, running as fast as his legs could take him. And then, they didn't touch the planks anymore. The old corsair snarled venomously as he levitated helplessly a meter or so off the ship. Doruk chuckled haughtily as he watched the hapless mariner.

"The proper end of every pirate is at the end of a rope, be it hanging, gibbeting or keelhauling," Doruk lectured. Gunderson stared wild-eyed as a rope from the rigging formed itself into a noose and began to snake towards him. He struggled against muscles that refused to obey him.

"Worry not," Doruk said soothingly. "You'll die with your weapons in your hand."

Gunderson yelled; he snarled and screamed. Spite roared through his veins. He drew his head back and viciously spat in Doruk's face. The sorcerer flinched and turned away. The spell broke, and Gunderson landed heavily on the deck. He saw his chance and threw his ax.

Doruk turned just in time to see the hunk of steel screaming towards him. He raised a hand and twisted it. The ax stopped dead in the air and then dropped. He looked up at Gunderson with a grin. His face immediately became one of horror. While Doruk had focused on the ax, Gunderson hadn't stopped moving. The corsair had turned on his heels and hurled his shield like an oversized discus. The mass of wood and metal collided with Doruk's skull. There wasn't much left of it after that.

Gunderson walked over and retrieved his shield. He coughed, trying to catch his breath and cursed old age creeping on him. The deck was empty, the Tersians having retreated at the sight of their fallen sorcerer. Gunderson looked around; more Tersian warships were closing in, but he didn't think there was enough time. Once again, death in battle had eluded him, and Vutan could not be fooled. Coughing and disappointed, Gunderson hurried towards the stern. In the distance, he could see the familiar sails of the *Osebirk*. He'd have to thank Charles later for trailing the ship, even if it was against orders. The old mariner leaped overboard and began to swim for safety. Death would have to come for him another day.

*****

ORUZ SURVEYED THE FORTRESS SHIP with his own eyes. It appeared to be abandoned, and that made his skin crawl. His crewmen were still fishing their fellow sailors out of the water, all of them frantically babbling that the corsairs had put up a savage fight and that Doruk and Erdem were dead.

"Then why did they abandon the ship?" Oruz demanded.

"No explanation, sir," one of his officers said. "They insist there was still at least one corsair aboard before they got away."

"Ran, you mean," Oruz sniffed.

"Correct, sir."

"The deck looks empty, sir!' a marine up in the rigging called. "Shall we try to board her?" Oruz hesitated and then shook his head. His men seemed to fidget uncomfortably.

"Are we just going to wait here?" his first officer asked. Oruz buried his head in his hands.

"If you were a corsair, what would drive you to sail one of our fortress ships back to us, give us a savage beating, and then abandon ship?" Oruz demanded.

"Probably a lack of courage, sir." a marine offered.

"No, no, it can't be that!' Oruz scolded. "They bravely charged our lines despite being outnumbered! What changed?"

"It is quaint that they only fired one volley from the guns. You'd think they'd have wanted to use them for all their worth," an officer speculated aloud. Oruz stared at him. The admiral's blood froze in his veins.

"Sorcerers, blink us out of here!" Oruz shouted.

"What? But where to? Which direction?" the cabal leader asked in bewilderment.

"Anywhere but–"

There was a deafening, deck-shattering explosion. Whether he was launched from the deck or his ship had disintegrated beneath him, or both, he didn't know. But he did figure out what caused this. The corsairs had jam-packed the whole fortress ship with powder. Three gun decks' worth, plus whatever other explosives they could get their hands on, was stuffed onto the ship and then put on a slow fuse. Cannonballs and the cannons themselves added to the screaming shrapnel that flew in all directions. The corsairs never intended for the Tersians to have their fortress ship back, and they were going to ensure that a few more sank with it.

Oruz awoke to a nightmare. What remained of his ship was a roaring inferno floundering into the depths. His whole body screamed with pain, and the carmine color of the water told him he was bleeding. At least his mind felt as sharp as it had ever been.

"Always knew this day would come," the old admiral sighed. Painfully, he splashed his way towards a drifting board just large enough for someone to take shelter on temporarily. Someone, or perhaps a jinn. Oruz slammed Yera's bottle on the wood and uncorked it. There was a flash of light, and Yera materialized on the makeshift raft. She stared in shock at everything around her and then backed away from the water that lapped at the wood.

"Yera," Oruz coughed. "You have served me well, so I shall make one last request: take yourself far from here. Go where you wish, but do not die here with me."

Yera stared at him for a moment. Then she gestured towards him. Oruz shook a hand dismissively.

"I make no request for myself. I know my place, and I will take no wish from you. My home is the sea, certainly no place for one such as you, a being made of fire. I would not have your bottle trapped to my bones in the depths. Go! Save yourself! You are free!"

Yera looked at him sadly, and there was a final flash of light. The jinn and her bottle were gone. Oruz leaned onto the plank and wondered how long it would take before it became waterlogged. Further off, he could see the sails of the corsair flotilla. Against all odds, they were going to escape. A chuckle came to his lips. There they went, the enemies of all nations. Villains all, and yet he couldn't help but admire them. After all, if it weren't for a few of the good ones, nations would grow lazy and become the enemies of man themselves.

The old admiral began to paddle. It felt like the right thing to do. He

Chapter Twenty

began to sing an old sea shanty, despite the rumble of the waves, the cries of the dying, and the ships burning around him. Death came for all men. It was up to you how you greeted him.

CHAPTER **21**

Two Weeks Later

DOOM CAME TO REYAIS and then, it was over. Prophets of the apocalypse often fail to mention this fact: the end comes, the chapter closes, and then something new begins. Some say that it's because the Holy enjoys making new beginnings.

Haggard longshoremen made their way back to the harbor, patched it up, and then waited for work. They didn't have to wait long. First, the Dhaliese sea-clanners returned seeking shelter from the coming ship-breaking storms. It was hurricane season now, and Reyais had one of the few harbors that dependably offered shelter from the worst of the weather. Then the sea-clanners raised the Shah's standard in the harbor, an orange field with a majestic fruit tree at its center. Reyais, a lost and orphaned old empire, switched from the negligent hands of Ta'Geh to the patronage of the Dhaliese Shah. The locals began to piece their lives back together. The tax collectors would be different, but life was going to go on and it probably wasn't too different from what they were used to experiencing.

The Dhaliese sea-clanners focused on getting the harbor back in working order first and felt the rest of the city could wait. Most of Reyais's survivors had migrated to the shoreside neighborhoods anyway. The communities in the upper parts of Reyais were still uninhabitable. After the Dhaliese came Danarian merchantmen, also looking for shelter from the coming storms, and after them came the Arazumi. The Republic's bronze cog on a blue field rose once again

341

in the ruins of their old embassy. The hurricanes were coming, but that didn't mean business couldn't continue. And with business came other curious affairs.

Two sea captains from different nations met on the docks. Behind them were two very different piles of goods. One hurriedly took notes while the other enthusiastically chattered on.

"And that's how Grandma Lola was able to get the tavern up and running again, *kip-kip,*" Samir explained. "Festival customers, and the plumbing issues that come with them, are awful, Cousin."

"I'm willing to give a little coin to ensure the repairs are done," Leon offered, pulling his coat tighter over him to ward off the chilly, damp wind. "It's been a while since I've seen Grandma Lola so this'll remind her that her faraway grandson hasn't forgotten her."

"Oh, don't worry, Cousin, she's refusing all help from anyone unless it's Uncle Baruum. The word has already gotten out: the Shah wants him to govern this island now," Samir murmured furtively. Leon's eyebrows shot up into his cap.

"Uncle Baruum a governor? Can a sea-clanner even be the governor of something that's on land?"

"It's rare, but not unheard-of, *kip-kip*. It's probably for the best. I heard a rumor that the Shah is refusing to restore the old Regent's Palace up on the hill. He thinks it's cursed, especially with that business with the dragon. So Uncle Baruum is getting a fancy seaside home. Besides, your scientists say the air up there is still poisoned."

"So I've been told," Leon said. "Can't say I've seen it for myself. I just make sure our ships are properly loaded and navigate safely out of here. The landlubbers can have the rest of the city for all I care."

"Agreed, Cousin! Now, I assume you'll want your purple yams, coffee, and durians?"

"Ugh, I'll take the coffee and yams. I don't understand why mother loves these durians so much," Leon said, rolling his eyes. "But I'll make sure they get the first fast steamer out of here. And here is your gingerbread, clocks, spruce beer, and something new: chocolate."

"Chocolate?" Samir asked curiously.

"A new confection made by the Southern Traders Company. Mother and Father love it, and it seems everyone else in the Republic loves it as well. Between you and me, I think purple yams are better."

"I see, I see. Well, I'll make sure Grandma Lola gets first pick of this chocolate then, *kip-kip*."

"You'll want to sneak a package off for yourself, Samir. Grandma Lola may not be too keen on sharing after she's had some."

"Right you are, Cousin. What Grandma Lola doesn't know won't hurt her."

***

SOME DISTANCE FROM THE HARBOR was a battered plaza. There were still piles of ash and pumice waiting to be hauled away, and most of the buildings were better off demolished, but it still played host to a handful of people. Most of the activity came from a rather strange, cobbled-together outpost.

Otto cast a bleary eye towards the Palace and thoughtfully slurped his coffee. A few fires were continuing to smolder in the ruins. Plumes of ash and smoke continued to rise lazily from the upper city. Jagged crevices, basements, and even wells vented the noxious fumes. The laboratory men also warned that lethal levels of different toxic gases were also present in the noisome air. Venturing beyond the outpost without a gas mask was strictly forbidden though that was a stricture that enforced itself.

Behind him, Jord lit his pipe, filling the air with the smell of sweet tobacco. Other guards were around, sullen and quiet in the cold, damp plaza. The men mainly occupied themselves with cleaning their weapons and keeping warm.

"Wait, wait, and more waiting," Jord sighed. "It can weigh heavily on a man, all this waiting."

"There are worse things we could be doing that fall under the official points in our job description," Otto rationalized, though his heart wasn't in it.

"I don't think our friends are enjoying it either, although they're doing the very same thing," Jord said and gestured towards the Dhaliese.

Their Dhaliese neighbors were quiet and didn't make many attempts to communicate with the Long Steel men. The Shah's soldiers wore green cloaks over their plated mail armor and each carried a flintlock musket and sword. They busied themselves with the challenge of keeping their powder dry though keeping warm also tugged at their minds. The streets were quiet against the murmur of the wind, and the locals had no interest in resisting their new Dhaliese masters. Quite the contrary, they more than welcomed the charity and food that came

Chapter Twenty-One

in. A stern voice, not a musket, was all that was required to scold off the crowds and tell them to come back tomorrow.

The hearts and minds of the locals weren't the purpose of this outpost. Otto looked over when he heard the tapping of the telegraph set. He waited until the operator was done before he said anything.

"Are we expecting another delivery, Michael?"

"Yes," Michael replied, nudging his headset into a more comfortable position with his stump. "This one is for the Dhaliese. It should be here in five minutes or so."

"How are you adjusting to using your weak hand?"

"I'm getting better," Michael said, smiling timidly. "I can still understand the telegraph codes as well as the next operator. I'm still needed."

"My grandmother would say, 'You're alive, so you're needed,'" Jord murmured.

"I suppose. Hold on, sirs, I need to telegraph for a relief team."

They heard their guests before they saw them. No one ever accused an Arazumi petrol engine of being subtle. A tractor, its driver, and a team of eight men emerged from the smoke and foggy ruins. The whole assembly was covered in soot and dusted with ash and particles of pumice. They pulled up to the outpost and unloaded two wooden crates, dropping them closer towards the Dhaliese.

"Yours," one of the workers declared.

"Since you said that in Northern, I don't think our Dhaliese friends understood you," Jord explained.

The worker hurriedly flipped open one of the crates. Within was a smorgasbord of jewelry with all the precious metals represented in the collection. A healthy layer of coins padded the bottom, and a few gold ingots peeked out from the pile. The worker closed the lid and then made a dramatic bow.

"Property of the Shah," he said. The Dhaliese quickly moved to take the boxes away.

Otto studied the workers with pursed lips and hard eyes. They all wore a drab uniform of dark brown, and none seemed interested in removing their fully enclosed gas masks and brimmed helmets. Four of the workers carried tools, either a pickaxe or shovel, and there were yet more implements strapped to the tractor. The other four men had repeaters, firearms that seemed morbidly over-equipped for work in ruins. Embroidered at the top of their sleeves were the letters "B.O.A." The Bureau of Artifacts men were a strange bunch. They talked little, explained even less, and appeared out of the blue at the oddest times.

Nine more B.O.A. men, the relief workers Michael talked about, arrived at the opposite side of the outpost and replaced their counterparts at the tractor. The machine's fuel tank was given a top off, and the fresh team turned around to head back into the poisonous ruins.

"Another team just wired that they've returned. This time the delivery is for us," Michael reported.

"Mhm," Otto murmured.

Chapter Twenty-One

There was something wrong with this new team of excavators. Lead plates were attached to the crates on the back of the tractor. One of the men didn't carry anything. Instead, he cradled his severely burned hand. The B.O.A. men ignored the Dhaliese altogether and looked intently on just driving by back towards the docks. Undeterred, the Dhaliese scolded them in their language and pointed towards the crates.

"You could at least show them the crates," Jord said over the engine. "Everyone here knows the deal we have with the Shah. These men just want to do their jobs and make sure we're not hoodwinking them."

One of the taciturn workers pulled the heavy lead cover off one of the crates revealing a pile of pumice and broken up chunks of hardened lava. This done, the worker promptly shut the lid and turned to move away. A Dhaliese guard barked and motioned towards the other crate, gesturing with his hand that it should be opened too. The B.O.A. man stared impassively through his cold mask and then pointed towards his whimpering comrade with the burned hand. The Dhaliese promptly lost interest and backed away. Satisfied, the excavators continued their journey uninterrupted towards the docks.

"They can be a bunch of arseholes," Jord grumbled as soon as they were gone.

"I never understood why simple artifacts have to be so heavily guarded," Otto said in agreement.

"Maybe they're not just simple artifacts then."

"All the more reason to distrust them, especially when they don't seem to be in a hurry to explain."

Ritual | F. Arburg

At the docks, Kassia waited under a broad tent. Scientists like her from different fields were also present, though only a few looked happy. The geologists had plenty to do, and one of Kassia's fellow chemists hummed while he did a few preliminary tests on the interesting samples that got brought in. Otherwise, the rest of them, Kassia included, felt like they were just there to take notes, and the Bureau of Artifact agents were hurriedly collecting those notes afterward, anyway.

Another excavation team came in. Kassia knew better than to try talking to them. Standing around and quietly observing made your life easier. One of the crates was lifted off the tractor, and its lead plates removed. The contents of the box were then carried into the corner and dumped into the sea. Kassia wondered if any of the Dhaliese would notice the pieces of pumice mysteriously appearing by their ships long after the eruption, but the B.O.A. men didn't seem to care.

"The artifact must remain sealed," one of the excavators declared, pointing towards the final crate. "It gave Jamieson a nasty scorching when he handled it."

A senior B.O.A. agent took out a file and began to fill it out. His questions were all in monotone, and his eyes never left the paper as he filled it out.

"Did you follow all safety protocols?"

"Yes, sir."

"I hope your accounts will reflect that when we ask you to each file one individually. Please describe the item."

Chapter Twenty-One

"It looks like a crown or other decorative headgear with a single glowing gemstone at its center. We–"

"What led you to believe it was anomalous?"

"The glow didn't look natural, sir."

"And where did you find it?"

"The ruin looked consistent with a noble's house, sir."

"Very well. Stow it aboard the ship and make sure it is sent to Miskgate. Jamieson, report to the medical personnel immediately, where one of our clerks will take an account from you. The rest of you are to file a report, as well. I suggest you do that while you rest."

Kassia tried not to shake her head. The B.O.A. didn't say much, but they got touchy about their work and were prone to giving short but sharp lectures about the importance and dangers of studying anomalous relics. They didn't seem to understand that most people took offense to their mannerisms, not just to their jobs.

She waited until her shift was over after lunch and then made her way towards the east part of town. The locals smiled and waved at her but kept their distance. A small rule had developed in the last week among the locals. A group of Arazumi at the harbor with crates of preserved food and medicines was a relief station. In contrast, a solitary or small band of Arazumi were strangers, best treated with suspicion. Kassia made it to the east gate and stumbled upon Otto and Jord, who had been waiting for her arrival. It looked like the two had found a stranger to chat up while they waited.

"It's good to see you survived, Sheriff," Jord said to the local, offering him a bag of tobacco. The crusty older man eagerly took it with a chuckle and placed it in his cart where a bored donkey waited.

"I wouldn't have made it out without Ass's help. Also, I thank you for the gift, sir Raermak."

"Are you still keeping the peace in Reyais?" Otto asked curiously.

"Hm? Oh no, not anymore. Ass and I are retired," Hector admitted. "I live up in Klimmick's Hollow now. I spend my days fishing and foraging for food to sell here before I go home. If someone doesn't have anything to barter with, I at least make sure they get a fish and a potato. There's something quite funny about the potatoes; they're growing pretty damn fast around here. Quite strange but welcomed, all things considered."

"Would you happen to have noticed a young girl around? Dark hair and eyes, freckles, goes by the name of Sophie?" Jord asked.

"Don't know of any Sophies around, but I'll ask if I see anyone matching that description. Did you lose someone in the evacuation?"

"You could say that. Also, have you seen any dragons about?" Jord inquired further. Hector stared at him, his pipe shifting about as if helping the old man look for the words he wanted to say.

"You didn't get any weird mold in that tobacco of yours, did you, sir Raermak?"

"A dragon attacked the embassy the night we evacuated," Otto said patiently.

"No shite? A Blighting dragon? Well, I've heard nothing of a dragon.

Chapter Twenty-One

Even the druids seemed to have disappeared. We're just trying to survive here on the island, and we're most certainly not looking for more trouble."

"I think we can all hope nothing else comes your way. There's been enough trouble here to last a lifetime," Jord muttered.

"On that, we can both agree," Hector replied, climbing back up on his cart of salty fishes and tubers. "Now, I must be off if I'm going to get home before it's too dark. It was good seeing you Arazumi again. You're all good in my book. Farewell!"

"Old friend?" Kassia asked as soon as Hector was gone.

"Yes, and as you probably heard, still no sign of Sophie," Otto said.

"It's discouraging," Jord added.

"Do you think she could be living in the city ruins, the parts still occluded with poisonous gas?" Kassia offered.

"The arseholes of B.O.A. have consistently said no one is living in the upper ruins anymore," Otto replied. "One second you have breathable oxygen, the next you're choking on ash, or worse."

"Yes, but Sophie wasn't a normal person," Kassia said.

"I suppose."

"Hey, you two," Jord interrupted. "I'm not the only one seeing this, am I?"

There, perched on the very tip of his pipe, was an iridescent blue butterfly. Three pairs of eyes locked onto the insect. The butterfly flapped its wings and lazily took off, fluttering about towards the shore.

"We follow it," Kassia declared, promptly marching after it. "That's Sophie's work, I know it."

"What makes you so certain?" Jord asked.

"Butterflies aren't native to Reyais."

"That's a rather specific bit of information that has nothing to do with chemistry, Kassie," Otto remarked.

"She left a book on entomology open in the library once. She was reading about butterflies."

"That was a really specific fact to be found in that book," Otto said in bewilderment.

"Don't get entomologists started. Don't," Kassia sighed.

The trio followed the elegant insect gently stumbling its way along the beach. It wasn't the fastest guide, and the three were able to marvel at the flotsam that came to rest on the sands. Detritus from the battle was still washing up. There were ruined packages of all sorts, piles of wood, a plethora of bottles, and blurry soaked books were in abundance.

"I'm surprised the locals haven't turned that into kindling," Jord said.

"They've probably had their fill of fire," Otto said.

"Sure, but they still need to cook food and boil water," the giant replied.

"I propose an experiment," Kassia declared and hurried towards a bottle she spied in the sand. "This appears to be a half-full but otherwise perfectly sealed cask of whiskey. Jord, you tasted a mystery bottle without care, so are you interested in this?"

Jord turned towards it with interest but then waved a dismissive hand. "It's probably salty by now. Besides, gin is superior to whiskey."

"The locals are probably treating themselves to salvaged booze," Otto suggested. "Why settle for tea when the alcohol helps you forget?"

"Hey, hurry along, you two. The butterfly just rounded the corner up there," Kassia warned and quickened her pace.

They almost missed it. Facing the sea was a near-vertical wall of stone. They would have trotted past the small grotto in the edifice of the rock if they hadn't been looking for the butterfly flapping around in the entrance. Confident that it had their attention, it bumbled further into the cave and then gently dissipated into blue mist.

"I got an electric torch, hold on," Otto announced and produced it from his coat.

They made their way through the tunnel, straightening up as the grotto steadily widened the further they walked. A few breathless moments passed before they noticed a strange glow at the end of the tunnel. Otto turned off his light and they fanned out. They had scarcely made it into the wide rocky room when they saw someone standing there to greet them. She held her arms out for a hug.

"Sophie!"

"I'm sorry it took so long to figure out you were here," she said after the embraces were done. "I've been busy."

"Trying to survive?" Kassia asked worriedly.

"Oh no, I've been helping others survive. It's a lot of work learning magic."

Sophie had made a humble, if bizarre, abode here in the grotto. A small smokeless fire burned in the center of the room, keeping it warm and causing the sizable crystal in the ceiling to glow and amplify the light. A bed was piled down with furs in the corner while a calico cat busily groomed herself on the blankets. Tables and crates were organized along the walls, and nearly all of them were laden down with tomes. Spheres of magic hovered over each one, slowly turning the indecipherable Tersian script on the pages into recognizable Northern.

"It's a shame, really," Sophie said. "The Tersians focused on destructive spells in their grimoires. A thousand different ways to turn a person inside out but hardly one that will heal a disease, mend a limb or nourish the starving. These books would all be a waste if I hadn't gotten creative and thought of ways to redirect that destructiveness into something more...healthy."

"I'm surprised the grimoires weren't destroyed in the water," Jord said.

"Me too, but I suppose the magic contained within helped preserve the writing," Sophie speculated.

Chapter Twenty-One

"What exactly have you been doing with all this information?" Kassia asked curiously.

"It's really subtle, but I figured out the first thing I could do was use magic to help the vegetables and plants grow. I've mostly been focusing on the areas around the city, though sometimes I send a bit of energy up towards Klimmick," Sophie said with a proud smile.

"Hector's observation wasn't off then," Otto murmured. "The potatoes really have been growing more quickly."

"I found a peach that washed up onshore yesterday. I'm going to see if I can make a peach tree grow!" Sophie squeaked excitedly.

"Now, now, don't get too carried away," Kassia warned. "If you do anything too strange, people are going to start speculating there's a witch about or something." It was then that she finally noticed that Sophie wore a simple but rugged dark cloak and dress. Her eyes fell on the cat again.

"Oh," Kassia said.

"I've decided to embrace it, being a witch. I'm already learning magic on my own, and I use it when it's needed. People are going to gossip and speculate, anyway. I know enough to protect myself now."

"Speaking of, how did you escape from the dragon?" Jord demanded.

"I...uh, well, um. I blew it up."

"You blew it up? You exploded a dragon?" Otto said, a skeptical eyebrow reaching for his hairline.

Sophie nodded.

"Yes, I think she can protect herself," Jord said, a broad smile forming above his beard.

"I'm trying not to do that anymore, not unless I really have to. It's easy, and that's the problem. You can't simply explode something that's in your way. It's a lot harder to, well, make potatoes grow, or heal a city, but that makes more people happy in the end," Sophie said quietly.

"I was going to suggest you come home with us," Kassia admitted as she surveyed the room again. "But I think Reyais needs you. All the experts figure that even with all the aid pouring in from Dhalinur and Arazum, the people of the island will have a hard couple of years ahead of them. Then the aid will probably dry up because the ash may affect regional crop yields. You might be the unseen differential that'll throw the numbers off."

"That was a compliment, right?" Sophie asked curiously.

"Yes, yes, it was."

"I'm sorry I don't have more food for you all," Sophie said, quickly noticing the lack of plates on her collection of tables.

"Don't worry about it, kid," Otto chuckled and handed her a package he produced from his coat. "Have my box of these. It's called 'chocolate.'"

"Otto," Kassia scolded.

Chapter Twenty-One

"And you can have my bottle of spruce beer," Jord said, placing the vessel on one of the tables.

"Jord!"

"What? It's not particularly strong. Fine, drink it sparingly, pup, not all in one go."

They stayed as long as they could, but eventually, the Arazumi had to return before someone noticed their absence. Sophie bid them farewell and promised she would send them messages regularly by butterfly. Kassia, Jord, and Otto nodded, hugged her, and silently wondered how a magic butterfly would carry a letter, but they kept their thoughts to themselves. Sometimes you had to accept the inexplicable but nonetheless beautiful things in life.

Sophie waited till they left and then began her trek up the mountain. She levitated most of the way up and then walked when the release of magic began to tire her. Nothing bothered her as she hiked through the night-shrouded forest. Even the druids kept their distance from her. The last witch on the island had provoked the dragon, and she was the witch that ended it.

She made her way up to the peak, just below the mouth of the still smoldering volcano. She found a place to wait on the windswept stone and admired the moon and stars above. On her right side, etched into the rock, was an unbroken chain of intricate runes. The carving was less than ten centimeters from top to bottom, but it stretched far out into the distance until it disappeared. Sophie waited until she heard a rhythmic tapping. It came from her left side, and there was a musical hint to it, the sound of metal carving into stone. She looked over when it was closer to her. There was the hammer, chisel, and crystal she enchanted yesterday to carry out this task. She watched the tools float in a synchronized dance only they knew, the crystal tapping along each rune the chisel carved out until finally, the runes formed an unbroken chain around the whole mountain. Sophie smiled and pressed a hand to it, channeling everything she had learned so far into the carving.

"I never knew you," Sophie said, knowing that this was the final resting place of the witch that caused so much pain. "I don't know your name. I only know what you did and what you would have done to me. What you did was wrong. You hurt so many people, but I'll make sure that I'll rebuild and heal where you destroyed. You meant to sacrifice me, but I've become stronger than you."

The crystal tapped the runes one last time, and the carving lit up, pure as moonlight. It glowed for a moment and then faded away until only cold stone remained. Sophie smiled to herself and began her walk home. Reyais could now stumble along that long journey called healing.

***

THE SUN AND SAND WERE WARM AND PLEASANT. The breeze smelled of fragrant flowers and citrus fruits. In the distance, she could hear the men carousing and smell the barbecue roasting on the fires they tended. She could also smell the rum heavy in the air despite the bottle of brandy she was nursing in her other hand. Mirabelle was happy and didn't understand why the other captains had to ruin it with their unending complaints.

"Are you sure, Davos?" Hernan Corba demanded. "If the Shah takes over Reyais, well, that means fewer letters of mark for us. The Shah was never as generous with those like Reyais was."

Chapter Twenty-One

"Reyais was generous?" Ivan grumbled. "Do you not remember the last couple of weeks?"

"Reyais was generous when it mattered," Hernan said petulantly.

"I'm certain," Davos asserted. "I'm a sea-clanner, aren't I? I was one of the first people to know about the orders."

"The sun is setting on people like us, pups," Gunderson sighed. For once, he wasn't sharpening a blade. He sat on the beach and seemed to be gazing sadly out into the waves.

"I'm not going back to Arazum," Hernan complained. "I'd rather die with my ship sinking around me than go back to them."

"I'm not too fond of how Empress Nathalie runs Danaria myself," Ivan said. Mirabelle didn't say anything. Saying ill of the empress wasn't treason if you were on an unmarked tropical island in the Southern Archipelago.

She read and re-read the letter in front of her. Gilroy said it had arrived at the ship a few days before they left and had been forgotten in all the commotion prior to the exodus. The first sheet of parchment was a brief personal note from Seth thanking her for her service and that she didn't have to worry about him because his job was "almost over." The second sheet of parchment was more official. On the authority of Danaria's Witch Hunters, it was an order that Mirabelle's old estate be returned to her.

She had smiled when she first read it but it faded with each subsequent reading. With its land and mansion, the old estate had been home, certainly. It was also comfortable, easier to run, and she never once worried about it sinking or running aground. But it belonged to her late husband, a man whose very name, and everything else about him, was disappearing into the forgotten past. When the coup happened, the Danarian loyalists had negotiated the help of the Arazumi, who sent an expedition force to put Empress Nathalie back on the throne. They also had put her late husband into the ground. Nathalie was reinstalled and seized the estates of those who rebelled. Was it ever hers to take away? Did the estate ever really belong to Mirabelle? In the mansion, she was just a noblewoman. On the *Lauria,* she was captain. She was master of her fate and could go wherever the wind was blowing. Sometimes she could even sail against it.

"Then let's create our own place," Mirabelle said, getting to her feet and standing among the moaning captains. They looked up at her in bewilderment.

"We're not kings and chancellors. The nations can go hang," Hernan sneered.

"No one is saying we need to raise taxes and build armies," Mirabelle told him. "And let's not forget how awful Reyais was. I'm saying we can do better than Reyais. They want to call us enemies of all nations but those same governments are murderers and thieves themselves. At least we're honest about it. We'll create our own island or islands, and welcome in the forgotten and rejected and protect our own."

"That's...that's crazy talk," Ivan scoffed.

"We just ran the largest blockade anyone has seen in, well, ever!" Mirabelle said with raised arms. "We're corsairs! We see crazy, and we do it! We just need to put our heads together, pool our resources, and raise the black flag!"

Gunderson got up from where he was sitting, brushed himself off, and

Chapter Twenty-One

walked up to Mirabelle. The old man raised a veiny, wry arm and drew his sword before planting it in the sand.

"I'm in. We can run our separate ways and die, or we can band together and look after our own. I know which side I'm choosing."

"If Gunderson is in, then I am as well," Davos said. He too stepped forward and stuck one of his machetes into the soil.

One by one, the other captains came forward and joined their weapon with the others. Some skeptically held out at first while others whined and nay-said but eventually were won over until even irascible Hernan was brought into the fold.

"A floating corsair republic in exile. Who would have thought," Gunderson chuckled to himself. "And we have Mirabelle to thank."

"You can thank me with another bottle of brandy. We can draft up the code in the morning. There's no more Reyais for us to go to, so it's up to us to dream better. So here's to us, the enemies of all nations!"

Mirabelle led them in the cheer. Then, she waited till they had gone their separate ways. She looked back to where the *Lauria* was anchored in the shallows and smiled to herself. She tore the declaration to pieces and watched them as the wind scattered them. Finally, she had what mattered to her the most: freedom. There were no more anchors to hold her down, and all that was left to do was order full sails and see where the wind would take her.

www.ingramcontent.com/pod-product-compliance
Lightning Source LLC
Chambersburg PA
CBHW010840190726
48286CB00012BA/2918